SPAC

GUIDE

TO

THE

GALAXY

002

C. ROCHELLE

CONTENTS

Copyright © 2025 C. Rochelle

First Printing: 2025

All rights reserved. No part of this publication may be reproduced,
distributed, or transmitted in any form or by any means without the prior
written permission of the author, except in the case of brief quotations
embodied in critical reviews and certain other noncommercial uses
permitted by copyright law. **It may not be used for AI training, learning,
or AI in any form.**

No part of this book was produced using AI.

The characters and events portrayed in this book are fictitious. Any similarity
to real persons, living or dead, is coincidental and not intended by the author.
All characters in this story are 18 years of age and older, and all sexual acts
are consensual. Any mentions of Star Wars or David Bowie, etc. in this book
are for *parody* purposes only and not to be confused with licensed use of
material owned by Lucasfilm/Walt Disney Company, Warner Music, etc.

If you've read this far, you are a space wizard!

ISBN: 9798317382544

Paperback cover and character art by Kristin Lemonde
(@lemonade_doodles)
Editing by Alexa at Fiction Fix
Cover design & interior formatting by divineconception (C. Rochelle)
www.c-rochelle.com

TYPOS & LANGUAGES

While many people have gone over this book to find typos and other mistakes, we are only human. **If you spot an error, please do NOT report it to Amazon.** I *want* to hear from you if there's an issue, so I can fix it. Send me an email at **crochelle.author@gmail.com** or **use the form** found pinned in my FB group or in my links on TT & IG.

SLANG NOTE: There is always a bit of slang peppered into my writing. When in doubt, use Google, or contact me using the methods above if you truly believe it's a typo.

FIRST, A NOTE ON ALIEN LANGUAGES/SPECIES: Unlike with Earth Boys Are Easy, I chose to show all conversations in alien languages being translated into American English (thanks to Micah's handy translator device!), with Stellarian being italicized (see **Formatting Notes**), but we do still have occasional "sci-fi" words thrown in to keep things interesting.

I've included a short glossary in the back of the book for your convenience.

As mentioned in the **Reading Order** callout on the **Warnings, Content & Triggers** page, while I still feel you can start your Villains in Space adventure with Earth Boys Are Easy, there *were* some important developments that occurred for Ziggy and Micah in Rabble: End Game (Villainous Things, Book 5, which occurs *between* Earth Boys and Space Daddy's Guide to the Galaxy) that inevitably need to be mentioned.

The most important being that Ziggy and the parent who knowingly abandoned him (Theo, formerly "he who shall not be named") *finally* reconciled. It was a long time coming, but also required two fully-faceted character arcs of their own first (in separate series), so it wasn't something I could simply squeeze into Earth Boys (or this book) and be done with it.

If it's important to you to see this reconciliation happen on-page (since sometimes, we can't help bringing our own *personal* baggage to these *fictional* worlds), you can find it in Chapter 38 of Rabble: End Game (although, I highly recommend fully reading up to that moment, for the full character/relationship arcs).

I'm acknowledging that some readers are going to get annoyed by what they see as fractured storytelling (like how I felt when Mando and Grogu were reunited in *The Book of Boba Fett* instead of *The Mandalorian* proper...). In this case, it was unavoidable, due to End Game being an all-in reunion book, starring thirteen, deeply-intertwined main characters.

However, I did my best within Space Daddy's Guide to the Galaxy to get you caught up to speed on any necessary backstory, without info dumping *and* without detracting from the main storyline of Villains in Space... and the main COUPLE —Micah and Ziggy.

Because what also happened in End Game was the formation of a resonance-induced polycule. This wasn't done for salacious reasons, or to "ruin" anyone's existing relationships or make them less "special." Anyone who thinks that should perhaps familiarize themselves with my back catalog (hint: it's full of loving polycules!) and *definitely* educate themselves on real-life polyamory.

The main reason this storyline came to be was simply because I realized I had created an interesting "problem" (not really) for myself as a writer when it came to Stellarian resonance.

As clearly explained in several of my books (Enter the Multi-Vers, Earth Boys, *and* End Game), creators and offspring have the same resonance (well, a combined *harmony* of resonance), and since their mates *also* have that resonance, it makes sense that polycules might form within the family unit.

Just like with real-life polyamory, this does not mean "everybody's fucking everybody"—some relationships within the polycule are purely platonic—or that anyone is "cheating." There is open communication and negotiations along the way (along with moments of miscommunication, confusion, and jealousy—*just like in real life!).*

Anyway, these extended family members (because that's what the alien polycule is—a *family*) will make brief cameos in Space Daddy's Guide to the Galaxy—through texts, phone calls, and family video calls, but *not* in person (because, again, Micah and Ziggy are the focus of this trilogy). **I will speak more on why it was *so incredibly important* for Ziggy especially to find this family in my Author's Note & Acknowledgements at the end of the book.**

Yes, you can head to Patreon for the extra spicy "Horny Glo Worms" bonus content, but in the main storyline we don't see much action beyond an innocent kiss in End Game (with all parties present and approving) and continuous, shameless flirting (horny glo worms indeed...).

In the end, I ask that my readers accept that this poly-cule *exists,* because I (THE AUTHOR) wrote it into existence. End stop. If you don't like it, write your own damn book.

Love is LOVE, in all forms, no matter how many individuals are involved. That's the vibe in this house (always has been), so if you disagree, then my books—my space—may not be for you.

I will say that any negativity I've received over the alien poly-cule has been few and far between, and seems to be the result of a lack of reading comprehension (and self-awareness) more than anything. Those who get it, GET IT, and seats are always open at my Weird-Ho's table for those who do (or are willing to learn).

With love and gratitude,

-C

Space Daddy's Guide to the Galaxy is the second book in the Villains in Space trilogy, all of which will star Ziggy and Micah as our MCs/idiots-in-love (in space!). While each book is a standalone space adventure you DO need to read the trilogy in order, starting with Earth Boys Are Easy.

Reading Order: Chronologically, Earth Boys occurred between Enter the Multi-Vers (Villainous Things, Book 4) and Rabble: End Game (VT, Book 5), while Space Daddy occurs after the "Happy Winter-Ween" bonus special found in Villainous All the Way (VT, Book 6/bonus collection).

I do feel you can start with Earth Boys Are Easy then orbit back to the main Villainous Things series to catch up on the larger universe lore, but there *were* some important developments that occurred for Ziggy and Micah in Rabble: End Game that inevitably needed to be mentioned in this book. ****Please see the "Off-Page Developments Note" that precedes this section****

And, please do not hesitate to email the author directly with any questions or suggestions for adding to the TWs.

NOW THE GOOD STUFF

Content, Tropes & Kinks (may contain SPOILERS):

- Green. Flag. Men. (One is still kind of morally gray tho)
- Established MM couple (still experiencing idiots-in-love moments).

- Grumpy/sunshine, hurt/comfort, found family & all the schmoopy feels.
- The usual unhinged humor + witty banter.
- Micah levels up as a space wizard.
- Ziggy has a Commander Babygirl kink.
- Swoonworthy mutual obsession and respect (forever each other's hype girl).
- Sci-fi lite.
- Spice melange but make it a witchy bitch crystal.
- Twisty plot where our boys don't know who to trust (EVERYONE'S A SUSPECT).
- More is revealed about supe origins (the lore continues...)!
- Rabble cameos (especially our alien polycule—***see Off-Page Developments Note***—but only through text and family video calls).
- Just a pair of space sloots continuing to enjoy the fancy peen buffet from the alien skinsuit closet.
- Tendril Touchy Time is still elite.
- The breeding kink is only eclipsed by the competency kink.
- The safe word is still Stormtrooper (but "free use" has been established, let's be real).
- The action starts out with a bang (literally).
- Xenomorphs are creepy hot.
- Reclaiming your power by fucking the alien that almost ate you.
- A primal chase scene (because scarousal is part of the fun!).
- Brats gonna brat by keeping their fine asses to themselves ("Lower your shields!")
- Ziggy. Begging.
- Men whimpering.

- RIP Han Solo pants. Again.
- When the skinsuit has a Venom tongue…
- The cock "cage" is part of the fun *("Anything is a dildo if you're brave enough!")*
- Ziggy continues to unalive Micah (and us) with his filthy mouth.
- Skinsuit induced language barriers.
- All our Grogu + Mando Space Daddy dreams come true with the arrival of "the most adorable little ball of Big Mad" we've ever seen (but they're just a baby).
- Please Note: The little creature friend is a NEWBORN, and while they are more active than a human newborn would be, you shouldn't expect the level of interactiveness and personality we got with Daisy in Putting Out for a Hero. They sleep a lot.
- Micah embraces his inner "white woman finds a cougar kitten."
- Unsurprisingly, Ziggy lacks any semblance of natural parenting skills (blame Theo), so (under much duress) calls *Zion* for parenting tips.
- All Stellarians are brats.
- Ziggy learns about wet dreams.
- Blowies on the *MTV Cribs* roof deck.
- A very sneaky finger.
- Micah doesn't know how to take a compliment (especially when he "was gonna gobble your dick anyway—no need to butter [him] up.")
- The joy of turning your significant other into a sloppy mess though a mix of praise and degradation.
- Space Daddy doesn't NEED more (or any) weapons, but that won't stop him from buying them (big guns = big boners, all around).
- Space fiancés—no take backsies.

- Smexy fangs being put to good use ("Mark me up, Space Daddy!").
- Kink confessions during Tendril Touchy Time.
- Ziggy. Talking. Micah. Through. It.
- Plenty of edging, orgasm denial, and "good boys," because Ziggy loves to make Micah squirm before he explodes.
- Ziggy ruthlessly teases Micah about a certain set of twins back on Earth.
- A double-donged skinsuit—with KNOTS! (Full disclosure: There is no DP in this scene. Boo, hiss! I promise, you'll enjoy what happens instead...)
- Using "somno fun-time powers" on your stellar collision so you can lick the cum out of their ass while they rest (as we do).
- Knowing your partner is capable of greatness and using whatever means necessary until they accept this inarguable truth ("Get on the goddamn bed. Your training isn't done.")
- Just a stern Jedi Master and his slutty little student.
- Micah uses his very impressive superpowers to make a triple tentacle dildo.
- "C'mon, babygirl. Fuck yourself for your Space Daddy."
- Commander Babygirl stands on business when it comes to this bad bitch partnership.
- Micah discovers his Dommy Mommy vibes.
- It's a good thing Ziggy doesn't overreact when Micah's in danger... said no one.
- ZIGGY FINALLY SAYS THE L-WORD!!!
- Ultimate. Codependency. Achieved.
- "Fuck me from the inside."

- That unconditional support we love from these two ("I trust you—even if you don't trust yourself.")
- *A trope that is one of the author's absolute favorites, and it's killing her not to include it in this list, but she doesn't want to ruin the surprise... (hint: just hold out for the deathpond)*
- Dr. Micah does not play.
- Realizing you not only have a lot in common with your greatest enemy but that the actual enemy may be within.
- All the stretching, blow jobs, frotting, rimming, dicks (and other appendages) in asses (and other openings), tendril bondage, biting/mate marking, etc because this is a (sci-fi) MM romance with two adventurous little space sluts.

Bonus epilogue-specific CWs:

- SOMNO FUN-TIME x INFINITY!
- Commander Babygirl, reporting for booty ("Your safe word is Grogu and your ass is *mine* tonight.").
- Space Daddy submitting (bad bitch in the streets, good boy in the sheets).
- "All you need to do is beg me for it like a good boy."
- Tendril Touchy Time (for REAL).
- The mpreg vibes are vibing *(to be continued...)*

NOT Triggers. More like FYIs:

- "Excessive" (not really) use of they/them pronouns. Stellarians (and most other aliens encountered in this series) are nonbinary at birth (*see updated **Nonbinary is Normative Note**, below*).

Therefore, our MCs don't assume gender until told otherwise (and even then, they respect the individual's right to choose—like with their alien baby).

- As mentioned above in the **Reading Order** section, there *were* some important developments that occurred for Ziggy and Micah in Rabble: End Game (Villainous Things, Book 5—which occurred between Earth Boys and this book) that inevitably needed to be mentioned. I did my best within Space Daddy's Guide to the Galaxy to get you caught up to speed on any necessary backstory, without info dumping *and* without detracting from the main storyline of Villains in Space... and the main COUPLE—Micah and Ziggy. While I understand that this may be a frustrating reading experience for some, it was unavoidable (and I am unapologetic to those who are big mad that the polycule exists). Please see the **Off-Page Developments** note that precedes these CW/TWs for more info.

Possible triggers (please also check above list and note this section may contain SPOILERS):

- An extremely misleading paperback cover design. By the time our boys landed on "Not-Hoth," it was dead of February here in Maine and I just could NOT write about anyone existing in the snow. Sorry not sorry for the bait and switch, bishes.
- Questionable adoption process of a ferocious alien creature (who's really just a baby).
- Conflicting parenting methods (*someone* suggested the boiler room would make a good nursery...)

- The real-life challenges of new parenthood—including resentment and loss of intimacy (thank F for nanny bots!). This may not be YOUR experience, but it is someone's.
- Ziggy fighting (non-descriptive) intrusive thoughts/urges to potentially *hurt* the child he's supposed to be protecting. **There are external influences making him feel this way, combined with him also not fully understanding his own naturally protective feelings. In the end no harm comes to the baby alien and Ziggy is a very devoted Space Dad (don't tell him I said that tho).**
- The breeding kink is STRONG in this book (more so than normal, which is saying a lot in a C. Rochelle book), and is now veering into the topic of actual mpreg with these two. **PLEASE NOTE: There is no mpreg in this book (at least… not between our two MCs…) but with how things are going, you might want to expect it in book 3 (and not from who you'd think…).**
- That being said, there are also some BIG (conflicted) FEELINGS about pregnancy/parenthood, specifically from our resident alien abandoned sad boi.
- Micah has big feelings of his own over his inability to get mpregged, to be identified as "mated" by other aliens, or to change skinsuits the way Ziggy can (**see updated **Body Dysmorphia and Infertility** note, below**)
- Violence (against others) as foreplay (these are NON-humans we're talking about).
- ON THAT NOTE… As usual, kink and other sexual experiences are explored in ways that could be

deemed unsafe were the MCs human (but prior discussion is key with these two CONSENT KINGS).

- Sweary dialogue.
- Naughty, medium-dark humor.
- Unhinged (some might say excessive) inner thoughts.
- Non-descriptive violence that includes excessive threats (usually with tendrils unleashed), exploding aliens & alien goo, electrocution, rampages, Ziggy blowing up everything in sight when his mate goes missing for two minutes, and the countless beheadings of Hydra-style aliens.
- On that note, there are aliens with snake heads (as Indiana Jones says, "why did it have to be snakes?")
- Vague references to Micah's parents' death, which I suppose is another thing that happened "off-page" in End Game but whatever (GOOD RIDDANCE).
- Ziggy getting briefly triggered by the sight of Honnor armored up and going into battle (because of past events).
- Ziggy temporarily has his tendrils trapped inside him, triggering the extremely uncomfortable—almost claustrophobic—panic that goes along with that.
- Nerdy pet names used as both nicknames and honorifics.
- Using religious phrases in an overtly sexual context (oh my god/Jesus Christ), along with the use of the words slut/brat/whore/etc in the bedroom (consensually and enthusiastically).
- The word bitch is also used, but as a compliment (eg. Bad Bitch Mercenary, which Ziggy—and Micah!—are).

- Still more dick eating (*Corpus spongiosum is tasty, y'all!*).
- The love confessions continue to take their sweet time (Micah has known since day one, but is waiting on skittish Ziggy. Meanwhile Zig is turning it into an existential crisis, as usual. I promise, you will SWOON once it finally happens in this book!).
- Ziggy continues telling little white lies that are more about self-protection or fear of negatively affecting Micah and *ohmyfuckinggawd, Zig, what is the matter with you?*
- Dr. Micah is fully booked and working overtime (and continues to carry the team).
- Miscommunication (of course) and relatable relationship growing pains, considering one person is a communication king and the other is an emotionally constipated alien learning to "human" (but we get a good grovel out of it).
- Even Micah clams up at one point and Ziggy (quite hypocritically…) loses his mind while not quite understanding the concept of "personal space."
- Old self-worth baggage rears its ugly head (on both sides—Micah is determined to be "useful" and Ziggy is doing everything to prove he isn't "weak" Le sigh).
- Continued murky gray morality on the whole body snatching business, and what is done with those bodies (in the end, Ziggy is a symbiotic alien, so we all just need to deal with it).
- A cutthroat, dubious moral code for supes (and aliens!) that isn't meant to be understood by normies. "It's how the game is played."
- Parody references to Star Wars and other Alien-related franchises (Zig just can't escape those

"Hollywood Aliens"), David Bowie music and movies, Candyland, Trumpet of the Swan, *MTV Cribs*, ACME Corporation, Jeff Goldblum/*The Fly*, Audrey II/Twoey/*Little Shop of Horrors*, Transformers, Dr. Seuss, and Superman's Fortress of Solitude. ****Please see note on parody usage rights in the Copyright section.****

———

NONBINARY IS NORMATIVE IN SPACE — UPDATE:

Being an alien whose true form is a cluster of stars, Stellarians are nonbinary by nature. They do occasionally end up identifying as male or female, or a mix of both, over the course of their very long lives, but nonbinary with they/them pronouns is to be assumed until stated otherwise.

There are occasional instances (mostly in Earth Boys) where a side character is potentially misgendered due to their outward—vessel's—appearance before it's understood that there's a Stellarian inside. **This is because, while nonbinary is the norm in space, there *are* some alien species who typically identify as he/him or she/her.** While misgendering would be considered harmful behavior in our world, it's a common situation for these symbiotic, body snatching aliens to find themselves in, and not one they take issue with*.

However, in *this* book, the species they encounter are all treated as nonbinary, so the only gendering we see is for Ziggy, Micah, and the family back on Earth.

*Regardless of what is considered normative in my

fictional world, please take care of yourself while reading if this situation would be triggering to you.

——

BODY DYSMORPHIA AND INFERTILITY NOTE — UPDATE:

We previously established that Ziggy identifies as he/him and prefers his male presenting Earthling form above all others—including his true form—for reasons that were explained in Earth Boys. **I wouldn't classify Ziggy's struggle in Earth Boys as body dysmorphia (after discussing his situation with a few in the trans community at the time), but I still asked that those who struggle with it please take care of themselves while reading.**

In this book, Micah battles frustrations over how he *can't* change his appearance the way Ziggy can—not because he doesn't identify as his Earthling form but because he wants to be able to truly (in alien terms) "mate" with his mate. **This *could* be triggering to those who've experienced infertility (especially the feelings of inadequacy that come with that experience), so I also wanted to flag it.**

In general, I like to err on the side of caution when it comes to my readers' potential triggers. Your mental health is more important to me than page reads.

A NOTE ON SUPERHERO & VILLAIN IDENTITIES

A SUPE'S IDENTITY IS SACRED!

In this world I've created, superheroes and villains (and aliens undercover as such) are supposed to guard ALL secret identities from normies—including their own, that of their family/clan, and even their enemies. When one supe addresses another as their supe name, that is a not-so-subtle way of saying they are considered the enemy at that moment. (Siblings may also do this just to mess with each other.)

Some supes like the Suarez twins have "civilian names," for use around normies (since they went to normie art school). In Micah's case, he wasn't integrated into normie society enough to need one, and with Ziggy (and Zion), Deathball was really the only time they mixed with the public (and it was still "masked," in a way). And Theo... well he was just Theo.

OUR MCs:
Exo Tech = Supe name
Micah Salah = Secret identity

Star Hopper = Supe name
Ziggy Andromeda = Secret identity

Scaled Justice = Supe name
Zion Salah = Secret identity

Shock = Supe name
Andre Acosta = Civilian name
Andre (Dre) Suarez = Secret identity

Awe = Supe name
Gabriel Acosta = Civilian name
Gabriel (Gabe) Suarez = Secret identity

Theo Coatl = Secret identity/celebrity persona

Space Daddy's Guide to the Galaxy not only features texting and the usual internal monologue, but Stellarian and "mind-speak."

Below is how I formatted each, to try to avoid confusion:

TEXTS:
Name Bolded: *Left-aligned and italicized for others.*

                    Right-aligned, italicized & bolded for POV texter.

INTERNAL MONOLOGUE:
Left-aligned and italicized.

STELLARIAN:
"Left-aligned and italicized but within a paragraph with dialogue tags."

MIND-SPEAK:

"Left-aligned, italicized with quotation marks for non-POV mind-speaker."

"Right-aligned, italicized with quotation marks for POV mind-speaker."

FLASHBACKS (to dialogue previously spoken):

> *"Left aligned, italicized and indented with quotation marks."*

ELECTRONIC COMMUNICATION (between planets and ships)
:The planet/base will be left aligned and italicized, between colons:

> - The ship answers within hyphenated bulleted lists, left aligned and indented.

THE LODGER 79 CROSS
SECTION

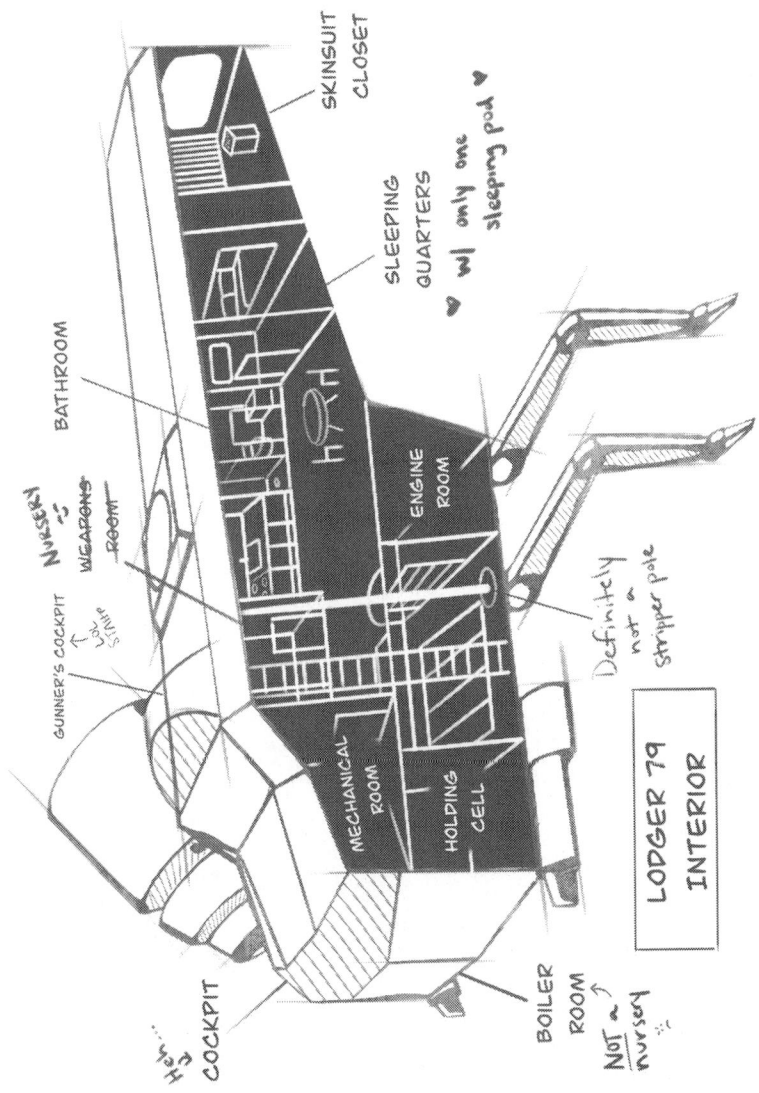

SKINSUIT CLOSET

SLEEPING QUARTERS
♥ w/ only one sleeping pod ♥

BATHROOM

NURSERY
WEAPONS ROOM
Vol Server?

GUNNER'S COCKPIT

MECHANICAL ROOM

HOLDING CELL

ENGINE ROOM

Definitely not a stripper pole

Heh—
COCKPIT

BOILER ROOM
Not a nursery

LODGER 79 INTERIOR

STALK C. ROCHELLE

Stalk me in all the places!
(by joining my Clubhouse of Smut on Patreon, my Little
Sinners FB Group, and subscribing to my newsletter)

For those who love green flag men in the streets, space sloots in the sheets

I was *pissed* at Ziggy Andromeda.

It was an unfamiliar, uncomfortable feeling. I'd never been truly *mad* at him before—not when he was refusing to admit he had obvious feelings for me, not even when he'd put me to sleep to fight Astrum Force Command by himself.

Clearly, he needed me as backup then...

But noooo—today, *I had to stay behind.*

My angry muttering nearly drowned out the echo of my Han Solo boots stomping down the metal gangway of the Lodger 79, but no one was around to hear me anyway.

Since I've been underestimated once again.

The worst part was, my Space Daddy was the *last* person I ever thought would do me dirty like that. Even with Zig being a lone-wolf mercenary before we met, he'd always made it clear no matter what happened—no matter what skinsuit he wore or what roles we had to play—we were *partners.*

C. ROCHELLE

Equals in every way.

Jk, I guess.

Thanks to this swoon-worthy mutual respect, I'd assisted him on every mission since the day I first hitched a ride to Stellaria with his Celestial Cube. Granted, my man had no choice at first, thanks to a little white lie about me exploding if he moved out of range, but *still.*

What babygirl wants, babygirl gets!

I angrily huffed as I refocused on my self-appointed task of carrying yet another armful of Ziggy's seemingly endless collection of guns from the weapons room to the kitchen.

Besides keeping me distracted—*kind of*—from my self-pity spiral, there was a reason for my cleaning frenzy. We'd landed on Marox hours ago for a high-level mission—to rescue a mysterious alien baby so coveted, an anonymous someone was willing to pay big money to steal it from someone else.

Kind of dramatic, if you ask me...

But what do I know?

In my opinion, we had a bigger issue than intergalactic babynapping. The Lodger only had one sleeping pod, and no way in *hell* was I giving up Tendril Touchy Time for our guest to have somewhere to sleep, no matter how adorable.

During our journey to Marox, I'd pointed out the obvious—that a baby needed a nursery. Ziggy had responded by flinging open the door to the goddamn *boiler room* and impatiently gesturing inside. In his mind, the warmth from the nine thousand degree equipment would create the perfect cozy cocoon for our tiny, helpless guest.

Space Daddy chose violence.

At the time, I responded by taking several deep breaths, all while reminding myself my alien didn't possess a nurturing bone in his borrowed body, through no fault of his own.

'Blame Theo' is the company motto.

I grumbled under my breath as I dumped my deadly haul on the kitchen table. Even though it pained me, I could begrudgingly acknowledge the Stellarian responsible for Ziggy's emotional constipation had sufficiently groveled since our last space adventure.

My man's still the better *man, though.*

As pissy as I currently felt, I was incredibly proud of Ziggy for *accepting* this apology. Putting aside hundreds of years of resentment in favor of forgiveness showed immense personal growth on his part, even if other factors might have drop-kicked the process.

Like the tropical island forced proximity situation, plus the subtle and not-so-subtle nudges from me and Theo's stellar collisions, supervillain twins Andre and Gabriel Suarez.

Aaaaand an unexpected kiss between Gabe and I that was reso-nance-induced and approved of by all parties involved.

Just stellar collision things.

My lips tingled at the memory—followed by my asshole clenching at the memory of Ziggy *wrecking* me afterward—and before I knew it, my phone was in my hands.

My original hop into the final frontier had been a little... *spontaneous,* so I hadn't fully worked out how to stay in touch with family and friends. My return to space was way more planned, so I'd had time to invent a satellite feature for the *Lodger* that kept us connected to select cell phones back on Earth.

Texting with Gabe would make me feel so much better right now...

I stared at my phone for a good fifteen seconds before sighing and setting it aside. While I *was* angry at Zig for dismissing my competency, I needed to resolve things directly with him instead of contacting my Earth-bound "boyfriend" for a sweet hit of schmoopy dopamine.

I guess I'll be an adult about it.

Hmph.

With another sigh, I headed back to the weapons room for the final load. The space was about the size of a freight elevator, which seemed cozy enough for a nursery, the walls lined with what were obviously custom gun racks.

Too bad.

Zig was just going to have to find somewhere else for his excessive, and slightly unnecessary, weapons collection.

He has built-in samurai tendrils, for chrissakes!

Stupid, sexy, razor-sharp tendrils...

I started angrily trudging toward the kitchen again, only for the outdoor motion alarm to suddenly go off. Of course, the security app was on my phone in the opposite direction of the cockpit, so I unceremoniously dumped my latest armful of guns onto the gangway floor and chose to investigate at the source.

It's probably just Ziggy returning from his solo *mission.*

Good.

Perfect timing to go sleep in the weapons room.

Once in the cockpit, I peered through the windows, trying to catch a glimpse of whatever set off the alarm. Unfortunately, I couldn't see past the swaying palm fronds surrounding us, since Zig insisted on landing the Lodger in the middle of the goddamn jungle for added camouflage on top of the cloaking device.

Well, the camo is working both ways right now.

I slumped into the captain's chair, displaying my best pout while awaiting his inevitable star hop.

Only for Ziggy not to appear.

That's... weird.

I leaned forward and turned on the night vision scope, frowning when all that accomplished was providing an unobstructed view of the *top* of the jungle canopy.

Next time, I'll *park the spaceship.*

The motion alarm wailed again, and my indignation started to fade.

What if Ziggy's too injured to star hop?

I actually didn't know if a Stellarian *could* be injured enough to inhibit star hopping, but once the thought planted itself in my head, the roots of anxiety began to grow. It didn't take long for me to envision the love of my life crawling toward the ship, bleeding out while I wasted precious seconds being big mad over getting left behind.

I need to rescue him!!!

Before my brain could catch up to my actions, I was in the landing bay and entering the secret code—*rudely,* not *my birthday*—to deploy the ramp.

Wait.

What the hell is wrong with me?

Realizing I'd almost done something incredibly stupid, I activated my shields, covering myself in a transparent, protective layer of my own invention that not even a Stellarian could get through.

Then I deployed the ramp.

Only to find Ziggy waiting for me at the bottom.

Well... that *worked out.*

His appearance momentarily startled me, despite my relief, because he was inhabiting his most terrifying form yet.

Maroxians were vaguely humanoid, if only because of the bipedal aspect, but that was where the similarities ended. This particular skinsuit was closer to a xenomorph, with its inky-black exoskeleton, sleek aerodynamic head, disconcerting lack of eyes, and an extremely impressive tongue.

Hot.

I wasn't being sarcastic. Yes, I probably would have pissed myself if faced with one of these predators IRL, but with *Ziggy* behind the wheel, the grotesque became gorgeous.

Because it's him.

Wait...

Is that him?

"Z-Zig?" I whispered, the *pull* I normally felt in his presence nowhere to be found.

That was when I realized the Maroxian at the bottom of the ramp was not only empty-handed, but had made no move to enter the ship. It was simply watching me, its creepily sightless head lowered and its elongated body coiled in a crouch, as if preparing to pounce.

Oh, fuck.

I dove for the keypad, but it was too late. The *not*-Ziggy nightmare was already bounding up the closing ramp on all fours —its claws gouging the metal as it released an ear-splitting shriek.

Fuck, fuck, fuck!

Operating on instinct alone, I used my powers to conjure a series of darts before blindly firing. Without waiting to see if they made contact, I threw myself through the door leading back inside the ship.

The Maroxian's howl implied my aim was accurate. Unfortunately, the hit didn't slow my opponent in the least as it tackled me before I could fully close the door.

I screamed—more from fear than pain—but managed to lengthen my steel toe spikes beyond my shields to kick the alien off me, power up my supespeed, and start running.

Ya boy needs a weapon!

As impressive as Ziggy thought my superpowers were, I *did* have my limitations. Yes, I could form basic weapons out of inorganic matter, including earthly guns, but that didn't mean

I could match the offensive technology needed to survive out here in space.

The only reason I'd been able to take down Astrum Force's Head Commander—besides feeding off my grief over Ziggy's supposed death—was because I'd obsessively studied my man's tendrils and battle techniques. Unfortunately, after being told I *wasn't* setting foot on Marox, I'd stopped all research on its inhabitants out of bratty protest.

Not the smartest move, in hindsight...

In the interest of said hindsight, I quickly extended my high-tech glasses to 360 mode and immediately wished I hadn't. The Maroxian was close enough that if I hadn't had my shields up, I would have felt its breath on my neck.

Probably would have smelled it too.

My lungs screamed from exertion as I rounded the corner, but the sight of the weapons I'd discarded on the gangway gave me a second wind. I dove into the mountain of ammunition like it was a pile of autumn leaves, grabbed the first thing I could, and twisted onto my back before pulling the trigger.

The Maroxian yowled in pain, stumbling backward and pausing only long enough to glance down at the fucking *harpoon* sticking out of its midsection before releasing a bone-chilling growl.

Imma die.

My superhuman strength was fading, making my shields waver alarmingly. Meanwhile, my intergalactic opponent seemed mildly irritated at being majorly disemboweled, clearly more than ready to go twenty more rounds.

Ziggy's gonna be so pissed if I die...

At the thought of my man, the piece of him permanently lodged inside me pulsed—*hard*—and my hand moved of its own volition to grab what looked like a goddamn rocket launcher.

Why not go out with a bang?

The Maroxian screeched a battle cry and leaped for my jugular. I fired, releasing a screech of my own as the propulsion tossed me backward into the pile. When death didn't arrive, I tentatively opened my eyes, but all I could see beyond my visor was a thick coating of green goo dripping down my shields.

Gross.

I swiped the viscous goop away, only to discover the entire gangway section—floor to ceiling—along with every inch of *me* was covered in what was clearly the remains of my opponent.

So fucking gross.

Blowing out a shaky breath, I slowly stood on even shakier legs, determined to clean up this mess before Ziggy returned. A faint sound had me snapping my attention farther down the gangway, and my shoulders and spirit sank.

Because *another* Maroxian was waiting for me.

My stellar collision is in trouble.

Must. Get. To. My. Mate.

Those were my only thoughts two minutes ago as I switched tactics partway through my mission, abandoning my original plan of espionage in favor of simply securing the asset and star hopping to my ship.

When I'd materialized on the gangway, close to where I'd felt Micah's vibrations, my borrowed hearts nearly stopped.

What in Stellaria's name happened here?!

Micah was standing—barely—and covered in a strange green substance with a Torrid Blaster dangling from his hand.

A blaster he was now aiming at me.

"Get the *fuck* off my ship!" he growled in the trade language, making my borrowed dick twitch with what a "bad bitch" he was being.

So cute and threatening...

When he cocked the blaster, I realized he was too keyed up to realize it was *me* in this Maroxian skinsuit, which meant I had about a millisecond to react before he fired.

I *could* deflect the blast with my tendrils, but I was still holding the asset in my claws, so I star hopped again—this time, materializing directly beside him.

"It's me, my..." I crooned as non-threateningly as possible, wincing as I realized there was no direct translation in this language for either his name or what he was to me. *"Celestial catastrophe."*

That works, given the situation.

"Wha—oh, *thank fuck,*" Micah replied in his native tongue, able to understand the Maroxian language thanks to his implanted translation device. "I maybe could have fought another one, but sheesh! That was a *lot."*

Wait, what?

He dropped the gun onto the pile of weapons he was inexplicably standing in and moved to hug me before rearing back. "Ugh. Hold on. I'm covered in... alien... goo."

He paused to gingerly dissolve his shields. This was a process that normally fascinated me, but the reality of the situation was starting to settle in, and my true form did not like it one bit.

"You... fought a Maroxian?" I carefully asked as a few wayward tendrils unfurled, *needing* to touch him—to confirm he was unharmed. "How did a Maroxian get onto the ship?"

"Uh, haha, yeah, soooo, about that..." Micah laughed nervously, shifting on his feet and tripping over the goo-covered weapons littering the floor. "I may have... accidentally let one in, thinking it was you. But, *as you can see,* I took care of the problem."

A Maroxian tried to hurt what was mine?

I AM GOING TO KILL THEM ALL!

"Hey! What's that you're holding?" My mate's smooth voice momentarily distracted me from imminent violence.

If I'd had visible eyes, I would have slow-blinked. Instead, I followed his gaze down to my prize.

"It's. An. Egg," I gritted out, practically shaking at this point.

I still want to kill them all.

"Huh," he replied, cocking his head as he reached for it, either oblivious to or ignoring my simmering rage. "I was expecting an actual *baby.*"

"Yes, well..." I grunted, more than happy to hand off the beach ball-sized object and follow closely behind as he began skipping down the gangway. "Nothing about this mission went to plan."

Micah stiffened but didn't turn around, and I couldn't help but notice how he then completed his journey by *stomping* into my weapons room.

Which is apparently no longer my weapons room...

"What?" I gaped, my confusion temporarily eclipsing my haywire protective instincts. "What... did you *do?*"

I winced again as I *felt* Micah's reaction to my primitive words but, yet again, I lacked the language to better express myself.

Which would be happening even if I was back in my Earthling form, I'm sure.

"Well, *partner,*" he snapped, spinning to face me, his tone making me straighten. "While you were out on a *very important* yet *solo* mission, your little housewife was at home, working on the nursery."

My... wife?

The word had such a visceral effect on me, I was lost for words. Unfortunately, this hesitation only seemed to increase Micah's irritation. With a huff, he turned away again, and I mutely watched as he carefully placed the oversized egg in an empty dry goods container lined with satin.

Specifically, the pile of kimonos Theo gave me as a goodbye present.

This makeshift bedding wasn't an issue, as I wanted nothing less than to dress like an aging Hollywood starlet. If anything, I puffed up with pride that Micah had come up with this solution on his own.

My mate is such a good provider.

Mine.

The possessive *need* to claim him roiled beneath the surface, but Micah was obviously upset, and we'd been together long enough for me to know he needed to *communicate* first.

Dr. Micah requires a session.

"It would not have been safe for you to come," I explained yet again. "Maroxians *eat* most every other species in the galaxy. They might have seen you as food."

"I would have been fine!" he shouted, angrily gesturing toward the innards-spattered gangway. "Clearly, I fought off a man-eating Maroxian all by myself—"

My vision went red as I advanced, backing him against the wall. "I know you did. Feeling your terror while being unable to reach you was excruciating."

Micah's plump bottom lip trembled, but I knew he'd prefer I shared my thoughts—my *feelings*—than hold anything inside.

Talk about excruciating.

The stellar collision bond we shared allowed both of us to sense the other's emotions to some extent—similar to how a Stellarian's tendrils tasted the air—but the piece of myself I'd left inside my mate gave me unfettered access to his inner workings.

Almost as if we're a single organism.

Just how I like it.

What I had no intention of sharing was that the main reason I hadn't immediately star hopped back to the ship was because of how delicate the mission was.

Astrum Force—and the anonymous benefactor of said mission—was counting on *me* to grab that stupid egg, which meant I'd been forced to make a split-second decision that now sat in my gut like a stone.

What if I left intel behind that could have helped us?

What if Micah hadn't won the fight?

The lack of intel I could work with—*hopefully*—but if something had happened to my stellar collision before I'd reached him, I never would have forgiven myself.

And then I definitely would have killed everyone.

Micah swallowed thickly. "I-I'm sorry, Zig—"

No, I'm sorry, sunshine.

"It was for the best," I interrupted, my unavoidably harsh tone making him flinch. "If I'd arrived in time to find that Maroxian attacking you, it would still be alive, because I'd force it to watch as I removed every one of its appendages. Slowly. Painfully."

My mate was shuddering, and for one, horrifying moment, I feared I'd triggered him. Here I was, *cornering* his much smaller, more fragile form while resembling the very same alien he'd just eliminated.

I keep fucking things up.

"Zig," Micah gasped, his lashes fluttering. "I'm *trying* to be mad over here, but then you have to talk about slicing up our enemies..."

I chuckled, which came out as more of a dry wheeze with these vocal chords. "You want to be mad at me?"

"Yes. I mean, no... I dunno," he mumbled. "What I really want is for you to show me I'm yours."

"I would enjoy nothing more," I rasped, lowering my head before remembering my appearance. "Let me first go swap out this skinsuit—"

"No!" Micah yelped before his cheeks darkened with an enticing blush. "I want you... like *this.*"

My massive jaw dropped. "You *do?*"

I shouldn't have been surprised. My stellar collision had an insatiable appetite, and he'd made it clear from the start he wanted me in *all* forms.

My perfect slut.

"Are you... certain?" I asked, even as my exoskeleton-covered cock extended to press insistently against his stomach. "You've only just survived an encounter with a Maroxian—"

"And that's exactly why I want it." Micah jutted out his chin, daring me to argue. "I want to run from my nightmare, but this time, when it catches me, I want it to fuck me into the gangway floor."

"Did you say *run?*" I choked out, stumbling back a few feet as my—and my skinsuit's—predatory instincts dangerously flared to life.

Micah swallowed again, his gaze sweeping over me hungrily as he inched toward the doorway. "Yeah, I did. My safe word is Stormtrooper, and right now, I'm your Earthling prey."

And then, he raced into the hall.

Well.

What babygirl wants, babygirl gets.

3

MICAH

Catch me when you can, Space Daddy!

It was a question of *when*, not *if*, because this was Zig we were talking about and, besides the fact he was wearing a skinsuit I already knew was faster than me, my man played to win.

That doesn't mean I won't give him a chase to remember.

The instant my boots connected with the alien goo-covered gangway, I conjured a set of crampons, digging the spikes into the slippery metal so I stayed upright long enough not to fall on my ass.

It wasn't until I reached the kitchen that I heard Maroxian-Ziggy release a bone-chilling yowl and start his pursuit, and a split second of panic had me breaking into a cold sweat.

Focus, Micah!

It's just Zig.

And you're a bad bitch.

There weren't many places to go in the Lodger, and as tempting as it was to make a beeline for the bedroom, descending to the lower level would drag out the foreplay a little longer.

First, I need to slow him down.

The majority of Zig's displaced weapons were still scattered around the kitchen, and while I didn't know how all of them worked, I recognized a few, like the Iota Bombs. These acorn-sized explosives were more of a distraction than anything, but the flashes of light they gave off were enough to temporarily blind whoever triggered them.

Maroxian-Ziggy's monstrous shadow appeared in the doorway, so I tossed a handful in his direction and made my escape, sliding down the fireman's pole I'd *begged* him to install alongside the utilitarian ladder.

Because... c'mon!

The bombs exploded the same moment I hit the lower deck, and I heard Ziggy curse in Maroxian before growling in annoyance over his temporary loss of sight.

Determined not to give him any edge this time, I reactivated my shields, masking my scent before slipping into the stifling-hot boiler room.

Aka, the not-nursery.

I remained motionless until the sound of his sharp talons scraping the metal floor faded into the distance. Then, I traded out my crampons and slipped from the room, silently sneaking back the way I came.

I'd barely made it a few feet when the hair on the back of my neck raised—leaving me with the distinct impression I was being watched—but when I peered over my shoulder, the gangway was empty.

And deathly silent.

This does not bode well.

The ladder was in sight, but I only took one more step before a strange sound had me freezing mid-step. It was a husky, rhythmic hiss that sounded like laughter.

It was also coming from directly above me.

Like that one dumbass in every horror movie, I slowly looked up. Ambush predator that he was, Ziggy was plastered to the ceiling, his armored Maroxian form molded around the pipes and lighting, awaiting the moment I realized it was all over.

Not yet, it's not!

I threw myself toward the ladder, screaming when—like my earlier, way less sexy chase—claws closed around my ankle and dragged me to the floor.

Thanks to instinctual panic, my safe word was on the tip of my tongue, but my dick was also hard enough to punch through my shields, straight into the metal beneath me, so it was clear which head was in charge.

"Lower. Your. Shields," Ziggy growled in my ear, caging me beneath his unfamiliar body, reminding me how much bigger he was in this form.

My hands closed around the fireman's pole in a defiant grip. "No."

Yeah, I was still a little salty over being left behind, and a *lot* salty over how easily he'd caught me.

What better way to brat out than to keep my fine ass to myself?

"I can't smell—" Ziggy cut himself off, panting in growly breaths that only made me harder. "All I smell is the Maroxian who attacked you. I must fix that."

Fix it?

I knew Zig was limited to the vocabulary of whatever skinsuit he occupied in that moment—*hello, celestial catastrophe*—but he was also a man who chose his words carefully.

"*Nothing about this mission went to plan.*"

He thinks he fucked up his directives...

But it's actually my *fault.*

With a sigh, I twisted my body to look at him over my shoulder. "I shouldn't have opened the bay door. The motion alarms went off, and I couldn't see what was out there through the scope. I-I thought you might be hurt and unable to star hop..."

Maroxian-Ziggy cocked his head—an oddly curious expression on such an inhuman face. "You... wanted to save me?"

I huffed, annoyed at this big idiot all over again. "Of *course* I wanted to save you, Zig! You aren't the only one who gets worried when we're apart. At least in your case, you can *feel it* when I need help."

Ziggy froze, probably because I was getting myself all worked up. Tears pricked my eyelids as the anxiety and relief I'd been holding in flooded my system now that the adrenaline of the chase was gone.

"Lower your shields, *star brightness*," he said, gentler this time, and I stifled a smile at his ad-libbing what was most likely supposed to be 'sunshine.' "I *need* to be inside you."

I bit back my customary reminder that he already *was*, but I knew even that permanently embedded piece wasn't enough for Ziggy Andromeda. If my man could live inside me completely, he would be the happiest little body snatcher in all the galaxies.

But that's not what he's talking about at the moment...

My gaze lowered to where Ziggy's Maroxian dick rested on my inaccessible ass—my lower back, really, thanks to its ridiculous length. It was long, yes, but the most exciting feature was the almost cock cage-like exoskeleton surrounding every inch of it, save for the dripping head.

"Please..." Ziggy mumbled low—as close to a whine as his current vessel allowed—rubbing himself against me, leaving a trail of precum on my shields.

Well, if I must.

Besides wanting to continue my all-access tour of the skinsuit closet, my proud Stellarian *begging* was my kryptonite, so I didn't waste another second before lowering my defenses.

Aaaand Zig didn't waste a second before he struck.

I yelped as his tail swung around, securely binding my wrists to the pole while his claws tore off everything I wore below the belt.

RIP, Han Solo pants.

Again.

Successfully immobilized, I could only watch in scaroused horror as his massive, fanged mouth opened—releasing his long, slimy black tongue.

Okay, why is that kinda...

"FUCK!" I shouted as Ziggy wrenched my ass cheeks apart, claws digging into my flesh as his mile-long tongue punched its way into my hole. "Holy fuck, Zig, just... *fuck!"*

Of course, he'd rimmed me before—in multiple forms—but this was the first skinsuit with a Venom-worthy appendage.

We were all *thinking it. Don't play.*

I writhed beneath him as it tunneled deeper, teasing my p-spot just enough to make me whine, the squelching sounds mixing with my helpless noises and Ziggy's growls until the gangway echoed with obscenity.

More, more, more!

All I knew was I would need to peruse the closet again after this, because the only time I'd experienced this glorious of a sensation was from Ziggy's tendrils.

Plus the tentacle dildo I'd created back home, pre-space adventures.

Nothing like the real thing nowadays.

"My mate," he growled after withdrawing his tongue, making me moan. "Mine to taste... to claim... to *devour..."*

Zig's brain had clearly gone bye-bye to primal la-la land, so I couldn't be sure if he meant that last part literally, but I also did not give a single fuck.

"Devour me," I whimpered as he licked a hot stripe up my center again. "I need more."

My brain might have been on its way to la-la land as well, but I was still coherent enough to know exactly which words to say to push his feral buttons.

"Get inside me. Please... *breed me.*"

That did it, as I barely registered a full second before Ziggy notched his armored cock at my opening, viciously pushing past my tight ring.

Okay, maybe not as tight as it used to be, but look what I'm dealing with here!

It was a good thing I'd spent the past several months gorging myself at the weird peen buffet, because, while the stretch was wild—magnified by the cage-like texture skipping over my prostate—the only pain I felt was the *good* kind.

There's nothing better than being stuffed full of alien appendages.

"Mine..." Ziggy rumbled, sawing his way in like he truly wanted to rip me open to nest inside. "Mine to drench with my seed, to fertilize and inseminate."

Ehhh...

It appeared the word 'breed' was not in the Maroxian vocabulary, but I could work with whatever my man gave me. After all, mating vibes were quite literally universal.

"Mine to impregnate."

That's the one!

Impregnate sounded close enough to mpreg to get my motor running. It didn't hurt that it reminded me of when I'd worn Ziggy's armor to the Muonova to pretend-capture him, only to have my dick-drunk Stellarian *beg* me to—

"Tear me apart, Space Daddy!" I blurted out in a sudden gush of inspiration.

Ziggy lowered himself with a growl, rubbery skin gliding over mine as razor-sharp teeth grazed the back of my neck. I instinctively squealed, clenching around him, and he cursed before placing a clawed hand on my nape instead.

No bedroom bites from this *skinsuit, thank you very much.*

I could live without the nibbles, especially with Ziggy holding me down so he could jackhammer into my ass with frenzied abandon. We'd played with ridged dicks before, but this was next level—like an actual piece of machinery wrecking my hole.

Anything is a dildo if you're brave enough!

"Yes, Zig! Yes, Space Daddy! Fuck me, breed me, mpreg me. Fill me with your cum. I'm yours to tear the fuck apart. Pump me full of Stellarian super space babies, *pleeeeease!*"

Never mind that this wasn't at all how Stellarians reproduced. I was happily babbling slutty nonsense, drooling on the gangway and so close to climax, I could taste it.

Like heaven.

Precum was pulsing from my throbbing dick, smearing all over the metal floor as the weight of Ziggy's thrusts provided unrelenting friction.

What I wouldn't give to turn the tables and breed his ass.

It wasn't the first time I'd envisioned mpregging my stellar collision, of somehow lodging a permanent piece of myself inside *him*.

And the obvious way to do that is to make babies with my Space Daddy.

This thought had me clamping down on the bulldozer currently rearranging my internal organs and howling through my orgasm, painting the floor with so much cum, it felt like a goddamn slip 'n slide.

Wheee!

"All. Mine," Ziggy snarled, his pelvis flush against my ass while his caged cock continued to piston inside me, pumping me so full, his 'seed' ran down my legs.

Okay, so maybe "drenched" was the right word...

We caught our collective breath for a few minutes while Ziggy massaged my wrists and nuzzled his terrifying face against the back of my neck.

To no one's surprise, he withdrew his monster cock before sliding down my body until he was in prime position to unleash that magic tongue again. I melted into a puddle— literally—as he burrowed into my ass, collecting every drop before rolling me over and licking the cum from my sweaty abs.

So gross yet so sweet.

Tears blurred my vision again, but this time, it was from grati- tude. Watching a creature who'd tried to kill me be so loving and gentle reminded me how perfect Ziggy was for me—not just with the way he protected me, but with how he always provided exactly what I needed.

He has certainly come a long way with the aftercare.

Closing my eyes, I allowed the soothing motion of his tongue to wash away my cum *and* my anxiety, bringing me back to baseline with his signature sexy competency.

Until the motion alarm went off again.

The one that meant something was *inside* the ship.

4

ZIGGY

Time to kill them all.

Reclaiming my mate had dulled the nearly unhinged possessiveness pulsing beneath the surface, but the thought of *another* predator nearby had me growing feral all over again.

Mine, mine, mine!

"Fuck..." Micah gasped, hurriedly yanking on his pants. "I swear, Zig, only one Maroxian got in before I closed the bayceee—"

His babbling turned into a yelp as I grabbed him around the waist and star hopped us to the cockpit. As soon as I determined the space was clear of threats, I engaged the lockdown doors and initialized an internal heat scan of the entire ship.

Let's see where you're hiding.

So I can kill you.

"Do you think they've come for the egg?" Micah whispered loudly. "Would they realize it was gone already?"

"Doubtful." I frowned at the odd data displayed on my dashboard. "The Maroxians had the egg in a custom incubator with barely any security." I glanced at my stellar collision and smirked. "At least, not with any security I couldn't handle."

The incubator itself had been easy to infiltrate, and my tendrils made quick work of the single guard assigned to overnight duty. Maroxians may have been at the top of the food chain in *this* corner of the galaxy but this false sense of superiority had turned into a glaring blind spot on their part.

Because Stellarians are superior to Maroxians.

We are superior to most other species, actually.

Micah was staring at me with a glassy-eyed expression I knew well, further confirmed by the pheromones he pumped into the air.

Behave.

"You're so effortlessly sexy, I cannot," he murmured before snapping out of his stupor to squint at me. "Did you say *incubator?* Wait—is *that* the reason you tried to turn the boiler room into the nursery?!"

"Yes," I replied mildly, confused by how his agitation seemed to be rapidly accelerating into panic.

"Oh gawd!" he gasped, looking like he was going to make a run for it. "I need to... I can't believe I fucked this up too..."

What in Stellaria's name is he talking about?

For reasons I blamed entirely on his blessedly deceased parents, Micah's 'worth' was an ongoing conversation. *I* knew he was the most impressive creature in all the galaxies—had even procured a certificate from The Knowledge saying as much to hang on the cockpit wall—yet he *still* insisted on focusing on his supposed flaws.

An impossible task.

Since he has none.

When he glanced at the barricaded door again, I realized why he was about to charge into battle.

For the egg.

Sigh.

"Star brightness," I inwardly scowled that this borrowed form wasn't allowing me to refer to Micah as the *sunshine* he was. "The asset is safe and warm enough. It was close to hatching anyway…"

I trailed off as my gaze drifted back to my security monitor, realizing exactly what had set off the motion sensors.

Oh.

Well, this is inconvenient.

"W-what is it, Zig?" Micah's voice wavered, making me want to kill every Maroxian all over again.

But that's not the intruder we're dealing with.

"Just a vermin problem," I soothed, forcing a smile. "I'll handle it while you fly us out of here, all right?"

The way Micah's warm brown eyes lit up caused my guilt to roar to life all over again. I knew he loved driving the ship, and while that was reason enough to allow him to do it, at the moment, I was shamelessly using it as a distraction.

Just until I get the situation under control.

"Commander Babygirl, at your service!" He saluted, grinning wildly, and I was thankful my current form hid the blush caused by that moniker.

It was in reference to the first time Micah had topped me—shortly after we defeated Astrum Force Command and during what *he* called our "Captured by the Enemy Alien Meet-Cute" at the Muonova.

We'd switched roles a few times since then, but I'd never let down my defenses quite like I had that time.

The twenty strong drinks helped...

It certainly wasn't a hardship to let him claim me. Micah was the only creature alive I would ever submit to, because he was the only one I trusted enough to allow *myself* to give up control.

Plus, his cock is perfect.

Actually, my mate was perfect, inside and out, and while I'd once thought claiming *him* was as close to heaven as I could get, I'd since discovered how exquisite it felt to allow him inside me.

Breeding me.

I knew a breeding kink—which we both enthusiastically had—and actual procreation were completely different things. The issue for *me* was how blurred the lines had become.

How it's all I can think about.

If I was being completely honest, the promise of Micah "pumping me full of Stellarian super space babies" had been lingering in the forefront of my mind ever since he first brought it up on Kaalanesea.

Unfortunately, I had mixed feelings about the concept of *family*—for reasons I blamed entirely on my creator back on Earth. Yes, Theo had sufficiently groveled for his crimes of abandonment during our brief return to the planet, and I'd genuinely forgiven him, but my scars ran deep enough that I knew I still had work to do.

Eventually.

Right now, I had a mission to complete, so I buried my confusing desires as deep as possible, where not even Dr. Micah and his "unbilled therapy time" could find them.

Problem solved.

Trusting Micah to get us en route for Stellaria, I star hopped to my skinsuit closet. While this Maroxian disguise had been necessary for securing the asset—and surprisingly adept at making my mate come—I could admit, it wouldn't be the best option for luring a helpless, newly-hatched alien out of the ductwork of my ship.

It's far too large for the task.

As much as I was craving my Earthling skin—the identity I most related to—my true form would be the best fit for the job.

After carefully encasing my Maroxian skinsuit in carbonite, I hopped to the weapons room for a closer look at the situation.

Pieces of eggshell littered the crate, with a few larger chunks flung about the room, as if the asset had hatched in a hurry. My gaze took in the deep scratches traveling up the wall before focusing on the missing air vent cover.

The *mangled* air vent cover.

The one that looked as if it had been removed with extremely large, extremely *sharp* blades.

Hmm...

Perhaps 'helpless' wasn't the right word.

I didn't know exactly what species I was dealing with here, because no one did. The distress signal Astrum Force originally received—which Honnor and Bron were still trying to track—had simply mentioned the abduction of a youngling of great rarity and importance.

A creature that could "bring great power to whoever possessed it."

I growled low, furious once again that I'd been forced to choose between my high-level mission and my mate.

Fuck this.

Extending a few tendrils into the duct, I tasted the air, aiming to not only determine which direction the asset had gone, but its mental state.

The more frightened, the better.

Unfortunately, I couldn't get much of a reading. So, with an irritated sigh I felt all the way to my nonexistent bones, I floated upwards.

Only to come face-to-face with an impossibly large pair of glowing yellow eyes.

What in Stellaria's—

Before I could finish the thought, a dark shape was lunging for me, its sharp claws extended as an ear-splitting yowl echoed in the close confines of the air duct.

It was nearly impossible to catch a Stellarian off-guard, but I didn't have the luxury at the moment of examining *how* this creature had accomplished it. Recovering quickly, I dematerialized before it made contact, reappearing behind the little shit and unleashing dozens of tendrils to entrap and immobilize my prey.

Only when my tendrils tightened on empty air did I realize that—somehow—the creature had not only escaped my clutches, but it was already bounding away.

I AM GOING TO KILL IT!

Of course, I knew I *couldn't* kill the "rare and important'" asset I'd been assigned to rescue, but the insult was enough to make me see red.

And no one said anything about not teaching it a lesson.

With this satisfying compromise in mind, I took off after my prey, smirking inwardly when I found it backed into a corner and hissing wildly.

Time to learn.

"Is everything okay up there, Zig?" Micah's muffled voice sounded below us, instantly silencing the creature. "Do you, um... need my help?"

My mate's translation device meant he could now understand Stellarian, so I called back to say I had the situation under control.

Because I do.

Thanks to my night vision and the glow from my tendrils, I was finally able to take a closer look at what I was dealing with.

I could make out a thick coat of shaggy, chestnut-colored fur, along with pointed ears drawn back as it hunched low, attempting to squeeze itself into a ball. Its enormous eyes were locked on me, unblinking, while a thin, hairless tail twitched against the metal wall behind it, but I couldn't be sure what the movement meant.

Since I can't get a read on this thing.

Its front paws and pangolin claws were lowered—which I took as a good sign—but I could see even larger claws on its hind feet as well. In sharp contrast, two tiny fangs peeked out as it started to hiss under its breath and, all at once, I realized it reminded me of the Earthling *felis catus.*

I'm facing off with a fucking house cat.

It scuttled further into the corner, revealing a circular grate I recognized as being part of the kitchen's new range hood system. A plan immediately sprang to mind, and I knew just the man to help me accomplish it.

Aside from his impressive brain, one of the many things I admired about my mate were his superpowers—his seemingly magical ability to create almost anything out of thin air.

Well, out of inorganic matter.

What I also appreciated was knowing he hadn't gone far. While Micah's inherent helpfulness had been taken advantage of by his parents, I tried not to make him feel as if his only worth was what he could offer me. However, at the moment, I needed my *partner* to capture the creature before it escaped.

Strategy in place, I called out to Micah again, explaining I was going to open the grate above the range and that he needed to be ready with an impenetrable cage of some kind.

His reply of affirmation had *our* prey cocking its head, almost curiously, but then the movement of my tendrils sliding toward the grate caused it to growl and crouch lower, clearly preparing to pounce—or make a break for it again.

Fuck. This.

I wasn't what you'd call nurturing on a good day, and with how thin my patience was, I honestly didn't care to make this entrapment easier on the source of my irritation.

Striking before it could, I wrapped a tendril around my prey, pinning its front limbs against its body, holding the writhing, snarling creature in place as I turned my attention to removing the grate.

A rapid grinding filled the cramped space—like an engine attempting to turn over in an Earth-based automobile—and I could only watch in amazement as the house cat transformed into something incomprehensible.

The fur hanging from its face parted as thick tentacles emerged, and the end of its flicking tail ballooned before a ring of spikes appeared, like a medieval morning star.

Then, it opened its mouth, its jaw hinging wide like a snake swallowing its prey whole, the tiny fangs extending to enormous canines nestled in two rows of equally deadly teeth.

By Stellaria...

I snatched my tendrils away and unleashed a dozen more, sharpening the ends for battle as I debated how to best subdue my opponent.

Unsurprisingly, the creature in question didn't wait for me to decide. It took one look at my weapons and dove downward, slicing clear through the metal surrounding the range hood grate and disappearing to the kitchen below.

Where my mate is...

With a battle cry that shook the shredded metal surrounding me, I flew after it, my essence freezing in my proverbial veins to find Micah backed against the wall with the extremely angry asset stalking toward him.

Maybe I will *kill it after all.*

What the hell is that thing?

And why is it so cuuuuute?

While my brain *knew* it was an alien of some kind, I quickly decided it was also a cuddly kitty—albeit, the anime version, able to transform into a deadly monster at any moment.

What else is new around here?

After departing Marox and setting a course for Stellaria, I'd switched to autopilot and taken a closer look at what Ziggy was up to. Yes, he'd mentioned a "vermin" problem, but to a bad bitch like Zig, that could've meant anything from a single rat to a horde of Maroxians.

Once I'd determined the only heat signatures were coming from the ventilation system—*and just what my man was doing in there was anyone's guess*—I checked on the egg through the live feed of our closed circuit security system.

That's when I realized I needed to step in.

It wasn't that I thought Zig couldn't handle himself—even if I would prefer him to take me on *all* his missions—but stalking a helpless baby through the ductwork was not part of the assignment.

That man needs to shape up if we're ever going to have space babies together!

Ignoring the delulu vision of my Space Daddy becoming a *real* daddy, I'd refocused on reality—specifically on the immediate need to stop Zig from killing anyone he shouldn't.

After disengaging the lockdown doors, I'd hustled along the gangway, following the truly terrifying sounds of pursuit until I reached the kitchen. Picking my way through the various piles of weaponry, I'd tracked the situation to just above the stove's new range hood, which meant Ziggy had successfully trapped the newborn.

And that went about as well as expected.

I still wasn't exactly sure *what* had gone down in the ductwork, but I was currently covered in debris and engaged in a stare down with the most adorable little ball of Big Mad I'd ever seen.

They're really just a baby.

"*Put up your shields!*" Ziggy barked in Stellarian, and even though he was being ridiculously cautious in the face of such cuteness, I obeyed.

Because he's baby too...

Babygirl, really.

Luckily, my man seemed to be letting me take it from here,

though I could tell Zig would attack the instant anyone breathed wrong.

Looks like I need to lead by example.

While I also hadn't experienced nurturing parents, my older siblings—especially Zion—had always taken care of me. Plus, I *liked* kids and, with a family as large as mine, I was just used to having them around.

And the first rule of dealing with kids is to never show them fear.

"Hey, there..." I soothed in Earthling American English, more to relay a calm vibe than communicate with words.

Since my translation device isn't picking up on the language here.

When the furball continued to watch me warily, I slid down the wall into a crouch, then extended my hand—palm up— and did the only thing I could think of to diffuse the situation.

I pspsps'd.

"What are you doing?" Ziggy hissed, his incorporeal form pulsing with agitated glow.

Determined not to get distracted by his awe-inspiring appearance, I made the sound again, louder this time, so it would project beyond my shields.

Here, kitty, kitty, kitty.

What my stellar collision didn't understand was this was the universal language—trade language, if you will—for all things cute and cuddly. I felt no small amount of pride when the baby alien cocked their head before dropping to all fours, pointing their tail at me like a beacon and trotting closer.

There you go.

"See, Zig?" I huffed, disengaging my shields and dropping fully to the floor so they could clamber into my lap. "A little kindness goes a long way."

Ziggy huffed—as much as a cluster of stars could huff. "I was being kind."

By not killing it, he means.

I giggled as the creature hooked their baby sloth claws around my neck and snuggled closer. Moving slowly so I wouldn't disturb or frighten them, I wrapped my sweatshirt—Ziggy's, actually—around both of us and zipped my new furbaby into a kangaroo pouch.

Ziggy drifted closer, causing the little guy or girl—or nonbinary alien—to tense and growl low.

"You're scaring them!" I scolded, frantically shooing him away. "Go... change into the least threatening skinsuit you have."

I should have known which skinsuit he considered harmless, but when Ziggy disappeared, only to reappear a few seconds later, I sighed.

Earthling, of course.

"See, little one?" I pspsps'd again for good measure. "He's a friend."

Ziggy scoffed, continuing to eye his fellow alien with distrust. "I am not a *friend.*"

Sighing, I awkwardly struggled to my feet, stumbling a bit due to the unfamiliar redistribution of weight. When I glanced at Zig, his darkened gaze was drinking me in, especially the large lump hanging around my midsection, implying he *liked* how I looked right now.

I see you.

Breeding kink for the win.

"Well, you're *my* friend—my *best* friend," I teased. "So I don't think it should be *that* hard for you to be nice to everyone on board until we get to Stellaria."

He gave me a flat look. "This is a *job,* Micah. I'm a mercenary tasked with delivering an asset to Astrum Force Command. That is all."

Such a stubborn Space Daddy.

"Okay, but can we at least not call them 'an asset?'" I muttered. "They are a living thing."

Ziggy sighed, but his tasty lips were turning up at the corners despite his best efforts. "Very well. What would you like to call it?"

I opened my mouth, only to snap it closed again, unsure how to answer. It felt weird to randomly give the creature a name without knowing anything about their culture or what language they spoke.

They're not a pet.

"Pspsps…" a little voice whispered from deep within my sweatshirt cocoon, and I laughed as inspiration struck.

"Pedro," I blurted out.

"Pedro?" Ziggy arched an eyebrow.

"Yeah," I powered on, fucking delighted by the internet humor-inspired opportunity I'd been blessed with. "Pedro Pspspscal."

Ziggy huffed a laugh, unable to resist my antics, as usual. "You're naming it after the actor from *The Mandalorian?*"

I SEE YOU!

My man always tried to act annoyed whenever I made him take a goddamn break and watch sci-fi with me. This *may* have had something to do with my constant questions about 'accuracy' while he was trying to enjoy the show, but it was mostly because Zig didn't know how to relax.

"Well, duh." I cackled, earning me a trilling sound from within my makeshift baby carrier. "You know I'm a ho for anything Mando. A *Mand-HO-lorian,* if you will."

Yes, I crack myself up.

Deal with it.

Ziggy's gaze darkened again. "Like how you react when I'm wearing my armor?"

I rolled my eyes, even as my cheeks heated. "Again, duh. I *told* you I had to hustle to my room for some privacy the first time I saw you suited up."

Insta-boner.

Like the cocky bastard he was, Zig smiled smugly and advanced. "You *did* tell me, but you never elaborated. What exactly did you imagine while chasing relief, babygirl? My gloved fingers inside you, fucking you slow until your cum decorated my sexy Stellarian armor?"

"Zig!" I gasped, wiping the drool from my mouth before covering Pedro's ears. "Not in front of the baby!"

But... yes.

He rolled his eyes this time. "It doesn't understand what we're saying, Micah."

"They," I corrected before glancing down.

Pedro's enormous eyes were closed, their little face tucked against my chest as they faintly snored.

Ugh, so cute.

"Do you know what species they are?" I asked. "Now that they've hatched, I mean."

Ziggy frowned and peered closer. "I do not, but once we deliver it... *them* to Astrum Force, tests can be conducted."

"Tests?!" I hissed, lowering my voice when my bundle stirred. "I'm not letting a bunch of Stellarians cut Pedro open with their katana-tendrils."

Over my dead body.

My katana-wielding alien smiled kindly. "This was a rescue mission, sunshine, which means we will need to determine where this creature came from—so we can return them to their home planet." He paused as something like regret passed over his deceptively boyish face. "Remember, this isn't the old Astrum Force. I promise, Honnor would never allow anything bad to happen to your... friend."

He's trying.

"I know," I muttered, slightly embarrassed I'd implied his kind would treat Pedro like a lab rat. "I'm just... feeling protective, I guess..."

Ziggy hummed, his gaze growing hooded again. "I noticed."

I bet you did.

"Do you like what you see, Space Daddy?" I covered Pedro's ears once again, unable to resist flirting with my man. "Does it get you thinking about what Gabe said—about how pretty I'd look all knocked up?"

You'd look pretty too.

"Careful, Micah," he warned in a tone that made my toes curl. "Before I wreck you all over again."

As tempting as that threat was, even I could admit I was legitimately sore from Maroxian monster cock.

Plus, we have a mission to complete!

I smirked, determined to get in the last word anyway. "Lemme just go put the baby to bed..." When Ziggy's eyes lit up, I laughed. "So we can *clean* this disaster of a ship together! Get your mind out of the gutter, sheesh."

My man growled in annoyance but dutifully turned and began gathering the weapons I'd dumped here earlier.

And if I took an extra moment to admire the way his ass flexed in his slutty gray sweatpants... Well, who could blame me?

We'll be alone again soon enough...

Ignoring how weirdly *sad* that made me, I headed toward the weapons-room-nursery, dutifully focused on settling Pedro into their crib before tackling the Maroxian goo situation on the gangway.

Just another day as a bad bish mercenary for Astrum Force.

6
ZIGGY

For as often as Micah referred to me as a "bad bish mercenary," I certainly didn't feel like one at the moment.

"Try making airplane noises," my mate nonsensically suggested as *Pedro* once again turned up their snout at the perfectly adequate spoonful of hatini I was graciously offering. "Err... spaceship noises?"

"Are you asking or telling?" I huffed, tossing the spoon in front of the insufferable creature who, of course, immediately grabbed the cutlery and threw it on the floor. "Besides, *why* in Stellaria's name would the sound of a quad engine, even the low speed of Mach 52, encourage *anyone* to eat?"

Instead of answering the question, Micah simply gazed at me with the same dreamy expression he got after I fucked him senseless.

And there's been a distinct lack of fucking since the asset hatched.

Excuse me—Pedro the Asset.

"Just keep trying, Zig," he murmured, fetching a fresh spoon and taking over. "This isn't the kind of thing you can be perfect at right away."

My bone-deep distaste for the task at hand suddenly made sense. There was no good reason for me to spend valuable time on anything I didn't naturally excel at—which wasn't much—or that I had no interest in.

Like spoon-feeding the cargo.

"Why not just put out food and water bowls for them?" I grumbled, glancing around the cluttered kitchen for a suitable spot.

Micah snapped back to focus, gasping dramatically. *"Zig!* Just because Pedro is cute and furry doesn't make them a *pet.* Plus, they have opposable thumbs, so they should be able to get the hang of this... with a little guidance."

I watched as Pedro snatched the second spoon out of Micah's hands and launched it across the room. It bounced off the cold storage unit and clattered onto the floor, joining the 'organized piles' of displaced weapons and causing the blood pressure in my Earthling form to rise alarmingly.

In the past, I may have responded to this emotional overwhelm by shutting down completely or letting off some steam in a Muonova bar brawl. Both responses helped in the moment, but it was never long before whatever had been bothering me bubbled to the surface again.

And Dr. Micah does not approve of my old methods.

We were about communication and solutions nowadays, and since I wasn't particularly eager to express my feelings of inadequacy to my mate, I focused on how to master this shortcoming.

"I need to... make a call." I abruptly stood, grimacing as I preemptively regretted my decision. "To your... brother."

Micah's eyes lit up with interest. "Oh? What do you need to talk to Zion about?"

The way he was clearly fighting a smile told me he knew damn well what the subject matter would be, but I refused to confirm his suspicions.

This is embarrassing enough as it is.

"I promised I'd confirm your wellbeing on a regular basis." A smug smile of my own broke through my terrible mood. "To ensure we don't repeat the 'space married' situation."

This was partly true. Zion Salah had asked for occasional 'proof of life' updates so he wouldn't worry unnecessarily about his younger brother. More importantly, digging up the past seemed to have successfully redirected Micah from the current issue at hand.

"Ughhhh..." my stellar collision dropped his head back and groaned, causing Pedro to blink at him owlishly. "I am *never* gonna live down my goodbye note, huh? Carve it on my tombstone, why don't ya..."

Unable to resist, I leaned down and kissed his perfect lips—using my hands to hold him in place, since I'd been told to keep my tendrils to myself in Pedro's presence.

Yet another reason to be done with this mission.

I was more than ready to have everything in its rightful place again—my ship pointed at the stars, my weapons back on their racks, and my mate impaled on my tendrils and cock.

That shouldn't be too much to ask.

However, I could also see how much properly feeding and watering Pedro meant to Micah, and since what was important to *him* was important to *me,* I was determined to do my duty and provide.

Which is why I need to talk to someone more knowledgeable than me.

More knowledgeable in this one area, that is.

"I'll be back shortly," I murmured, tearing myself away from my forever distraction.

"No prob. Tell Z I said hey." Micah smiled encouragingly before a mischievous curve to his lips distracted me all over again. "Go phone home."

Sigh.

Ignoring the Hollywood alien reference, I star hopped to the bedroom, sat on the sleeping pod mattress, and blew out a slow breath to collect myself.

You can do this, Ziggy.

You can... ask for... help.

I resolutely removed my phone from the intergalactic charging and Wi-Fi station Micah had created for us to stay connected with Earth before deciding a *text* would be less traumatizing than a phone call.

Hopefully.

Before I could change my mind, I brought up Zion's number and sent my missive into the ether.

> I have a question that requires immediate attention.

To my surprise—and slight dismay—the reply was nearly instantaneous.

ZION SALAH/SCALED JUSTICE
> Hello to you too, Space Husband! 👽 How may I share my expertise with you today?

Siiiigh...

> I need to know how to keep a child alive.

The reply wasn't quite as quick. The three dots appeared and disappeared a few times, followed by a silence so long, I assumed the clan leader had stepped away to deal with family business.

Unfortunately for me, *this* family business now had his undivided attention.

ZION SALAH/SCALED JUSTICE
> Any particular reason you're asking, Star Hopper?

I frowned at my phone screen, unsure why I was suddenly receiving the supe version of a light warning when it was a perfectly acceptable question.

> Because you have managed to maintain your offspring's existence for 10 Earthling years.

ZION SALAH/SCALED JUSTICE

> Okay, well, an Earthling kid might be a little different than... whatever you're dealing with up there, but the basics are probably the same.

I huffed, beyond annoyed I was being forced to *articulate* exactly what I needed. Then, I reminded myself the countless blows to the head from Zion's former profession were no doubt affecting his comprehension skills.

And the Lacertus DNA isn't helping.

With a deep breath, I tried again.

> Understanding what you consider "basics" will help me formulate a plan of action.

My phone abruptly rang, and my mild annoyance at the interruption morphed into horror once I realized Zion was *calling* me.

The things I do for my stellar collision.

"How the hell did no one clock you as an alien while you were here?" The eldest Salah's booming laugh rattled my eardrums as soon as I answered. "Your texts sound like a broken-down robot learning to *human.*"

"Just share the intel, Justice," I growled, tempted to star hop back to Earth and interrogate the hero properly.

Another way I usually relax.

All this did was earn me another laugh. "Cool your jets, space boy. Okay, so Earthling babies survive on breast milk or formula for the first six months. Carbs, fat, protein. Then, you slowly introduce solid foods, but it's gotta be stuff they can easily swallow, since they have no teeth."

No teeth?!

I narrowed my eyes, realizing perhaps the supposed "basics" were not quite as universal as this so-called expert had claimed.

"The asset has two rows of fangs," I countered before switching to an alternate angle. "Is there anything other than feeding and watering I should know about?"

Zion was silent for a moment before clearing his throat and continuing. "Some parents swear by co-sleeping—"

"No," I brusquely interrupted, because *no one* was getting between me and my mate in bed.

Even if a certain twin is occasionally allowed to play with us on a limited basis.

"Someone needs a nap, huh?" Zion chuckled before wisely refocusing when I didn't share his humor. "Okaaay... so an important part of raising kids is *enrichment.*"

Against my better judgement, I had to ask. "Enrichment?"

"You know, things to help their brain and motor skills develop..." He briefly covered the phone to reply to someone— probably Baltasar—who'd decided *now* was the time to involve themselves. "Like reading books to them or singing songs, playing with age-appropriate toys, tummy time..."

What in Stellaria's name is tummy time?

"Do Earthling children not have fully developed brains when

they're born?" I deflated, internally questioning *why* I'd chosen to ask a lower life form for tips in the first place.

Zion laughed. Again. "Of course not! Supes develop faster than normies, thanks to genetics and being trained in certain areas from a young age. In general, though, Earthling brains aren't finished developing until their mid-to-late 20s."

WHAT?!

Despite having lived on Earth for over fifty years, this was news to me, since I rarely bothered researching the early life cycle of whatever planet I was infiltrating. My marks were always full-grown adults, and most alien species could survive on their own soon after birth.

Even if they shouldn't have to.

Shaking off my own unpleasant memories of early childhood, I refocused on this shocking intel.

Wait.

"Does this mean Micah will become *smarter?*" I asked, unable to keep the excitement out of my voice.

My stellar collision was already one of the most impressive creatures I'd ever met, but he'd only recently turned 25 in Earth years. If his brain was still developing, there was no limit to how intelligent he might become.

I must breed him immediately.

"Have you managed to knock up my brother, Andromeda?" Zion's voice snapped me back to reality. "Is that why you're asking me all this?"

"W-what?" I stuttered, strangely caught off guard. "No. We are currently transporting a newborn of unknown origin to Stellaria and need to keep it... *them* alive until then. Besides, Micah and I aren't in compatible forms for reproduction and haven't discussed—"

"Hey, no judgement!" he interrupted my rambling with a huff. "Lord knows, Daisy wasn't exactly a planned pregnancy..." The muffled sound of Baltasar in the background again had Zion's tone turning serious. "But, uh, if you *were* in, you know... *compatible forms,* would it be possible?"

As much as my traitorous heart pounded at the idea of actually impregnating Micah—or having him do the same to me—this was *not* a topic I wished to discuss with Zion Salah.

The entire extended family would know by nightfall.

"In *your* case, *Lacertus,* you'd simply need Baltasar to develop the necessary female reproductive organs," I huffed, already mentally done with this useless conversation.

A crash followed by the sound of pounding feet had me frowning down at my phone.

"Thanks, Star Hopper," Zion chuckled darkly, his voice dropping the way it did when he took *his* true form. "Good luck with parenting."

Parenting?!

The miniature *Lacertus* abruptly hung up, which saved me from needing to reply to his closing words.

Small mercies.

Returning my phone to the charger, I star hopped to the kitchen, only to find the room empty. Unleashing a few exploratory tendrils, I found Micah and Pedro in the weapons room, and from the rhythmic vibrations surrounding them, I determined Micah was... singing.

Of course, my incredibly intelligent mate already knew about "enrichment."

Despite the resonance building in my chest, I stubbornly resisted the urge to *watch* him care for the child—to imagine this random creature was one we'd created together.

Just complete your mission, Ziggy.

Then you'll never need to worry about this again...

Reentering Stellaria's bubblegum pink atmosphere never got old.

I'd once asked Ziggy if everything here was glittery to camouflage a Stellarian's yassified true form, but he hadn't seemed eager to answer the question—which was answer enough for me.

The silence is LOUD with that one.

Regardless, I was looking forward to visiting some of our favorite local haunts—like the dunes where you could race tricked-out vehicles, or the "safest" bazaar in town.

Complete with the occasional blood puddle for ambience.

As much as I enjoyed our space adventures, I was also more than a little excited to play house until our next assignment. Ziggy preferred to exist in his Earthling skinsuit even here, and seeing him puttering around his modest home—cleaning his weapons, organizing his weapons, obsessively feeding and watering me—gave me all the domestic feels.

The first order of business was handing off Pedro to Honnor, which didn't sit right with me. I trusted Ziggy's maker implicitly, but walking into the audience chamber of Candyland Court always triggered me. This was probably thanks to the time Ziggy put me to sleep so he could fight the entire Astrum Force Command by himself, only for me to still need to face off against the Head Commander while thinking the love of my life was dead.

Good times... said no one.

To their credit, Honnor and their partner, Bron—the space dads, as I liked to call them—had put serious work into revamping Astrum Force. It was no longer a totalitarian dictatorship, and the missions assigned to its Star Units, or stray mercenaries like us, were more focused on humanitarian efforts than colonialism.

Case in point: Rescuing kidnapped alien babies and returning them to their natural habitat.

Wherever that is...

As if knowing I was thinking about them, Pedro made an adorable trilling sound and snuggled closer in their makeshift sweatshirt baby carrier.

Ugh.

"Hopefully, that creature isn't imprinting on you," Ziggy muttered as he strode beside me down the bustling Gumdrop Pass. "It will make the handoff difficult."

I sighed, doing my best to ignore how indifferent he sounded about the situation. Zig used this same emotionless tone in *most* public situations as part of his mercenary mask, but I'd thought a furry ball of cuteness might crack his stony exterior.

After all, I managed to do it!

In the end, he was a product of his orphaned upbringing, although he'd come a long way from the emotionally consti-pated, Deathball-playing 'hero' in a stolen skinsuit I'd first met at my family's house back on Earth.

Nowadays, he *talked* about his feelings—occasionally and only to me, and mostly when Dr. Micah was in session—but he was *trying.*

Baby steps.

So, while I didn't necessarily expect him to leap at the chance to fulfill my Mando and Grogu Space Daddy fantasy, I was determined to get at least one photo of them together before my dreams died.

"You're right." I dug Pedro out of their nest and held them out for the taking. "Maybe *you* should transport *the asset* from here."

Ziggy instinctively shrank from the bundle of joy, but as soon as he realized I was serious, he sighed and dutifully let Pedro climb him like a tree.

The instinct is real.

Once the little creature reached Zig's shoulders, they draped themselves around his neck like a scarf—creating the perfect photo op.

"Must you?" my man grumbled as I took at least twenty rapid-fire photos with my phone.

"Yup!" I cheerfully replied, taking twenty more.

I'd made it my mission to get the two of them acclimated to one another during our short flight back to Stellaria, mostly through the same form of trickery I was using now.

Forced proximity and big puppy dog eyes.

While they weren't the besties I'd hoped for—or the scrappy father-son duo I'd dreamed of—at least no one was *hissing* anymore.

Including Zig.

"There are the brave soldiers!" Bron called out in Stellarian the instant we walked through the doors.

This friendly greeting was in sharp contrast to the intimidating vibe of the last Astrum Force Command lineup. It helped that the twelve raised thrones they'd perched on to loom over us had been removed so everyone could be on equal footing during an audience. The walls of the audience chamber were still made of a stone so black, it sucked the light from the room, but Zig had explained this material was mined from deep within Stellaria's core, so it was meant to be more a show of pride than anything.

Whatever you say, Space Daddy.

It's still creepy.

Even with the new Head Commander being his maker, Ziggy had still worn his Stellarian armor for the occasion—which I greatly approved of—and of course, the commanding officers had done the same.

"No more Zeanidions?" I joked in English, knowing they could understand me even without my harp.

I only play that for Ziggy.

Bron was nothing but a swirl of stars behind the open visor of their helmet, but I could plainly *feel* their amusement. *"We grew tired of those terrestrial forms,"* they replied as Honnor wrapped up their nearby conversation with a Star Unit squadron leader and joined us. *"So back to the communal skinsuit closet they went!"*

I cringed and glanced at my stellar collision. I'd gotten a little tipsy during our last dinner with the space dads and let slip how much I enjoyed browsing Ziggy's closet and making him try on different outfits for me.

While I hadn't outright said *why* we played dress up, I'm sure the subtext had been loud and clear. Zig had been *horrified* by my confession—*what else is new?*—but Honnor and Bron responded by cackling their starry little heads off before dragging us both to the "communal skinsuit closet" for a family field trip.

The closet was located a few levels below the audience chamber—only accessible by star hopping, of course—and the sheer selection was awe-inspiring.

And boner-inspiring, if I'm being honest.

Since Honnor and Bron were as patient with my endless questions as Ziggy was, I also learned why a resource of this magnitude needed to exist. Star Units typically traveled to their destination together, either by star hopping or aboard a generic carrier ship with no room for the massive closet they'd need to outfit everyone, so they suited up before they left. This meant thousands of vessels were needed at any given moment, and those that weren't being used were left vacant, awaiting possession beneath our feet.

Which is weirdly... not creepy.

You might think there'd be mixed opinions on the ethics of Stellarian body-snatching habits, but besides the understandable fear this top predator inspired, the intergalactic consensus seemed to be that they were simply following their natural instincts.

It is what it is.

Hot, in my opinion.

I'd also discovered most Stellarians preferred their starry true form, either free floating or encased in their cozy, leather-lined armor. That is, unless they'd discovered a perfect candidate for their true purpose in life—as a muse melded with their ideal vessel.

Zig and I had accidentally discovered this arrangement during our final boss battle with Astrum Force Command, but most Stellarians weren't aware it was an option.

Because their leaders hid the truth from them.

And continue to...

The "True Stellarians"—as the rebellion called themselves— knew the truth, but even after returning to their home planet, they'd been hesitant to share with their less-enlightened brethren. Honnor explained it was too risky, that most Stellarians had been conditioned to believe conquest was their birthright, so *encouraging* them to take over someone's body with the hopes they'd leave them alive had the potential to go horribly wrong.

So, until it was deemed safe to spill the tea, the current focus was on goodwill missions—like rebuilding Kaalanesea—to educate these katana-wielding murder machines in the fine art of empathy and emotional intelligence first.

Dr. Micah has been consulting on an unofficial basis.

I would have been more involved in this mass deprogramming project, but Zig didn't want to risk me being asked to stay while he flew off on missions of his own.

Even if I was left behind on the ship for this last one...

"How did the extraction on Marox go?" Honnor asked, pure parental pride radiating from them as they observed Pedro perched on Ziggy's shoulders. *"No casualties, I see."*

Well...

I glanced at Ziggy, remembering how he'd advised we *not* talk about the Maroxian I fought and killed. Our mission was supposed to be covert—with no bloodshed—and an unnecessary trail of bodies would not look good for the new Astrum Force.

So, the old in-and-out is what we did.

Which is also true, in a way...

"Uneventful," Ziggy smoothly replied for both of us. "The security the Maroxians had guarding the asset was pitiful."

"Pedro," I added, wincing as all three Stellarians turned their attention to me.

"You named it?" Bron asked, tone dripping with amusement again.

"Yes, I named *them*," I corrected, annoyed these nonbinary star clusters weren't understanding the importance of a gender-neutral pronoun. "Because they're a living creature and just a baby and shouldn't be experimented on in any way."

Real smooth, Micah...

Unsurprisingly, it was Honnor who stepped in to calm me down. *"We have no intention of experimenting on Pedro, although we will need to gather a few samples to help determine their planet of origin."* They turned to Ziggy. *"Were you able to gather any intel during the mission?"*

What?

I had no idea snooping had been part of the plan but, then again, this mission hadn't exactly been a team effort.

My *partner* briefly glanced at me before straightening. "I... forgot."

What?!

This was clearly bullshit. Ziggy was the most meticulous creature I'd ever met. If he'd been unable to track anything down while on Marox, it was because the intel didn't exist.

Or...

"It was my fault!" I blurted out, making Ziggy tense. "I distracted him—as always—so he ran out of time."

And this is why I get left behind.

Bron hummed thoughtfully. *"Yes, our mates can be extremely distracting. It was all I could do to stay hidden when you captured Honnor in that tractor beam on Zeanides."*

"Oh, you mean *before* you attempted to kidnap me?" I replied dryly while Ziggy bristled at the terrifying memory.

"Yes." Bron chuckled in the musical way Stellarians could in their true form. *"That was fun."*

I wouldn't have called it that.

"It's all right, Ziggy." Honnor once again diffused the situation. *"It will be easier for us to identify the creature now that they've hatched."*

Honnor reached for Pedro but quickly withdrew their armor-covered hands when the newborn hissed and clung tighter to Ziggy.

"Ruh-roh, Zig!" I sang, beaming at my scowling stellar collision. "Looks like someone might have *imprinted* on someone else."

"No one has imprinted on me," he snapped as Bron snickered. "Pedro is simply a lifeform of lower intelligence with a barely developed brain!"

Is that *all he got out of his phone call with Zion?*

Because, yeah, big bro told me everything.

I rolled my eyes. "My bad. I forgot. All Stellarians are geniuses at birth."

"We are." Ziggy crossed his arms and sniffed haughtily, trying his hardest to look cool with a hissing furball peering over his shoulder. "We are one of the highest forms of intelligence in all the galaxies."

Sounds like someone wants a certificate.

"Perhaps you shouldn't make assumptions, my child," Honnor gently replied. *"You know better than most that not everything is as it seems when it comes to other species."*

Mic drop!

Ziggy didn't reply, but I knew he'd give his creator's words the consideration they deserved.

To their credit, Honnor didn't push. Instead, they patiently waited for Ziggy to unhook Pedro's claws from around his neck and hold the agitated creature out like a smelly sock, ripe for the taking.

It's okay, little guy.

Or girl.

Or... nonbinary alien.

I guess they'll figure that out soon enough.

Knowing the waterworks were on the way, I pulled Pedro into my arms for a goodbye snuggle.

"I'm gonna miss you, furbaby," I murmured as the expected tears threatened to fall.

"We promise, Pedro will be well looked after until we can safely return them to their home planet," Honnor soothed, and I felt Pedro go limp in my arms, as if suddenly overcome by exhaustion.

When I narrowed my eyes at Honnor, they chuckled before throwing in a blast of *our* shared resonance for good measure.

Cheater.

"If you would like, you may stop by the lab tomorrow while our scientists conduct their examination," Bron piped in.

I glanced at Ziggy, but my man was busy fiddling with his

Celestial Cube, apparently already done with the conversation *and* the orphaned alien baby.

Hmph.

While I wasn't super jazzed about seeing Pedro being poked and prodded, making sure no Stellarian scientist turned the creature into a lab rat had its appeal.

"I'll be there," I announced, lifting my chin. *"We'll* be there."

"What?" Ziggy snapped, but I was already handing Pedro off, glad the little alien seemed way more chill about the handoff than before, thanks to the sleepy ish.

I'm still gonna get emotional about it, though.

"Why did you offer to get involved?" Ziggy hissed as we headed back down Gumdrop Pass. "Our mission is over—"

"Maybe because I'm having a hard time letting go!" I barked angrily, which was a rare enough occurrence to have him snapping his mouth shut for the remainder of the walk.

Oops.

"I can fix things," he confidently stated once we stepped outside, and my salty attitude weakened in the face of such assured competency.

Oh, what will Space Daddy do?

Ziggy took my hands in his and gazed so intently into my eyes, my breath caught.

Wait.

Is he...?

"Micah Salah," he began, and I grew lightheaded, swaying unsteadily on my feet.

IS THIS HAPPENING?!

"Sunshine." He dipped his head and kissed me sweetly before straightening. "What you need is for me to feed you some cock."

As long as ya boy doesn't choke, I'll be good.

Now that I was fed, I could totally admit I'd thought Ziggy was popping the question *for real* outside Yasstrum Force HQ. *Then,* I'd assumed the cock being offered was the one encased in Space Daddy armor. Both would have greatly improved my mood, but shoving Stellarian street food into my mouth was also getting the job done.

What can I say?

I get hangry sometimes.

"Better?" Ziggy asked as I cleaned my plate—*err... banana leaf*—at the city's 'safest bazaar.' When I nodded, he smiled like he'd won the lottery, and I wondered how I could ever stay mad at this big idiot.

He's trying his best.

It had taken a few bites of *corpus spongiosum*—and one harrowing swallow—but I finally felt like I was back to baseline.

"I'm sorry I yelled..." I peeked up at him through my lashes. "I just got myself all worked up over saying goodbye to Pedro, but that didn't give me the right to take it out on you."

Ziggy reached across the small stone table and patted my cheek so hard, I almost choked on my last bite of Neluth dick. "I wasn't worried. You are far from the most frightening creature I've encountered."

Thanks.

"Yeah, you've mentioned that before." I lovingly rolled my eyes and took a sip of Orgon's milk, even though I still didn't know exactly what it was. "But you've yet to tell me more about the big skerry alien that's skerrier than you."

Ziggy cleared his throat before taking a sip of his milk, which was suspicious as fuck. Stellarians didn't need to eat or drink —not the way I did, anyway—so my man was clearly stalling.

When he noticed I was waiting impatiently for a reply, he pressed his lips together. "It's not an alien. Not... exactly."

My interest is piqued.

Unfortunately, my burning need to know was forced to wait as a commotion near the permanent stalls caught Ziggy's attention. I followed his gaze to find a creature with six snake heads involved in what looked like a heated debate with a slender green alien selling gemstones and bundles of herbs.

Intergalactic witchy bitch shit.

To my delight, Ziggy stood and began strolling toward the action, so I scampered after him, eager for the tea.

Stellaria's bazaars were a popular stop for aliens from all over, but it wasn't always easy to tell if these creatures were locals in stolen skin—or scale—suits. Every now and then, I caught glimpses of the starry auras indicating the vessel was occupied—an ability we still couldn't explain—but for the most part, I wasn't worried about being targeted for body snatching.

This skinsuit is taken, thank you very much.

The only Stellarians who seemed able to vaguely detect if a vessel was inhabited or not were the True Stellarians, although that was more based on vibes. Honnor and Bron made it sound like it was a mental block they'd had to overcome, but even with Ziggy knowing the truth, he hadn't magically developed the skill.

Maybe he just needs to practice?

Either way, Zig made sure everyone knew who I belonged to through an effective combination of death stares and removing body parts from anyone who dared to touch me.

Overt tactics aside, just the sight of his recognizable armor sent most aliens running in the other direction. He was such a pro at resting bitch face, you'd think Zig barely noticed the effect he had on others but, thanks to our bond, I knew their terror gave him a little thrill.

Hey, no judgement!

Skerry Space Daddy bricks me up too.

Despite Ziggy's strange hesitation to share which "not exactly an alien" was scarier than Stellarians, I also knew not much frightened him, so it was odd when he pulled me into the shadows of a nearby rock formation instead of taking a front row seat to the drama at the hippie cart.

"As I have told you, I do not carry karnilian!" the green-skinned stall owner hissed in the trade language, their large violet eyes darting around the crowd, as if concerned about eavesdroppers like us. "Possession of it has been outlawed for eons in most galaxies, including this one—"

"But not in ours," the snake-headed one rumbled before placing their clawed hands on the stall's counter and leaning toward the scowling vendor. "We know it is here—we can *feel* it—and if we have to search every gem stall at every bazaar on this planet, we will."

Jesus, dude—chill.

I glanced at Ziggy, who was intently watching the exchange with the focus of a predator, but I was obviously missing something. "Why do we care about this angry hydra-looking creature and their crystal collection?" I whispered, eager to know everything he did.

Ziggy shot me a proud look, as if me simply asking the question would get me another certificate on the cockpit wall.

"The Hydrassians use gemstones in their rituals, so their crystal collection is of no interest to me—even with *what* they are looking for." He returned his focus to the wildly gesticulating *Hydrassian.* "However, they are known to be peaceful... I can't recall ever seeing one behave so *aggressively.*"

"You have no authority here," the gem vendor huffed, bringing *my* attention back to the drama. "If you have a complaint against my business, you may take it up with the city...."

The vendor trailed off as Ziggy hissed and slapped his gloved hand over my eyes. I trusted there was a good reason for him blocking my view, even though it didn't sound like anyone was getting gruesomely murdered.

Plus, I'm a supe.

Murder is our love language.

A loud thud, like a body hitting the dirt, was followed by what was obviously the Hydrassian ransacking the stall in search of their precious *karnilian*.

I didn't get confirmation, as the next thing I knew, Ziggy was star hopping us away from the scene of the crime. When he uncovered my eyes, I saw we were in a different row of stalls that seemed oddly unfamiliar.

"Stay close," he growled under his breath, in full, boner-inducing mercenary mode. "This bazaar is nowhere near as safe."

I nodded, confused why we were suddenly on a Stellarian bazaar tour but instinctively knowing now wasn't the time for my questions.

Even though I am dying to ask all *the questions.*

Ziggy effortlessly cleared a path through the bazaar, simply by looking mean and tasty, and it was no hardship to ride his armor-covered ass. Unfortunately, I was following so close behind, I almost crashed into him when he abruptly stopped, but I managed to save face by casually strolling around my man to see where we'd ended up.

At another witchy bitch stall.

One that already looks like it's been hit.

"W-why are *you* here?" The willowy vendor shrank from my man, their oversized eyes widening further. "I did not contact Astrum Force—"

"Why didn't you?" Ziggy interrupted. "Were you not the victim of a crime?"

"I-I..." they stuttered, telling us without telling us it was because Astrum Force was terrifying as fuck until recently.

And Zig's not doing much to change that reputation...

"Was anything stolen?" I gently asked, stepping in to play good cop.

The vendor shook their head. "No. *No.* I did not have what they—"

"The Hydrassian," Ziggy brusquely interrupted.

"Y-yes..." Our unfortunate interrogation subject nodded rapidly. "What the Hydrassian was looking for is something I do not sell—would *never* sell."

"Karnilian," Zig cut to the chase once again.

The vendor swallowed thickly and nodded once, as if not wanting to even say the word.

MY INTEREST IS PIQUED!

Ziggy pulled out his Celestial Cube, causing the vendor to gasp in alarm, but my man simply began tapping various buttons, outwardly ignoring the reaction while inwardly soaking it in.

Such a sexy psychopath.

"Did the Hydrassian hypnotize you?" Zig calmly asked, snapping his gaze to his fellow alien, intently watching their face.

"I..." The vendor furrowed their brow and gingerly touched their temple, drawing my attention to how their skin was darker there—as if a bruise was forming. "I do not know. The last thing I remember was the Hydrassian saying they would 'use whatever force necessary to uncover the stone.' Then, I awakened to this..." They trailed off, gesturing with elegant fingers to the mess surrounding them.

So that's why Ziggy covered my eyes.

Witchy bitch hypnosis shit.

My man pocketed his cube and nodded decisively. "Astrum Force is sending a team to investigate." When the vendor sharply inhaled, he sighed heavily. "You have nothing to fear. They simply want to collect evidence and determine motive."

Dr. Micah is so proud right now.

"Watch out, Zig. Your *empathy* is showing," I teased as we walked away, earning me the side-eye of loving exasperation I couldn't get enough of.

Once we reached a quiet corner of the bustling market, he turned to face me. "It wasn't about *empathy,*" he huffed, clearly offended by the idea. "The investigation will be easier to conduct if that vendor isn't cowering in the corner like a helpless child."

So close.

"Ah, yes, because what would you know about cowering when you were born a bad bish..." I grumbled, although *my* exasperation was just as loving. "Because baby Stellarians are just wielding those katana tendrils at conception, huh?"

Ziggy's lips twisted. *"Novas.* That's what young Stellarians are called. And…" He cleared his throat, looking mildly embarrassed. "My tendrils didn't attain optimal precision until around age 50."

No way in hell was I letting *this* salacious intel pass me by. "Wait. Does that mean 50 is considered Stellarian puberty? Did your resonance change octaves around that age too? What about wet dreams? Did you ever just imagine a hot cluster of stars while sleeping and wake up covered in, like, *space dust?"*

Ziggy had been patiently waiting out my excited babbling, per usual, but at the mention of nocturnal emissions, he squinted. "What in Stellaria's name are wet dreams?"

Uhhh…

I sometimes forgot Zig had a *very* different childhood than me, not least of all because he lacked an actual corporeal form.

Dude must have blown his own mind the first time he jerked off.

Grimacing, I rubbed the back of my neck. "Um… well, when Earthlings reach a certain age—usually 11 to 14—their bodies start changing for adulthood, so there's a *lot* of hormones just coursing through our systems. And for guys especially, we sometimes wake up a little, uh, sticky, if you know what I mean…"

Sex Ed with Space Daddy.

Ziggy slow-blinked before running his gaze down my body so intently, I *felt* it. "And do *adult* Earthlings experience wet dreams?"

I was starting to get a little hot under the collar of my Han Solo vest, but I powered on in the name of biology. "Sometimes. It's not super common, though. I hadn't had one in *years* until—"

Oh, fuck.

As usual, my mouth started to run away from me, and, *as usual,* Ziggy zeroed in on my weakness like the predator he was.

"Until *when,* Micah?" His voice was dangerously low as he backed me against the stone wall surrounding the bazaar, his much larger body blocking out the light from the setting Stellarian sun.

His scent and proximity were making me dizzy, and if I'd possessed a will to resist, I would have already folded. At this point, I'd seen Ziggy interrogate several suspects, and while his—much scarier, but no less boner-inducing—methods were effective, I often wondered why he didn't just turn on the Space Daddy sex appeal to coax out the intel he was after.

Lord knows I'm *powerless to resist it.*

"Until *you* moved into my family's house," I whispered, my mouth dry and my dick deciding confession time was also playtime. "After that, I soaked my sheets almost every night."

He hummed in approval, lowering his face to drag his nose up my neck, inhaling deeply—savoring the lust I was no doubt pumping into the air. "And what did you dream about, babygirl?" he purred. "What filthy little fantasies made you so *wet?*

Lord. Have. Mercy.

If Ziggy hadn't been pressed against me, holding me up with his bulk, I would have already melted into a puddle on the dusty bazaar ground.

"All sorts of wild stuff," I eloquently gasped, scrabbling at the sides of his armor, *needing* to get inside and touch his skin. "I-I didn't know what you were under this hot bod, so my mind just made up a million scenarios where you were fucking me with a variety of alien appendages."

I mean...

Ziggy pulled back with a laugh. "No wonder you enjoy my skinsuit closet so much."

I grinned at him, sliding my hands up his armored pecs. "You know it, but only because it's *you* behind the wheel."

Just so we're clear.

My stellar collision's warm smile turned into a smirk. "Well, then. It sounds like you may need a reminder of what I really am beneath this *hot bod.*"

Yes, please.

9

ZIGGY

There were countless reasons my mate was perfect for me, but one of my favorites—besides his beautiful brain—was how *desperate* he was for my cock.

Figuratively speaking. And skinsuit-dependent, of course.

"I swear to gawd, Zig... This better not be another veiled offer to feed me *corpus spongiosum,* because ya boy needs the real thingggggg..."

His adorable scolding turned into a squeak of surprise as I abruptly star hopped us to the roof of my Stellarian house. The urge to take him to the Lodger's sleeping pod—our *nest*, in my mind—was strong, but I wanted to give him a unique experience tonight.

Something a bit more... personal.

"Excuse you, sir!" Micah exclaimed after we landed. "Why were you holding out on me with the *MTV Cribs*-style roof deck? Look at this boss setup! I just wanna kick back with a frilly little drink—"

"I'll give you something to drink if you'd like," I smoothly interrupted, tapping my gloved fingers against the metal covering my crotch in hopes of distracting him from the loaded question.

Unsurprisingly, it worked, as Micah's earthy brown eyes snapped to my cock with the naturally ingrained predatory focus all supes possessed.

Including those who rarely flexed their powers on the battlefield.

Even with the obscene amount of satisfaction I felt over his parents' deaths, there were also times I *begrudgingly* appreciated that, by underestimating him, they'd indirectly kept my precious mate out of harm's way.

Even if I haven't always managed to do the same.

While immense pride had almost eclipsed the anxiety I'd felt upon discovering Micah standing over the remains of the Maroxian who'd infiltrated my ship, I'd also meant what I said about murdering everyone had anything happened to him. I knew my mate could handle himself—had defeated Astrum Force's Head Commander when I failed to finish the job—so I tried my hardest to tamp down my protective instincts when they flared up.

The last thing I wanted was for Micah to ever feel coddled, or for his well-earned self-confidence to be eroded by my actions.

Since he is *the most impressive creature I've ever met.*

The mission on Marox required I leave him behind, but usually, I *preferred* having my stellar collision by my side, because I knew I could count on him to display a level of competence most lacked.

So perfect.

So incredibly attractive.

"You're so goddamn hot in your armor, Space Daddy," Micah murmured breathlessly, gliding his hands along the flexible metal as he lowered himself to his knees. "We *need* to figure out a way for you to fuck me while still wearing it."

Now that's an idea...

Micah deftly worked open the hidden fasteners holding my armor together, and I couldn't help smiling as I recalled how he'd struggled to remove it the first time he wore it as Commander Babygirl.

He looks hot in my armor as well.

My cock slapped against my abs once it was freed, painfully hard from not only the sight of my perfect mate kneeling before me, but the memory of that night. It had not only been the first time Micah had topped me—the first person to *ever* top me in my Earthling form—it was the only time another's tendrils had tangled with mine.

Fuck, I want to do that again...

Wait, what?

"What are you thinking about, Zig?"

Micah's voice snapped me back to the present, and I realized he was standing again, cupping my face in his hands, tilting it downward so his lips could brush mine.

"You," I answered truthfully, enjoying the feel of his clothed body flush with my naked one. "The first time you topped me, to be exact," I added, *almost* truthfully, while finishing the remainder of the thought in my head.

Your tendrils specifically.

Micah blushed and attempted to cover his face before I stopped him. "Gah! I was such a nervous wreck that night... I'm shocked you even let me top you again after that mediocre performance."

"It was perfect," I vehemently replied, wishing I could somehow convey all I meant by that through our bond alone. *"Everything* about it was perfect."

Everything.

I knew Micah thrived on clear communication, and while I'd made strides to match his candor, I wasn't sure *how* to articulate what I wanted in this moment.

Because I don't understand why I want it at all.

My stellar collision blushed deeper before grabbing my hand and leading me toward my "boss setup." It consisted of an enormous slab of intricately carved petrified wood surrounded by two equally ornate benches topped with hand-spun silk cushions stuffed with Raspun's wool.

All stolen from the palace of my first kill.

It may have seemed morbid for me to display my prizes in this way, like hunting trophies or spoils of war, but I had my reasons. My generically furnished housing was originally given to me as charity in exchange for pledging loyalty to Astrum Force Command, but *this* space was all mine. It represented the freedom my mercenary work had provided me after the limitations of my orphaned upbringing—the moment when I was finally in control of my own trajectory.

Or so I'd believed...

I hadn't been up here since discovering the old Astrum Force had simply used me as a rebel-born social experiment. However, thanks to Micah, I knew I'd still *earned* everything I'd accomplished, including this open-air refuge.

So why not share it with my perfect mate?

"Still deep in thought over there?" Micah laughed, kneeling between my thighs after I sat on the bench, not seeming at all offended by how distracted I was. "Still thinking about the time I rocked your world at the Muonova?"

Yes.

I cleared my throat. "Actually, I was... thinking about how important it was to bring you here. How... *happy* I am that you're mine."

Alarm bells rang in my head, trying to convince me I was showing too much weakness, but I tamped down my deeply ingrained flight instincts, determined to *show* my mate how true my words were.

Even if I'm not telling him all my desires.

Baby steps, as Dr. Micah would say.

Apparently, I wasn't the only one caught off guard by my confession. My stellar collision was frozen with his hands around my shaft, his mouth centimeters from my dripping crown as he gaped up at me.

"Jesus, Zig." Micah blinked rapidly and dropped his gaze. "I was gonna gobble your dick anyway—no need to butter me up."

Now *he* was deflecting, most likely because my sensitive mate was trying to appear tough while his system flooded with emotions. Thanks to our bond, however, and the piece of my essence still inside him, he couldn't hide from me.

And the last thing I ever want is for Micah to shut me out.

Not like I've tried to do to him.

Another thing I lo... *liked* most about my mate was that he didn't push me into necessary discomfort until I was ready, so the least I could do was the same for him.

We'll focus on other things for now.

"I'm *also* thinking about how expertly you swallow my cock," I purred, using a tendril to gently guide him into doing just that. "How much you enjoy choking on it."

"Mmph mmph..." Micah agreed, running his hands up my thighs as his eyelashes fluttered closed and bliss flavored the air.

I groaned when he bottomed out, hot and wet, his tongue lapping at anything it could reach while his throat tightened around me.

Perfection.

"You were made to take me, babygirl," I stated, caressing his face with my hand before sliding it down to his neck—feeling how perfectly I filled his throat. "Not just your mouth, but your ass..."

I unleashed a few more tendrils to unbutton and unzip his pants before sliding one down the back and between his juicy cheeks, ghosting over his hole.

"Zigmphhh…" Micah tried to speak, but I pushed his head down, feeling his hole flutter in response.

Such a slut.

Micah not only had a safe word—*Stormtrooper*—but a few non-verbal actions to use if he actually wanted me to stop while his mouth was otherwise engaged. However, "free use" had already been established between us, and with the way he was gazing up at me, eyes glassy and mouth stuffed full of cock, I knew he was giving me unrestricted permission.

My slut.

"For example," I continued, lazily thrusting into his mouth as I began breaching his ass with a naturally lubed tendril. "Your hole is still so perfectly tight—just for me."

Micah whimpered and squirmed, so I wrapped two tendrils around his thighs to wrench them open and hold him in place. Then, I added another to his ass.

"Even though I wasn't your first, this hole is mine," I growled, still wishing he'd give me names so I could eliminate any rivals outside of our clan. "Just like this perfect cock is mine."

Micah's whimper turned into a whine as I burrowed a tendril into the front of his pants to retrieve his cock, loosely coiling around his shaft, stroking in a rhythm I knew was slower than he preferred.

Let's see how sloppy you can get.

"So perfect," I praised as saliva overflowed from the corners of his mouth, dripping down my length to coat my sac. "Such a sloppy slut, made just for me."

Micah's body had gone limp, indicating he was more than happy to let me fuck his mouth and ass how I saw fit, although I noticed how he thrusted into the tendril wrapped around him—as if he couldn't help himself.

"Are you thinking about fucking *my* ass, babygirl?" I tried to snarl, but my voice caught as he unexpectedly slipped a finger behind my balls to circle my hole. "Of... holding me down with your... tendrils again while you take what's yours?"

It was all I could think about, even if I was certain my stellar collision didn't share my newfound fixation with our tendrils touching.

Because why would he?

Micah understood that my kind reproduced by using our tendrils to harvest essence from each other, but he would never experience the biological *need* to create another Stellarian in this way.

A need I never thought I'd experience either...

Prior to meeting my stellar collision, the very idea of reproduction "for the glory and continuation of Stellaria" had made me ill. Thanks to Dr. Micah, I knew this was mostly because of my own abandonment issues, but it was also something I'd simply had no interest in.

Now, it was attempting to consume my thoughts, despite being a moot point anyway. While incredibly accurate, Micah's gorgeous tendrils were man-made, so combining our essence would be imposs—

My unruly thoughts were cut short as Micah unfurled his tendrils the same moment he slipped his spit-covered finger into my ass. I choked on air, doubling over with a groan as I immediately unloaded down his throat.

BY STELLARIA!

Micah clenched around me, his cries muffled by my pulsing cock as he spilled across the rooftop with a near-violent shudder of his own. Terrified I was truly choking him, I withdrew my tendrils from his ass, yanked him off me by the hair, and wrenched open his mouth with my hands, checking for blockages.

He laughed, batting me away and using the back of his hand to wipe the overflow of cum from his chin. "Calm down, Space Daddy! I'm fine. Ya boy knew what he was in for with that sneaky finger... Buuuut it didn't seem like you minded, hmm?"

I huffed as he waggled his eyebrows suggestively. "Of course, I didn't mind, Micah. I *like* you being inside me..."

Fuck.

I want his tendrils inside me...

"Yeah, you do." Micah stood and straddled my lap, his spent cock smearing cum on my still-heaving abs as he licked his way into my mouth. "Because your ass belongs to me too."

Oh, no...

It no longer seemed to matter what I *thought* I wanted, because my tendrils were now wrapping around my mate's mechanical ones of their own accord—desperate to combine my essence with his.

Hesitantly surrendering to the situation, I pulled him closer, wrapping us both in a cocoon of starry light while my resonance hummed in approval of our physical connection.

I am in so much trouble.

Ziggy Andromeda was acting squirrely.

Squirrelier than usual, I mean.

Unfortunately for my man, I could sense his emotions to some extent, and while my stellar collision sonar wasn't as enhanced as his, I could still tell he was bunched up about *something*.

"Is this about me sticking a finger in your ass?" I blurted out, no longer able to hold it in.

What?

We all know I have no filter.

"E-excuse me?" Ziggy choked out, his pale skin blushing adorably beneath his murder freckles.

"You're acting weird, dude," I huffed, apparently more confident than him that no one around us understood Earthling American English. "And I need to know if I did something wrong."

Because I'm sensitive, goddamnit!

Ziggy's expression softened. "No, sunshine. This isn't about anything you did." When I continued to stare at him expectantly, he sighed and shifted awkwardly on his feet. "However, I... would rather work through it on my own a bit before discussing it with you... if you don't mind."

Oh.

Well, I suppose I can't argue with that.

As nosey as I was, I respected his answer. To be honest, I was downright *proud* of this emotionally constipated alien admitting something was wrong in the first place, much less *communicating* he needed time to process.

And that deserves to be celebrated.

"Roger that." I nodded decisively and steered the conversation to safer waters. "So which gun are we buying today?"

We'd stopped at the shop of Ziggy's favorite weapons merchant, which happened to be located near Astrum Force's laboratories. Even though I was *dying* to see Pedro again, I'd encouraged the detour, because if there was one thing Space Daddy enjoyed—*besides fucking me senseless, of course*—it was adding to his already overflowing arsenal.

And what Space Daddy wants, Space Daddy gets.

Ziggy smiled gratefully before returning his focus to the merchandise spread out on the crystal case before us. "I'm having trouble deciding," he murmured, which was even *more* off-brand than him talking about feelings. "Which one do you think I should buy?"

Gasp!

It may have seemed like overkill—*literally*—for a creature with built-in Samurai tendrils to own so many weapons, but I was more than happy to be the enabler. I was far better at conjuring up defensive shields than creating complex alien weaponry, so the selection at shops like this always impressed *me*—even if I was pretty pleased with how my wannabe Stellarian tendrils had turned out.

Although they're nowhere near as cool as Zig's...

Even with how excessive it was, I found my man's murder weapon collection as sexy as his skinsuit closet—*almost*—so being asked to weigh in on the newest addition had me feeling like a kid in a candy store.

"Let me see..." I rubbed my hands together, evil villain-style. "Which one will make us look like the baddest bitches in all the galaxies?"

Ziggy snorted but patiently waited for me to decide. I ran my hands over the merchandise, pausing at a futuristic looking crossbow—*because then we could get medieval on someone's ass*—before my gaze fell on a humorously oversized, neon green and orange ray gun that clearly came from the intergalactic department of ACME Corporation.

Beep beep—that's the one!

I grinned as Ziggy picked it up, only to grow impatient as he lingered on testing its heft, pressing buttons, staring down the scope, and generally taking *forever* to hand it to me.

"C'mon, Zig," I whined, reaching for my prize with grabby hands. "I wanna—*hoooly shit!* Jesus, that's heavy..."

He snickered as I almost dropped the deceptively light-looking gun. When I glared, Ziggy gracefully moved behind me, curling his body around mine to demonstrate how to support its weight.

Maybe I can just balance it on my erection...

I sighed before letting him take it back. "Yeah, I don't think this one's gonna work for me—not unless I hold it with my tendrils."

Ziggy tensed, and I wondered if maybe it was considered *uncouth* for Stellarians to use their tendrils for anything other than tasting emotions or disemboweling enemies.

Or making babies...

"*You* look badass holding it, though." I gave him an exaggerated once-over. "It kind of reminds me of something Bowie would've used as a prop during his *Spiders from Mars* tour."

Put your ray gun to my head.

My stellar collision's face lit up, but he tried to play it off with a scowl. "Actually, it was called the Ziggy Stardust Tour, although *Ziggy Stardust and the Spiders from Mars* was only one of the albums being promoted."

Such a hot boomer.

"Wait..." I feigned ignorance, as if I hadn't mentally catalogued *every* piece of personal intel this alien had ever spilled. "Were *you* the inspiration for *The Man Who Fell to Earth?* Or a starry-eyed groupie, touring with the band?"

Ziggy rolled his eyes as he paid the gun merchant with the usual, yet-to-be-explained handful of skeletal remains that passed for currency around here.

It's probably better not to know.

"The Man Who Fell to Earth didn't come out until a few years later, but it was based on a novel from a decade prior." He cleared his throat, squirming awkwardly once again. "However, I *did* tour with Bowie for a bit. In a way..."

What?!

"You did?" I yelped, my eyes nearly bugging out of my skull. "You never told me you were a Bowie roadie!"

"I would hardly call myself a roadie, Micah," Ziggy murmured distractedly, searching his utility belt for where to attach his shiny new ray gun. "I was simply stalking the tour in my true form until we made it to Kansas City. That's where I found this skinsuit."

My chest tightened as I remembered the heartbreaking story he'd once shared. How he'd stumbled upon a dying Midwestern boy who had never been accepted by his family —who'd thought Ziggy was an angel delivering him to heaven.

A heaven he'd already been denied entry to because of who he loved.

"And then, once the tour arrived on the West Coast, I *sensed* I should stick around," Ziggy hurriedly continued, unsurprisingly *not* wanting to linger on that moment of vulnerability. "Make that area of the country my home base while I created my superhero identity."

Star Hopper, the Deathball player.

I quickly conjured up a holster for his new toy, earning me another coveted smile. "Were you.... picking up on Theo's resonance?" I hesitantly asked, not wanting to reopen old wounds but curious if Ziggy knew what was happening at the time.

My heart swelled with pride again as he carefully considered his reply instead of shutting down like he had in the past when his wayward parent was brought up.

"No, I don't believe resonance was to blame," he finally replied once we were out on the glittering Stellarian streets again. "It was more like a... gut feeling. An intuition, perhaps? I would call it the sixth sense I've developed over the years from hunting my prey."

Hot.

Before I could coax him into more horny war stories, we reached our destination—a shimmering pearlescent door set in an otherwise nondescript building.

As nondescript as this yassified planet can be.

The instant we stepped through the door, a Stellarian materialized before us in true starry form.

"Ahh, welcome!" they greeted us in musical tones. *"You must be Ziggy and Micah Andromeda."*

Oh.

My.

God.

MICAH ANDROMEDA!!!

"That's us!" I enthusiastically replied in the trade language.

Ziggy choked on air, but then he somehow slammed his emotions shut before I could get a read on them.

You can't escape destiny, Space Daddy.

We're already space fiancés—no take backsies.

"How is Pedro?" I blurted out, since there was something I was currently more invested in than our marital status. "Can we see them?"

Luckily, the Stellarian didn't seem offended by my pushiness. *"Of course! We have already taken a fur sample and conducted a basic physical exam but were then told you insisted on being present before we drew blood."*

Drew blood?!

Oh, right.

For testing.

Irrational worry still had me anxiously wringing my hands as we followed our guide down a sterile white hallway, and it was only Ziggy's steady grip on my shoulder that stopped me from bolting ahead to find our alien baby.

Calm down, mother hen.

I'd only been responsible for Pedro's wellbeing for a couple of days, but apparently, that was long enough to grow attached.

Maybe I imprinted on them...

I was surprised but relieved to see Honnor waiting for us inside the lab, even if their Stellarian armor was blinding me with the glare from the fluorescents above.

Craning my neck, I searched for our little creature friend. "Where's—"

C. ROCHELLE

"Pedro?" Honnor replied, clearly amused by the familiarity as he stepped aside to reveal a cowering ball of fur. *"She's right here."*

She?

Before I could confirm what I'd heard, the feral tumbleweed was launching themselves—*herself?*—into Ziggy's arms.

Squee!

"She?" Zig calmly addressed Honnor, determined to play it cool despite the cuteness.

"Yes," his maker replied, turning to grab a small collection kit before handing it to me. *"Whatever species Pedro is, she appears to be a female."*

I swallowed thickly, wondering why *I* was suddenly the one in charge of gathering a blood sample from...

"Well, I'm still going to call them Pedro," I snipped as I readied the needle and syringe. "It's gender neutral enough."

Executive decision.

Blowing out a slow breath, I took a step toward the alien before pausing, unsure how to proceed.

What if I hurt them?

Sensing my distress, Ziggy shifted Pedro's position, stretching out their little arm and firmly holding it in place so I could aim for a vein.

What if they don't have veins?!

"Allow me, sunshine," my man offered when I continued to

98

hesitate, unleashing a tendril to deftly snatch the syringe from my hand.

Unsurprisingly, Pedro did *not* like the sight of those starry katanas, but they only released a single hiss before slumping in Ziggy's hold—as if suddenly overcome by exhaustion.

Sleep powers, more likely.

"Thank you…" Zig murmured, glancing at his creator, and my heart warmed to see him accepting the help he deserved.

Equally unsurprising was that a Stellarian was able to locate a vein on a shaggy fur-covered creature almost immediately. As soon as the blood sample was acquired and handed off to the lab tech, Honnor released our patient from their doze.

That was stressful!

"Now, let's commence a more thorough physical examination." Honnor nodded at the tech before gesturing toward a metal countertop that looked freshly cleaned. *"There was an odd breastplate formation I would like to take a closer look at—"*

The other Stellarian reached for Pedro with starry tendrils, but then froze when a siren abruptly blared outside.

"What is that?!" I hissed, grabbing the alien baby from Zig and clutching them against my chest while peering around the windowless room.

Honnor was already barking orders into their Celestial Cube, so I looked at my man for answers.

Ziggy's pale skin had gone even paler. "Air raid alarm," he murmured, his gaze growing distant. "It appears Stellaria is under attack."

To say I was triggered by the sight of my maker suited up in their Star Unit-issued armor and headed into battle was an understatement.

What if...

Just like when they...

"I'll be fine, Ziggy," Honnor stepped closer and placed a hand on my chest, coaxing my resonance into answering theirs. *"Initial reports indicate the approaching ships are carrying Irathians. This will be child's play."*

"Are I-Irathians not dangerous?" Micah stuttered, his voice muffled behind the shields he'd already activated to cover himself and Pedro.

Finally, some self-preservation!

"Oh, they are incredibly dangerous—to those with corporeal forms," my maker distractedly replied while glancing at an incoming message on their cube. *"But Irathians are flesh-eaters, and since we have no flesh to devour..."*

"Like zombies?!" Micah squeaked.

Honnor didn't correct what was an accurate assessment, but their next words surprised me. *"It would be best if the three of you took the Lodger and escaped elsewhere for now—in case Pedro is the asset they're after."*

"Pedro is not—" Micah tried to protest, but I placed a hand on his back as best I could through his shields.

You are an asset too, babygirl.

My most precious asset.

"Why would the Irathians want this creature?" I frowned, glancing down at Pedro. "It was the Maroxians I stole from, and they are not allies."

An explosion from outside had Honnor's attention understandably wavering. *"I do not know, my child, but right now, you need to leave."*

Glorified babysitting was not how I'd expected my day to go, but that wasn't why I continued to hesitate.

What if...

My maker softened, no doubt picking up on my concern better than I could articulate it. *"I promise, I will contact you as soon as the battle is over."*

Thank you.

I could only manage a curt nod in reply, but when Micah immediately blasted me with additional comfort through our bond, I smiled gratefully at my mate. With directives clarified, I star hopped both the assets back to my ship—straight to my weapons room.

Which I apparently won't be getting back anytime soon.

"I'll get Pedro settled while you fly us out of here." Micah flashed me a strained smile in a sorry attempt to disguise the anxiety I could feel pouring off him. "Help us, Space Daddy— you're our only hope."

I knew he was simply attempting to lighten the mood with a *Star Wars* reference, but his words felt like a punch to the gut.

My mate needs me to get him out of danger.

They both do...

The Lodger 79's cloaking device was activated, so I wasn't worried about the Irathians spotting us before we took off, but leaving the planet undetected could still be an issue.

Star hopping to the cockpit, I grimly assessed the battle already raging in the sky. Since Stellaria was a popular outpost, and most who stopped here were experienced—and bloodthirsty—enough to join the fray, there were a wide variety of aliens involved, making the situation even more chaotic.

I should be out there, fighting for my planet.

Not that I have the credentials...

With a scowl, I refocused on my directives, reminding myself *if* Pedro was the reason for this attack, getting them off my planet was as important a task as fighting Irathians in a Star Force squadron.

Even if it feels like running away.

After adjusting various controls, I eased the Lodger into ignition, hovering a few feet off the ground while I decided where to go.

Stellaria's moons weren't an option, since I didn't want to compromise an established hideout, and the idea of potentially bringing the fight to a peaceful planet like Kaalanesea *yet again* left a bad taste in my mouth.

The Irathians weren't official allies of the Stellarians, but—until today—we wouldn't have considered them enemies either. With this unprecedented attack, however, I was now questioning who in the galaxy we could trust.

What would Din Djarin do?

"Hey Zig!" Micah appeared so suddenly at my side, I wondered if he'd star hopped. "Is there a *reason* we're, um, *not* leaving the raging war zone?"

I huffed. "To be honest, sunshine, I'm not entirely sure *where* would be safest for us to go."

Past Ziggy would *never* have admitted he didn't know what to do—and present day Ziggy still wouldn't have uttered the words to anyone else but him—but this Earthling had somehow convinced me to let down my guard, almost from the moment we met.

Another impressive superpower.

The trust I had in my stellar collision was ingrained but also earned. Micah's parents may have expected him to use his powers to ensure *others* succeeded, but he'd also never resented that assignment.

My mate *enjoyed* helping others, was the kindest soul I'd ever met, and even once I dared to show him vulnerability, he never took advantage of what others—what I—saw as a weakness. With how his beautiful mind worked, he was more interested in focusing on solutions than problems, and there was nothing I admired in him more.

He probably already came up with a solution—

"What if we went somewhere densely populated?" He shrugged and dropped his gaze, as if I might dismiss his input the way everyone else in his life had. "You know... hide in plain sight? I mean, only if you think—"

I gripped his chin so he'd look at me, relieved he'd lowered his shield. "Must I remind you that you are my *partner* in all things, and that includes our missions?"

He averted his gaze again, and I frowned as *uncertainty* flavored the air.

Does he not believe me?

"Hiding in plain sight is an exceptional plan," I added, in case he needed the validation. "So we'll head to the nearest Muonova."

Micah remained silent, but I was satisfied with our plan. Turning in my chair, I faced the dashboard to set our course, focusing all my attention on maneuvering my ship to safety.

And my precious cargo.

It wasn't until we were clear of Stellaria's atmosphere that my stellar collision spoke again. "Not to be a Debbie Downer, but... I'm not sure bringing a baby to a *bar* is the best idea."

I huffed, unsure who this "Debbie" was and why their uneducated opinion held any weight here. "Muonovas are neutral zones where enemies and allies must coexist or risk being black-bagged."

Micah furrowed his brow. "Do you mean blacklisted?"

"No," I replied, disabling our cloaking device once we were out on the Intergalactic Highway so as not to seem suspicious. "Black-bagged. Forcibly removed and never heard from again. It would be bad for business if Muonovas were nothing but violence and bar brawls."

Even if that's still a large part of the appeal.

At least, for me *it is.*

When my mate continued to taste like uncertainty, I swiveled to face him, realizing reassurances were needed. "I promise, sunshine, I will protect Pedro from harm. We will simply stick to the more... family friendly areas of the Muonova, like the market district."

Not to be confused with the neighboring red light district.

Micah's eyes lit up. "Oh, right! I forgot about the market." He chewed his bottom lip for a moment, his big, beautiful brain whirring away. "Hey, maybe we could stock up on supplies for Pedro while we're there?"

I nodded thoughtfully. "Yes. If we find a vendor from the Yaaritzi galaxy, they might carry metalwork strong enough to prevent Pedro from infiltrating the air ducts again."

My mate snickered. "Baby proofing the ship isn't a bad idea, but I was talking about toys and games and stuff."

Toys and games?

"For... *enrichment?*" I rolled the word over my tongue, still processing the foreign concept Zion had mentioned during our phone conversation.

Novas weren't encouraged to play—at least, not under the regime I grew up with. I'd learned how to kill my opponent from the inside and out, how to be useful to Stellarian society as a whole, but I couldn't recall ever participating in a 'game' until I played Deathball as an undercover superhero on Earth.

A sport that would have been better with actual deaths...

"Exactly." Micah climbed onto the captain's chair with me, straddling my lap and cupping my face before grinning wildly. "Look at you, being a good Space Daddy to our little alien baby."

I huffed, annoyed when my dick stirred once again at the idea of "making space babies" with my stellar collision.

This is ridiculous.

"I am simply utilizing the intel your brother shared on keeping a child alive." I frowned. "Apparently, there's more to it than simply providing food, water, and shelter."

Micah delivered a sweet kiss to my lips that instantly settled me. "Yeah, there's more to it, but we'll just have to figure it out as we go."

I don't like the sound of that.

"You seem to already know what to do," I muttered sourly, even as I gazed at him in admiration. "A natural provider."

The perfect mate.

It was Micah's turn to huff, his cheeks darkening deliciously. "I wouldn't say it's totally natural... I just had a good role model."

"Who?" I scoffed, angry on his behalf all over again. "Your parents were terrible to you—to *all* your siblings."

Worse than Theo.

And that's saying a lot.

"Zion, silly," he laughed, carding his hands through my hair in a way that made me purr. "He was younger than I am now when he had Daisy, but big bro stepped up! I was barely a teenager when she was born, but it blew my mind to see the way he cared for her, despite our parents' disapproval. And he had to figure it out on the fly, you know? I mean, he'd always taken care of the rest of us in his own way, but this was different. It was... unconditional."

My borrowed heart broke for my mate once again. If there was one thing I'd observed during my time as a supposed superhero, it was that *all* supe families—heroes and villains alike—operated on extremely conditional terms. Clans were aligned, in marriage and business, through ironclad contracts, and even those related to you were expected to prove themselves 'useful' at every turn.

Or be culled from the herd.

"It sounds like how you... care for me," I mused, unleashing a few tendrils to wrap around him, pulling him closer.

Perhaps even love me?

Micah sniffled and rapidly blinked, adorably trying not to cry. "Y-yeah. And how you... care for me too..."

Yes.

If there was one thing I knew, it was that what I felt for Micah was unconditional. I may have since reunited with both my makers, and inherited a much larger family in the process— through resonance and otherwise—but none of these connections were as strong as what I had with my stellar collision. Articulating those emotions were proving to be a challenge, but there was nothing my mate could ever do to change that irrefutable fact.

Nuzzling my face into Micah's neck, I deeply inhaled, allowing his sunshiney scent to smooth out my lingering concerns.

I can do this.

"We'll figure this out, Zig," he murmured, expertly knowing what I needed to hear. "Together."

We can do this.

Together.

12

MICAH

How the hell are we going to figure this out?

It had been a while since Ziggy first took me to the Muonova's market district—and even then, we'd only visited the more *adult*-focused stalls—so I hadn't realized how vast of an area it was.

Aaaaand I'm already confused...

Besides the glaring lack of signage, there didn't seem to be what one would call a kid's section—or a universal idea of what that even meant among such a wide variety of species.

"I'll be right back..." I murmured to Zig after spotting a blob-shaped creature herding mini-blobs through the crowded aisle. "Gonna ask that one a few questions."

My man tore his gaze from the selection of high-tech weapons he was perusing—*because of course he was*—to squint at my target, no doubt assessing the threat to my wellbeing.

What does he think they're gonna do?

Absorb me into their blobness?

As soon as he nodded in approval, I approached the blob as non-threateningly as possible before addressing them in the trade language. "Excuse me? I couldn't help noticing you have offspring—"

"They are not for sale," the blob curtly interrupted before reaching out with blobby arms to gather their children close.

Before absorbing them into their blobness.

Well, okay then.

"Oh! I wasn't interested in..." I stammered before gesturing at Ziggy. "We have, uh, offspring of our own but are unfamiliar with where to shop for them. Could you please direct me where to find supplies for offspring... things...?"

I don't even know what I'm asking for!

The blob-parent peered around me to assess my family situation. When I followed their gaze—*I think? Where are the eyes?* —I sighed.

I'd asked Ziggy *not* to wear his Stellarian armor today, for a better chance of inspiring goodwill among our fellow shoppers, but he was apparently incapable of appearing like anything other than a bad bitch.

Usually, I can't complain, but...

The current issue was that he was holding the sci-fi version of an AK-47 directly above where Pedro was bundled up in their homemade baby sling. A furry paw appeared from the folds of the sweatshirt, and I could only watch in resignation as Zig lowered the gun so "our offspring" could wrap their pangolin claws around the trigger in the correct way.

Space Dad of the Year...

I turned to face the blob again, expecting to find whatever their version of side-eye was. Instead, they were animatedly gesturing for me to follow them to a worn metallic panel barely hanging on to a nearby wall.

"We... are... here," they haltingly spoke while pointing at a hieroglyph that looked like a minimalist skull. "The death sector."

That tracks.

It was no shock that one of the only areas of the market Ziggy was familiar with was Ye Olde Death Sector, but I staunchly focused on the pleasant surprise of there being an actual map.

"You go here," the blob concluded, stabbing a blobby finger at a section marked with what was possibly an egg.

Or a bomb.

Unclear.

"Thank you." I pressed my palms together and bowed my head, assuming that was the universal gesture for gratitude.

"Most welcome," my savior replied with a blobby bow of their own. "Good luck with your *Trol!*"

Trol?

My translation device didn't recognize the word, but before I could get clarification, the alien released their offspring from blob time-out and continued on their way.

Ziggy appeared at my side, brow furrowing as he squinted at the map he should have goddamn known about.

"You were… asking for directions?" he murmured in wonder, as if the concept was as foreign to him as expressing emotions.

No wonder he identifies as a man…

"Well, yeah!" I exclaimed. "And the very nice blob told me this," I pointed at our destination on the map, "is where to find offspring things."

At least, I hope it is…

Ziggy nodded once before grabbing my wrist and abruptly star hopping us to the bomb-egg sector.

"I thought we were keeping a low profile," I hissed under my breath, even if I was secretly glad we'd skipped what looked like a forty minute walk.

My ass is still a little sore from rooftop tendril tango.

That bratty Stellarian chuckled. "There are a few alien species who can fade in and out of invisibility, so our sudden disappearance and reappearance will not result in undue attention. Not to mention, *any* of the creatures here could be a Stellarian."

I instinctively looked around, interested to see if I could spot a hint of tendrils glimmering above anyone. Unfortunately, this area of the market had adopted the same futuristic design choices as the death sector. Every visible surface was sleek, shiny metal, creating a dizzying funhouse mirror effect while reflecting the overhead glow that fluctuated between purple, blue, and pink.

Gotta make that merchandise look fancy with the bi-lighting!

Even offspring things…

My gaze snagged on a stall with rows of carved wooden objects, reminding me of the all-natural teething toys my sister Rose insisted on for all her kids.

I led the way, grabbing an item vaguely shaped like a baby rattle before experimentally holding it out for Pedro. A clawed paw appeared to accept the toy before disappearing into the depths of Ziggy's kangaroo pouch once again. A moment later, the toy was loudly spat onto the counter with the wooden ball at the end missing a jagged chunk.

Oops.

"Try this one." The unbothered vendor handed me a *metal* version with a ridged surface that reminded me of a meat tenderizer.

"Uhhh..." I grimaced. "I'm not sure that's safe for—"

Pedro snatched it directly from the vendor, and the enrichment must have hit, as all that emerged this time was the sound of grinding metal and contented cooing.

"It cleans the teeth," the vendor sagely explained while accepting payment from Ziggy. "And maintains incisor sharpness."

Bitey enrichment.

I nodded in thanks before we moved on to the next stall. By the time we'd visited every vendor in the first row, I'd taken over baby sling duties, and Zig had star hopped three loads of purchases back to the ship.

What baby Pedro wants, baby Pedro gets.

While waiting for my man to return from his latest door dash, I stumbled upon a corner lot filled with robots of all shapes and sizes, fenced in by shelves of accessories and mods.

Is this a freakin' droid shop?!

I had no idea why something like this was being offered in the bomb-egg sector, but I couldn't seem to locate anyone in charge to ask what their purpose was.

Let's be real, Imma want one anyway.

Some of the droids were basic, little more than geometric trash cans on wheels, but most were humanoid shaped. I was relieved none were covered in skin—since I *was* alone in this creepy back alley full of lifeless automatons—but I couldn't stop my nerdy little engineering heart from beating a little faster at the sight of so much tech.

And I know someone else who'll appreciate this...

Digging out my phone, I snapped a few photos of a bright gold, blinged-out model and immediately texted them to Gabe.

> I'm thinking 'bout recruiting a new crew member.

To no surprise—probably thanks to him being an actual psychic—Gabe replied almost instantaneously.

EARTH ANGEL

> Bruh, did you make that?! 🙀 Is there anything you can't do? 🖤

I smiled down at my phone, my cheeks heating at the thought of someone as impressive as Gabriel Suarez thinking *I* was cool.

I'm such a dork.

Pedro made a little trilling sound from within their nest, and I peeked inside, finding their enormous yellow eyes rhythmically blinking up at me, like a cat showing they were happy.

Gah! So cute!

EARTH ANGEL

Dre wants me to ask if it's a sex bot 😶

I could clearly picture Gabe's twin lurking over his shoulder, reading his texts while inserting himself into everyone else's business, as usual.

He should know by now that I clap back.

It is. Now, Dre has someone to play with the next time you come visit.

Unless he wants to take Ziggy up on his offer...

EARTH ANGEL

Dude just star hopped away like a skerred little bitch! 😂😂😂

I cackled, pleased I'd knocked the more intimidating twin off his game.

Prolly gonna go jerk off while thinking about Space Daddy.

EARTH ANGEL

Fair. I know I would.

Wait, what?

Before I could make my slutty bestie spill, a hissing voice speaking the trade language had my hair standing on end.

"You are searching for a nanny bot, yes?"

Nanny bot?

I turned to face who I assumed was the robot vendor, hustling for a sale, only to come face to... *faces* with a Hydrassian.

Eek.

With Zion's supe form being a giant lizard—an *alien* lizard—you'd think encountering extraterrestrial reptiles wouldn't faze me. But it was one thing to observe a creature with multiple snakeheads from afar, and an entirely different experience to have a multitude of unblinking reptilian eyes fixed on you.

Pedro must have felt equally unnerved, because they were burrowed deep in their pouch, unmoving and quiet as death.

It's okay, P—I've got this.

Realizing the Hydrassian had caught me in the corner of the lot farthest from the main drag, I flashed my most charming smile. "Why would I require a nanny bot?"

All six snakeheads zeroed in on the baby sling. "Because you have offspring. May we see it?"

How 'bout no?

"My offspring is sleeping," I replied in a light tone even as I discreetly raised my shields around both of us. "And my *mate* will be back any moment."

I retreated, only to have the Hydrassian advance, backing me into a corner. While I felt fairly confident I could escape—or hold my own in a fight—I did *not* appreciate having my personal space disrespected.

Read the room, dude.

The... creepy robot abandoned lot...

Releasing a slow breath, I sent as many DANGER vibes to Ziggy as I could without alerting the alien in front of me that I was anything other than completely calm.

"You do not appear to be mated." The Hydrassian judgmentally looked me over, and I bristled.

What the fuck does that *mean?*

"Well, he is." Ziggy suddenly appeared behind my opponent, making all twelve reptilian eyes widen in alarm. "To me."

13

I can't leave him alone for a minute.

It didn't shock me anymore that trouble followed Micah everywhere he went, but this magnetism for disaster was making my protective instincts go haywire.

"Celestial catastrophe" may be the perfect distinction after all...

While I'd been *trying* my best to tamp down the urge to rescue my mate at the slightest threat, there were still instances— like this one—where I clearly needed to step in with a few threats, possibly some violence.

What a hardship.

"You are S-Stellarians...." the Hydrassian I was now restraining with my tendrils idiotically observed.

Micah's chest—where a piece of me was permanently lodged —puffed up with pride at being classified as such.

I wish it was true...

"Fuck yes, we are!" he crowed, shooting me a wink before glaring at our captive. "So maybe you should think twice about cornering one who's just trying to shop for a nanny bot, huh?"

Nanny bot?

My gaze flickered to a bright gold droid next to Micah, and I realized my perfect mate had discovered a solution for our noticeable *lack* of "Tendril Touchy Time."

We are taking a bot with us.

"We simply wished to offer *our* services instead." The Hydrassian's sibilant tone brought me back to the task at hand.

Interrogation.

My favorite thing.

"Exactly *why* would we allow *you* anywhere near our offspring?" I snarled, oddly enraged at the idea, considering Pedro wasn't actually mine.

"Because we know what it issss..." they hissed, vainly straining against my tendrils. "What it is *worth.*"

"Worth?" Micah wrapped his arms around the contents of the baby sling before growling. "You think we'd *SELL* OUR CHILD?!"

Commander Babygirl is angry.

So fucking attractive.

The Hydrassian briefly shrank from my stellar collision's intensity before scoffing. "You think you would be given the *opportunity* to sell? Killing you both would be a far easier solution, especially with how many planets—how many *galaxies*—are searching for the *Trol.*"

Trol?

"Trol..." Micah murmured, most likely as confused as I was.

"Is that why I've spotted no less than six Hydrassians following us today?" I scoffed in return. "Including the two currently hiding in the stall directly across from us—no doubt waiting for you to die and get out of their way?"

Because you will be dying.

"What?" Micah yelped, his pretty brown eyes widening as he glanced around. "I mean, yeah! Why are Hydrassians following us?"

An excellent question.

"Answer him." I tightened my hold, allowing my tendrils to grow sharp along their edges, just to hear the creature cry out in pain. "And don't try to deny it."

The Hydrassian choked out a dry cough. "A fellow mercenary, we see. Come now, Stellarian... We all do what we need to in order to survive."

What?!

"Hydrassian's are not *mercenaries,*" I snapped, confused by this unexpected intel. "You are seers. *Recluses.* The only time you leave your humid planet is to gather supplies for your ridiculous rituals."

Supplies like...

"This wouldn't have anything to do with *karnilian,* would it?" I growled, thinking of the oddly agitated Hydrassian on

Stellaria attacking gem dealers in search of the illegal stone.

My captive paused before releasing a chorus of laughter from all six heads. "Of course, a *Stellarian* would know nothing about the source of karnilian's power. Such a formidable species has no need of 'ridiculous rituals' to ensure victory in battle, hmm?"

Ridiculous indeed.

"These rituals sound like how the ancient Greeks consulted oracles before battles and other major decisions," Micah murmured thoughtfully. "They believed the answers were divinely inspired and could predict the outcome of..." He trailed off before eyeing the alien shrewdly. "Do your rituals predict or *determine?*"

The Hydrassian made a sound of admiration. "Ah, how refreshing. A Stellarian who does not assume *undefeated* means *impossible to defeat.*"

Because he's not a Stellarian...

I inwardly cursed. The full extent of my knowledge on karnilian was that it was illegal—in my galaxy, Invenio-Astralis, and most I'd visited. In fact, the only planet within reasonable distance of Stellaria that allowed the stone and its related rituals was...

Lacertus.

Speaking of predictable.

The reptilian species had once been considered a worthy foe for my kind, but then we evolved—perfecting star hopping to evade their agile flight and developing an immunity to their paralyzing power drain. Now, they could barely bring us a challenge.

Do they honestly think a silly little rock is going to give them an advantage?

"So, it was the *Lacertus* who hired you," I sighed, more annoyed by this sad excuse for a mercenary than anything. "They hired you to track down the karnilian and this... *Trol,* whatever that is. As if possession of either of those assets will change the fact Stellarians *are*—and forever will be—undefeated by those lumbering lizards."

"Zig..." Micah warned, but I'd had enough.

I didn't want to spend another minute in this sector, or in this Muonova, or be on glorified babysitting duty while Honnor and their Star Units were defending my home from invaders. All I wanted was to complete this mission and move on to the next with my stellar collision by my side.

"Careful, Stellarian..." the Hydrassian chuckled low, dropping to their knees as I released them, accepting the inevitable. "Imperial blind spots may be the end of your empire."

Enough!

With a snarl, I sliced my tendrils through the air, cleanly decapitating all six of our captive's heads in one stroke.

"Gross," Micah grimaced as he attempted to wipe the Hydrassian's black blood off his shields—which only resulted in him smearing it around even more. "I wasn't expecting you to go full Alien Rambo until we were done interrogating."

"I was done," I snapped. "There was nothing this self-proclaimed *mercenary* could tell me that I didn't already know."

Micah deactivated his blood-covered shields with a huff. "Is that so? I'm not gonna lie, Zig—I'm having serious déjà vu from the *last* time you refused to humor any perspectives that didn't confirm your own biases."

What is he talking about?

"It's not a bias to suspect the *Lacertus* are behind this, Micah," I scoffed, tossing aside the fallen Hydrassian so I could step closer. "They have *never* accepted their inferiority, so it's unsurprising that they—"

I paused my history lesson to unleash another set of tendrils, snatching the second Hydrassian who *thought* they were sneaking up on us and decapitating them as well.

"ZIG!" Micah shouted, now wiping Hydrassian blood directly off his skin and clothes.

Oops.

"Well..." I cleared my throat. "That's why you shouldn't lower your shields until—"

Sigh.

I turned to face the third—and hopefully, for everyone's sake, *final*—Hydrassian, letting them get close enough to satisfy my bloodlust before sweeping a razor-sharp tendril toward their necks.

Only to have a set of mechanical tendrils intercept.

"No, Zig." Micah's stern tone mixed with the way his tendrils coiled around mine had me melting...

Now is not the time, Ziggy.

"I've got this." My mate smoothly released me and entrapped the now fleeing Hydrassian before it could escape. "Just let me handle it."

Commander Babygirl is reporting for duty I see...

To my immense disappointment, Micah didn't reel in our prey to finish him off. I was partially appeased when, instead, he swung his tendrils and slammed the Hydrassian into a nearby metal wall so hard, it bent.

Hot.

"Whoops!" My mate winced before clearing his throat and rallying. "Who are you working for? Tell us, and maybe we won't kill you."

Slightly less hot.

"Micah..." I sighed. "I already told you. They were hired by—"

"The Irathians," our captive croaked before one of their heads swiveled to the last one I killed. "We are unsure who sent the others."

WHAT?!

The Irathians may have terrified lesser species, but they were barely a blip on Stellaria's radar. They also had never struck me as intelligent enough for strategic thinking, so the idea of them attacking my planet while simultaneously sending a mercenary after us...

No.

This mercenary was already here.

They all were.

They're everywhere...

"We need to leave, Micah." I kept my tone calm while unleashing dozens of tendrils to search the area for more lurking opportunists. "Now."

My mate froze before nodding hurriedly. "Okay, so what do I..." His gaze drifted to the trapped Hydrassian before he swallowed hard.

Oh, sunshine.

One of things I respected most about Micah was his natural affinity to *help* instead of *harm*. It wasn't an ideal trait for a mercenary to possess, but I had no intention of making him change who he was.

I'm happy to be the cold-blooded killer in this partnership.

Secure in our roles, I neatly ended our final opponent then grabbed my sputtering—and blood-covered—mate in one tendril, snatched the golden 'nanny bot' in another, and star hopped us back to our ship.

"What is the point of me saying we might let them live if you just kill everyone we interrogate?"

I finished rinsing shampoo from my Earthling hair before peering around the frosted partition of the Lodger's single occupancy shower stall.

Single occupancy despite my best efforts.

"The point is that they tell us more if they think they might be released." When Micah's pinched expression told me it had been a rhetorical question, I sighed. "I allowed the lone survivor of Theo's massacre to live."

And Theo, let's not forget.

It was Micah's turn to sigh as he refocused on bathing Pedro in the large basin we'd apparently bought for this purpose.

I thought it was to hold my weapons.

My mate had handed me the baby sling upon arrival before practically throwing himself in the shower, muttering about "itchy trigger fingers" while he aggressively scrubbed himself clean.

For once, I didn't mind being the one on baby duty, because it gave me time to think.

Assuming we'd run across *more* 'mercenaries' at the next Muonova, I'd simply picked a random direction before getting us back on the Intergalactic Highway. Then, I'd reactivated the Lodger's cloaking device and put us on autopilot while I contemplated our next move.

Learning *multiple* alien species had hired Hydrassians to scout for karnilian was jarring enough, but the revelation this search involved *Pedro* confirmed the creature was the reason Irathians had attacked Stellaria.

Which means we can't return until we've unloaded the asset.

I would have preferred to consult with Honnor and Bron on these new developments, but my maker had promised to contact me *after* the battle, so the least I could do was be patient.

But what if...

"What the fuck?" Micah muttered under his breath, leaning down to take a closer look at the soggy ball of fur in the basin.

Pedro appeared to be enjoying themselves—splashing and cooing in an oddly *baby-like* way—so it didn't seem like an emergency.

Plus, I have zero interest in participating in "bath time."

"Hey, Zig? Can you come look at this, please?"

Sigh.

Turning off the water, I grabbed a towel and wrapped it around my waist before exiting the shower stall. With how tiny the bathroom was, this put me directly above the basin, so I crouched down to better see what had Micah concerned.

"Sooo, Pedro's fur is thick as fuck and layered, which is probably why I didn't notice this until now…" he murmured, attention fixed on parting the fur on the creature's chest.

I sighed again. "If you're going to show me the defensive *tentacles* Pedro has, I am well acquainted."

And still slightly annoyed they caught me off guard.

Micah glanced up and smiled sweetly. Deceptively so. "Mmhmm… and have you noticed how Pedro hasn't felt the need to flash those tentacles since you started playing nice?"

Another rhetorical question, I presume.

"Although…" He chewed his lip, already puzzling through the next problem. "It's weird they didn't activate their defenses when the first Hydrassian showed up at the Muonova. Pedro was clearly uncomfortable…"

I frowned down at the creature splashing around the basin, remembering how they'd been curled up in the sling while I'd shopped for guns.

Until I lured them out for some "enrichment."

"They did…" I murmured. "It was a different sort of defense mechanism—similar to how novas are taught to curl inward to protect our core while our tendrils are still developing."

My stellar collision had abandoned his task in favor of gaping at me in awe. "Is your core more *fragile* than your tendrils?"

I shifted uncomfortably at the thought of sharing my secrets, but sternly reminded myself Micah would never use this intel against me.

Even if he is powerful enough to kill me.

"Yes," I haltingly replied. "The only way to destroy a Stellarian is to tear our core to pieces and return us to the stars."

Micah sharply inhaled, and I cursed my thoughtlessness, realizing exactly which traumatizing memory I'd just invoked.

"It's over quickly, sunshine, and relatively painless," I lied, attempting to calm his growing panic by sending soothing energy through our bond. "It's also an injury that's easy to reverse if a piece of that core happens to be permanently lodged inside our perfect mate."

That did the trick as he snapped back to scientific focus. "The piece of you inside me is from your *core?*" When I nodded, he beamed. "That's my favorite part of you! So pretty…"

To my absolute horror, I blushed. "Yes, well… a Stellarian has little control over the colors our true form displays. It's most likely a combination of our makers' hues and other genetic factors—"

"It's okay to be a pretty boy, Space Daddy," Micah purred, making me blush harder and scowl down at Pedro. "Is that the only reason I'm able to glow for you?" he added, barely audible.

My gaze snapped to his face, sensing… *sorrow* in our bond. "Yes," I answered truthfully, knowing full well that wasn't what he—what *either* of us—wanted to hear.

Because you're not a Stellarian.

Now *my* sorrow joined his, but it didn't change how I felt.

"You are still my mate," I firmly reminded him. "My stellar collision."

Until I return to the stars.

"I know, Zig." Micah smiled gratefully although he sounded tired. "I guess I just feel like the odd Earthling out in our alien polycule."

Alien polycule?!

He snickered at my horrified expression, even if I had to admit it was an accurate assessment of the unprecedented relationship he and I had with Gabriel.

It also gave me an idea.

"If I left *more* of my core inside you—similar to how the twins were created..." I casually mused, attempting to mask how *feral* the idea made me. "I wonder if that may allow you to access some of my abilities, like—"

"Real tendrils?!" he shouted, accidentally startling Pedro into stillness. "That would be way cooler than the wannabe tendrils I made—"

"Your tendrils are *perfect!*" I snarled, eliciting a squawk from Pedro, who then blinked up at both of us with concern.

Do they... think we're fighting?

While I could admit I'd felt called to protect and comfort Theo's stellar collisions during our recent excursion on Earth, I could at least blame that reaction on the resonance we shared.

Yet, here I was, suddenly *compelled* to stop a random, newly-hatched alien with zero connection to me from being upset.

What is happening to me?!

Before I could tamp it down, my resonance hummed soothingly, causing Micah's chest to glow in response.

Then, so did Pedro's.

What.

"Oh!" Micah exclaimed, gently pawing at the creature's layers of fur once again. *"That's* what I wanted to show you. Our baby is glowing!"

Our.

Baby.

I could only stare, slack-jawed, at the reddish glow emanating from the center of Pedro's chest, pulsing in time with their happy trilling sounds.

"Do you think there's a Stellarian in there?" Micah whispered, looking far too invested in the idea.

For science, no doubt.

Unleashing an invisible tendril to hover over Pedro, I discreetly tested the air for the minuscule energetic surges certain creatures gave off, but I sensed nothing more than the usual vibrations found among my fellow space travelers.

Which doesn't mean much, considering how insidious some of us are.

I cleared my throat and warily glanced at Micah. "It would help if I could get inside and take a look around..."

He cocked his head, observing me silently for a moment. "Are you asking for permission?"

I huffed, not appreciating how observant he was at this moment. "Well, yes. I can't ask *them,* so it seemed the polite thing to do."

Micah smirked. "So polite." He returned his gaze to Pedro and ran a hand through their soggy fur, eliciting another happy trill. "If you promise to be as quick as possible, and gentle... I just don't want—"

"I promise, I will be quick and gentle." It was my turn to smirk. "The opposite of how I am with you."

He huffed as his cheeks darkened. "Not in front of the baby, Zig!"

Resisting the urge to remind him this creature had no idea what we were saying, I focused on my assignment from Commander Babygirl.

Undetected—*temporary*—infiltration.

First, I sedated Pedro with my sleep powers, similar to how Honnor had when we took a blood sample, before carefully snaking a tendril down their throat. I couldn't exactly 'see' inside their body while doing this, but with how sensitive my tendrils were to touch, scent, and vibrations, I was confident I could get a useful reading of some kind.

Oddly, the deeper I traveled, the more energetic resistance I came up against while also feeling *compelled* to keep going—to reach whatever was luring me in.

I need to find it.

An offhand comment Honnor had made about "an odd breastplate formation" had me branching out once I reached the chest cavity, sending tendrils shooting off in various directions to locate the source of the glow.

I need to make it mine...

Fuck.

I was having a difficult time ignoring my natural instincts to take over, but I chalked it up to the now-outdated Stellarian mindset of complete subjugation as the only option when it came to our vessels.

That's not who you are anymore, Ziggy.

It's not why you're here—

I froze as the source of the red glow suddenly washed over me, unobstructed by Pedro's natural defenses. It was an almost maddening amount of energy, vibrating my synapses with the promise of ultimate supremacy

So. Much. Power.

All mine...

With a gasp, I snatched my tendril out of Pedro's slack mouth and put as much distance between us as possible in the tiny bathroom.

"What happened?!" Micah hissed, his panicked gaze darting between us like he didn't know who to attend to. "Is everything okay?"

My chest heaved, my tendrils roiling beneath the surface as I locked them down tight. "There's something in there, something more powerful than anything I've ever encountered. I need... I need to..."

I need my maker.

Honnor must have sensed my distress, as the alert lighting built into the walls began flashing, indicating an incoming message from Astrum Force Command.

Thank fuck.

"I don't think *Pedro* is a danger to us, sunshine," I soothed, wanting to be clear before I disappeared. "But if you could get them settled in the weapons... the nursery and then meet me in the cockpit..."

"You got it, Zig." He nodded resolutely, gently lifting a still sleepy Pedro from the basin and wrapping them in a towel. "You can count on me."

Thank. Fuck.

I star hopped away before my mate could fully pick up on how shaken I was, stopping in the bedroom to pull on some clothes before heading to the cockpit.

Once there, I sat heavily in my captain's chair and dropped my head into my hands, running through a few of the breathing exercises Micah had taught me.

What in Stellaria's name was that?

I would have preferred to wait until my capable partner rejoined me, and for my frazzled nerves to return to baseline, but when an urgent *call* came through, I immediately answered.

"Ziggy?" Honnor's recognizable armor filled the holographic screen above my dashboard, and I breathed a sigh of relief to see it looked intact.

"We have a problem," I croaked, uncharacteristically uncaring if I sounded weak and helpless.

I need help.

"We do," my maker agreed with a nod before flipping open their visor to show me their true form beneath. "It appears that asset of yours is made of karnilian."

I got Pedro dried off and put down for a nap as quickly as possible, but I still ended up needing a recap on the tea in the cockpit.

Since I guess they couldn't wait for me to get started...

"Wait a min..." I spun in the second captain's chair we'd installed—the one I usually ignored in favor of Ziggy's lap. "You're telling me Pedro has a *gemstone* inside them? Like a... like a *troll doll?!*"

Unsurprisingly, all Stellarians involved in this holographic video call stared at me blankly.

"The only trolls I remember on Earth were those in ancient legends..." Bron mused. *"Then again, I haven't visited the planet in at least one thousand years, so circumstances may have changed."*

I snorted, imagining the space dads disguised as humans in the Middle Ages. "The trolls I'm talking about weren't *real.* They were these little plastic dolls with crazy colorful hair and little gems embedded in their belly that you'd rub for good luck."

This explanation apparently only confused the issue. *"Good luck with vanquishing your enemies?"* Honnor asked. *"Because that would match why karnilian is so sought after..."*

"No!" I cackled before the rest of their statement caught up. "Wait. Karnilian helps you vanquish your enemies?"

Well, fuck.

The space dads glanced at each other. *"Many believe it does,"* Honnor carefully replied. *"More specifically, many believe the stone bestows courage, strength, protection, and good luck on whoever owns it—or on whoever has a Hydrassian in their pocket to tell them who will be victorious in battle."*

A shiver ran down my spine at the memory of the first Hydrassian Zig had killed at the Muonova—how they hadn't corrected me when I asked if their rituals could not just *predict* but *determine* who would win.

"Is that why the Hydrassian was searching every gem stall on Stellaria?" Ziggy asked. "To make predictions for the Irathians' attack?"

Bron chuckled smugly. *"Obviously not. Otherwise, the Irathians would have known not to attempt something as pointless as invading Stellaria."*

"And that Hydrassian claims they weren't working for the Irathians—or anyone else, for that matter," Honnor added before growing thoughtful. *"At least, not in the capacity you recently experienced..."*

Apparently, Zig had already told them about the gaggle of mercenaries we'd encountered—and eliminated—at the Muonova.

Since the debriefing started without me.

"Do you have the Hydrassian in custody?" I piped in, stubbornly determined to be included.

"Of course," Honnor absently replied, distracted by an incoming message on their Celestial Cube. *"Although, they haven't provided much intel—aside from confirming Pedro was most likely the asset the Irathians were after."*

"I'd like to talk to them," I boldly continued, swallowing the urge to ask for permission or apologize for my demands.

Or to remind them Pedro isn't just an asset.

Honnor cocked their head at me but then nodded once. *"Very well. I'm connecting the feed to their holding cell now."*

Oh, okay...

I hadn't expected my request to be granted *this very minute,* but I was hell-bent on at least looking like I knew what I was doing.

Gotta be useful.

"More questions...?" The Hydrassian we'd seen at the bazaar was suddenly displayed as a hologram floating over the dash, all six snakeheads squinting at the camera.

"Until you give us something we can work with, yes," I snapped in the trade language, too annoyed by the entire situation to play games.

Ziggy cleared his throat and shifted awkwardly in his chair, and I had to fight a smile at the distinct *horniness* flavoring the air.

Space Daddy likes me in Commander Babygirl mode.

The Hydrassian sneered. "We already told your *superiors* we were simply answering the call of the karnilian on your planet—that it had been so long since we heard its song."

At this point, I realized Hydrassians spoke in the royal "we," probably because of having multiple heads. I was still wondering if each head was a separate entity with different thoughts—and whether they meant it literally when they said they could *hear* the karnilian's song—but asking how their abilities worked would only make me look even more clueless than I already was.

Fake it 'til ya make it!

Refocusing, I channeled my inner bad bitch to continue the interrogation. "And how many of your fellow mercenaries happened to be searching Stellaria alongside you—"

"WE ARE NOT MERCENARIES!" the Hydrassian boomed, and it was only thanks to my deeply ingrained supe instincts of Big Dickery that I didn't flinch.

"Hmm…" I hummed in a bored tone. "That's odd. We encountered no less than six Hydrassian mercenaries in a neighboring Muonova, with at least one working for the Irathians… the same Irathians who recently attacked Stellaria —where *you* were found sniffing around."

It doesn't look good, dude.

The prisoner sighed heavily, seeming to understand they needed to start talking or face the thunder. "We assume *those* so-called mercenaries," their voice dripped with disdain, "are from a younger generation of Hydrassians. With karnilian growing scarcer by the day, some have claimed there is more money to be found tracking down the stone than waiting for it to appear on our doorstep in exchange for our talents."

Okay, so Hydrassian Millennials also believe in hustle culture...

"We'll ask you one more time," Ziggy joined in with his skerry Space Daddy growl. "Why were you on Stellaria looking for a stone you know full well is illegal in our galaxy?"

The Hydrassian huffed, clearly offended. "We were sent to Stellaria to shop for basic ritual supplies. The instant we left our ship, we felt the pull of karnilian from... *somewhere* nearby. That was when we began searching for it."

So their witchy bitch senses are only so exact.

Good to know...

"What were you planning to do with the karnilian once you found it?" I asked. "Since you claim to not be associated with the Irathians or any other third party species seeking the stone for personal gain."

A blast of *pride* from Ziggy had me sitting up straighter, even as I kept my gaze locked on our subject.

What I wouldn't give for the twins' mind-reading abilities right now.

The Hydrassian was silent for a moment, observing me with the same level of intensity—as if they were trying to sus out how much *I* knew as well.

"We were hoping to get it somewhere safe," they carefully replied. "As mentioned, karnilian is rare nowadays, and the source of the stone even rarer."

"Trols," I filled in the blanks as confidently as possible, using deductive reasoning to finally name what Pedro was.

Our furry little alien troll doll.

"Yes." The Hydrassian nodded all six heads in unison. "We have not seen a Trol in at least a few hundred years—not since their planet disappeared."

Disappeared?!

"Disappeared?" Ziggy stepped in as my anxiety skyrocketed.

"That is what the elders say." Our tea-spiller shrugged. "Historically, our planet had a direct link with Trols, along with contracted trade agreements so we could ethically harvest the stone for our rituals. However, one day, communication simply... stopped. When an envoy was sent to investigate, there was reportedly nothing at the coordinates except empty space."

Well, fuck.

The plan had been to return Pedro to their planet once we figured out where it was, but now, it sounded like there might be no way home for our baby Trol.

"How would one *harvest* the stone? Ethically, of course..." Ziggy pressed in an oddly fervent tone I'd never heard from him before.

At least, not outside of the bedroom.

Now the Hydrassian was squinting at Zig with obvious suspicion. "The only ethical way is to cut out the karnilian from the Trol after they die of natural causes. Otherwise, you are essentially removing the very piece of their essence keeping them alive."

"Oh," Ziggy choked out before growing silent, and it took everything in my power not to react to the uncharacteristic anxiety I could now feel coming from *him* through our bond.

"Well…" I cleared my throat, redirecting the Hydrassian's attention back to me. "That explains why it's become a scarce resource."

"Indeed," they softly replied. "Especially as each stone can only be used for a single ritual before turning to dust itself."

Well.

Fuck.

Now, the silence was heavy on *all* sides, and I wasn't sure what else to ask—not until I debriefed with the others.

"Thank you." I smiled grimly at the Hydrassian. "This was extremely helpful."

"You are most welcome." The Hydrassian inclined their heads respectfully. "We only ask if you find the source of the karnilian we sensed on Stellaria, you guard it with your lives."

That's the plan.

The feed to the holding cell cut, replaced by holograms of Honnor and Bron, who appeared equally grim.

"Well done, Micah," Bron attempted a cheerful tone. *"You acquired more intel from the Hydrassian than we were able to."*

I almost pointed out it was probably because I wasn't using the Stellarian strong-arm method, but I bit my tongue. "Yeah... Well, I just want to be *useful.*"

"You are *always* useful!" Ziggy vehemently hissed as he sexily glared at me. "You are useful simply by *existing.*"

Oh.

Okay, then.

Honnor cleared their throat before piping in, *"You all should return to Stellaria as soon as possible—"*

"No!" Ziggy barked, displaying an increasing level of aggression, even for him. "We are not bringing a *beacon* of war to Stellaria's doorstep—not when we haven't identified every species hunting for it. For... *them.*"

"So you would rather send out a beacon from your lone ship rather than allow our Star Units to protect you?" Honnor gently asked.

Ziggy looked like he was fighting one hell of an internal battle, so I stepped in, assuming my Space Daddy had a good reason for wanting to keep the situation as is.

"I could create shields for Pedro," I offered. "When mine is activated, Ziggy can't even smell me, so maybe it would also block the *song* of the stone?"

Honnor nodded thoughtfully. *"Yes, that could work. It would be helpful if we could test its effectiveness in some way—"*

"Send us the Hydrassian you have in custody," Ziggy interrupted, staring down his maker as if they might say no. "Give them whatever ritual supplies they need and then Star Hop them to my ship. I would like to ask the *elders* of their planet some questions."

Now we're talking!

I was ridiculously excited about the idea of visiting a new planet as the badass team we were, but I attempted to keep my cool while the space dads deliberated.

Wouldn't want to ruin my bad bitch persona.

"*Very well,*" Honnor agreed, and I fist pumped in response. "*And now that we know what sort of creature—what sort of situation—we have here, we will start gathering intel on our end.*"

"*While creating a distraction...*" Bron added in a mischievous tone I'd come to realize *all* Stellarians possessed.

Shit-stirrers, all of them.

When Honnor turned to their partner with an expectant stare, Bron elaborated, "*I'll simply leak that a few Irathian survivors managed to escape with the asset. Let their planet be the target for a while.*"

Ice cold.

"Were there any survivors?" I grinned, already knowing the answer.

"*No.*" Bron chuckled. "*Worthy opponents for Stellarians are almost as rare as karnilian.*"

"Be careful of imperial blind spots," Ziggy murmured under his breath, but before I could reply, he raised his voice and addressed the hologram. "I'll send our current coordinates so you can transfer the prisoner to our custody."

The space dads signed off and the line went dead, leaving us in silence once again.

"Zig..." I swiveled my chair to face him. "What happened when you were inside Pedro? Are you okay—"

"Nothing," he snapped, abruptly standing and staring straight ahead to the endless galaxy beyond. "I'm fine."

He obviously *wasn't,* but I knew from experience, my man only talked through his issues when he was good and ready. So I begrudgingly gave him the space he needed and nodded once before following him from the cockpit to prepare for our new *prisoner.*

And for whatever comes next.

16

MICAH

Apparently, what came next was Ziggy looking like a Wookie.

While I *had* flipped through his skinsuit closet from end to end at this point, my body-snatching alien's 'outfits' were encased in carbonite when not in use. This shrink-wrap effect either left nothing up to the imagination or more questions than answers, depending on whether the vessels were covered in skin, scales, or fur.

Or a Sasquatch-level pelt.

Which... I'm not hating...

"Dang, Zig. If you wanted me to roll all over you like a bearskin rug, all you had to do was ask," I teased, eye-fucking his full furry splendor, knowing it would get a reaction from my man.

He didn't disappoint. Ziggy's ferociously furry face morphed into a grumpy scowl before he replied in the trade language. "Presenting myself as a Borque seemed appropriate for our current situation. They are a fierce but relatively peaceful species Hydrassians will be familiar with and, therefore, *comfortable* encountering in their world."

I nodded solemnly, drinking in how he chose to attach the baby sling to *himself* for the mission ahead. It also didn't escape my notice that Pedro was gurgling up a storm in my arms, reaching for Ziggy with clawed grabby hands.

"Makes sense," I breezily replied. "And it's just a happy accident you chose a skinsuit that looks as close to a certain someone as possible, hmm?"

I see you.

After quickly checking the karnilian-masking shields I'd created for Pedro before we allowed the Hydrassian on board, I handed our furbaby to their *favorite*—furry—space dad, before staring at Ziggy expectantly.

"It crossed my mind that choosing a visually similar skinsuit might help disguise what Pedro is to those unfamiliar with Trols," Ziggy huffed as he focused on settling his Mini-Me into their cozy kangaroo pouch. "This is an intel-gathering mission, so I'd rather not engage in combat unless necessary."

We have wildly different definitions of "necessary" when it comes to violence.

My attention snagged on another part of his redirection. "Okay, but... wouldn't it be safe to assume Hydrassians are familiar with Trols? At least the elders will be, right?"

Ziggy cocked his head. "Yes. However, between your shields masking the karnilian and Pedro staying out of sight, it should be assumed they're nothing but my—*our*—offspring."

I seeeee youuuu....

"We could also leave Pedro on the ship," I continued teasing, physically unable to give this poor man a break. "I managed to get the nanny bot up and running—"

"Well, *I* would prefer to test out the nanny bot while we're present," Ziggy sniffed, trying so hard to act indifferent. "To ensure everything functions correctly."

I. See. You.

Before I could continue my second favorite hobby—after Tendril Touchy Time—Ziggy added, "And I'm uncertain how much the other species on the planet know about Trols, so I'd rather keep Pedro close."

Wait.

"Other species?" I yelped. "What? I thought all these planets we've been going to were *homogenous...*"

Borque-Ziggy gave me an odd, accidentally threatening look. "Why would you think that? Humans may be the dominant species on Earth—supes, I should say—but that doesn't mean *your* planet only supports life for a single species, correct?"

"Hmm..." I replied, forcibly stopping myself from asking a million follow-up questions to this bombshell. "I just *assumed*, since I haven't really *seen* other species anywhere... except on Stellaria."

A smirk twitched the fur covering Ziggy's lips. "Just because you haven't noticed other species doesn't mean they're not there, noticing *you.*"

Well, that's not creepy or anything.

"Okay, then," I huffed, crossing my arms, annoyed yet again

that I was being given only partial intel. "What other creatures should I be looking out for on Hydrassianidesellaria?"

Yeah... I don't know what the planet is called...

Ziggy raised his furry paw to his mouth for a pretend cough. *"Dionaea.* The planet is called *Dionaea*—after the *dominant* species."

I chewed on my bottom lip, dredging up my rusty Latin to remember what on Earth was in the *Dionaea* genus.

Oh, gawd...

"Are you telling me there are going to be giant *flies* on this planet?!" I gasped, clutching my Han Solo vest dramatically. "Like... Jeff Goldblum-sized flies?"

Jeff Goldblum—smash.

The Fly—pass.

There was no mistaking the baffled expression on Borque-Ziggy's face. "I'm talking about *Dionaea muscipula,* Micah. I believe Earthlings have welcomed adolescent versions into their society as 'Venus flytraps.' Unwisely, I might add."

"EXCUSE YOU?!" I shouted, startling Pedro into popping their furry little head out of the baby sling.

Okay, but that's adorable...

After quickly snapping a dozen photos with my phone, I refocused. "Venus flytraps are actually aliens? I thought that was just *Little Shop of Horrors* lore." My blood ran cold as the rest of his statement caught up with me. "Wait... so what we have on Earth are only adolescents?"

Ziggy nodded. "Yes, and as long as Earthlings aren't stupid enough to feed the adolescents *human* blood, they will remain a manageable, relatively safe size, unlike what's on *Dionaea.*" He paused to give me a hard look. "So stay away from the tree line once we're there."

DULY FUCKING NOTED!

"You don't have one of those in your skinsuit closet, do you?" I shuddered as I checked my own shields. "Because ya boy is also swiping left on man-eating plants."

Along with Lacertus and those creepy giant spider things...

Arachs.

He made a chuffing sound that was probably a laugh. "Very well. I will add *Dionaea muscipula* to the *extremely short list* of skinsuits you're uninterested in. Any others you can think of at the moment?"

I ignored his painfully accurate dig in favor of giving his Wookie wardrobe an exaggerated once-over.

No doubt noticing my perusal, Borque-Ziggy grinned, exposing a pair of vampire-worthy canines that promised fun, bitey times ahead. His fur—*pelt?*—was pin-straight, chestnut brown, and so glossy, it reflected the various lights blinking in the landing bay, indicating our imminent arrival on *Dionaea.* It was also *thick,* because when my gaze drifted south, there was no way to tell what he was packing below the proverbial belt.

Since I don't think my man is wearing any clothes beneath all that fur.

The thought of some random Hydrassians—or oversized house plants—seeing Ziggy naked made near-psychotic *jealousy* blast through me, but I banished the ridiculous concern. Western Earthling standards of so-called "decency" didn't apply in outer space, as I'd come to learn many times over during our adventures, and I doubted the snake-headed seers would find him attractive anyway.

While we're on the subject...

"I would also like to remove Hydrassians from the body snatcher buffet menu," I added decisively. "Anything reptilian, really..."

It's all a little too close to big bro's supe form.

"Noted," he chuckled. "I don't believe I *have* a Hydrassian in my closet anyway, since I've never needed one for a mission before." Those big canines came into view again. "Perhaps I should add to the collection today—"

"No, Zig," I mock-scolded, knowing he was only kidding.

During one of his *many* sessions with Dr. Micah, Ziggy had confessed that, since leaving behind the twin Kaalanesean kings, it no longer felt right to take over any bodies he hadn't already acquired.

While I appreciated the sentiment, I'd told my Stellarian not to promise anything that went against his nature. Inhabiting another's body was what he was meant to do—even if his *true* purpose in life was to provide inspiration to his stellar collision.

That's me, bitches.

Before I disappeared down the Ziggy-fucking-me-from-the-inside fantasy rabbit hole I'd been inhabiting lately, I refocused once again. "On that note, shouldn't we be letting our Hydrassian out of their holding cell now that we've landed?"

There *was* a small holding cell on the Lodger 79—only accessible by star hopping—and even though the Hydrassian we'd liberated from the space dads wasn't technically a *prisoner,* there was quite literally nowhere else to put them on the ship.

Aside from the boiler room.

Ziggy nodded before disappearing, reappearing a moment later with six sputtering snake heads attached to a lizard creature.

"There is no need to treat us so roughly! We have already agreed to take you to the elders—"

"Yes, you have," Borque-Ziggy loomed all seven-and-a-half feet of hairy goodness over our tour guide. "And it shouldn't need to be said, but if you reveal what I am—what either of us are—I will wipe out your entire settlement."

Babygirl boner imminent!

"Understood," the Hydrassian shook themselves free before noticing the baby sling. "You... have a child?" They glanced at me, confused. "Together?"

I grinned, unable to hide my excitement over both Pedro's karnilian-masking shields working *and* this alien thinking we'd gotten down to baby-making.

Only in spirit, unfortunately.

"That's none of your concern," Ziggy growled, placing a protective paw over the sling, making me swoon. "Now," he practically shoved his fellow alien down the deployed ramp, "take us to the elders."

"It wasn't our intention to pry," the Hydrassian muttered, sneaking another peek at Pedro's bundled form. "We were simply unaware Stellarians reproduced at all. Not much is known about your kind, aside from your reputation for killing other aliens indiscriminately."

Ziggy didn't respond as we walked a blessedly foliage-free path toward a nearby mountain range, but I sensed the tension ratcheting up a few degrees.

This already does not bode well.

"You shouldn't believe everything you hear," I replied, earning *me* a warning growl from my man. "I mean, *yes,* Stellarians *can* kill any alien in the... *our* paths, but that's not our purpose in life."

I could tell Ziggy didn't approve of the loose lips I was exhibiting, but my tea spilling was strategic.

Trust equals more tea.

The Hydrassian hummed thoughtfully. "That is unexpected, and in stark contrast to most war-minded species. When one's only goal is to conquer, it does not leave much room for nuance."

All or nothing.

"Do species come to you for predictions on anything other than war?" I asked, genuinely curious.

The Hydrassian seemed surprised. "Yes, occasionally— although the desire for love, marriage, or offspring is not usually treated with quite the same sense of *urgency* as the lust for war."

Ya boy begs to differ.

"And is karnilian used for those rituals as well?" I asked, even *more* genuinely curious.

Incredibly invested, you could say.

The Hydrassian laughed sadly, leading us through a cleverly disguised opening in a craggy rock face. "No, the stones used for domestic matters are far more common and easily acquired without bloodshed."

Of course.

As we followed our guide into the depths of the mountain, I was reminded of when we visited the True Stellarians hiding on the three moons of Invenio-Astralis.

Genero, Interitus, and Apotelesma.

Birth, death, and the effect of the stars on human destiny.

Pedro had *also* been displaced from their planet of origin—a refugee hiding in plain sight—and if anyone could help us get them home, it was possibly a species with no skin in the game aside from guiding others toward what may or may not already be written in the stars.

17

ZIGGY

Having Pedro as close to me as possible had blessedly dulled the distracting and uncontrollable pull I felt toward the creature.

A pull I must now do my best to ignore.

I hadn't told Honnor what I was struggling with—only confirmed I'd encountered the karnilian inside Pedro first-hand. It was troubling enough that our kind hadn't known of Trols, or *why* the stone was sought after by both our enemies and allies alike. The last thing I needed was to put a target on *my* back by admitting the stone was calling to me. All it would do would be to add undue stress to my maker's respon-sibilities as Head Commander of Astrum Force.

A role originally meant for me.

While I'd been flattered to be offered the position after Micah and I disposed of the old guard, I'd immediately turned down the opportunity. Recognition from Astrum Force no longer held the same appeal for me it once did. In fact, the very idea of what their leadership represented left a sour taste in my mouth only Honnor's dedication to the cause lessened.

I also greatly enjoyed the autonomy I'd discovered as a mercenary—how it allowed me to disappear into space with only my stellar collision by my side.

And whatever... valuable assets we acquire along the way.

The biggest reason I rejected the idea of becoming Head Commander, however, was that I wasn't leader material. Yes, I'd adopted a heroic *team player* disguise on Earth, but that had been a self-serving means to an end—nothing more.

In reality, I was an orphaned Stellarian at the bottom of the societal barrel. Before everything came to light, I wasn't even qualified to wear the official insignia of a Star Unit *soldier,* much less become a squadron leader or commander. This lone wolf persona had become such a vital part of my identity, I couldn't imagine a situation where I would be seen as an authority figure to so many others.

The *power* that came with a position like that was overwhelming to think about.

Overwhelming... Intoxicating...

Tempting.

"Zig?" Micah's clear voice snapped me back to reality—to the dank yet well-lit tunnel we currently walked through. "Is everything okay with... Pedro?"

It was clear my mate was more concerned about *me,* but didn't want to alert our guide that anything was wrong.

I should tell him what's going on.

I should tell him everything going on with me...

"Our child is fine," I calmly replied, noticing how he brightened at my public declaration. "However, we should be mindful of how long we spend away from the ship."

As I'd hoped, my clumsy attempts at parental caretaking successfully distracted him from whatever anxiety he'd picked up on through our bond.

"You're such a good Space Daddy," Micah dreamily replied, and I had to focus all my concentration on *not* getting an erection while caretaking.

Especially considering this skinsuit has two *cocks.*

"We must admit," the annoyingly chatty Hydrassian called over their shoulder. "Discovering that Stellarians can be *nurturing* is another pleasant surprise."

That's debatable.

Yes, nurturing Stellarians existed, but *I* hadn't been nurtured by *anyone* until I'd met Micah. While Stellaria's foundling system wasn't cruel by any means, it had a utilitarian focus meant to shape useful members of society more than meet emotional needs. Only the basics were taught, like how to fight and how to reproduce for the glory and continuation of our kind.

That was also why I'd had no idea how resonance worked—or that it was apparently commonplace for the stellar collisions of makers and offspring to also form bonds with each other. When Gabriel started resonating for Micah during our last visit to Earth, I'd been completely caught off guard, mostly because it *didn't* make me want to murder the supervillain and everyone else in my path. Instead, I'd found it intriguing

—attractive, even—and Micah and I had been exploring it together ever since.

Well... mostly together.

Since returning from our latest visit to Earth, I'd done some solo reconnaissance work of my own, spying on Stellarian family units with more than two members to find working examples of this phenomenon.

Alien polycules, as Micah would say.

These polycules weren't unusual, but they also weren't necessarily the standard. Honnor and Bron were as close to mated as our kind got without a stellar collision bond, but, despite being together for two hundred and fifty years, they'd never added more Stellarians to their family unit or created offspring with each other.

"Too many authoritarian regimes to overthrow," Honnor always says.

My maker was mostly joking, but there was also an air of truth to their words. Even without the old Astrum Force manipulating the message, a Stellarian's *need* to dominate was deeply ingrained, and they had therefore stepped into the role of Head Commander effortlessly.

I bet I could have handled it better...

Despite my traitorous thoughts, I had absolutely zero interest in *taking* the position from Honnor, especially as they had been the one who originally tried to convince me to accept it. Our relationship was good, all things considered, and certainly less complicated than my history with Theo. Then again, neither of my makers were what I would call *nurturing*.

I suppose Zion Salah is the best example I have.

And my mate...

"Micah." I gritted my teeth, forcing the words out before I could stop myself. "Would you please take Pedro from me for a bit?"

It was an experiment—a test to see if my stellar collision being in possession of the karnilian would be considered enough of a threat for my true form to react.

I hope not.

"Sure thing, Zig." Micah smiled warmly and stepped closer, trusting me when he possibly shouldn't.

If I hurt him, I will return myself to the stars.

The Hydrassian patiently waited as we readjusted, awkwardly angling our bodies so Pedro stayed hidden during the transfer. Thanks to the light sleep powers I'd used before we left the ship, the Trol didn't make a sound, but I wondered if perhaps they also instinctively understood this was a precarious situation.

After the hand-off, I slowly backed up, ready to snatch the baby sling away from Micah at the first sign of agitation. Luckily, the only emotion stirred up by the sight of him holding *our child* was an increased sense of protectiveness.

Thank fuck.

I *did* notice a slight twinge of discomfort from no longer having Pedro nestled against me, but I easily buried it beneath logic. Without the sling in my way, I could unleash my tendrils more freely, which would come in handy if I needed to protect what was mine.

Hydrassians weren't what I would consider *dangerous,* but they had fairly advanced hypnotic abilities—ones Stellarians were immune to. This skill was usually reserved for use during rituals or while escaping predators, but I'd witnessed this very Hydrassian use it to incapacitate a harmless gem vendor who got in their way.

And we possess the very thing they were searching for...

Seeing we were ready, our guide continued walking, and I refocused on my admittedly loose plan for acquiring the intel we needed. I would first ask nicely and then respond to any resistance with force.

Foolproof, in my opinion.

My internal strategizing was abruptly interrupted as we reached a cavernous antechamber, lit up from the flickering light of bioluminescence-powered sconces. My gaze traveled upward, noting the layers of sedimentary rock that varied from dark basalt gray to glossy volcanic black, interspersed with thin lines of rich brown that reminded me of Micah's eyes.

I wonder how this cave was formed...

"We bring visitors seeking counsel!" our Hydrassian guide called out, their request echoing off the cavern walls, wrenching me from my thoughts. "They wish to speak with Uulvin."

This announcement resulted in a flurry of activity, with Hydrassians racing in various directions, presumably to prepare for our audience. We'd been told Uulvin was the oldest of their kind on *Dionaea*—older even than the last reign of Astrum Force Command. While it was a gamble to talk to someone with enough expertise to possibly identify us, I needed information only an elder could provide.

But first, let's see how chatty this Hydrassian can be...

"Do many seek Uulvin's counsel specifically?" I asked as they led us to a bench carved from the same unusual rock and covered in worn, tasseled pillows.

Our guide snorted derisively. "They *seek,* but Uulvin only offers the gift of their sight to those willing to pay what such profound abilities are worth."

How charitable.

Those looking for advice on domestic matters would not possess pockets half as deep as those with a well-armed military at their fingertips. So, of course, the 'war-minded' pilgrims were the ones who kept this supposedly neutral facility running.

"Is part of that payment *karnilian?*" I gritted out, annoyed at how *unsurprising* this intel was. "Because we brought no such asset with us."

As far as you know, anyway.

No doubt picking up on my emotions, Micah discreetly activated his shield. While this provided an additional layer of masking for Pedro, along with protection for both of them, it also stopped me from being able to smell my mate.

Not the safest move, considering my mood...

Oblivious to the encroaching danger, the Hydrassian gestured a clawed hand toward the packs attached to my belt. "The iridium coins we've heard clinking around since we left the ship should be sufficient compensation for our stores."

A smirk curled my lip beneath the fur. "Was *that* why you were harassing gem vendors on my planet? You were shopping for 'ritual supplies' for your most valued customers, hmm?"

I didn't truly believe these seers were hoarding caches of karnilian on the premises, but my bold question managed to strike a nerve, as evidenced by the now-glaring Hydrassian clamping their mouths shut and stomping away without another word.

Looks like the interrogation is over.

"Uulvin will see you now!" a new set of voices rang out, and I spied a younger Hydrassian waving us toward another tunnel branching off the main cavern.

"Please try not to kill anyone," Micah murmured under his breath as we crossed the room. "We come in peace, remember?"

I huffed but nodded. "I will do my best to behave, but whether anyone dies depends entirely on them."

On how they *behave.*

Micah sighed but didn't reply, and we followed our new guide down the tunnel in silence. My mate knew we were here to learn more about Pedro's home planet—on what remained of it, if anything—but he wasn't aware my interest in reuniting the creature with their own kind was now tainted by... an incredibly distracting pull.

A pull I will *do my best to ignore.*

We entered a much smaller chamber, shockingly bright thanks to the light reflecting off the pumice walls. Seated on a cushion in the center of the room was an ancient Hydrassian I assumed was Uulvin, but that wasn't what caught my attention.

The two adult *Dionaea muscipula* flanking the elder did, along with the Celestial Cube resting in Uulvin's scaled hand.

Fuck.

"Have a seat, Stellarian," the seer croaked as six incredibly sly smiles stretched over their faces. "We have much to discuss."

18
MICAH

Luckily, my shields were already activated, because the terrifying sight of two man-eating-sized Venus flytraps had me freezing like a deer in the goddamn headlights.

Eek!

I only had a moment to register that the Hydrassian was holding *a Celestial Cube* before Ziggy grabbed me with his big Borque paws, no doubt about to star hop us away from danger.

Except... nothing happened.

"You will not be able to star hop, I'm afraid," Uulvin casually said, as if they *weren't* proving to be the witchiest bitch on the block. "Not with what was used to construct these caves."

"Where did this rock come from?" Ziggy demanded, baring his teeth like the bad bitch *he* was, even as he pumped uncharacteristic *panic* through our bond. "No natural material on any planet can stop a Stellarian—"

"The rock is from deep within our planet's core," the Hydrassian interrupted with a wave of the clawed hand *not* holding the cube. "However, the *shields* incorporated into the design were created by those with the power to do so."

This sounds familiar...

Apparently on the same witchy wavelength, Uulvin's gaze—all *six* of their gazes—focused on me before they continued. "It is similar to what your *companion* has for shields, although their version seems more advanced than ours. Fascinating."

That's my cue to bring the thunder!

Not wanting to escalate the situation, I held off on unleashing my mechanical tendrils, but I still wanted these fools to know I was kind of a bad bitch myself.

A little dark rain cloud at least...

"Yeah, well, I created my own shields—with my *powers*," I replied, keeping my voice as steady as possible, forcing myself to stay calm for Ziggy's sake. "And if you attempt to hurt us, you will witness the full force of what I can do."

I hope.

My bad bitch card was still valid as the Hydrassian's many eyes widened. The two oversized house plants responded by rustling their enormous leaves—almost making me turn my brown pants browner—but then I realized they were communicating with each other.

They better not be saying "feed me"...

Unfortunately, my language translator didn't seem to speak Twoey. Luckily, Uulvin was ready to interpret.

"We mean you no harm!" the seer exclaimed. "These precautions are for *our* protection. One can never be too careful, especially when dealing with a species as formidable as the Stellarians."

"How could you tell we're Stellarians?" Ziggy growled, so pissed off, *I* almost shrank from his bottomless rage.

"We can see your aura," Uulvin addressed him coolly before turning their attention back to me. "And while *yours* matches in tone, it is decidedly fainter... as if your Stellarian is simply coexisting within you, like the old times—"

"You know about that?!" I excitedly cut in before attempting to back pedal. "I mean, of course you do—you're the oldest Hydrassian here. Not that you *look* old! You actually look fabulous for your age. Slay, queen."

Sigh.

Bad bitch card revoked.

By some miracle, the Hydrassian didn't immediately tell their attack plants to turn me into fertilizer. Instead, they laughed heartily with all six snake heads, immediately diffusing the tension in the room—at least for me.

Ziggy was still tense as fuck, but I sent my man the motherload of chill vibes, silently begging him *not* to go full Alien Rambo so we could get the intel we came for.

And maybe some extra intel while we're at it...

"We know about a Stellarian's true purpose, yes," the seer answered my original question, smiling toothily while gesturing at the two empty cushions across from them. "And if you hand over that iridium you are carrying, it would be my pleasure to share my knowledge with you."

Ziggy made a disgruntled sound as I dragged him forward. "I bet you would. Shall I give you my entire purse now, or will you be teasing scraps of intel for more coin as we go?"

Here we go.

I sat with a sigh, careful to keep Pedro curled up and hidden in their sling while I got comfy on the cushion. To no one's surprise, the True Stellarian in the room chose to stand, for maximum grumpy-guy-looming effect.

"The entire purse would suffice," Uulvin sniffed—a true queen refreshingly uninterested in measuring dicks with anyone.

Slay.

Ziggy apparently knew a fellow bad bitch when he saw one, as he huffed begrudgingly before unhooking his coin purse and tossed it onto the floor next to the seer. Instead of dumping it out and counting like *I* would have done, Uulvin simply placed a hand on the pack and grew eerily still.

Are they...?

"An impressive amount of this incredibly *rare* metal," the Hydrassian mused before squinting at me. "Did you create this?"

The answer was yes, but I wasn't sure if using counterfeit coins would disqualify us from receiving witchy bitch services, so I redirected. "Is it enough for you to tell us everything we want to know?"

They continued to intently stare until Ziggy stepped closer with a warning growl, flashing those smexy fangs again.

"The coin is more than sufficient," Uulvin replied, oddly unconcerned about the katana-wielding murder machine in the room. "You *will* need to lower your shields—"

"No," Ziggy snarled, practically pulsing with rage.

We probably have a time limit on Alien Rambo emerging...

The seer sighed heavily and glanced at my big, skerry protector. "As we have said, Stellarian, I mean you and your mate no harm." Their unnerving focus returned to me. "However, I am unable to do my job if I cannot access their chakras."

Witchy bitch status verified.

I squared my shoulders. "I'll only lower *my* shields if you also promise not to hurt our child."

All six snakeheads snapped to the baby sling, looking as confused as their reptilian faces allowed. "Of course. We have no interest in harming your child—"

"Or take our child from us," I continued, desperate for answers but needing to diffuse the Stellarian-shaped ticking time bomb in our midst. "Or take... anything associated with our child."

Please, just don't hurt them.

Now the Hydrassian was invested, and curious enough to concede to my mad negotiating skills. "You have our word, little..."

"Earthling," I replied with a sigh of relief, wanting to give them *something* to show my gratitude. "Although not all Earthlings are like me."

Then, I lowered my shield.

Well... most of it.

"No one is like you," Ziggy murmured appreciatively. "Not in any galaxy."

Staaaahp.

I absolutely did *not* want to get sniffly in front of this snake-headed witch and their killer flytraps, but Uulvin simply chuckled warmly. "It is unsurprising you would think so, with the Earthling being your *stellar collision."*

"You can tell I'm his stellar collision?!" I shouted, like Captain Obvious of the S.S. Dumbass, before attempting to recover some of my cool. "Is it a physical thing or..."

Do I still need to put a ring the size of Saturn on my space fiancé?

"Energetic," the seer replied matter-of-factly. "Your energies align perfectly. We would guess your Stellarian here recognized their match when you met."

Oh?

I turned to blink up at Ziggy expectantly. "Yes." He cleared his throat, caving immediately. "I felt a *pull* toward you when we met. However, I mistook it for the... usual interest."

Ohhhh???

He flashed me a smirk. "The usual interest in taking over your body completely as my next vessel."

Asshole.

"And have you?" Uulvin cut in, leaning forward with interest. "Taken over completely?"

Ziggy snapped his attention to the seer and swallowed thickly. "Not... completely, but we have—"

He cut himself off this time, and for a moment, I assumed it was because he didn't want to continue sharing in front of an audience.

No... that's not it.

All at once, I realized that—thanks to his disconnected childhood and the old Astrum Force's single-minded regime—the big idiot *still* didn't trust himself.

I trust you, Space Daddy.

"Not completely," I confidently filled in the blanks, keeping my gaze locked on his. "But you did fully inhabit this vessel with me—when we worked *together* to take down Astrum Force."

Like a couple of bad bitches.

Uulvin hissed, and I grimaced, hoping what got confessed in the cave stayed in the cave.

"We did not realize we were in the presence of the one—the *ones*," they nodded at both of us, "who were foretold to free their fellow Stellarians."

Borque-Ziggy frowned, which looked grumpy-cute as hell. "How do you know about that?"

Who's Captain Obvious now?

The Hydrassian scoffed and held up their Celestial Cube. "Because your last Astrum Force commanders once used *this* to pay us for our prophecy, yet they refused to listen when we warned of their inevitable downfall." Uulvin grinned triumphantly. "They were entirely uninterested in humoring the prediction that an orphaned Stellarian born of two rebels would somehow topple their empire of lies."

"But I didn't..." Ziggy stuttered, glancing down at me. "I didn't do it alone."

"Is refusing to listen a Stellarian trait?" Uulvin huffed, dismissively tossing the cube aside—probably because they didn't possess the DNA needed to even operate it. "Of *course,* you did not do it alone! The only way you could have fulfilled your destiny was by fully connecting with your stellar collision. That is the entire point!"

Tell him!

Ziggy *finally* sank down onto his assigned cushion, looking like a lost little Wookie puppy dog who'd just had his mind blown.

It's okay, Space Daddy.

Let the witchy bitches consult the chakras.

I had a million stellar collision-related questions of my own, but I didn't want to embarrass Zig by asking a complete stranger if we could ever get to baby-making for *real.*

Even I know when to have a filter.

Instead, I refocused on the reason we'd traveled to this planet. The one currently snoozing, safely curled up against my non-existent womb. The one in danger.

The one I might be putting in more danger...

"Are you able to see *anyone's* destiny?" I carefully asked, still unsure how much to reveal.

Uulvin nodded decisively. "We see what the stars wish to show us—past, present, and future—but *only* if it has been written."

That's gonna have to be good enough.

"What about our *child*?" I began, placing my hand over Pedro's sleeping form as Ziggy tensed all over again. "Can you tell us *their* destiny?"

Tell us how to get them home.

Uulvin intently stared at the baby sling once again before glancing at me. "Tricky Earthling... In order for me to get a clear reading, you will need to lower the child's shields as well."

I...

Even though *this* was what we'd come for, I hesitated. I still wasn't completely sure how the Hydrassian—or their leafy bodyguards—might react to seeing Pedro, but mostly, I was concerned about Ziggy's reaction. He'd been acting *more* possessive than usual lately, and I didn't want to set him off again by revealing our precious 'asset' to those he might consider a threat.

I don't know what to do.

"We will show you the child if you release my tendrils," Ziggy gritted out, and my jaw dropped.

What?

WHAT?!

I'd had no idea he couldn't access his tendrils this whole time, and a fresh wave of anxiety bubbled up in my chest.

How powerful is *this witchy bitch?*

"The precautions were for *our* protection," Uulvin sighed, as if what they'd done wasn't completely uncalled for. "We should *all* trust each other, we suppose..."

They must have released whatever—possibly mental—hold they had on him, as Ziggy unleashed his tendrils with an unearthly growl, aiming two dozen razor-sharp points at the Hydrassian and the *Dionaea muscipula.*

"Zig, no!" I hollered, unleashing *my* tendrils as well.

Before I could stop him from inflicting unnecessary violence once again, Ziggy froze and then retracted his tendrils until they hovered around me and Pedro like a barbed wire fence.

Jesus...

The oversized plants were flapping their leaves and snapping their jaws but blessedly *not* moving their roots to attack us. Uulvin, on the other hand, looked as unbothered as they'd been when we first walked into the room.

Bish probably saw this coming.

The seer coolly addressed Ziggy. "After you leave here today, we want you to remember how it felt to be trapped within this room—within your vessel—unable to connect to your true purpose or to your stellar collision. *That* is how your fellow Stellarians felt as they blindly went about their lives beneath the old Astrum Force rule, except they were *unaware* of their bondage until you came along to liberate them. You may be able to topple regimes, Stellarian, but you cannot fight destiny. Embrace it. Otherwise, it will eat you alive from the inside out."

Tough love from the queen.

Ziggy wisely retracted his tendrils and kept his trap shut, so Uulvin refocused on me.

On where Pedro was still hidden.

"Show us the child," the Hydrassian soothed, only marginally easing my anxiety. "Let us tell you what the stars have to say about their destiny."

With a deep breath, I reached into the baby sling and lifted Pedro out of their hiding place, hoping I wasn't about to ruin everything.

Please don't let this be a mistake...

This was a mistake.

The instant Micah dropped Pedro's shields, I could *feel* the karnilian calling to me, and Uulvin reacted in kind.

The seer gasped, flinching backwards in alarm. "Where did you find that?" they hissed, their many eyes darting around, as if suspecting we'd smuggled more in. "How do you have a Trol in your possession—a *newborn* Trol?!"

I lessened my sleep powers so Pedro could awaken and be aware of the situation, in case we needed to fight our way out of here. Unsurprisingly, the little Trol squeaked in surprise to find themselves in such a strange environment, and they immediately wiggled out of Micah's hold to scamper onto my back.

Mine.

True to form, my mate jumped in as peacemaker. "An anonymous tip sent us to Marox to rescue the egg. It hatched on the way to Stellaria, but then the Irathians attacked our planet, so back into space we went."

This shockingly succinct summary provided me with the perfect opportunity to get answers of my own. "Yes, and it still hasn't been explained how the Irathians knew we had the Trol... although there *was* a Hydrassian coincidentally harassing gem vendors about karnilian a day prior. Apparently, your kind has taken to mercenary work lately—"

"We have *never* condoned using our unique skills to acquire karnilian for our clients," Uulvin huffed. "Those who do so are defying destiny itself."

The *Dionaea muscipula* began rustling their leaves again, and Uulvin half-turned to listen while Micah frowned and fiddled with his translator device.

"A strong possibility..." the Hydrassian murmured before facing us again. "They say, perhaps the Irathians knew their limits, so they sent the Stellarians to Marox to do the dirty work for them."

I opened my mouth to argue before snapping it closed again. Whoever had called in the original assignment paid handsomely, but they'd also left no way of alerting them once the job was complete. They'd simply assured Astrum Force they would "be in contact."

A full-scale attack certainly would have been one way to make contact...

At this point, it could've been *anyone* masterminding this series of events and, judging from the lack of updates coming from Honnor, I wasn't the only one fumbling in the dark here.

How many imperial blind spots do we have?!

"No one is untouchable in our world, Stellarian—never forget that," Uulvin effortlessly addressed my unspoken thoughts, making me narrow my eyes.

I tightened my mental walls before replying. "Except Hydrassians, hmm? Your kind are too *valuable* to worry about attacks or manipulations from other species."

Uulvin glanced at Pedro again before returning their focus to my face. "Mmm... so valuable that others will stop at nothing to covet our talents to advance their own empires. Perhaps we should have followed in the footsteps of the Trols and disappeared completely."

There was a *bitterness* in their tone that caught my attention, but something more important took precedence. "When you say 'disappeared completely,' do you mean their planet no longer exists, or..."

The Hydrassian stared at me for a long moment before laughing humorlessly. "Your defenses are almost as good as your mate's."

"Stop trying to read our minds and answer the question," I growled, proud Micah had apparently locked them out but still angry this sorcerer had somehow trapped my tendrils inside me.

"We want you to remember how it felt."

Oh, I'll remember.

"The answer depends on your intentions," Uulvin replied, continuing to judgmentally observe me. "Do you mean to return this youngling to their home and leave them be, or is there another reason you wish to locate the Trols?"

I froze, oddly unsure how to answer, and a slow smirk stretched across Uulvin's six faces.

Micah hurriedly came to my defense. "Of *course* we want to return Pedro to their home! I mean, I'm probably gonna cry when we do it, no lie, but it's the right thing to do."

The right thing to do...

"Pedro?" Uulvin repeated, snapping me from my existential crisis.

The latest existential crisis.

"Uh, yeah... I named them." Micah rubbed the back of his neck, his delicious blush distracting me as always. "I wanted them to feel like they had a family, you know? Like they belonged, even if it was just temporary."

You belong with me.

Forever.

Pedro rested their little chin on my shoulder and purred, settling my agitation in a way I thought only Micah was able to do.

Uulvin hadn't taken their eyes off me. "Family is vital to survival—a universal truth across species—although sometimes, that family is one you find along the way."

"We know a thing or two about that, don't we, Zig?" Micah laughed nervously, no doubt picking up on the tension still lingering in the air.

"We do," I replied, holding Uulvin's gaze, daring the seer to challenge me. "And I protect what's mine."

All mine.

To my surprise, the Hydrassian nodded, seeming satisfied with my reply. "Well, then you will understand why we cannot give you information on the Trol's home planet—"

"What?!" I shouted, making Pedro skitter down my back.

"...but my sibling could," Uulvin added absently, ignoring my interruption.

"Very well," I snapped, determined to keep us on track. "Then we would like to speak to your sibling."

"You cannot," they curtly retorted, and it was all I could do to not unleash my tendrils again, intel be damned.

"What happened to your sibling?" Micah quietly asked, and when I sharply glanced at him, I saw my mate watching the Hydrassian with *empathy* written all over his gorgeous face.

Ugh.

As usual, my mate had picked up on an emotional element to the conversation I'd been too focused on my end goal to notice.

Why is it so hard to human?

"Uuktar was abducted many moons ago," Uulvin replied, dropping their gaze. "By the *Lacertus.*"

"*WHAT?!*" I bellowed, and Pedro yelped, scurrying back into the baby sling on Micah's lap.

My outburst earned me more judgment from the Hydrassian. "Yes, well, why pay for services when you can simply enslave your own personal seer instead?"

I need to tell Honnor!

Wait...

"What good is a seer with no karnilian?" I muttered as the pieces started to come together only to remain infuriatingly out of reach. "Is that why they paid mercenaries to locate the stone for them...?"

Or why they called in an anonymous tip about an egg, perhaps?

Uulvin hummed, back to watching me like a predator. "As I hope you realize by now, Stellarian, the *Lacertus* are not your *only* enemy. However, they are the ones you will need to target if you wish to find the answers you seek."

It was my turn to narrow my eyes. "By rescuing your sibling?"

They nodded.

This is ridiculous.

I huffed. "So now *you're* calling in a Stellarian to do your dirty work for you—"

"No," Uulvin brusquely stated. "We are asking the Stellarian who freed their people for help. The *honorable* Stellarian who chose uncomfortable truth over lies of supposed supremacy."

Oh.

Oh, fuck.

I truly didn't know how to address this assessment. "I'm not—"

"You *are*, Zig," Micah stated, equally sure. "Deal with it." Before I could reply, he turned to Uulvin. "What do we need to know to rescue your sibling?"

The only reason I didn't continue arguing was that he'd apparently gone into Commander Babygirl mode again, and I was powerless to resist. That, and it gave me the opportunity to *think*.

To plan my next move...

The seer brightened. "We can give you the coordinates for where they are holding my sibling."

"Then I will simply star hop in and out. Done." I rolled my eyes and gestured at the walls surrounding us in annoyance. "After we leave this cursed cave—"

"Wrong," Uulvin barked, silencing me. "The *Lacertus* employed those who created this very technology to protect their prisoner from Stellarians like you—technology your stellar collision can also conjure at will..."

"Wait," Micah sat up straighter, an excitement I knew well making his brown eyes sparkle. "Are you saying there are others like me? Supes... I mean, *aliens* who can manipulate inorganic matter?"

The scientist has awakened.

Uulvin bobbed their heads. "In a way. You will need to talk to these matter manipulators in order to learn how to dissolve the barrier surrounding Uuktar."

"The barrier..." I mumbled, struggling to keep up as my attention was drawn to the baby sling.

Micah should reactivate Pedro's shields...

As if *he* was suddenly a mind-reader, my mate did exactly that, and I breathed a sigh of relief as I was able to *focus* again.

"Uuktar, you said?" I repeated, determined to get the facts and get out.

"Yes," Uulvin snapped, their patience obviously wearing thin. "Our sibling. Our *family.*"

I glanced at my stellar collision, who gazed at me with so much hope in his expression, I was momentarily lost for words.

Does he actually think I'd say no to anything he wants?

"We will go speak to these *matter manipulators.*" I nodded at my mate before glancing at Uulvin. "And do our best to save your... family."

Then, I can focus on mine.

Micah's grin was dazzling. "It sounds like we're going on another adventure, Zig. For science!"

For science.

I had to admit, I was a bit curious about the possibility of discovering more creatures like Micah. It wasn't that I expected any of them to be half as impressive, but I wanted to know if my mate was something more than just an *Earthling.*

Something even more perfect for me.

"Very well." I rose before helping Micah stand beside me. "What are these matter manipulators called, and where would we find them?"

The Hydrassian was back to smiling slyly. "They're called the Eki, and while *you'll* be fine on their planet in your current vessel," they eyed my pelt appraisingly, "your stellar collision will need something warmer to wear."

While I knew Ziggy wanted to leave the star hop cockblock cave as quickly as possible— and understandably so—there was one thing I *needed* to do first.

Take a selfie with the Dionaea muscipula, duh.

This was mostly because I wanted to send a photo to a certain Mafia Queen back on Earth, so I could show the tiny tyrant his miniature "carnivorous child" ain't shit.

How you like them apples, croissant-muncher?

Once Zig, Pedro, and I were back on the Lodger and en route to the ice-planet EX-36740–locally known as Ekistron—I realized there was something else on the space mercenary to-do list.

The family video call.

While we occasionally did check-ins like this with Zion and Balty—and only rarely with Simon, which was just fine with him and Ziggy—I insisted on regular face time with Theo and the twins. It wasn't just because I wanted to see Gabe. I legitimately felt it was important, especially for Zig, to maintain a strong connection with those who shared our resonance.

Our Stellarian family.

Or... alien polycule, whatever.

Ziggy had insisted on changing back into his Earthling outfit for the call—*much to my disappointment*—but he reminded me he'd be in Borque-mode again once we landed on Ekistron. I didn't push, since I understood he wanted to be wearing the skinsuit he felt most comfortable in for a situation he was still getting used to.

Plus, my man probably didn't want to hear the Wookie jokes.

Since this crew is merciless.

However, there *was* a different celebrity appearance I wanted to surprise the others with on today's call.

"Holy shit, is that a *space cat?!*"

Gabe was sitting front and center when the feed kicked on, his ridiculously attractive face framed by the long, luxurious hair he'd no doubt left down just for me. However, the sweet supervillain only had eyes for the furry creature friend perched in my lap.

"Not quite," I laughed, already feeling the piece of Ziggy inside me positively reacting to the visual. "Although I *did* name them Pedro Pspspscal."

A snort brought my attention to the twin in the background, his black shit-kicker boots propped up and slightly blocking the view of his equally attractive face.

Not that I'd ever tell him that.

"Hey, Dre, how's it hanging?" I cheerfully called out, just to get an amused smirk out of his grumpy ass.

"A little to the right," he replied, which was as close to a greeting as I would get. "So where did the new pet come from? Don't tell me you went all 'white woman adopts a cougar kitten' or something..."

How dare!

But accurate.

"That's classified," Ziggy cut in, attempting to shut down questions in the most ineffective way possible. "Where's Theo?"

Dre dropped his feet to the floor and slung an arm behind his twin, cocking his head as he stared Ziggy down. "That's classified."

"I'm here, I'm here!" Theo sang out before coming into view. More specifically, his neon blue *crotch* came into view.

MY EYES!

The eccentric artist flopped onto the couch on Gabe's other side, wearing nothing but his signature bold-print kimono and tiny, bikini-cut bathing suit while holding a plate full of what looked like barbecue ribs.

"T had a big interview this morning for his latest installation, so he didn't eat lunch," Gabe explained with an apologetic shrug, reminding me the *time difference* between us was something we could never quite figure out.

Fuck, I miss them.

Well... most of them.

"And being Stellarian, Theo also didn't *need* to eat right this minute," Dre added with a glare at his chaotic brat. "He also didn't need to choose something so messy to eat on the extremely expensive couch."

Thoughts and prayers, Dom Daddy Dre.

"Calm down, Demon," Theo unwisely dismissed his handler with a wave of his hand. "We already know blood and cum wash out of the fabric soooo..." He leaned closer to the screen and peered at Pedro. "What in Stellaria's name is *that?*"

"It's a Trol," Ziggy replied, suddenly totally cool with spilling this 'classified information.'

"A *troll?*" Dre repeated with a scoff. "Welp. It will fit right in with *this* family."

"They, not *it,"* Ziggy corrected while keeping his gaze locked on his maker. "Have you ever heard of a Trol, Theo?"

Theo noisily licked BBQ sauce off his fingers. "Can't say I have. Ugly little thing, aren't they?"

I gasped and covered Pedro's ears as Gabe whirled on his stellar collision. "Are you blind, old man? They are the cutest goddamn thing I've ever seen!" He then turned back around to smile shyly at me, blushing as he added, "Well, *almost* the cutest."

Gah!

Ziggy snorted as Dre rolled his eyes, but I could *feel* the happy resonance buzzing from all sides.

I see you fools.

"Ruh-roh, angel," Theo mumbled through a mouthful of meat. "Looks like it might be time for another conjugal visit."

Ohmyfuckinggaaaawd!

My face went up in flames, but I couldn't even use my hands to hide behind, since I needed them to hold onto Pedro.

Luckily, Ziggy came to my rescue to get us back on track. "Visits won't be safe until this mission is complete."

I knew he was *trying* to redirect, but all he was doing was piquing *everyone's* interest.

Does he not understand this is the Stellarian Tea Party?

"Is... Pedro *dangerous?*" Gabe chewed on his bottom lip, his pretty blue eyes flitting between my face and the creature in my lap.

"No, they're just a baby," I soothed before lifting one of Pedro's paws and waving it at the camera. "Although check out these claws."

Even Dre leaned forward as Gabe murmured appreciatively under his breath. And when Pedro chose that moment to yawn extra wide, both twins grinned like kids on Christmas over the two rows of sharp little teefs.

"Looks like it's nap time," I explained, awkwardly punching in some numbers on my phone while trying not to drop the star of the show. "Lemme just get the nanny bot in here..."

Gabe's eyes lit up as the enormous robot clanked into the kitchen. I'd been slightly concerned at first that Zig grabbed one so big, but it turned out, this one was also programmed to *protect* its charges, not just change diapers and such.

Or, in our case, empty the litter box.

"SWOL-E in the house." Dre whistled as the nanny bot took Pedro from me, gentle despite its bulk. "Dude looks like they could take down a Transformer."

I wonder if Transformers are real...

"Wait, so *did* you make that?" Gabe asked, his assessing gaze running over the gleaming gold surface like the industrial designer he was. "You never texted back when I asked."

Oh, shit.

"Yeah, sorry about that." I rubbed the back of my neck and grimaced. "A creepy snake-headed alien snuck up on me and started asking questions about Pedro and nanny bots, so I got distracted. And no, I didn't make it—"

"You were texting on your phone when I left you in the Muonova?" Ziggy hissed. "What if the Hydrassian had attacked first?"

"Hydrassians don't randomly attack," Theo scoffed. "Although why one was loitering at a Muonova in the nanny bot section—"

"They do when they're being paid as mercenaries!" Ziggy barked, causing everyone to freeze and the nanny bot— SWOL-E, because that was its official name now—to swivel Pedro away from my stellar collision.

Pshhh... As if Ziggy would ever hurt our furbaby.

Theo set aside his plate, calmly wiping his hands and clasping them in his lap before facing the camera, as serious as I'd ever seen him.

"Why are a bunch of fortune tellers behaving like mercenaries, Ziggy?" His normally breezy voice had turned cold and calculating. "Does it have anything to do with that adorable space cat of yours?"

Judging by how the twins were gaping at their stellar collision, it wasn't often they saw their chaos gremlin in bad bitch mode. I was also a little weirded out, but then I reminded myself Theo *was* a Stellarian and had once worn his own Space Daddy armor to fight with a Star Unit for Astrum Force.

Before slaughtering his entire squadron and escaping to Earth...

So the mood changes track.

Only Ziggy seemed unbothered by Business Theo joining the chat. "Younger Hydrassians are accepting payment from various species to use their talents to track down karnilian." When his maker's eyebrow raised, Zig added, "Have you ever heard of *that?*"

"Of course I have," Theo replied in that same eerily emotionless tone. "Karnilian conquers planets. At least, it has the potential to... in the right hands."

Or the wrong ones...

"You didn't answer my question, Ziggy," Theo continued, switching to Stellarian. *"Does the Trol have something to do with the most sought after gem in the galaxies?"*

Gulp.

Theo knew I had a translation device, and the twins appeared to be following, so I assumed he was attempting to encrypt our conversation from potential eavesdroppers.

This is getting serious.

Ziggy nodded once, almost imperceptibly. *"The karnilian is inside the Trol. I've..."* He cleared his throat and blew out a slow breath. *"I've seen it... felt what it can do..."*

Oh, is that *what freaked him out so badly?*

So much had happened since that fateful bath time, Dr. Micah hadn't been able to drag Ziggy out of his shell for a session. I *had* noticed my man being extra protective of Pedro, but I had hoped it was more about them forming a bond.

Please don't tell me it's just about the gemstone...

Theo watched Ziggy closely as the nanny bot left the room with a sleepy Pedro in its arms. *"And the Hydrassians can feel it as well, can't they? They could be tracking you down this very minute."*

Gabe gasped dramatically, and even Dre looked marginally concerned, so I wildly gestured at the air around us, confident Ziggy could translate my interpretive dance.

He didn't disappoint. *"Micah has surrounded the entire ship with a karnilian-blocking shield, and when we took Pedro to the Hydrassian elders on Dionaea, he created one for the creature—"*

"You visited those creepy psychics?" Theo scoffed before smirking and gesturing at his stellar collisions. *"I wonder if that's where these two creepy psychics got their powers..."*

"You know damn well who we got our powers from," Dre

sighed in English before addressing Ziggy. "Can Hydrassians read minds, though?"

Ziggy smirked. *"They certainly tried."* His grin faded. *"The elder did manage to somehow trap my tendrils inside me..."*

Theo growled and glared at his psychic Dom. "Well, *that* sounds familiar, hmm?"

Dre chuckled and winked at me. "Brats were bratting."

"It was a horrible feeling," Ziggy snapped. "It would be like you two being unable to get into anyone's head—including each other's."

Oh, snap.

That landed, as both twins looked horrified at the thought. Satisfied his point was made, Ziggy switched back to Stellarian.

"They also possessed technology to stop me from star hopping, similar to Micah's shields, but not as advanced." He paused to smile proudly at me. *"We are on our way to meet the matter manipulators who created the Hydrassian's shields—to see what we can learn from them."*

"Cool," Gabe whispered, wide-eyed, before sobering. "Will you be safe, though?"

Oh, angel.

Theo had a soft spot for his subby baby, as he immediately stepped in to soothe. *"I assume they are headed for Ekistron, so they will be fine. No one wants to go to that frigid place. It's like that Not-Hoth planet you read about in your slutty books about strapping blue aliens fucking Earthlings."*

"Read me to filth, why don't you!" Gabe groaned, dropping his pretty face into his hands as Dre cackled. Then he peeked at me through his fingers. "They resonate for each other. It's hot."

I smiled reassuringly at the other piece of my heart. "Drop the link, bestie. We can start a slutty book club."

"Sluts gotta slut," Dre piped in.

"Perhaps you should join the club too, Andre," Ziggy purred. "See what all the fuss is about."

Space Daddy leaves no crumbs!

As usually happened when Ziggy reminded Dre about *his* repressed fantasies, the scarier twin had nothing to say.

Theo, however, did.

"Oh, how I would pay to see that!" he chortled before we *all* gaped at him. "What? This family is already twisted enough. What's one more taboo log on the damnation fire?"

I mean...

"All joking aside, Ziggy," Theo slipped back into Stellarian and searched his offspring's face. *"If you need somewhere to hide out, I will protect you."*

GAH!

As usual, Ziggy refused to show how deeply *I* knew those words affected him. *"Honnor made a similar offer, but the last thing I want to do is bring danger to anyone's doorstep. We will be fine."* He proudly gazed at me again. *"My partner and I have a plan."*

Heck yes, we do!

"Very well." Theo nodded and reached for his lunch, back to Earthling-speak once again. "Please keep in touch. I would hate to be forced to reconnect with the one Stellarian I reproduced with," he mock-gagged, "just to track you down."

This crew can only handle so much 'family.'

We said our goodbyes, and I turned to my *partner.* "So what else do we need to do to prep for Not-Hoth? I've got my winter-wear ready, and you're changing back into your sexy Sasquatch fit..."

Ziggy eyes flared with heat. "I am. At this very minute, in fact, so perhaps it's time to put all that *prep* to good use."

SWOL-E was the best purchase ever!

Not that we actually paid for it...

All thoughts of nanny bots disappeared as Ziggy appeared in the bedroom in full Borque splendor.

I'd asked if we should kick things off with a little game of chase, but he'd explained the predator instinct wasn't as strong in this skinsuit as others—partly because Borques were vegetarians.

Those fangs, tho...

"My what big teeth you have!" I crooned, clutching the blanket to my chest in mock-fear.

Ziggy cocked his furry head, somehow relaying amused confusion in his current form. "Is this another obscure Earth-ling reference?"

Sigh.

"Not obscure if you grew up as an Earthling," I laughed, scooting to one end of the sleeping pod to make room for his lanky form to join me. "Long story short, a talking wolf wants to eat a little girl, so he eats her grandmother instead. Then, he puts on the granny's clothes and hides in bed until the girl shows up and is like, 'my, what big teeth you have?' Wolf-gran says, 'The better to eat you with,' and then, you know, eats the little girl."

I am totally Stormtroopering skinsuit sexy times right now...

Thankfully, Ziggy was used to my runaway train of thoughts and more than capable of getting this horny little engine back on track.

He pulled the blanket off me before running his hungry gaze over my already naked body. "I see... Does this mean you want me to *eat* you, Micah?"

Chew-chew!

"I mean," I trailed off, distracted by him lowering his face to my ankle and working his way up my leg, lightly nipping along the way. "I wouldn't say *vore* is a kink of mine... but I do like it when you nibble on me a little. Or a-a lot."

Mark me up, Space Daddy.

Ziggy knew exactly what I liked as he gave my inner thigh a hard nip that made me yelp before he licked away the sting.

He chuckled evilly and continued his path up my body, purposefully avoiding my dick in favor of tracing my abs with his impressive tongue. "Any other favorite kinks I should know about?"

I released a shaky laugh as he reached my nipples, lightly dragging his fangs over them while I squirmed.

"It would p-probably be easier for me to tell you which kinks I *don't* have," I joked, attempting to tilt my hips to find some furry friction.

Ziggy growled and grabbed my hip with an enormous paw, holding me down while hovering his sexy as fuck Sasquatch face over mine. "Behave and tell me what you like."

"Yes, Space Daddy..." I whispered, melting into the mattress like the happy ho I was. "I like somno and role-play and whatever it's called when I plug your cum inside me."

"Mmm... yes, you love it when I breed you, don't you, baby-girl?" he purred, lowering his face to my neck.

He gets me.

"Yes!" I gasped as he ran his fangs over my sensitive skin, glad our filthy pillow talk matched up, thanks to this skinsuit knowing the trade language. "And I... I love to breed you too."

I just love you.

Ziggy froze, and for one terrifying moment, I thought I might have said that last part out loud, but then he shuddered and resumed torturing my neck.

"I love... that too," he murmured, unleashing a few tendrils. "I love being inside you."

As if to demonstrate his point, Ziggy pushed a tendril into my ass, stretching and lubing me up while I whimpered and writhed beneath him.

"Your tendrils are my kink too," I added breathlessly.

And probably unnecessarily.

I used to think I had a *tentacle* fetish—judging by my home-made toy collection back on Earth—but Ziggy's tendrils, his true form in general, more than fulfilled my desires.

Fuck, I just want him to live inside me.

I want to live inside him too...

My thoughts drifted to our witchy reading with the Hydrassian, where they revealed our destiny had been written in the stars—*together.* The only way we *could* have taken down the old Astrum Force Command was apparently by becoming one, by having each other's backs both figuratively and literally.

Before visiting The Knowledge on Kaalanesea, I'd told Ziggy there was nothing I could learn about his kind that would change how I felt about him. Later that evening—when I was stuffed full of twin Kaala cock—I'd also told him I'd wait however long it took for him to work through his feelings for me. While all of the above was, and always would be, true, I was also *dying* to drop the L-word on his skittish ass.

So if he could hurry up with the love confession, I'd appreciate it.

"More..." I begged, adding a "fuck, yes," when he forced another tendril into my hole.

"You love being full, huh?" Ziggy astutely observed, reminding me that 'talking me through it' was *another* kink of mine.

There are too many to count at this point.

"Does it remind you of when I fucked you with *two* cocks on Kaalanesea?" he continued ruthlessly as precum poured out of me. "As *twins.*"

"Ziiiig..." I whined. "Please don't tease me about Gabe and Dre right now. I'm... I'm so close already. Have mercy."

And don't even mention topping Dre, I beg.

Ziggy chuckled darkly against my neck before raising his head to gaze down at me. "I wasn't talking about them specifically. I was asking if *double penetration* might be another kink of yours..."

He punctuated his words with a thrust of his fur-covered hips, nudging something against me that immediately caught my attention.

Two somethings.

I pulled the smut train emergency break, pushing him off me and scrambling to sit. With a huffing laugh, Ziggy sat back on his heels, giving me an unobstructed view of the monster cock emerging from beneath his soft pelt.

The *two* monster cocks.

My mouth watered at the sight—pulsing veins beneath chestnut-colored skin with a deliciously intimidating thickness running from the dripping crowns to where they disappeared under his fur.

"Lordt," I choked out, eyes on my prizes and grabby hands reaching of their own accord, despite the risks to my digestive tract.

Ziggy slid his tendrils from my ass and used them to pull me closer. "My eager slut... You think you can take all of me into that tight little hole?"

LORDT!

"I..." I trailed off as *more* of his cocks emerged.

Unfortunately, it was painfully obvious that putting the two together would be unmanageably thick—beyond even what I took from him as Cock-jizz the Zeanidion.

Hmph.

"Well, I *want* to," I muttered petulantly, accepting I was being *too* ambitious in this case.

Even science has its limits...

"We'll start with one," Ziggy calmly replied, although I noticed him lubricating *both* with his tendrils. "You can milk it with your perfect ass while you come all over the other."

Lordt. Have. Mercy.

My sneaky stellar collision knew exactly what he was doing with that filthy mouth of his, judging by his equally filthy smirk. But all thoughts of clapping back evaporated as he effortlessly lifted me into the air before lining up just one of his cocks with my eager little hole.

Ya boy is ready for descent.

"Breathe, babygirl," Ziggy soothed, working his way in with slow, steady thrusts, deeper and deeper. "Let me in."

"Nnngh..." I whined, burying my face in his furry neck and gripping his broad shoulders for dear life.

He grabbed my ass cheeks with his paws, spreading me wide as he continued to push me down onto his thick length. The stretch was almost unbearable, painful in the best way, and I was thankful he'd thought to wrap a tendril around my cock and squeeze before I could blow too soon.

Because I never want this to end.

"Fuck, Zig," I mumbled, my body shuddering as my rim hit his balls. "Please…"

I wasn't even sure what I was asking for, but my stellar collision knew. He loosened his hold on my shaft and pulled me closer, nestling my throbbing cock against the one *not* buried in my guts and wrapping a tendril around both of us together.

I'm not gonna survive this.

"I've… got you," he panted, holding me open as he used his tendrils to slowly raise and lower me. "Mine…"

At this point, I was almost beyond speech, and it sounded like Ziggy was struggling with words as well, but there was one more thing I needed to say.

Besides that other thing…

"Breed me," I murmured, essentially giving my Space Daddy the green light to wreck my ass.

Even with how eager I was to be wrecked, Ziggy never gave me more than I could handle. Yes, he increased his pace, but it was controlled—the drag of his one cock against mine and the other against my p-spot just enough to have me dancing on the edge of release, sobbing into his fur while I slowly unraveled.

"More..." I managed to croak, no longer able to see through my tears. "I can handle more. P-please..."

"Good boy," he gritted out, tightening his grip on my ass, betraying just how much he'd been holding himself back. "Because I still need to give you my knot."

What...

My dick-drunk brain had barely given two slutty thumbs up when Ziggy abruptly slammed me down onto what I'd mistakenly thought were his balls. And, as usually happened with his knot-blessed skinsuits, the instant he locked into place, my vision whited out, and I exploded all over both of us.

When I came to, Zig was *still* pumping cum deep into my ass with his long fangs buried in my neck like a Wookie vampire.

"F-f-fuuuuuuck..." I moaned as *more* cum pulsed out of me, coating his fur-covered chest and abs, combining with the release shooting out of his second cock.

He must have "somno fun-timed" me at that point, because when I opened my eyes again, I was flat on my back, free from the knot but with Ziggy's Borque head between my thighs as he gently lapped at my incredibly sore little hole.

Ground Control to Commander Babygirl.

"Fuck," I repeated, craning my neck to sleepily gaze down at him. "What's the damage?"

He pulled back to intently stare at his handiwork, smug satisfaction written all over his furry face.

"You look perfectly wrecked," he purred before shifting his gaze to my face. "How do you feel?"

While I knew he was legitimately checking on my wellbeing, I was also aware my man wanted the dirtiest of details.

Such a perv.

"So fucking wrecked," I sighed, noticing the way his eyes flared at my confirmation. "And also so fucking thankful you *didn't* give me both cocks like I was begging for, Jesus *Christ.*"

Ziggy huffed a laugh before maneuvering himself in the pod until he was stretched out beside me.

"I will always give you what you want... within reason." His gaze traveled down my bitten and slightly bruised body. "You can handle more than the average Earthling, but I know I still need to be careful with you."

Tears blurred my vision yet again. "I-I wish I could change forms like you can, so I... so we..."

I was too frustrated and exhausted to finish my sentence, but my big, scary alien who was only soft for me knew just what to say to calm me down.

"Sunshine..." He pulled me against him so I could *feel* the resonance vibrating in his chest just for me. "It doesn't matter *what* form either of us are in. You are my stellar collision, my mate, my other half. You are mine."

The words I wanted to say so badly were on the tip of my tongue, but I was too overcome to do anything aside from cuddle closer and sniffle into his furry chest until I fell asleep again.

Micah was acting strangely.

Stranger than usual, that is.

Despite touching down on Ekistron an hour ago—despite how excited my mate had been to explore a new planet—we remained on the ship. Pedro had been fed and tucked into their baby sling by the nanny bot, and I had gathered as many weapons as needed for the journey ahead, but Micah still hadn't emerged from the bathroom.

Has something upset him?

I didn't know the answer to that, which was highly unusual in itself. In this relationship, *I* was the one who buried my emotions, who pushed others away and struggled to talk about whatever I was going through. In contrast, Micah was an open book who thrived on communication—who shared every thought that materialized in his impressive brain—but he'd seemed distant since playtime last night.

I didn't... injure him, did I?!

At this point, Micah had enthusiastically enjoyed numerous skinsuits from my collection—had mounted appendages that even the bravest superheroes on Earth may have shied away from. Last night had seemed like no exception, even if we'd been limited in what we could do.

And I thought he could handle what we did...

The issue was, fully denying my babygirl anything was a superpower I didn't possess. When he'd asked for both cocks, I'd given him what I could, and when he'd begged for more, I hadn't hesitated to knot him, even if I'd immediately put him under so he wouldn't feel any pain while I finished.

Plus, 'somno-fun time' is my favorite.

The mood had noticeably shifted after he awoke, but then he'd fallen asleep again before I could check in about it. Since then, my attention had been on preparing for Ekistron, so it wasn't until we were ready to leave that I noticed the bathroom door between us and remembered his tears.

I am a terrible mate.

Now I was questioning if perhaps I *didn't* know what Micah could handle in bed—if it might be better for me to change into a less threatening skinsuit to help *him* relax.

To help me relax as well.

Deciding that was the first logical step toward fixing whatever I'd broken, I quickly star hopped to my closet to slip back into my Earthling form. Then, I returned, steeled my spine, and approached the closed bathroom door before raising my hand to politely knock, just like he'd taught me.

But then, I froze.

What if he doesn't want me bothering him?

Not wishing to intrude but also physically unable to walk away from my mate when he was in need, I did the *next* logical thing.

I unleashed a few tendrils to slip through the cracks and investigate.

Strange...

For how long he'd been in the bathroom, I'd assumed Micah would have showered, but he still smelled like sex—like *me.* While this pleased me on a primal level, it was uncharacteristic behavior from my fastidious mate. Stranger still was that he seemed to be simply standing in place, most likely facing the small mirror above the sink—since there was nowhere else to go—staring into it.

Radiating *hurt.*

Oh fuck...

Dozens of tendrils emerged as my protective instincts went haywire. This was followed by a nearly suffocating wave of panic as I wondered whether the threat here wasn't skinsuit-specific, but *me.*

What if I did injure him?

Why didn't he use his safe word?

What if he's crying again?!

"Just come in, Zig. The door's unlocked."

The words had barely registered before I was flinging open the door and crowding into the small space along with him.

"What's wrong?!" I barked, louder than I intended, my gaze immediately dropping to the way his hand was pulling aside the collar of his shirt—exposing the fresh bite marks on his neck and shoulder.

Marks I'd put there.

Fuck, fuck, fuck...

"You changed your skinsuit?" he murmured, releasing his shirt and eyeing me as well. "I thought you were wearing the Borque because the fur would protect you from the elements."

You are the one who needs protecting.

"I decided to change into something with fewer... *teeth*," I gritted out, wondering why he wasn't simply answering my question. "Something less *threatening*."

"Oh, okay." He turned back to the mirror and absently rubbed his neck. "If that's what you think is best."

"I do," I replied, still watching him closely, subtly tasting the air around him with hair-thin tendrils, desperate for clues.

Micah's gaze lifted to track the movement in the mirror's reflection, even though he shouldn't have been able to see me move at all.

"Is there a problem, Zig?" he asked, turning to face me again with a furrowed brow and clear annoyance.

"You tell me," I snapped, the instinct to connect with him—*to claim him*—clawing beneath my stolen skin.

No, Ziggy.

This is what got you into this mess in the first place.

He huffed. "I just want to know why you're clocking me instead of communicating. If you wanna talk about something, then *talk.*"

While this blunt way of speaking was one of the countless reasons I admired my stellar collision, all I could focus on at the moment was how *on edge* Micah sounded, how he was still emanating distress.

"Very well... I could possibly use the piece of my core inside you to fix the marks on your neck—to heal them faster." The words were tumbling out of me, with no hope of stopping them, and Micah's eyes widened as my sorry attempts at a solution continued. "It might require me putting *more* of myself inside you, but it would only be temporary."

"What the heck are you talking about?" Micah scoffed. "Why would I want to *erase* the marks you gave me?"

"Because I hurt you!" I shouted, my tendrils undulated awkwardly in the cramped space. "Because I have failed at controlling the urge to mark you as my mate. You can't hide from me, Micah. I can *feel* your distress now, just like I could feel it last night after I..." My horrified gaze dropped to his lower half. "Unless it's elsewhere you're hurt..."

Is that why he didn't shower?

Because he's in too much pain?!

"Breathe, Zig, *breeeeeathe.*" Micah's cool hands were suddenly cupping my face, his touch settling me, if only somewhat.

"I'm not in physical pain. I mean, I do hurt a little, but it's the *good* kind of hurt, ya know?"

Frustration replaced my blind panic. "Then what am I picking up on? You are upset about *something* but are not telling me what it is!"

I knew full well I was being hypocritical and, judging by the smile my mate was failing to hide, he was about to bluntly point my hypocrisy out to me.

Dr. Micah has arrived.

"Yeah... It's rough when someone you deeply care about is hurting but doesn't seem to trust you enough to talk about it, huh?"

Ouch.

Before I could reply, Micah continued, "There *is* something I'm kind of upset about, but... it's really just my own shit that snuck up on me out of nowhere, so I was trying to leave you out of it."

I scoffed. "I don't *want* to be left out of it. I want to know everything."

Because you are mine.

Micah sighed and turned to the mirror before pulling aside the neck of his shirt again. "I'm actually upset at how *fast* these marks are already healing, thanks to my supe DNA. *Alien* DNA, whatever, although... not alien enough."

The last part was spoken so bitterly, I could taste it, and I was confused why we were back on this subject again. "Micah, I told you last night, you are my mate, no matter what—"

SPACE DADDY'S GUIDE TO THE GALAXY

"Not *really,* though, right?" Micah interrupted in a sharp tone. "Not in a way anyone out here would recognize."

Is this about getting space married?

I was about to suggest we go look at Micah's "Space-Married to my Space Husband" Pinterest board for the millionth time —*anything to help*—but he blew out a breath and continued.

"I'm sorry, Zig." He smiled apologetically before averting his gaze. "It's just... The first Hydrassian who cornered me at the Muonova said I 'didn't appear to be mated', and I guess that stuck with me more than I thought."

What?!

Oh.

I cleared my throat, knowing we were entering dangerous territory. "Many species leave marks on their mates while breeding them," I carefully explained. "However, due to how textured most alien skin is—never mind scales, fur, and various protective gear—most of these marks wouldn't be visible to the average bystander anyway."

And that's not what we're talking about here.

"What I believe the Hydrassian was referring to was..." I faltered, but forced myself to soldier on, "how you don't *smell* mated."

Micah's gorgeous face scrunched into pure confusion before a glimmer of understanding appeared. "Well, I *did* have my shields up... despite my dumbass mistake of texting Gabe when I should have been paying attention to my surroundings."

Sigh.

The urge to pause the current conversation—to remind Micah yet again of how capable he was—was strong, but it would be even *more* hypocritical of me to not share my knowledge on the issue at hand in favor of avoiding the subject.

Even if it's my issues about to be brought to light.

"Yes, your shields are quite adept at blocking your scent but, regardless, you would smell a certain way to others if you had been *successfully* mated." When his confusion persisted, I blew out a slow breath. "If you currently were, or had ever been, *impregnated.*"

Micah's eyes became comically large as every inch of visible skin darkened with an enticing blush. Most distracting of all was the raw *lust* now flavoring the air.

From both of us.

Just as quickly, his distress rose to the surface again, along with his snippy tone. "Yeah, well, then I'm never gonna smell mated, am I? Because that's not something we can do."

Now *my* distress was no doubt joining his as I struggled to answer in a way that wouldn't make things worse.

Or alert him to my own conflicted feelings on the subject.

The truth was, we *could* figure it out if we both wanted. I could take an Earthling female form, or any alien vessel with the ability to be impregnated by a different species. Likewise, I could find a skinsuit capable of using a male Earthling's body as an incubator, although that scenario probably wouldn't be ideal for him.

I've already been told ovipositing is out.

We could even mimic the way Stellarians reproduced with each other using Micah's tendrils, and if another Stellarian were involved....

Nope.

We are not going there right now.

By some miracle, I was saved from a lengthy reply by the blaring sound of an incoming communication in the Lodger's cockpit.

Micah flinched, so I quickly explained, "This is a standard notification—most likely the Eki inquiring about the nature of our business on their planet. While I *did* send out a peaceful signal when we entered their atmosphere, it's considered... *impolite* to withhold intent upon landing, so we need to clarify."

So we don't get disintegrated.

"Oh, shit! Okay, well, let me just..." Micah grabbed his sweatshirt off the towel rack and grabbed his phone before frantically stuffing it in his pocket.

"I'll take care of it, sunshine," I soothed. "Why don't you go grab winter layers for both of us." I hesitated. "Unless you *want* me in the Borque's skinsuit again...?"

This is confusing.

Micah smiled softly, although there was a hint of sadness in his expression and the air. "Zig, you are *my* mate too, no matter which form you take. Whatever you're most comfortable doing is fine with me."

While his sincerity warmed something inside me, I suspected

there was a deeper meaning to his words—one that didn't sit right with me at all.

Because a relationship isn't just about what I want.

"Very well, but we *will* continue this conversation later... *partner*," I said, staunchly burying my instinctive terror in favor of basking in the sunshine of Micah's grateful smile.

One baby situation at a time.

ZIGGY

:We require your ship's manifest before granting you access to our city:

I shielded my eyes against the glare, sweeping my gaze over the blindingly white landscape outside the cockpit window, wondering where this so-called "city" was located.

Perhaps they've cloaked it in some way?

Theo hadn't been exaggerating when he said no one came to Ekistron. While the Eki were renowned for their engineering powers, not much was known about how they lived. Exactly why a species as advanced as they were chose to inhabit a barren wasteland was beyond me, but I was willing to play by anyone's rules—*temporarily*—if it got me what I wanted.

What my babygirl wants, that is.

:Start with life forms, including artificial intelligence:

I began entering my reply into the communicator, knowing this was standard, if not tiresome, protocol.

- Two adult males, 21 and 25 years, Earthlings from
03-Via Lactea.
- One droid, model GRX-5L.

:Do you possess documentation for the droid?:

We did not, of course, considering I hadn't *paid* for the nanny bot before star hopping away from the scene of multiple murders.

Oops.

- Documentation destroyed during a skirmish with
Stellarians.

Mentioning my kind usually frightened others enough to let the subject drop. It helped that a prevalent superstition claimed those who said our name three times resulted in us materializing like harbingers of doom.

And here I am.

:Proceed:

- One newborn, female.

:Species?:

Fuck.

- Unknown.

The ignorance tactic was a gamble, but, along with betting on the Eki being unfamiliar with Earthlings, I was hoping this highly intelligent species would grant us entry based on their deeply ingrained scientific curiosity.

As opposed to other species who eliminate potential threats without question.

Unfortunately, the lack of response stretched on so long, I began to question the merit of my strategy.

Perhaps I should mention Uulvin sent us...

The seer had actually cautioned *against* mentioning them— only because the Eki were notoriously suspicious—so I'd decided to make up a story about how we ended up here.

It's easy enough to fool these lesser species.

"Tell them about my powers." My mate appeared at my side, bundled in a puffy insulated coat for the impending cold, yet still flavoring the air with his familiar scent.

Mine.

"You'll be activating your shields once we leave the ship, I assume..." I sighed as I dutifully typed, already growing agitated over the knowledge I'd be unable to smell him for much of our visit.

I hate it.

> - Earthling adult male, 25 years, possesses similar
> powers to the Eki.

"No," he softly replied, causing me to spin in my captain's chair to face him.

"Micah..." I warned. Even if I was personally conflicted on

his shields, his safety was my top priority. "If this is about *others* not being able to smell me on you—"

"It's not," he brusquely interrupted, his gaze drifting to the communicator screen as it chimed with a reply. "But I think it will look weird if only one Earthling has a shield, and I would never want to... trap your tendrils like that."

Oh, sunshine...

I grimaced. "Well, I would offer to change skinsuits, but I've already told them to expect two Earthlings..." I trailed off as I turned to read the message.

:Standby for Nuclei City hatch:

What in Stellaria's name does that *mean?*

"Presenting ourselves as a *pair* of Earthlings is a good cover, Zig." Micah placed a hand on my shoulder and squeezed, drawing my attention back to him. "It will help sell the idea that we're mates."

Enough of this!

With an annoyed huff, I roughly pulled him down onto my lap, determined to put this silly misconception to bed.

"We *are* mates," I growled, claiming his mouth with mine until he melted against me, licking and biting until he understood who he belonged to. "We are space fiancés."

Micah laughed and playfully shoved me away. "Yeah, we are. Although..." He looked down at his bare hand with exaggerated disapproval. "I still don't see a ring on this eligible finger."

With another huff, I grabbed his hand and raised the finger in question to my mouth, biting down on the first knuckle with my blunt Earthling teeth, hard enough to leave a mark.

Since, apparently, he likes me to mark him up.

"There." I met his shocked gaze with an innocent smile. "Now you have a ring."

"Dammit, Zig," he grumbled, although a smile twitched his equally abused lips as he admired my gift. "I really didn't want to be rocking a boner when they opened the hatch for us."

Opened the hatch...?

My confusion turned to alarm as the endless tundra outside the cockpit window shuddered so violently, the Lodger shook.

"Wait for it," Micah murmured, grabbing my hand before I could reactively fly us from danger.

Trusting my stellar collision's calm, I watched as a split appeared in the snow-covered ground before two massive, yet oddly silent, trap doors swung upward, revealing the neon orange glow of a city below.

Nuclei City...

"Knew it!" Micah crowed. When I eyed him curiously, he shrugged. "I did some research on the geological history of Ekistron and, apparently, the planet was once *covered* in now-extinct shield volcanoes. At some point, an ice age hit, making the surface unlivable, but then the Eki realized the lava tubes left over from volcanic times created the perfect subterranean infrastructure for underground living. Pretty cool, huh?"

"Indeed," I murmured, impressed as always with my impressive mate but also wondering how I'd missed this detail myself.

I'm losing my touch.

"The location of Nuclei City isn't documented, Zig," Micah added, either sensing my frustration or simply knowing me well enough. "I just made an educated guess."

Of course, you did.

"More educated than me, sunshine," I chuckled. "Hunting down undocumented intel is usually my specialty."

He frowned, so I deposited one last kiss before gently sliding him onto his own captain's chair. While I *could* fly the Lodger with my mate in my lap—as we'd done many, *many* times before—the angle with which we'd be entering the city required my full concentration to maneuver. I also wanted to pass through the hatch as quickly as possible, assuming the Eki would prefer to seal it up again before any passing ships spotted it from above.

The better to keep that intel undocumented.

At this point in my mercenary career, I'd visited dozens of technically-advanced planets—had materialized in the middle of New York City when I first arrived on Earth—but I had never experienced nose diving between two underground skyscrapers in order to land on an area the size of a helipad.

A helipad surrounded by flowing lava.

In fact, it appeared the entire city was powered by lava—from the ground-level streets to the towering buildings seemingly carved from the rock itself. Lava flowed in thin rivulets everywhere I looked, like a naturally-occurring alternative to neon tube lighting.

It's fairly impressive.

Although still not as impressive as my mate.

"I... guess my educated guess was only half-educated," Mach laughed nervously. "Maybe those volcanoes aren't as extinct as I thought they were."

"It's all right, sunshine," I soothed as we landed. "I'm assuming the Eki are using their powers to keep the lava under control."

He chewed on his bottom lip, radiating nervousness. "I've never attempted to control something I didn't create myself... Do you think they'll teach me how to do that?"

Exactly how generous the Eki planned to be remained to be seen. While it was promising they had allowed us into their secret city—especially with the vague manifest I provided— their alliances and agenda were unconfirmed.

They better not try to hurt my mate.

Or attempt to take Pedro away from us...

The visceral protectiveness that shot through me at the thought of these creatures attempting to harm the Trol surprised me. Then, I remembered the karnilian—how the stone hadn't stopped calling to me since I'd come in contact with it days ago.

"Micah..." I put the ship in standby and turned to face my entire universe. "About Pedro..."

How am I going to explain this?

"It's okay, Space Daddy—I've already activated Pedro's shields." His smile was nearly as bright as the lava's glow reflecting off his face. "And I know to let *you* take the lead on explaining how we got the egg, but otherwise, not tell the Eki *anything* about our little bundle of joy."

As usual, Micah talking about Pedro as if they were *our* child made my instincts glitch, and I realized now wasn't the time for a deep discussion anyway—not when our hosts were waiting.

And I am perfectly fine with delaying the conversation.

The nanny bot lumbered into view with Pedro attached, and, again, I had to fight the urge not to snatch the sling for myself. Besides the Eki already knowing the "little bundle of joy" wasn't biologically ours, it would probably be best to downplay any attachment to Pedro—to redirect all attention to my mate.

"Should we tell them *you* have powers too?" Micah asked as I pulled on the puffer jacket I didn't need, for appearances' sake. "Or make it sound like I'm an Earthling anomaly?"

I considered my answer as I star hopped our party to the landing bay. While I understood Micah's hesitation to draw attention to his home planet, I begrudgingly believed honesty would be best in this circumstance.

Honesty to a point.

"Eki value innovation and discovery over the idea of conquering other planets," I replied. "Yes, meeting you may make them curious about Earth, but we are many light years away from your galaxy. Telling them about the existence of superheroes and villains probably won't make the trip worth their while." I paused to tap in the code to open the ramp. "And to answer your question—let's keep *me* off their radar for now. Tell them I'm a powerless normie."

So if I need to kill them, they won't see me coming.

My mate nodded thoughtfully as the ramp deployed, the light from outside the ship illuminating his perfection in an orange glow once again. "Do you think they'll like me?"

What?

This was the *last* question I expected him to ask, and one I had no easy answer for. If there was one thing I'd learned in all my years of infiltrating various vessels and societies, it was that *some* experiences were universal while others were as varied as the stars in the sky.

"I believe they will *respect* you," I carefully replied. "Because anyone who doesn't lacks intelligence, and the Eki are an extremely intelligent species."

Unfortunately, I sensed this was *not* what Micah wanted to hear, but then the ramp hit the ground with a resounding clang, and we collectively walked to where a trio of hooded figures awaited.

The Eki.

"You didn't tell me they were *space wizards!*" I hiss-whispered to Ziggy in English, earning me an amused snort in return.

This was the best way to describe what I saw, since the three Eki standing at the bottom of the ramp were wearing full-length Jedi robes that sparkled with pinpricks of orange light.

Are those lava *robes?!*

Talk about the fit being fire...

Even though I was practically vibrating with excitement by the time we reached our welcome committee, I was determined to play it cool—to at least *pretend* I was a chill bad bitch in front of the yassified space wizards.

"Greetings!" I called out in the trade language with a little bow of my head, because why not? "We are grateful for your hospitality."

Please don't kill us.

I didn't *really* think we were in danger, but I also knew if the Eki caught a whiff of us being a threat, they wouldn't hesitate to turn us into space dust.

So, as usual, we're playing Hide the Stellarian.

Besides being hella built, even by supe standards, Zig was fairly unassuming in Earthling form. Thanks to his adorable freckles and fresh-faced good looks—plus the ski lodge-inspired outfits we were both rocking—nothing about my man overtly screamed "danger."

Except that weapon between his legs—ayoooo!

All jokes aside, Ziggy *looked* younger than me, thanks to the age of his chosen skinsuit. That, combined with his lack of Space Daddy armor, made my protective instincts buzz beneath the surface alongside my enthusiasm.

They better not try to hurt my mate.

Or attempt to take Pedro away from us...

"You are welcome in our city, *Earthlings*," one Eki spoke from the depths of their wizard robe. "Assuming you come here in good faith."

To illustrate we'd better not fuck around, the Eki waved a velvety black hand toward the lava encircling us, causing it to dance over the edge of its designated aqueduct in a mesmerizing display.

I am so impressed right now!

Of course I'd seen supes command fire before, but it was my understanding that spark was generated from within. There *were* some who influenced the weather, while others could cause earthquakes or tidal waves, but these powers were still specific to what they could directly control.

My brother Isaiah, for example, could physically connect to the Earth's core and *shock* it into causing earthquakes or tidal waves—like a defibrillator restarting a heart. Unfortunately, once the quake or wave had started, he no longer had control.

And Izzy is known for leaving a trail of destruction in his wake...

But what the Eki was doing with the lava wasn't chaos. It was easeful control, despite there being no direct line between the manipulator and the matter manipulated.

Suddenly remembering our host's *welcoming* words, I smiled warmly and respectfully bowed my head again.

Playing *his* part of helpless human, Ziggy mirrored my actions while replying for both of us. "Our purpose here is to simply learn from you and—"

Before my man could finish his sentence, the Eki flicked their wrist, creating a wall of lava between us they immediately threw in our direction.

JESUS!

Instead of reacting as a Stellarian—by either unleashing his tendrils or star hopping us away—Ziggy placed his vulnerable Earthling body in front of mine, fully prepared to take the brunt of the attack to keep up appearances.

Not on my watch, you don't.

Before his murder freckles could get murdered, I surrounded my little family—including SWOL-E—with an impenetrable shield. Then, I glared at our not-so-gracious hosts.

"We told you we came in peace!" I hollered, knowing I should probably watch my tone but being too pissed off to care. "Why would you endanger my mate and my..."

My stolen nanny bot and questionably adopted child.

"We simply wished to test the truth of the manifest you provided," the Eki on my shit list calmly replied. "And determine which one of you possessed the supposedly similar powers."

I huffed, annoyed to find I respected their caution, if not their methods. "We have no reason to lie. If you had just *asked* which one of us had powers like yours, I would have told you it was me."

Unsurprisingly, the Eki were as unapologetic as any alien or supe who shot first and asked questions later.

And since I clearly passed their little test—

My petulant thoughts were cut short as another Eki stepped forward and touched my shield, dissolving it instantly.

Jk.

"You are failing to pull enough varied particles from the air," they nonchalantly remarked as I gaped.

"Good to know," I muttered, sufficiently humbled.

Duly fucking noted, murder wizard.

"Your mate does not possess powers?" another Eki asked as all three hoods turned to stare at Ziggy.

Hearing Zig openly referred to as my *mate* made our bond shimmer with approval, but I could tell he was struggling to remain respectfully non-aggressive after the unexpected attack. Meanwhile, our hosts were clearly addressing *me* with the big questions, as if my powers automatically made me the one in charge.

Commander Babygirl, reporting for duty.

I cleared my throat and stood a little straighter, desperate to salvage my rep. "On Earth, some of the population has powers while others don't. We are not entirely sure why."

That wasn't completely true. We'd learned a *lot* about supe DNA in the past couple of years, but there were still quite a few unanswered questions floating around.

Gotta keep the franchise going.

"I have never met anyone with powers like mine before," I added, bringing their focus back to me. "Even my parents and siblings all had... *have* different powers."

The two Eki in the background began whispering amongst themselves, but they kept their voices too low for my translation device to pick up on.

"And the baby has not displayed powers either?" The first Eki pointed a long finger at where Pedro was curled up inside SWOL-E's sling, making me tense.

"N-not that we're aware of," I stammered, which was the truth... in a way. "We discovered the egg, and then they hatched on our ship, but we don't know what species they are."

"Where did you find the egg?" the one in front of me asked as they cocked their head, staring into my soul from deep within their hood.

"Stellaria," Ziggy replied, saving me from fucking this whole thing up.

The best partner.

"You *stole* from the Stellarians?!" they hissed while the others gasped and looked skyward, as if the infamous body snatchers might appear at any moment.

Who's gonna tell them?

Not me...

"No," Ziggy continued, so effortlessly cool and sexy, I almost swooned. "The egg had been abandoned near a gem dealer's stall. Before we could attempt to find the parents, Irathians attacked the planet."

"Irathians?" they all murmured, their confusion apparent even without being able to see their faces.

I was pumping so much pride through our bond, I *knew* my man could feel it, but when I glanced at Ziggy, his pretty blue eyes were fixed on the Eki.

So effortlessly badass.

"Yes," he confirmed, continuing to watch our hosts closely. "It seemed like odd behavior from what we've heard... Unless you know otherwise?"

Space Daddy is on the case!

Hunting down undocumented intel...

Guilt gnawed at me once again as I thought of the potential intel Ziggy left behind on Marox in favor of rescuing *my* dumb ass when I let a goddamn Maroxian onto the ship.

"It certainly sounds like ill-advised behavior," the first Eki mused before glancing at the others. "Bad advice, perhaps?"

There was something off about their tone, but Ziggy shrugged, flashing that goofy jock smile from when he was undercover back on Earth. "Yeah, well, it didn't concern us, so we grabbed the egg and flew to the nearest Muonova."

"Why not simply leave the egg behind?" our interrogator asked.

My gaze snapped to where I *thought* their eyes might be. "Because it was a helpless baby!" I blurted out, breaking our script by getting emotional all over again. "Because no one else was around to protect it."

"Because it's what heroes do," Ziggy quietly added, but when I glanced at him, I could tell he *thought* he was only talking about *me.*

Why don't you see yourself the way I do, Zig?

"May we see the baby?" One of the backup Eki stepped forward. "Perhaps we will recognize what it is."

I only hesitated for a moment, knowing any longer would seem suspicious. "O-of course," I stuttered, turning to reach inside the sling. "But I'd prefer to keep their shields up, if you don't mind..."

Obviously, these creatures could remove my lame shields if they wanted, but I didn't want to risk anyone *sensing* the karnilian.

And I'm really hoping they don't recognize what Pedro is...

With a deep breath, I lifted the sleeping Trol out of the sling, cradling them in my arms as I turned to face our hosts once again. The Eki went perfectly still in the way only supernatural creatures could, and I immediately knew the jig was up.

They know exactly what Pedro is.

"So what do you think?" Ziggy interrupted in a big, dumb cheerful voice. "Ever seen something like this before?"

My man was one of the most observant people I'd ever met—if you didn't count identifying *big feelings*—so I knew he'd noticed the Eki's reaction, despite how he was playing up the himbo vibes.

A master of disguise.

"No," the first Eki replied, lying through their wizard teeth. "Who sent you here?"

"A couple of Kaalas we met at the Muonova," my man smoothly improvised like the pro he was.

Okay, so I guess this *is our story...*

"They saw *my mate* using his powers and mentioned there was a planet full of 'matter manipulators' like him," Zig continued babbling, as if he didn't have a single thought in his pretty head. "I guess they have a famous library, so they know this stuff. The Knowing, or something."

"The Knowledge," the Eki in charge corrected before stepping closer to Pedro. "They did not know what this creature was?"

Ziggy glanced at the curled up Trol and shrugged. "It sleeps a lot, so it was hidden in the sling."

By some miracle, the Eki seemed satisfied with this answer—with all the masterful half-truths Ziggy fed them. While we *had* discussed our story a bit beforehand, I knew my man liked to pivot if he sensed things were going sideways.

And pivot he did...

Meanwhile, I was over here just praying I hadn't fucked things up with my emotion-fueled input. It had been the whole-truth that I'd never met another supe like me, and despite Ziggy being weirdly impressed with my powers, most everyone else in my life had always brushed them off.

Ekistron was my chance to level up, to actually become a bad bitch like my stellar collision. Yes, I'd managed to finish off the last corrupt commander in Astrum Force, but whether I could truly back up Ziggy in battle remained to be seen.

He insisted I was fine the way I was—that I didn't need to prove my 'usefulness' with him—but I wanted to offer more to this relationship than comic relief and a fantastic ass.

Listen, I know my strengths.

So, while my first priority on this planet was protecting Pedro, followed closely by making sure Ziggy's cover didn't get blown, I was also desperately hoping these 'matter manipulators' were going to teach me all their space wizard ways.

Pick me, please, coach!

"Your shields might impress a lesser species," the first Eki addressed me. "Unfortunately, by *our* standards, they are lacking."

"Okay, t-thank you," I stuttered as my dreams were dashed with a single sentence.

I could *feel* Ziggy about to step in, but I shook my head at him.

This is my loss, not yours.

"However," the Eki continued, "it fascinates us that a creature such as yourself can manipulate matter at all. You have potential, and we would like to help you hone your powers during your stay with us."

Oh.

My.

Gawd.

Like a Padawan!

"I would be honored." I bowed my head again to hide my ridiculous excitement. "When do we begin?"

The Eki in charge gestured at the Lodger. "Gather what you need, and we will show you to your rooms. We can begin your training after you are settled in and ready."

I was born ready.

With that, they turned to their companions and began discussing something in hushed tones again, but I wasn't even offended by the blatant dismissal. I was pumped for this opportunity, practically vibrating out of my skin with unhinged excitement for what lay ahead.

Ya boy is gonna be a space wizard!

25
MICAH

An hour later, I was pacing the small space while Ziggy lounged on the bed and Pedro pounced on invisible dust mites.

They kind of are *a space cat.*

The building we were staying in was unsurprisingly created from lava rock—from the ceiling to the floor, and including the furniture. The beds were covered in various furs for comfort, like those ice hotels back on Earth, but the temperature was pleasantly warm beneath the surface of Ekistron.

Must be all that lava...

The Eki *controlling* lava was blowing my mind, even if it wasn't outside the realm of possibility for someone like me. It was more that I'd just never used my powers in that way before.

Never been asked, *more like it...*

You would think having a kid who could control inorganic components—which were found everywhere on Earth, including within organic matter—would be seen as a valuable asset in a supe family. It *was,* but only for utilitarian things, like fixing the crumbling foundation of my parents' estate or creating handy tools to enhance my siblings' more badass powers.

I remembered the time my mother was hosting a superhero dignitary who asked about the stone walkway they were strolling down. Not only had she referred to the person who created it—*me*—as "the hired help," she'd completely missed the opportunity to point out how the design was based on chemical compounds found in the human body.

All that star stuff we're made of.

Despite how impressive—or *not* impressive, depending on who you asked—my powers were, I'd only ever used them on material I was in direct contact with. In theory, lava's inorganic makeup meant I *should* be able to manipulate it, but I wasn't understanding *how.*

"Why are you worried about this, Micah?" Ziggy murmured, effortlessly picking up on my nerves, even with his eyes on Pedro. "You were born with these powers. The Eki are simply showing you how to better utilize them."

"But what if I *can't?*" I whined, dramatically flopping onto the bed next to him as another wave of self-doubt washed over me. "Yeah, my powers are *vaguely* similar to theirs, but that doesn't mean—"

"I have no doubt you can," Ziggy interrupted, gaze shifting to me even as he dangled a random piece of rope over the side of the bed for Pedro to play with.

That looks like "enrichment" to me, Space Daddy.

"Uhh…" I eloquently replied. "You seem pretty sure of yourself, Zig."

"I am," he fired back, *patting his lap* until Pedro hopped up to join him with a ferocious little yowl.

So cute!

Both of them.

"Okay, fine, fine," I chuckled, basking in the confidence he had in me before a new thought floated to the surface. "Maybe that's why they're agreeing to train me—because they recognize I have the matter manipulator Force or something?"

Like Obi-Wan Kenobi and Anakin Skywalker.

More like Yoda and Luke, let's be real…

Ziggy hummed noncommittally. "Perhaps. Or it's because they're trying to figure out why we're *actually* here."

My blood ran cold as I sat up and turned to gape at him. "You don't think they believe the story we gave them?"

Now I was sweating, but my stellar collision looked as unbothered as always. "I don't believe they're as clueless about Pedro as they let on."

"I got the same vibes!" I shouted before lowering my voice—as if anyone around here spoke Earthling American English. "And Pedro's shields were up, so it wasn't the call of the karnilian or whatever."

Ziggy cleared his throat and dropped his gaze to the Trol

curled up in his lap. "Yes, well... you should keep Pedro's shields up while we're here regardless—"

"What's the point?" I huffed, annoyed at my lack of skill all over again. "You saw how that Eki just *dissolved* my shields like it was nothing."

Hmph.

"And you can learn to do that too, sunshine," he soothed, filling me with comfort from the inside out. "If the Eki wanted us dead, they would have tried harder to kill us."

"That's not as reassuring as you think, Zig," I laughed, even as I blasted *him* with schmoopy gratitude in return. "I have to ask, though... Why did you make up that story about the Kaalas? I know Uulvin said don't mention them by name, but we're really gonna pretend this was a complete coincidence?"

Ziggy was quiet for a long moment, absently running his hands through Pedro's fur as the creature purred up a storm.

"Something isn't adding up here." His gaze met mine. "And since *we* haven't been given the full story of *why* they let us into a notoriously unwelcoming city, I figured I'd return the favor."

I sighed heavily, even if I understood where he was coming from. Knowledge was power, no matter what planet you were on, and—as a supe—I was well-versed in the ways people withheld intel for personal gain.

"Well, as long as you don't think it's a bad idea for me to train with them..." I tried to play it cool, even though I assumed my man could see—*feel*—right through my nonchalant posturing.

He smiled softly. "I think it's a very good idea, and I also believe the offer to train you is genuine."

That was all the reassurance I needed, because Ziggy *was* skilled at reading others, even with his tendrils under wraps.

"Okay!" I stood and jumped in place a few times, hyping myself up. "Then I should probably go find the Eki who offered—"

As if on cue, a soft knock on the door had me hustling to answer. When I swung the—lava rock, of course—door wide, my space wizard sensei was calmly standing on the other side with their hands tucked into the sleeves of their sparkly robe.

I wonder what they look like under there...

"H-hi, hello!" I switched to the trade language and stepped back. "Please come in."

They took a single step inside the room before clocking Zig and Pedro on the bed. "The accommodations are to your liking? Would you have preferred a single room?"

"Yes! And, uh, no. Two rooms is better for me and my... mate..." I trailed off as my face heated.

Because I need uninterrupted Tendril Touchy Time, thanks for asking.

"What should we call you?" Ziggy called from the bed, probably picking up on my slutty embarrassment and wanting to redirect.

"Leeloo," the Eki replied, and my excitement returned with a vengeance.

Like Lilo and Stitch?

Or The Fifth Element?!

MULTIPASS!!!

Yes, my nerdy taste in entertainment knew no bounds, but devouring sci-fi content had always been the best way to give my busy brain a break while feeding my obsession with space.

Until my very own alien landed on my doorstep.

Now I'm just obsessed with him.

"I'm Ziggy," my partner continued, since I was still gaping like a fool. "And this is Micah."

"Zig-ee," Leeloo repeated before turning their literally hooded gaze on me. "My-kuh."

"That's me!" I waved for no good goddamn reason. "It's a name from the Bible... which is a, um, book where we come from. A fiction book. Open to interpretation. Anyway, I've always liked my name because it sounds like *mica*, which is what we call crystallized silicate minerals that show up in metamorphic, sedimentary, and igneous rock... Kind of like what you've got going on here..."

The Eki was staring at me with either rapt interest or deep confusion, but I had no way of knowing which one.

And this is why I was single before I met Ziggy.

"And this is Pedro," my space fiancé cheerfully called out, saving my dumb ass once again—this time from myself.

Partners 'til the end.

Leeloo snapped their attention to the pair on the bed. "You named them?"

"Well, yeah." I rubbed the back of my neck, wondering if it was considered weird in outer space to name highly coveted talismans. "We think of Pedro as family."

The Eki hadn't taken their gaze off the Trol. "Is that why you feel... *called* to protect them?"

Ziggy tensed, placing a protective hand on Pedro as Leeloo stepped closer.

Ooh, Space Daddy in the house!

"Yes," I blurted out, eager to draw Leeloo's attention away from the Trol. "It's like a... paternal instinct? I mean, we don't have children of our own yet, so—"

Oh, no...

This time, I tried to rescue my own damn self by slamming my mouth shut and throwing away the key, but the damage had been done. Ziggy's baby blues had gone as round as twin moons, and the sound he choked out could only be described as a death rattle.

Way to Stormtrooper the baby discussion, Micah.

Leeloo nearly blew their own hood off with how quickly they glanced between us before producing a rasping sound of their own.

Are they... laughing at us?

Fair.

"Let us focus on training for now, My-kuh," they blessedly redirected. "Before your mate disappears into thin air."

THEY KNOW!

Now, we *both* tensed, but I instantly realized my Jedi Master was making a joke.

Okay, Leeloo. I see you.

"Yeah," I laughed awkwardly. "I would like that, and I *appreciate* the training. Again, thank you."

The Eki inclined their head as Ziggy piped in, "May I join the training session? To watch?"

Yes fucking please.

The raw *relief* that coursed through me left no doubt in my mind that I *needed* my Space Daddy by my side for this exercise—as moral support.

My forever hype girl.

Leeloo considered for a moment before nodding at Ziggy. "Of course, you may accompany your mate, as long as you maintain a safe distance from the exercises. I would caution against bringing the child with you, however, as we would not want to place them in harm's way."

Ah, fuck.

We *all* knew Pedro would be fine, but if Ziggy and I insisted they come along, it might contradict my claim of possessing paternal instincts to protect the 'helpless' baby.

"The droid you have will suffice as protection while you are away," Leeloo crisply added, apparently wanting to get this show on the road. "The GRX-5L is known for swiftly delivering death to anyone aside from the designated caregivers—assuming you have programmed it to do so."

Uhhh...

"I... *think* I did," I replied with a grimace. "It didn't exactly come with instructions."

"You also have nothing to fear in our city." Leeloo stepped closer before inclining their head. "Shall we proceed?"

I nodded, and Ziggy immediately stood, carrying Pedro to the nanny bot in the adjoining room. While I knew he was just playing his role of supposedly less impressive mate, I couldn't help how my chest grew tight at the sight of my stellar collision caring for the little furbaby.

Our pretend baby.

Fuck.

I want to mpreg that man so fucking bad.

Leeloo cleared their throat, and for one horrifying moment, I wondered if Eki could taste emotions in the air as well.

I will throw myself into the nearest volcano if that's the case.

To my relief, they simply whispered conspiratorially, "I promise to steer the discussion away from *children* in front of your frightened mate."

Leeloo has your number, Zig!

I had to hide my laugh beneath a cough. "Yeah... He might need a little time to warm up to the idea."

The Eki followed my gaze to where Ziggy appeared to be fussing over arranging Pedro just so in SWOL-E's baby sling.

"He will come around eventually," Leeloo replied sagely,

earning them infinite points in my book. "For now, let us see what *you* can do."

I nodded and blew out a breath, determined to give this my all and not fuck up too badly.

You've got this, Micah.

I hope....

Why isn't he getting this?

At this point, Micah had been demonstrating his abilities to Leeloo for hours—quite impressively, I might add—but he was clearly losing patience with himself. The Eki seemed confident my stellar collision could accomplish everything they'd been demonstrating for him, but whenever he attempted to manipulate an object from afar, he faltered.

My mate should *be able to do this.*

He can do anything!

Granted, I hadn't yet encountered an Eki when I'd declared Micah as the most impressive creature in all the galaxies, but their powers seemed comparable. They both could conjure complex objects from simple, inorganic particles, including weapons and shields even a Stellarian couldn't infiltrate.

Uulvin said Micah's shields were more advanced than the Eki's.

I wonder what they meant by that...

While Micah regrouped, my gaze drifted to our surroundings. The makeshift training ring was an otherwise vacant helipad positioned below what I assumed was another surface level entry point. Unlike where the Lodger was parked, this one was on the outskirts of the city, with towering skyscrapers in one direction and what appeared to be farmland in the other, judging by the recently tilled, no doubt nutrient-rich volcanic soil.

All this did was deepen the mystery surrounding this species. Between the crops, the fortified city, and the nature of their powers, the Eki were a wholly self-sufficient society.

So why did they let us in?

And why take outside jobs on other planets?

"I-I'm not sure this is gonna work," Micah announced in a shaky voice, bringing my attention back to him.

"It will," Leeloo decisively replied. "Try again."

My mate puffed out a breath and refocused on the thin gutter of lava surrounding the helipad with an expression so uncharacteristically serious, I wondered if another Stellarian had taken over.

Impossible.

Since I'm the only one allowed inside him.

"I can't do it," Micah sighed after a full minute of no results, his shoulders drooping in defeat. "I just don't have the space wizard Force."

Oh, sunshine.

Watching the most important person in my life struggle—combined with keeping *my* abilities under wraps—was making me restless, but I wasn't sure how to help.

Or if he wants *my help at all...*

Leeloo cocked their hooded head. "How do you create your shields, My-kuh?"

Micah chewed his bottom lip. "Well... I combine whatever particles are on hand and *push* them outward. With *my* shield, I'm kind of just... holding everything in place about a millimeter above my skin."

So incredibly impressive.

The Eki hummed thoughtfully. "What about when you create shields for others—like with the child?"

Micah adorably scrunched up his face, and I realized his amazing abilities came so naturally to him, he rarely thought about how they worked.

"In that case, I think I'm... *pulling in* particles from the air," he murmured, gesturing vaguely. "And then sealing the shields around whoever—"

"Show me on Zig-ee," Leeloo interrupted, and I froze.

What?!

Micah met my gaze before nervously glancing at Leeloo. "I-I'm not sure..."

The Eki clasped their hands behind their back and stepped closer. "Surely you have shielded your less powerful mate before?"

"He…" Micah cleared his throat, radiating anxiety. "He doesn't like it. Gets… claustrophobic."

Now, Leeloo was staring at *me,* and I knew our hesitation was starting to look suspicious.

Fuck.

"It's all right, Micah." I smiled brightly, sending soothing energy through our bond. "If it helps your training, I don't mind."

I definitely minded. Just the *idea* of being encased in an impenetrable barrier was making my true form writhe beneath the surface, wanting to star hop away from the threat.

Breathe, Ziggy.

Micah is not a threat.

"Pretend he is your enemy," Leeloo coolly said, and Micah shrank backwards. "So instead of creating shields to *protect* Zig-ee, create a cage to *trap* him."

It took every ounce of self-control to remain outwardly calm, but I schooled my Earthling face into a placid mask and nodded at my mate.

Let's get this over with.

"I'm sorry, Zig," Micah whispered before he stripped me of everything I was.

The instant the shields locked tight, the discomfort I'd experienced while in Uulvin's cave washed over me—only this time, it felt magnified, like a tidal wave of distress.

Because it's being caused by my mate.

My body was vibrating with the need to flee, and since a Stellarian rarely backed down from a fight, this *helplessness* was simultaneously terrifying and humiliating.

"He truly hates this, hmm?" Leeloo calmly observed, circling me like a predator. "Such a *visceral* reaction."

"Yeah..." Micah eyed me with concern as I inwardly unraveled. "It's not his favorite. Can I remove—"

"Your shields are still lacking... something." The Eki raised a hand, hovering it over the invisible surface, taunting me with freedom.

Let. Me. Out.

Instead of dissolving my prison like I knew they could, Leeloo glanced at Micah. "You are familiar with Stellarians, correct?"

My mate blinked. "Y-yes. We were on Stellaria recently, when we found the egg—"

"Do you understand *how* they take over another's body?" the Eki continued conversationally. "How the process works, that is."

Letmeoutletmeout...

Micah was visibly sweating, shifting on his feet as his gaze darted between us. "From what I've heard, they connect to their host like synapses in the brain and then control the bodily systems from there?"

He replied as if he wasn't certain, but my stellar collision knew firsthand what it felt like for me to control his movements from the inside out. It was a trick we *both* enjoyed. I would force him to touch himself during playtime, to bring himself to the edge of completion, only to stop right before he tumbled over the edge.

Usually while keeping him under.

Not even the thought of my mate at the mercy of my desires could quell the panic bubbling up within me, so I begged for help in the only way I could.

LET ME OUT!

Micah gasped as his hand uncontrollably jerked upward, reaching for the shields entrapping me as I desperately manipulated the piece of my core lodged inside him.

Please...

"Not yet!" Leeloo lifted a scolding finger, making me *rage*. "I need you to think about how a Stellarian controls living cells —organic matter, if you will. It's a similar process to how *we* control inorganic material."

Even though I could *feel* his growing anxiety on my behalf, Micah gave the suggestion careful consideration. "But I can't connect with the lava directly..."

"You can," the Eki interrupted, still sounding as patient as when this exercise began. "It is a series of smaller chain reactions, from particle to particle, until you connect with your mark. You are already doing it when you *create* items—like with your shields—but you can use this same method for destructive purposes, to both assemble and disassemble."

Despite my distress, I couldn't help recalling when we'd first learned of a similar duality from the lone Stellarian survivor of Theo's massacre.

"Earthlings are capable of both destruction and creation, so why not us?"

The signs were always there. Even Stellaria's two smaller moons—*Genero* and *Interitus*—translated as *creation* and *destruction.*

Meanwhile, our largest moon, *Apotelesma,* meant *the effect of the stars on human destiny,* because it was humans—Earthlings—specifically who were uniquely suited for us to meld our consciousness with. As Bron had once explained, humans and Stellarians were the perfect symbiotic match.

"A species easily inspired to create and destroy, and a creature eager to serve as inspiration for either."

Like a pair of muses.

Like stellar collisions.

There was a time I'd felt I couldn't handle the weight of this knowledge, especially after being raised to believe a Stellarian's only purpose was to conquer everything in their path. Now I knew the narrative had been a lie. We were made to benevolently coexist with our hosts, to collaboratively guide their thoughts toward a common goal.

Like true partners.

"Could you imagine if you were able to combine *your* power with that of a Stellarian's, My-kuh?" Leeloo asked.

Excuse me?

I snapped back to the present to witness Micah's anxiety give way to signature scientific curiosity. "That would be awesome, actually."

"It would." The Eki's gaze drifted to the empty air above Micah's head before returning to his face. "I want you to *pretend* you have command over both realms—inorganic and organic. Lead with the inorganic matter and use it to *push* the organic. Mastering that will allow you to cause greater chain reactions, to create stronger and *larger* shields."

Micah's cheeks darkened as he shyly dropped his gaze. "I *did* create shields large enough to protect an entire building once..."

And an entire island.

Leeloo nodded once, as if coming to a decision. "It sounds like you already have everything you need inside you."

Again, Micah and I froze, and I internally cursed being unable to unleash my tendrils to taste whether the Eki was harboring any suspicions about our unique connection.

"In other words..." they breezily continued. "You simply need to trust what you are made of. Trust *yourself.*"

"What I'm made of..." Micah murmured before shaking his head and refocusing on his assignment with renewed determination.

It was my turn to gasp as he pulled from the piece of me inside him, guiding our *combined* energy through the air to manipulate the lava upward into a perfectly controlled arc. The glowing substance hovered in the air for a moment before gracefully returning to the aqueduct without a drop spilled.

Amazing.

But... why not simply do it himself?

"Well done!" Leeloo clapped their hands before glancing at me. "You may release your mate now."

Thank fuck.

Micah immediately dissolved my shields, and it was only thanks to my finely-honed self-control that I hid the raw *relief* coursing through me.

Let's never do that again.

My stellar collision gave me an apologetic smile before turning to the Eki. "Thank you for your guidance, Leeloo. I *think* I understand what it takes now."

Hmph...

I wasn't sure I agreed with that statement. Yes, Leeloo had waxed poetic about leading the organic with the inorganic, but the only particles Micah had just manipulated were *air* and *lava*.

No carbon detected.

My heart sank as I realized why my mate still believed *I* needed to be involved.

He still doesn't believe in himself.

This exceptionally powerful superhuman seemed determined to dismiss his own greatness, despite being worlds more impressive than me, than almost everyone I'd ever encountered in my travels.

Sounds like some one-on-one training is needed.

"Will that be all for today, Leeloo?" I called out, ensuring my tone relayed there was only one correct answer to that question.

The Eki wisely inclined their head before silently leading us back into the heart of the city. I dutifully plodded after them as Micah chatted away, exercising my self-control yet again to not immediately star hop my mate to our room.

Because it's time for him to learn.

Ziggy Andromeda was *pissed.*

No.

That's... lust?

After getting Leeloo to promise another training session, Zig and I said our goodbyes before checking on Pedro. The Trol had still been curled up in SWOL-E's baby sling—safely shielded—but when I'd suggested waking them up to feed, my man practically dragged me into the room next door.

For one terrible moment, I thought Ziggy was *mad* at me for how badly I'd sucked today, but then I realized it was my own baggage muddying the waters again.

It was my *parents* who would punish me for a less than perfect performance, by either ignoring my existence completely or reminding me that existence was dependent on how useful I could be to the family.

Ziggy wasn't like that. If anything, he was *overly* confident in my abilities. It reminded me of how my sister Rose weirdly praised her younger kids every time they used the potty—as if normal bodily functions deserved all the gold stars.

Maybe they do?

The issue was that, aside from Zig, I had barely any experience with someone blindly supporting me with no ulterior motive. On the flip side, I had absolutely zero issue blasting my man with unconditional fangirling, but that was *different*.

He's legitimately amazing!

"Get on the goddamn bed," Ziggy growled the instant the door shut behind us in our own room. "Your training isn't done."

His skerry Space Daddy tone made me instinctively freeze, but I quickly realized he was staring at me like I was his next and last meal. This meant the only parts of me in any real danger were whatever hole—or *holes*—he had his sights set on.

And I am HERE FOR IT!

"Ohhh... Are we gonna play stern Jedi Master and slutty student?" I purred as I stripped off my clothes and crawled onto the lava rock bed. "Because ya boy is more than ready to handle that lightsaber of yours—"

I didn't even get the chance to finish my nerdy flirting before a half dozen lightsabers shot out of Ziggy's skinsuit and sexily tossed me onto the mattress.

Here for this too.

"The only thing you will be handling is a toy," he snarled, releasing his hold on me so he could also undress.

Wait.

What?

"W-what do you mean?" I stuttered, as if I didn't know full well what he was talking about.

Being fifth in line and relatively unimportant in my family, there hadn't been many chances for me to find partners, much less get them alone in my room. Plus, my tastes definitely skewed toward the... *inhuman* realm, thanks to my entertainment preferences, but besides my eldest brother and his fellow Deathball players, shapeshifting supes were fairly rare.

So I got creative!

A combo of boredom, horniness, and necessity were to blame for the dragon's hoard of dildos I'd created over the years, but now, I had my own hot-bod body snatcher to fulfill my wildest dreams. And while it hadn't bothered me to tell Ziggy about these blessedly now destroyed homemade toys, I was suddenly regretting mentioning them at all.

Maybe he's talking about a random toy he smuggled off the ship?

"I want you to create a toy," Ziggy clarified in a stern Jedi Master voice that bricked me right up, despite confirming my worst nightmare. "Like the ones you used to make when we first met—when you were soaking your sheets, imagining me fucking you with my *alien appendages.*"

Oh, no...

I could feel my entire body flushing, because the idea of

showing Ziggy *physical proof* of what I used to think he was under his Earthling exterior was beyond humiliating.

Even if my boner is still going strong.

"Ziiiig..." I whined, even as I sat up and made room for him on the bed. "It's just... the fantasies I made up were so... silly."

And nowhere near as perfect as the real thing.

"Micah." He grabbed my chin and forced me to look at him. "Sunshine. *Babygirl.* Nothing you do is silly. Besides how much I'm going to enjoy this, I want to see what you can do. Show me, *please...*"

Not the begging!

"You really don't play fair," I grumbled, not for the first time, but I was finding it hard to stay mad.

Ziggy was clearly trying to support me in his usual over-bearing yet incredibly sexy way. The least I could do was use my powers to conjure up a dildo.

I awkwardly cleared my throat. "Okay, sooo... My guesses about what you were working with were kind of all over the place and mostly based on Hollywood aliens, full disclosure, but *this* one was my favorite."

Blowing out a steady breath, I pulled from the medical-grade silicone fragment embedded in my wrist—among other handy materials—and started forming a flared base.

Safety first!

Ziggy's attentive gaze was fixed on my hands as I then conjured a ridiculously thick, textured tentacle covered in bumps, ridges, and suction cups. I made the tentacle exactly as *long* as I liked it, which couldn't compare to the reach of a certain Stellarian's tendrils, but it was satisfying enough.

The Stellarian in question smirked. "Well now I see why you love *corpus spongiosum* so much."

Ignoring his sassy commentary, I powered on, adding two slightly smaller tentacles on either side of the main event before topping all of them off with twisted tips.

Ta daaaa!

Ziggy raised his eyebrows appreciatively. "Impressive. You've managed to take all of that in your tight little ass?"

Ughhh...

My man knew exactly what he was doing as I squirmed under his knowing gaze. "I mean, I've *tried*... but the two on the sides are mostly for external stimulation."

He hummed before holding out his hand. "May I see?"

With a laugh, I handed off my homemade tentacle dildo to my stellar collision, feeling weirdly proud as he examined the craftsmanship.

Gimme all the gold stars.

"Lie back and spread your legs," he commanded, and I obeyed without question.

Forever here for it!

"Are you gonna use my new toy on me, Space Daddy?" I teased as he lubed it up with one tendril while two others stretched and prepped me.

"No," he replied with a sly little smile full of bad intentions. "I think I'd be too jealous for that."

"Fuck," I sighed. "You're so fucking hot when you get all possessive and—"

"You're going to use it on yourself instead," he bluntly interrupted, holding out the now glistening toy for me to take.

WHAT?!

"Zig!" I yelped, wishing I could disappear into the layered furs on the lava rock bed. "Are you *trying* to embarrass me or something?"

His smile turned soft as he withdrew his tendrils from my ass. "No, sunshine, although I do love to see you squirm and blush."

Is that all you love?

Ziggy's gaze fell to the toy as I grabbed it with a huff. "I want to see your creation in action, Micah. You know I love to watch..."

What Space Daddy wants...

"Ugh, fine." I blushed all over again before spreading my legs wider and lining up the main tentacle's tip with my hole.

It's showtime.

With a slow exhale, I bore down and began pumping it in— back and forth, one thick inch at a time—grimacing as I realized I may have made this one a bit bigger than I remembered.

But quitters never win.

"Look at that," Ziggy murmured, his pretty blue eyes trained on the action. "Look at that needy, *greedy* hole trying to swallow all of it."

"ZIG!" I scolded, stopping my efforts to glare up at him. "If you want to see me take the full tentacle dick before I blow, you need to find something else to do with that filthy mouth."

He grinned wide and crawled toward me, but instead of swallowing down my dick as I'd hoped, he kept going—stretching out his hot muscles alongside me and tilting my face to his.

"Would this help you relax, sunshine?" Ziggy whispered, kissing me softly, drinking down my moans as I continued to work the toy inside me.

"Fuck, yes," I groaned, finally bottoming out. "I forgot how good this felt..."

Ziggy growled and *nipped* my lip. "Not as good as I feel inside you."

So cute and jelly.

"Nothing feels as good as you," I breathed against his lips, sliding the tentacle halfway out before pushing it back in. "You were made for me, Zig, made to be inside me... breeding me."

Filling me with space babies.

Ziggy tensed before shuddering and kissing me harder, licking his way into my mouth. "You were made for me too," he replied, adorably breathless when he came up for air. "For the same reasons..."

Oh?

I knew better than to Stormtrooper *tentacle* touchy time by making my skittish Stellarian repeat himself, but telling myself he'd *also* been thinking about getting mpregged gave me all the horny fuel I needed.

Losing myself in our kiss, I increased my pace, whimpering as the textured surface of the secondary tentacles rubbed along the sides of my sac with every stroke. My dick was leaking precum on my abs, but there was nothing I could do about it while handling this two-handed toy.

And I think I can get off just like this...

"Zig..." I panted, eyes squeezing shut. "I'm so close... I'm gonna..."

"I know, babygirl," he murmured, kissing me so sweetly. "But you need to work for it."

Wait...

My eyes flew open as he used the piece of his embedded core to rip my hands away from the dildo and pin them to the mattress overhead. Then, he secured my ankles in the same way, effortlessly immobilizing me from the inside while a tentacle dick hung halfway out of my ass.

"What the... what the *FUCK?!*" I shouted, my entire body shuddering as I stumbled back from the edge of release. "W-why would you—"

Ziggy ignored my sobs and continued casually kissing my neck like a fucking psychopath. "Because I want to see you use your powers to finish yourself off."

Ugggggghhhhh...

I'd completely forgotten this was supposed to be a *training exercise*. If I was going to be honest, I'd kind of assumed Zig was just adding another role-play word to his filthy talk vocabulary.

"Fine," I gritted out, immediately unleashing two mechanical arms to grasp the base of the dildo.

"No!" Ziggy barked before biting my neck so hard, I yelped. "No contraptions. No tendrils. And *no* using the piece of *me* inside you."

Oops.

My vision blurred with tears—more from horny frustration than anything. "Zig... I j-just need to get off. *P-please...*"

He gently licked at the bite mark, easing the sting while pumping soothing energy through our bond. "And I *want* you to get off... want to watch you come... but I'm going to need you to use your powers to do so."

"But those *are* my powers!" I wailed. "What the hell else am I supposed to use? The *air?!*"

Oh.

Sigh.

"That's right, Micah," he chuckled, lifting his head to smirk down at me. "I want you to use the *bad bitch* powers you learned today to move the toy inside you."

"But..." I searched his face, struggling in his hold more for the aesthetics at this point than anything. "But what if I *can't?*"

Because *that* was what was bothering me the most, and I suspected Ziggy knew it. I wasn't confident what I'd done today *could* be accomplished again—at least, not without his help.

He is *helping you, Micah.*

As if knowing I needed that extra push, Ziggy dipped his head, tenderly brushing his lips over mine again. "I know you can do it. C'mon, babygirl. Fuck yourself for your Space Daddy."

Fuuuuck...

That was all the encouragement I needed. With a slutty little moan, I gathered enough air particles to *push* the dildo inside me before *pulling* it out again—over and over, faster and deeper, in and out, using my powers to guide the textured tentacle over my prostate as it stretched me full.

Almost there.

Ziggy thrusted against my thigh—almost as if he couldn't help himself from seeking release along with me—and the glorious sight of him unraveling booted me over the edge. Clenching around the toy, I arched backwards, shooting a bucketload of cum over both of us, with my stellar collision's name on my lips.

"Good... boy..." he groaned, adding to the mess with a final thrust and a slutty little moan of his own.

Hot.

We both panted as we came down, and although I *was grateful* Zig had figured out a way for me to get out of my head, I was still a little salty about his methods.

You don't mess with another man's orgasm.

"Oh, you liked that, huh?" I grinned like a villain, deciding to tease. "You liked watching me come while thinking about me knocking you up?"

Ziggy sharply inhaled and lifted his head, looking like an alien deer in the headlights.

Gotcha.

"I..." he trailed off before swallowing thickly. "Yes."

His unexpected honesty instantly cleared my lingering annoyance. "Really? Is that... *that's* what you want?"

Ziggy dropped his gaze and *blushed,* making me feral. "It's all I can think about..."

I deserved all the gold stars for not immediately flipping his ass over to kickstart the baby-making, but I could hear the hesitation in his tone.

So this *is the thing he needed to work through on his own...*

"Zig." I cupped his handsome face with my hand and gently coaxed him into meeting my gaze. "It's all *I've* been thinking about too... But we don't have to talk about it now, and we definitely don't need to do anything until you're ready. Okay?"

He offered me a shy smile and nodded, and I dissolved my tentacle toy before rolling onto my side so I could kiss his big, stupid face some more.

I could do this all day.

We might have done just that—lazily kissing and rubbing our cum-covered bodies against each other—but if there was anything I'd learned, it was that this space ship couldn't catch a break.

Because a shrill alarm chose that moment to break the comfortable silence.

An alarm coming from the room next door.

Micah had barely sat up before I was dressed and flinging open the door between our rooms.

If Pedro is hurt, someone will die.

There *was* an injury, but it wasn't the Trol. The nanny bot was sprawled on the lava rock floor, halfway to the door, as if its legs had given out while headed for the exit. Closer inspection revealed the wiring connecting its joints had been gnawed through by what appeared to be two rows of sharp fangs.

Of course.

Unfortunately, the perpetrator was long gone, judging by the Pedro-sized hole clawed through the exterior rock wall.

"Holy shit!" Micah stumbled into the room, his Han Solo pants still unbuttoned and his "Y'all Need Science" tee shirt halfway over his head. "Is Pedro—"

"Pedro did this, yes," I sighed, more than a little impressed with the creature. "And now they are loose in Nuclei City."

"Shit," Micah repeated as he kneeled beside the droid and turned off the alarm before getting to work on repairs. "Maybe we *should* have fed them when we got back..."

I cleared my throat. "It's my understanding that if a baby is sleeping, you should let them sleep."

As soon as the damning evidence was out, I wished I could take it back, but I breathed through the discomfort, just like Dr. Micah had taught me.

He knows all my secrets anyway.

Almost all of them...

To his credit, Micah attempted to hide his smile while keeping his gaze on his task. "Oh, yeah? Is that something Zion told you?"

Sigh.

Nothing is sacred in this family.

"Your brother gave me barely usable intel," I huffed. "I did my *own* research."

Again, I tamped down the instinct to flee after such a confession and was rewarded for my efforts.

"You're such a good Space Daddy..." Micah murmured, gazing at me with glassy-eyed lust. "And your competence is so fucking hot."

The feeling is mutual.

The urge to take him back to bed was strong. While my mate had attempted to wipe our collective cum off himself, I could still smell it on him—tempting me to continue marking him as mine. But finding Pedro was the most pressing mission at the moment, especially as I wasn't convinced the Eki wouldn't try to claim the karnilian for themselves if given the chance.

Which gives me an idea...

Albeit a dangerous one.

"Are you able to remove Pedro's shields from afar?" I forced my tone to remain even—to not betray anything. "It would help me track them."

Micah chewed his bottom lip as he stood the repaired droid back on its feet and grabbed the baby sling for himself. "I could, but..." He turned to face me with an unreadable expression. "Do you really think that's a good idea? With how *some people* can sense the karnilian, I mean."

We stared at each other for a moment as I discreetly unleashed a few tendrils to better gauge if *I* was included in this concern.

As I should be.

Of course, nothing escaped my mate's notice. His gaze tracked the movements that *should* have been invisible before meeting mine, and I braced for being called out yet again for my unnecessarily duplicitous actions.

"I think Leeloo can see my aura, Zig."

Wait...

"What do you mean?" I carefully asked.

"They kept looking at the space over my head..." He gestured to demonstrate, although all *I* could see was empty air. "And it got me thinking about how *I* can sometimes tell if someone is a Stellarian or has a Stellarian riding shotgun inside them... Maybe the Eki have similar powers?"

Dread was clawing its way up my throat at the implications. "If Leeloo can see *your* aura, they know exactly what I am."

And they possess the technology to trap me here.

Which they've probably already done...

Needing confirmation before my anxiety consumed me, I opened the front door and stepped outside, immediately scanning the crowd for any sign we were being watched.

Despite Nuclei City's underground setting and unusual architecture, it operated like any intergalactic metropolis and, just like with most major cities, anonymity was almost a given. Countless Eki bustled past—entering and exiting various buildings or shopping at the nearby stalls—but none were paying me any mind.

They don't need to.

The instant I gathered my power, I knew it was futile. Just like how Micah had protected The Knowledge on Kaalanesea with Stellarian-proof shields when the planet was under attack, the Eki had fortified their entire city with an impenetrable barrier of pure power.

There's no way out.

Not unless they let me out...

My only saving grace was, I could still unleash my tendrils if need be, but it was probably only a matter of time before *that* was taken from me as well—since Micah had already demonstrated how easily I could be contained.

How will I protect my mate?

And...

"Is everything okay, Zig?" Micah was suddenly behind me, pressing his palm to my back, somewhat settling me.

"Yes," I lied. "But you need to lower Pedro's shields so we can find them and get them back on the Lodger."

Then, I can blast a way out of here.

"You got it," he replied, trusting me without question. "Okay, his shields are lowered."

He didn't need to tell me. A wave of almost suffocating power washed over me—*called* to my more primal instincts—sharpening my focus, promising me everything I'd ever wanted....

"Zig?" Micah dropped his hand, his voice wavering with uncertainty.

"This way," I growled, stalking in the direction of my prey, knowing my stellar collision would follow.

The Eki we passed continued to ignore us—or at least, they *pretended* to.

They know.

They all know.

Stellarians *were* rightfully feared, but we were ambush predators. Our supremacy lay in our ability to remain undetected within our vessels until it was too late. If this element of surprise was eliminated, we were more easily thwarted or captured. The first time Micah had mentioned seeing my tendrils—and again when he'd identified a Stellarian in the wild—unnerved me, but I trusted my mate implicitly.

Everyone else, not so much.

Most species didn't possess the technology to kill us, but with what I'd already seen of the Eki's powers, I wouldn't put it past them to be one of the few.

Breathe, Ziggy...

I couldn't seem to slow my racing heart or my panting breaths. I felt raw and exposed, like an open wound on a fragile skinsuit before it healed, with no means to force this feeling away. Dr. Micah would tell me to "lean into it"—to start by identifying my emotions.

Panic.

Helplessness.

Vulnerability.

Everything I hate.

"I've got you, Zig," Micah whispered as we finally left the city limits, and I could have *wept* with the relief that washed over me—from his words, his calming presence, and the lack of watchful eyes.

Now to find the karnilian.

I mean... the Trol.

It wasn't farmland we'd reached, but a series of lava tubes, burrowing deeper into the bedrock in various directions. I could easily sense which one Pedro had traveled down and, luckily, they seemed to have *stopped* moving, which would make retrieving them easier.

Since I can't fucking star hop.

Micah's high tech glasses had night vision to rival mine, so I knew the lack of light wouldn't be a problem. We entered the nearly pitch-black tunnel and continued in a silence that weighed heavier with each step, like a ticking clock counting down the seconds until my talkative mate couldn't take it any longer.

"Zig, are you sure we're going the right way—"

"Of course I'm sure!" I barked, sharper than I meant to, but my tone didn't discourage the one creature in all the galaxies who could match me.

"How do you know?" Micah asked, quieter this time, abruptly stopping in his tracks.

Fuck.

I stopped as well, because even with the karnilian mindlessly dragging me forward, the invisible string connecting me to my stellar collision was stronger.

"Because I can smell them, the same as when I track you," I lied again.

I lied, because the thought of Micah keeping me away from Pedro felt like a tendril to my borrowed heart.

"Fine." My stellar collision turned away too fast for me to properly read his expression, although the spike of anguish in our bond was crystal clear. "Let's just find our baby."

Our baby.

He wants that too...

Confessing my deepest desires to my mate earlier had been shockingly painless. It shouldn't have been a surprise, because there was always unconditional acceptance waiting for me when it came to my mate.

The worst part was knowing the same would happen in this instance. I should simply *tell* Micah what was troubling me about Pedro, because he wouldn't judge. If anything, he would offer a solution—*multiple* solutions, probably along with his support. Yet I still couldn't bring myself to admit how much control this ridiculous gemstone had over me.

It's making me weak.

A Stellarian is never weak.

With a growl, I stalked onward, fueled by the familiar well of self-loathing bubbling up to the surface.

> *"Karnilian conquers planets. At least, it has the potential to... in the right hands."*

Or the wrong ones...

Like me.

That feeling of worthlessness only grew when we rounded the corner to find Pedro perched on a pile of rubble as if nothing were amiss. I took a step forward but paused when Micah *immediately* reactivated their shields.

He knows.

Of course, he knows...

Again, we stared at each other, each of us refusing to be the first to name the issue, refusing to communicate.

I. Fucking. Hate. It.

"Pspsps…" Micah called, patting the baby sling he was wearing to encourage the creature to go to *him* instead of *me*.

It's probably for the best.

"What now?" I asked, partly to break the tension, but mostly because I *needed* him to step up and take control of the situation.

In case he needs to take control of *me*.

Please.

Micah arranged Pedro in the sling before glancing around. "Well, I was hoping to continue my training with Leeloo, but I'm getting the feeling…"

His voice trailed off as something behind me caught his eye. I instinctively spun, preparing to unleash my tendrils if necessary—ready to protect what was *mine*.

Both of them.

My brow furrowed to find nothing there, but Micah hurried past me, activating the headlamp feature on his glasses to illuminate the tunnel wall.

"Holy shit!" he whispered, and Pedro chittered in response, as if also excited about the discovery. "Look, Zig—*cave paintings!*"

Cave paintings weren't what I would call *rare* on other planets—climate and conflict dependent, of course—but they were generally only found in societies that valued creative expression and the preservation of accurate history over destructive supremacy and one-sided political narratives.

Hence why they are *so rare on Earth.*

C. ROCHELLE

And Stellaria...

Given what we knew of the Eki, I wasn't surprised to find them here. If nothing else, their existence proved just how long this species had lived underground. What else this discovery provided was a conversation starter—a way to redirect my scientifically-minded mate to safer waters than the proverbial elephant in the room.

The Trol in the lava tube, I should say.

I moved closer, feeling my anxiety lessen simply from having *both* these creatures in close proximity once again.

"What do you see..." I began, trailing off as the pictures came into view.

The scene before me sent a cold shiver down my spine. A large blue sphere dotted with green continents floated in a sea of stars. Farther down the wall were crude renditions of humanoid figures and the unmistakable arrival of *Lacertus* to their primitive world.

This much I already knew, thanks to similar discoveries on Earth. What caught my eye, however, were the starry auras hovering over certain Earthlings, spreading outward like invisible strings—like *tendrils*—back in time to what were apparently the *original* invaders to my stellar collision's home planet.

The Eki.

The mind-blowing discovery we'd just stumbled upon temporarily distracted me from Ziggy's ongoing emotional constipation.

Dr. Micah will *be bringing it up at our next session.*

Of course, it wasn't news to me that the *Lacertus*—along with Stellarians—invaded Earth once upon a time. My eldest brother turned into an apparently 'miniature' version of the oversized lizards when in supe form, and we now knew where *that* DNA came from. If the cave painting's timeline was to be believed, the Eki touched down on Earth *before* the *Lacertus* did, but it wasn't clear what they had to do with the events that followed.

Were they trying to protect Earth from the others?

Or... were they the ones we needed protection from...?

"We *need* to get off this planet, sunshine." Ziggy's voice in my ear startled me from my thoughts. "I can't—"

There was a hint of emotion in his tone—in our bond—that I rarely witnessed from my unflappable Space Daddy.

Fear.

"Are you... okay?" I switched off my headlamp and turned to face him, unsure what had spooked my man.

"No. I'm not," he replied, surprising me yet again with his honesty.

Since I know he's keeping something from me...

Pedro wriggled their top half out of the baby sling and reached for their favorite space dad, but before I could intervene, *Ziggy* leaped away.

What...

"If the Eki can *see* you have a piece of me inside you..." he pointed accusingly at the cave painting with a shaking finger, "then they know what *I* am!"

Is... that what he's upset about?

I suddenly felt like the biggest jerk in all the galaxies. I'd been suspecting Ziggy might be more invested in the karnilian inside Pedro than the Trol themself. Meanwhile, my ambush predator was legitimately losing his shit over whether the Eki could sniff him out.

"Zig, I need you to breathe." I stepped closer and placed my palms on his chest, knowing it helped. "Even if the Eki *are* aware you're a Stellarian, it doesn't mean they see you as a threat."

I hope.

"They don't need to!" he shouted, but I held my ground, knowing it wasn't *me* he was angry at. "This entire city is shielded. I can't... I can't *star hop*, Micah. Not to the surface, not even from here to the ship. I... We are *trapped* here!"

I had *never* seen Ziggy like this—not when he'd 'failed' his mission on Earth to capture Theo, not even when his entire worldview imploded upon discovering the truth about Astrum Force Command. This wasn't just concern over his powers being stifled. Zig was *triggered* and in danger of descending into a full-blown panic attack if I didn't step in quickly.

It's time for Commander Babygirl to take control.

"I don't believe the Eki created the shields to keep *you* in," I calmly stated, desperately wanting him to focus on the facts. "It's probably how they protect their city in general—"

"From Stellarians," he interrupted, crossing his arms, apparently not too scared to stop being stubborn as fuck.

"From *anyone!*" I exclaimed, throwing my hands into the air. "The shields I made for Pedro are all-purpose protection."

Although, yes, it's effectively Stellarian-proof...

Ziggy scowled, his gaze dropping to Pedro, who chirped and stretched their little pangolin claws in his direction again. This time, Space Daddy allowed them to leap into his arms, and I smiled to see how just having the little creature close seemed to settle him.

Why did I ever think he could hurt our baby?

"Yes, the shields you're able to create—for yourself and others—are quite impressive," Ziggy murmured, scratching behind Pedro's furry ears while they purred. "Unfortunately, everyone on this planet aside from the Trol can also create them, which means *anyone* could trap my tendrils at any moment if they wanted."

"Well, I would never do that—" I began, only to snap my mouth shut.

Because I already did.

Ziggy's gaze snapped to mine, and my heart sank to see the pain in his eyes.

Pain I put there.

"I'm sorry, Zig," I repeated, realizing how badly I'd fucked up. "I should have told Leeloo I didn't want to do it."

"It's fine, Micah," he replied, even though it clearly *wasn't*. "What's done is done."

Fuck, I really fucked up.

I thought back to our family video call, when Theo mentioned how horrific it was to have his tendrils trapped inside him. Dre accomplished *his* torture psychically—which was probably how Uulvin had accomplished it during our visit to *Dionaea*. Granted, Dre and Theo's relationship had a more sado-masochistic flavor than ours, but there had been real emotion behind Theo's words.

Because the last thing a Stellarian, or any supe, wants is to be seen as is weak.

Not being able to access their tendrils or star hop probably felt like losing a limb to a Stellarian. A more accurate comparison would be if someone took away *my* powers completely, leaving me unable to create or be useful—unable to protect those I cared about.

Oh.

That's what this is about.

"Zig…" I began, wanting to soothe him without dismissing his feelings. "You are the baddest bitch around. I know you have my back, and you'd protect Pedro with everything you had—even if that was nothing but your millions of guns!"

The tiniest smile tried to make an appearance, but there was still a dullness in his eyes I didn't know how to fix.

New tactic.

"I used to think a supe's powers were so random, especially when you looked at someone like me or Zion." Glancing over my shoulder, I tracked the moments in ancient history when various aliens landed on my planet before facing him again. "Now we know better with big bro, but what about me?"

I want to know the truth.

Ziggy sighed and nodded, already agreeing to my unspoken request to continue my training with Leeloo.

But that's not what I'm getting at.

"What the Eki can do—what I have the *potential* to do—is so incredibly tempting to learn, but I would *never* choose what *I* want over your comfort."

"Micah." Ziggy's stern Space Daddy voice had returned. "I *want* you to learn more about yourself, especially as your potential is limitless. This stop on our journey isn't about me.

I'm simply not... feeling like myself lately, and clearly, I'm not handling it well."

Sweet danger baby.

I pushed up on my toes to deliver a kiss to his kissable lips. "Okay, how 'bout this? I need to at least learn how to dissolve shields, so we can free Uulvin's sibling from the *Lacertus,* right? That would also be a handy skill to have in case anyone gets the foolish idea about putting unauthorized shields around what belongs to *me.*"

Because you're mine.

As usually happened when Commander Babygirl took the wheel, Zig straightened to attention like the good little soldier he was. I'd be lying if I said it didn't give me a thrill, because it was probably the only time he'd shown deference to *anyone* outside of his work with Astrum Force.

Who wouldn't *want all that power at your fingertips?*

"Yes." He slowly nodded before offering me a brave smile. "You being able to dissolve another's shields *would* make me feel better..."

But...

With a sharp inhale, I realized what he *wasn't* saying, the reassurances he still needed from me.

To not hurt him again.

"I promise I won't ever trap you with shields again." I swallowed thickly, blinking back tears I hoped he couldn't see.

"Unless you need to," he added quietly, that awful dullness creeping into his tone again.

"I can't imagine there *ever* being a reason for me to *need* to trap you," I scoffed, internally chastising myself for thinking otherwise. "We both know I need my bad bitch mercenary at my back."

Finally, a real smile lit up his handsome face, even in the dark. "I'll always have your back, sunshine."

Grinning wildly, I snapped a few photos of the cave paintings before taking his hand and leading him back toward Nuclei City. "I know you do, and I appreciate you compromising on this. *I'm* not getting nefarious vibes from Leeloo and the other Eki, but I also trust your intuition, so let's just be vigilant—together. Keep our enemies close and all that."

Ziggy was quiet for so long, I assumed that was the end of it, but when the city came into view at the end of the lava tube, he stopped walking and turned to face me.

"I'm honestly not sure if there *are* nefarious vibes, Micah. All I know is *something* feels off about this mission—this entire situation—but I can't identify what is setting off my... intuition." He dropped his gaze. "Like I said, I'm not feeling like myself lately. I'm... distracted and losing my touch—"

"You are *not* losing your touch," I lovingly scolded. "It might just be because of Pedro."

"What?!" he hissed, glancing up at me in alarm.

Silly Space Daddy.

So opposed to emotions.

"Priorities change when kids come along, Zig," I gently explained. "I've seen it with Zion and my sister Rose, and some of my older cousins. Unless you're a total asshole like

291

my parents, who were only interested in what their kids could do for *them,* it's not surprising that your focus might be a little more fractured than usual."

My man looked like he was going to legitimately throw up, so I backed off, taking his hand again and guiding him onward.

"C'mon, Space Daddy," I laughed, hoping to lighten the mood. "Let's increase my bad bitchery by a few points and then aim for the stars."

"And if the Eki won't let us leave?" Ziggy growled.

I shrugged, trying for nonchalance. "Then we'll just blast our way out of here."

Ziggy nodded. "That was my plan as well."

Of course it was.

"See," I teased, giving him a poke while Pedro chittered in approval. "We make a great team."

He smiled tightly, keeping his gaze locked on the city ahead. "Yes, we do."

30

MICAH

Back in the city, we stopped at the first market we saw to grab ingredients for dinner. I found it fascinating how all the fresh produce had been grown locally—and *underground*—but Ziggy was too on edge to share my nerdy enthusiasm for subterranean gardening.

He'll get it once I set up some hydroponics in the Lodger...

I was incredibly grateful my man had shared what was bothering him earlier, although I wished I could just erase his anxiety so we could move on. Unfortunately, that wasn't how this worked. What we needed to do was work through it together—continue to *communicate,* even if talking about feelings was Ziggy's least favorite thing.

Too bad it's my favorite thing!

Thanks to our discovery in the lava tubes, I now wasn't sure if the Eki could understand American English—our usual go-to secret language while in the company of other aliens. So somehow, against all odds, I managed to hold in *all* my thoughts on the situation until we returned to our rooms.

293

Seriously, gimme those gold stars.

"Some of this stuff must have come from other planets, huh?" I awkwardly segued as we spread out our purchases on the kitchen island. "Like... I recognize this can of Who Hash from the bazaar on Stellaria."

Ziggy breezed past my Dr. Seuss reference—probably because he didn't get it—and glanced at the can in my hand. "Yes, hatini comes from Kaalanesea. You enjoyed a homemade version of it the night we spent there, remember?"

That was *not* what I remembered from our night on Kaalanesea, but I wanted to keep our conversation on track.

We can't just be fucking all the time, sheesh.

"I wonder if traveling to other planets is the reason why no one here has been paying us too much attention," I mused, fiddling with the cooktop to boil some water.

Ziggy scowled down at the vegetables he was slicing—with his tendrils, of course. "Or they were *pretending* to ignore us."

Sigh.

While I understood *why* he felt paranoid, I needed him to center himself by refocusing on the facts.

"I dunno, Zig." I moved closer, wrapping my arms around his waist from behind. "We did get *some* side-eye today, but the vibes were more vague curiosity than horrified confusion. My hypothesis is that while the Eki might *know* about Earthlings—might know about our shared history, whatever that is—they just might have never seen one up close before. I mean, we're probably the first ones to ever set foot on their planet."

My man hummed thoughtfully as one iota of tension left his hot bod. "Perhaps they learned about Earth from The Knowledge... while trading with the Kaalas for Who Hash and Roast Beast."

And this is why we're getting space married.

I gave him a squeeze, partly to reward him for humoring the Seussian but also to stop him from escaping.

Since he's not gonna like what I say next.

"I want to ask Leeloo about the cave paintings, Zig."

As expected, he tried to shake me off, but I was one of eight siblings with an insane center of gravity. Nobody could match my pro wrestling-level Nelson hold—especially a Stellarian who couldn't star hop. I knew it wasn't fair to take advantage of his temporary disadvantage, but we *needed* to discuss this.

And I play to win.

Ziggy glared at me over his shoulder, big mad he'd been owned. "I don't think that's wise, Micah. In situations where you don't know what your opponent knows, it's always best to feign ignorance."

I glared back. "Like how you decided to not tell the Eki that Uulvin sent us."

Decided without me, I should say.

"That was because I'm not sure who to trust!" he snapped before sighing and dropped his head forward. "I trust *you,* sunshine. Only you."

I released him and leaned back against the countertop, crossing my arms as he turned to face me. "Last I checked, you also trust Honnor and Bron, and our family back on Earth. And that's good you trust me, but we still need to operate as a *team*. Each of us can step up and lead when we need to, but we're still partners. Got it?"

He nodded in agreement, and again, I felt a shiver of satisfaction at how this terrifying creature was deferring to *me*.

Who knew I had Dommy Mommy vibes?

"I know it's hard to believe, but I *can* keep my mouth shut if I need to." I chuckled, grabbing the chopped veggies from the island to add to the pot. "I'll test the waters a bit during my next training session—see what Leeloo knows before I decide to ask about the cave paintings... Feign ignorance, like the experts say."

That got a smile out of him, and we continued cooking in comfortable silence. Ziggy insisted on being the one to feed Pedro, so I quickly ate my hatini and stew before patching the wall in the next room. Then, I checked the repairs I'd made to poor SWOL-E's wiring before we put the Trol down to sleep in the baby sling.

Zig and I spent the evening cuddling in bed—kissing and chatting while he resonated and I played my *Trumpet of the Swan* harp until my eyelids grew too heavy to keep serenading my man anymore.

Who knows if I'm even in tune.

The next thing I knew, I was waking up to discover our furbaby sprawled across Ziggy's bare chest, snoozing away. When I peeked over the cozy pair, I spied a brand new, Pedro-sized hole, this time in the wall separating our rooms.

Why the hell didn't SWOL-E's alarm go off?

Maybe I should create shields around the nanny bot...

A knock on the door had me nearly falling off the bed, convinced an army of Eki had come for us.

"It's Leeloo." Ziggy calmly announced, carefully readjusting Pedro in his arms as he gracefully stood, all while keeping his gaze locked on the door.

Then, he unleashed his tendrils.

"What are you doing?" I hiss-whispered, stumbling into my pants and snatching a clean-ish tee from my bag before yanking it over my head. "Put those things away!"

He made an unbothered sound but faded his tendrils into the ether. Unfortunately, *I* could still see the shimmery aura surrounding them, which meant Leeloo might be able to as well.

"Be there in a minute!" I called out in the trade language. "Just let me—"

Just let me try to get this situation under control.

I gestured wildly at Zig's starry katanas as I inched closer to the door, but apparently, my man had once again gone rogue.

Stellarians are such shit stirrers!

"Come in!" he called out, smirking like the devil, and my stomach dropped to my nuts when the door swung wide.

Eek!

The Eki glided into the room, shimmery robes shimmering, but froze when their hooded gaze fell on Ziggy.

"Hey, Leeloo!" Ziggy cheerfully waved, flashing the same charming smile he used to give to the cameras during Death-ball tournaments. "Is it time for more training?"

It suddenly became clear what he was doing, other than giving me a heart attack. Zig was feigning ignorance— making it look like we didn't know *they* knew he was a Stellarian while also calling the Eki's bluff.

Since, judging by the tension in this room, they can see his tendrils just fine.

"Yes," Leeloo finally replied, continuing to watch him intently, and rightfully so, since he was out of his goddamn mind. "However, it would be best if My-kuh trained alone with me today."

EEK!

It was Ziggy's turn to freeze. "Where he goes, I go—" he growled, all faux friendliness gone.

"No," the Eki sternly shut him down. "My-kuh will come with me while *you* stay here to ensure the child doesn't escape again."

Okay, so Leeloo is actually the Dommy Mommy, got it.

Ziggy looked like he was about to Hulk out, but Leeloo's words were having the opposite effect on me. If the Eki hadn't taken advantage of our separation from Pedro yesterday to capture the creature, they weren't interested in the Trol, or the karnilian.

"It's all right, Zig," I cut in, using my best Commander Baby-girl tone but sticking to the trade language for transparency's sake. "I need to discuss a few things with Leeloo anyway."

Despite Ziggy's paranoia, the Eki weren't giving me shady vibes. I knew there was a risk with me going alone, but I wanted to play my cards differently than my stellar collision would.

Which means I need to handle this on my own.

A blast of concern shot through our bond as Zig met my gaze from across the room.

You trust me, remember?

My Space Daddy was a pro at appearing unreadable, but I saw the moment he relaxed—the moment he deferred to me *for real.*

Thank you.

Leeloo must have also sensed the shift, inclining their head respectfully. "I promise I will return your mate safe and sound, Zig-ee."

The best my overprotective Stellarian could offer was a tight smile in return, but then Pedro stirred in his arms, and his gaze dropped to the Trol.

"Oh!" I took a step toward them. "Pedro probably needs to eat—"

"Come, My-kuh. Zig-ee will take care of it," Leeloo interrupted. "Your mate is an excellent provider."

I could *feel* Space Daddy panic through our bond, even though that fool had already admitted he wanted space babies of our own. Still, I held my tongue and obediently followed my teacher outside.

"Forgive me for bringing up the subject again," Leeloo whispered once we started walking down the street. "I could not resist seeing Zig-ee's reaction."

Okay, so the Eki are shit stirrers too.

"He'll survive," I huffed a laugh. "I feel better with him watching Pedro anyway, since they *did* escape yesterday..."

I was totally leading the witness here, but I wanted to know what Leeloo knew before deciding how to proceed.

The Eki hummed. "Yes, I was informed about the hole in the exterior wall of your lodging—although, it seems *someone* used their powers to repair it."

Ugh.

While I was relieved Leeloo's intel of yesterday's adventure was limited to the structural damage we'd caused, I was still slightly embarrassed at being a bad houseguest.

"Yeah..." I rubbed the back of my neck. "I did my best, and I'll fix the, uh, new hole when I get back..."

Leeloo belly laughed, and it was such a *human* sound, I couldn't help joining in.

"The little one certainly keeps you busy," they murmured, gesturing for me to follow them through a bustling courtyard to a vacant table built from the same rock as everything else.

Wanting to talk in a common area was promising—unless they were planning a public execution. Banishing the morbid thought from my mind, I took one of the seats while Leeloo sat at the other. Another Eki appeared almost immediately with two steaming mugs of *something* in hand, and I realized we were seated at their version of an outdoor cafe. Several of the surrounding tables were occupied, mostly by couples or entire families, with everyone wearing the same glittering robes. I smiled when I spotted a pack of smaller Eki chasing each other around the courtyard while the adults talked, fascinated to see kid-versions of these mysterious aliens.

I wonder if they look like humans under there.

If they look like... me.

Even with *my* lack of a filter, I was aware this would be a rude question. For all I knew, the Eki wore robes for religious reasons, or because other species weren't supposed to look at them.

"Do you have many visitors to Nuclei City?" I awkwardly asked, unsure how else to break the ice.

"No," Leeloo bluntly replied, staring at me from the depths of their robe. "We do not allow outsiders in."

Eek.

"Oh..." I trailed off, glancing around to find many of the Eki had stopped their conversations to watch ours instead. "Soooo... you don't consider *Earthlings* to be outsiders?"

Leeloo took a sip of their drink, but I left mine untouched, no longer feeling as confident about handling this alone as I had a few minutes ago.

Ziggy will know if I'm in trouble, right?

"The Eki and Earthlings *do* have a history together, yes..." Leeloo mused. "But you already know that, don't you? From the cave paintings you discovered yesterday."

My instincts were screaming at me to raise my shields, but there wasn't really a point when this space wizard could dissolve them. Plus, I stubbornly wanted to continue this conversation in good faith, even if I was possibly about to be killed for my naivety.

I cleared my throat, noticing some Eki had stepped closer, watching our exchange like a pack of predators circling their prey. "Y-yeah, we saw some cave paintings," I mumbled, tamping down the urge to unleash my mechanical tendrils in case I was attacked. "Pedro wandered down a lava tube, so we had to find—"

"And how exactly did you find them, My-kuh?" Leeloo asked. "Or, should I say, how did *Zig-ee* locate the Trol?"

Ah, fuck.

Now the space cat was out of the bag, and I assumed lying would only make things worse.

"Ziggy has a really good sense of smell," I replied, which wasn't a lie but also wasn't the whole truth.

Because now I don't know who to trust.

Leeloo stared at me in silence for a full minute before making an amused sound. "Is *that* how you think your *powerless* mate tracked down one of the most coveted creatures in the galaxy?"

Wait.

"What do you mean?" I muttered, frowning as my previous suspicions reared their ugly heads.

Ziggy doesn't care about the stone...

Does he?

"You are correct," the Eki continued, as if I hadn't spoken. "Stellarians *do* have an acute sense of smell."

All the fucks.

This deception did *not* look good on our part, and with the Stellarians' reputation—which wasn't unfounded—I wouldn't be surprised if Leeloo assumed *we* were the ones with nefarious intent.

Or... just Ziggy...

I opened my mouth to speak, to desperately try to smooth things over, but then I felt the walls close in around me.

More specifically, a shield.

Leeloo tutted as the other Eki formed a tight circle around our table. "I hope you do not mind the precaution, My-kuh. We cannot have your mate tracking *you* down—not until we've finished our talk."

31
ZIGGY

Micah had only been gone for a few minutes when I felt his anxiety spike, but I refrained from charging into battle on his behalf..

He told you he could handle this, Ziggy.

It was a struggle, but I refocused as best I could on feeding Pedro leftover hatini, too distracted to care when they threw their spoon on the floor, as usual.

A natural behavior of certain species at this age, apparently.

My thoughts drifted to the concept of *Micah* as an Earthling child. Unsurprisingly, the Salahs had barely any family photos in their home while I was there, aside from professional portraits lining the hallways, but Micah displayed more candid snapshots in his bedroom, taped above his desk.

I knew this because as my mission on Earth drew to a close— and Micah and I had grown closer—I'd started sneaking into his bedroom in the middle of the night in my true form. At the time, I'd credited my overwhelming *need* to be close to him as simple curiosity, and the evidence supported this belief. When I wasn't watching him sleep, I focused on examining the sentimental possessions he had on display, determined to decode *why* I was drawn to this seemingly random Earthling.

My stellar collision all along.

We'd learned the truth about stellar collisions during our first adventure together and saw this harmony in action in the rebel hideout on the moon. Thanks to the different auras of various True Stellarians, Micah was able to identify which had taken full control of their skinsuits versus those coexisting with an equally aware host.

While I'd only melded my consciousness with Micah's once since then, I was happy with our current arrangement. The piece of my core that remained inside him served its purpose by allowing me to get a better read on his feelings—when he wasn't purposefully burying them.

I'm one to talk, I suppose...

Due to the piece being so small, I couldn't read his thoughts. Even if I *could,* however, I most likely wouldn't take advantage of this unfettered access out of respect for his privacy.

I do have some *morals.*

Those morals were hard to remember at the moment, as I anxiously awaited my mate's return. Micah may have insisted *he* wasn't suspicious of the Eki, but that didn't change the fact my most precious treasure was currently alone and unguarded among creatures *I* didn't fully trust.

Having Pedro under my watchful eye was appeasing me to some extent. Despite the fangs and other defensive enhancements I hadn't seen since I'd cornered the Trol in the air vent, they *were* just a baby. A baby who needed my protection.

A baby who could make me extremely powerful...

Stop it, Ziggy.

As with every time these intrusive thoughts crept in, I tried to put as much distance between myself and the karnilian as possible. With how small our rooms were, the best option was to step outside, but I didn't go far. I left the door cracked as I leaned against the door frame—not only to keep an eye on Pedro, but discourage them from making another hole in the wall to reach me.

Maybe they could gnaw through the shields trapping us in this city...

My gaze lifted to the ceiling high above us, extending my powers to subtly push against the invisible barrier, testing for weaknesses. Unsurprisingly, there were none, which begrudgingly impressed me.

Who is keeping the shields in place?

Leeloo? Or is it a collective effort?

My thoughts wandered to an offhand comment Honnor had made when we first met on *Apotelesma*. It was in reference to their fellow True Stellarians—how they'd all discovered their true purpose, not just by coexisting with their vessels, but by tuning in to each other.

They called this connection "the collective well."

There was a similar concept on Earth called the *collective unconscious,* coined by the Swiss psychotherapist Carl Jung. It referred to the matrix of objective experiences shared generationally by all humans, as opposed to the subjective experiences of one's personal life. He claimed it was the reason anthropologists discovered universal archetypes and mythologies in civilizations that otherwise had no physical contact with any others.

I had noticed a similar phenomenon during my travels among various alien species, but with how common trade between planets was, I'd always assumed *that* was how stories traveled as well.

What if certain species are more psychically connected than that?

I thought of the first time my resonance was sung to me—by Theo when we finally met on Earth. While I was incredibly overwhelmed at the time, I later marveled at how I *recognized* a tune I had never heard before.

A Stellarian's resonance was unique to them, a combination of their makers' resonances being passed down to their offspring. Stellar collisions were your perfect match, but everyone on the same wavelength also responded to the harmony of the family unit—sometimes in a platonically affectionate way, sometimes as something more.

I'd been told unrelated Stellarians could *hear* another's resonance, even if they didn't respond to it, which gave me an idea for the present moment.

Perhaps a little experiment is needed.

First, I scanned the hoods of the Eki passing me by, confirming Micah's observation that they seemed more interested in their own lives than mine. Then, I slowly allowed my resonance to build in my chest—starting with the low purr I demonstrated while in bed with my mate.

I noticed a few Eki closest to me cocking their heads inquisitively, but the evidence was inconclusive. So I increased the volume and intensity to what I would use to catch Micah's attention across the room.

This caused *more* Eki to turn and stare directly at me.

How is this possible?!

I had been too panicked yesterday to fully absorb what the cave paintings implied, thanks to discovering that Leeloo—the entire planet—knew I was a Stellarian. Now, I had no choice but to consider what we'd seen. If the timeline was to be believed, the Eki had landed on Earth prior to the *Lacertus* and Stellarians, which suggested *their* DNA may be part of the supe soup.

This wouldn't have surprised me. Micah desperately wanted to continue his training with Leeloo because he suspected the similarities between their powers went deeper than pure coincidence.

It was closer to synchronicity.

Another pillar of Jung's core concepts.

I abruptly stopped resonating, and the Eki who'd noticed continued about their day. This supported Micah's belief that they meant me no harm, despite knowing what I was. Either way, I was still unsettled while also aware enough to know a large part of my restlessness was because I was separated from my mate.

Another experiment will help.

This time, I resonated from the piece of myself within Micah, hoping to *internally* remind him of our connection, wherever he was. I expected a comforting squeeze in return, but the panicked pull I felt instead had me immediately realizing something was wrong.

With a growl, I unleashed countless tendrils—fully visible—uncaring how the locals might react. Those in my path leaped out of the way, but no one countered with an attack as I snaked my way through the streets in search of what was mine.

Only to not register a single trace of my mate.

Why can't I track him?!

My receptors being blocked reminded me of when Micah put up his shields in self-defense. This was all the confirmation I needed that he was in danger, and the only solution was to blast our way out of here.

With pleasure.

Maintaining an air of outward calm, I retracted my tendrils and slipped back inside our room to quickly pack up our belongings. Then, I placed Pedro in the nanny bot's baby sling and led the droid back to my ship before leaving them both in the cockpit behind the lockdown doors.

Which are hopefully strong enough to keep the Trol from escaping.

That no Eki had attempted to block me from boarding the Lodger implied Leeloo specifically, along with a small collection of minions, perhaps, were who I was up against. I couldn't be sure if their intent was to separate me from my stellar collision indefinitely, but the solution was obvious.

I'll simply smoke them out.

Resolutely climbing into the gunner's cockpit, I aimed for the closest uninhabited pile of rocks before disintegrating them with a rocket-powered grenade.

Just a warning shot.

As I'd hoped, this *finally* got the Eki's collective attention. I smirked as they all began scrambling for cover, although *why* they still weren't engaging in combat remained a mystery, as Leeloo suddenly appeared with a frightened looking Micah in tow.

Appeared out of thin air.

As if they'd star hopped...

"Ziggy, stop!" Micah shouted, his voice muffled between the cockpit dome and his shields. "I'm fine. Leeloo just needed to contain me long enough to talk."

Contain him?!

All at once, I realized the Eki had turned Micah's own technology against him, shielding my mate against his will, trapping his powers inside a prison of inorganic material.

No.

They're trapping the piece of me *in there.*

I grabbed the intercom mouthpiece and snarled into it. "Release his shields, Leeloo."

"No," the Eki replied defiantly.

Oh, you want to play that game?

I pivoted in my seat, aiming the guns at a row of buildings. While I took no pleasure in killing innocent civilians, if it was between them and my mate, I would destroy this entire planet—blast it into oblivion until no one remembered its name.

"Permission to come aboard," Leeloo called out, causing me to pause and remove my finger from the trigger.

That was... unexpected.

I grabbed the mouthpiece again. "Only if Micah comes with you."

The Eki inclined their head. "Of course. We will meet you in the cockpit."

Wait, what?

Without thinking, I star hopped to the cockpit, hoping to arrive before Leeloo got near Pedro.

Unfortunately, they beat me there.

"Ah, so you figured out star hopping *does* work within Nuclei City's shield."

"I..." I glanced down at myself in confusion before glaring at the Eki who'd effortlessly infiltrated my ship.

"You assumed we had stifled your powers," they coolly replied, "instead of considering that the shields over our city might be for *our* protection—against *any* species capable of star hopping."

"Only Stellarians can..." I began before Micah gave me a *look* that successfully silenced me.

Leeloo chuckled. "So quick to argue when, only moments ago, you *witnessed* another species star hopping..." They made an amused sound. "I know you will not want to hear this, Zig-ee, but the Eki were the first to do it."

They were?

I opened my mouth to argue—true to form, apparently—but then closed it again as Honnor's words from days ago flashed in my memory.

> *"Perhaps you shouldn't make assumptions, my child. You know better than most that not everything is as it seems when it comes to alien species."*

Siiiiigh.

"I simply want to talk." Leeloo's tone turned gentle—soothing—but I still wasn't pleased with the terms.

My ship, my rules.

"Remove. Micah's. Shields," I gritted out.

"No," Leeloo sighed, sounding more exhausted than anything. "Before you opened fire on my city, Micah was working on removing the shields himself."

Oh.

My mate had the nerve to look embarrassed, despite his impressive skills. "Yeah... Apparently, *dissolving* shields is part of Eki Powers 101, but I'm struggling over here..."

"Is *that* why I felt your panic?" I carefully asked, accessing the piece of me inside him to gauge his true feelings on the situation.

More embarrassment, but no fear.

Good.

He dropped his gaze. "I started panicking when I realized *we* were the ones behaving like a threat to the Eki, not the other way around. Aaaaand you blowing shit up didn't help."

Not sorry.

"Rational thought is often overshadowed by protective instincts when one's stellar collision is threatened." Leeloo huffed before chuckling self-deprecatingly. "I should know."

Wait.

I crossed my arms. "Next, you'll be telling me the Eki invented stellar collisions."

"Not invented, no... That would be our common ancestor." When I squinted, they cocked their head. "Are you finally understanding, Zig-ee?"

I wasn't. In fact, my thoughts were as confused and jumbled as they had been when Micah and I discovered the truth about Stellarians at The Knowledge.

Not the whole truth, apparently.

"Zig?" Micah's familiar voice cut through my growing anxiety, just as it had then, and when I met his gaze, he smiled encouragingly.

Supporting me, as always.

Unconditionally.

"I *don't* understand," I sighed before nodding at Leeloo. "But I'm willing to... listen."

In the interest of playing nice.

You would think nothing could surprise me at this point when it came to learning about Stellarians, but sharing a common ancestor with the Eki was the most unexpected intel yet.

Assuming it's even the truth...

32
ZIGGY

It was hard not to be suspicious of the alien seated across from me, especially as Micah was within their reach, still struggling to remove the shields they'd trapped him in.

"Ughhhh!" he exclaimed, dropping his head back with a groan. "Just when I think I've got it, I choke..."

Oh, sunshine.

Before I could offer encouragement, Leeloo beat me to it. "I am confident you can do this, My-kuh. Everything you need is already inside you."

Micah's gaze flickered to me before he mumbled, "Yeah... you've both said that."

It wasn't quite what *I* had said, but I wasn't about to share my unique training methods with my opponent.

"So, the Eki can star hop, have stellar collisions, and apparently pick up on resonance." I leaned back in my chair, partly to convey an air of indifference, but mostly so Pedro had

317

enough room to curl up in my lap. "Does that sound about right?"

"You are correct... to a point," Leeloo replied. "Eki can hear a Stellarian's resonance—most likely because we also resonated at one time—but it means nothing to us now. *My* kind identifies our stellar collisions by the pull we feel from our mate... or mates."

That had me sitting up, although I was careful to not displace the Trol. "You have multiple mates?"

Perhaps this is more common than I thought.

"Sometimes." Leeloo shrugged. "It helps with raising children to have more helping hands."

Like an alien polycule...

Now *Micah* was rapt with attention. "And how do the Eki reproduce? I mean... Gah! That was totally inappropriate to ask. *Jesus,* just ignore me..."

Leeloo laughed brightly. "With our tendrils, of course."

And then, to demonstrate their point, they unleashed a half dozen starry tendrils.

Of course, they did.

I didn't bother to hide my annoyance at this latest revelation. "Are the Eki nothing but superior Stellarians, then?"

Micah tried to give me another *look,* but I ignored it. I knew full well my anger was thanks to being raised under the old Astrum Force, with the unarguable narrative that our kind was simply *better* than other alien species.

It's still true.

Mostly.

To their credit, Leeloo didn't seem offended by my tone. "I would not call it *superior*—more like a different branch of evolution. One way to describe Eki might be... fully formed Stellarians."

"Fully formed?" Micah murmured.

The Eki nodded. "Yes. We also possess a starry core, with tendrils branching outward." They undulated theirs, possibly just to piss me off. "However, unlike Stellarians, *we* are permanently embedded in our vessels."

Oh.

My curiosity got the better of me. "If you reproduce with your tendrils and presumably start as novas, how do you become... this?" I gestured at their hooded figure.

Not that we know what you look like.

Leeloo made an amused sound. "Our bodies form around our core after birth, like the *shell* of some other species."

Micah openly gaped at the Eki. "Is *that* why you can create shields? Because it's how you keep your young safe until the vessel has fully developed?"

"Exactly!" Leeloo exclaimed, and I simultaneously appreciated and bristled at the pride in their voice. "Although, even the vessels we have now benefit from this protection. Our shields have always been defensive armor—nothing more."

There's my opening.

"Shields *do* seem to be your specialty," I drawled. "And the skill others are more than happy to pay you for."

The Eki froze and slowly turned to face me. "Our shields are not for sale."

I laughed derisively. "Is that so? Then why were we sent to Ekistron by those who knew of your shields—who have first-hand experience with your supposed 'defensive armor' being used as impenetrable *prisons?*"

Leeloo continued to stare at me, and for one, unnerving moment, I glimpsed two flares of fiery light from deep within their hood—exactly where their eyes would be.

I've faced worse.

"Who did you say sent you here again?" my opponent finally asked in a chilly tone. "A Neluth you met at a Muonova?"

I hesitated, momentarily forgetting which lie I had told when we landed.

Fuck.

"A pair of Kaalas." Micah stepped in to save me, like a true partner. "Although that wasn't exactly the truth."

So much for that.

I actually wasn't mad about my mate's confession. Leeloo was openly suspicious, so offering a half-truth like an olive branch could help smooth things over.

A half-truth for a full one.

"Who do you *think* sent us?" I asked, matching their depth-less stare. "Who would send us to Ekistron knowing we had *this* mysterious creature with us?"

Grabbing Pedro, I held up the squawking Trol for Leeloo to see.

"The creature *you* supposedly have never seen before..." I added, *daring* the Eki to look me in the eye and continue pretending they didn't know what we had in our possession.

In my *possession.*

Leeloo sighed. "That is a Trol. They are extremely rare, and the only source of karnilian—a gemstone said to promise victory to anyone who possesses it. But you know all this already, don't you, Zig-ee?"

"We *do* know..." Micah cautiously cut in, no doubt attempting to diffuse the situation.

Too late.

"I was talking to Zig-ee," Leeloo replied without taking their eyes off me.

"Does the name *Uulvin* mean anything to you?" I deflected— now willing to trade a truth to hide a deeper lie.

I could feel Micah's anxiety spiking, but I was too invested in dominating this exchange to stop.

A Stellarian never backs down.

Unfortunately, neither did an Eki. "Uulvin is a Hydrassian—a great and powerful seer. Well..." They chuckled darkly. "They *were* great and powerful once, until we took half of that power away."

"So we've heard," I shot back. "Now you know who sent us here. And *why.*"

"I do." Leeloo retracted their tendrils and rose from their chair before smoothing their *almost* human hands down the front of their robes. "And it appears our training is done."

"Wait!" Micah cried out, but the Eki had already dissolved the shields surrounding him with a wave of their hand. "I was... I was so close... "

"You were..." the Eki murmured before focusing on me again. "You *both* were, but I cannot help you. I refuse to aid anyone blinded by lies the way you are. I suggest you leave before I am forced to deal with you the same way the Hydrassians needed to be dealt with."

"Gladly," I growled. "And *you* are no longer welcome on my ship. I suggest you open the shields trapping us here before I blast my way out of this city and take a few of your buildings with me."

"Zig!" Micah scolded before standing so suddenly, his chair almost fell over. "Leeloo, *please*... We just want to get Pedro home. Uulvin told us their missing sibling knew where the Trols' planet was—that the only way to find it was—"

"To free Uuktar from the *Lacertus,* hmm?" The Eki turned to face Micah, as if I wasn't a threat at all.

Oh, but I am.

I'm your worst nightmare.

When Micah nodded, Leeloo sighed yet again. "I would advise you both to abandon this mission, but it does not seem as if your stellar collision is *truly* ready to listen."

"Not to someone who's feeding us lies of their own," I growled, rising to stand, relishing how I towered over them in this form.

The Eki sniffed, as undaunted by my bold accusations as any Stellarian would be.

"Not everything is as it seems when it comes to certain species," they continued, startling me with how closely they echoed Honnor's words. "Enjoy facing your greatest enemy, Zig-ee."

I will.

With a curt nod, Leeloo star hopped away, and I *felt* the shields surrounding Nuclei City start to dissipate, releasing us from this prison.

Thank fuck.

Micah slowly circled the table. "Give me Pedro."

"What?" I snapped, still agitated over the confrontation and itching to be gone from this wretched planet.

"I can take care of Pedro," he replied, oddly careful, "while you fly us out of here."

I nodded and handed the creature to my mate. "Yes. Get them settled for our journey and then meet me in the cockpit."

Micah abruptly looked away. "I-I actually think I'm gonna lie down. I'm not feeling so hot..."

I frowned, unleashing a few tendrils to determine if Leeloo's shields had somehow injured him, only to register...

Nothing.

"Very well," I muttered, confused why I couldn't get a read on my mate. "Then I will come meet *you* in the bedroom once I've set a course for Lacertus."

He swallowed thickly and nodded. "Okay..."

Something was wrong, but my first priority was getting the Lodger out of here before the Eki changed their mind.

It was a tense few minutes as we passed through the enormous hatch, and several more before Ekistron was nothing but a glowing white dot in the distance.

Good riddance.

I charted a path to Lacertus before switching to autopilot. It would take us at least until tomorrow to reach the planet, which meant I had plenty of time to attend to my stellar collision. With one last check on our coordinates, I star hopped to the bedroom.

At least, I *attempted* to.

I grunted as an invisible barrier blocked my path, tossing me to the gangway floor between the bedroom and kitchen instead of allowing me to reach my destination.

What in Stellaria's name...?

"Micah?" I hesitantly called out. "Are you... Is everything all right?"

I could hear him shuffling closer on the other side of the bedroom door before silence fell. It stretched on so long, I almost repeated my question, but then he spoke.

"Pedro and I are gonna sleep in here tonight, Zig," he replied in a flat tone. "Just let me know when we land."

"Why are you suddenly interested in co-sleeping?" I asked, mystified as to why *now* was the time to try out a new parenting technique.

Micah sighed, loud enough that I could hear it. "If you really wanna know, I need some space for tonight, okay? I'm not happy with how things just went down out there."

"With how Leeloo lied about their powers, you mean?" I huffed, annoyed all over again.

We should never have set foot on Ekistron.

The bedroom door slid open with a mechanical hiss to reveal my mate, but when I stepped forward, I hit his shields again.

"No, Zig," he snapped. "With how *you* just cock-blocked any chance for me to level up *my* powers."

Excuse me?

"That's not what happened!" I exclaimed. "Leeloo had no intention of helping you—of helping *us*. We have a mission to complete—"

"And just *how* are we supposed to complete the mission of freeing Uuktar when I can't dissolve shields I didn't fucking create?!" he shouted in reply.

I gaped at my mate, not only because Micah raising his voice to me was a rarity, but because his continued blindness to his own greatness was baffling.

How can I make you see what I see?

"Micah." I spread my hands beseechingly. "I *know* you can do it. All it will take is—"

"What? *What* will it take, Ziggy?" He stepped forward, soft brown eyes flashing dangerously. "The Force? Some magical Stellarian pixie dust? Thoughts and prayers?"

You believing in yourself the way I believe in you.

Even without our connection—which was still oddly stifled—I would have registered my mate's emotional pain. The worst part was knowing he thought *I* was the cause of it.

You are *the cause of it, Ziggy.*

"Sunshine..." I trailed off, unsure how to fix this. "You're my stellar collision. It's my responsibility to protect you."

"Yeah, well, it didn't feel like protection," he huffed. "It felt like you were stopping me from becoming as powerful as you."

WHAT?!

"What are you talking about?!" I shouted as shame and terror flooded my system. "You are already more powerful than me. I've told you countless times—you are the most impressive creature in all the galaxies."

Why don't you believe me?

Micah sighed. "You know... I'm starting to think that's just something you came up with so you don't have to tell me how you really feel."

Oh, fuck.

On the one hand, I couldn't fathom how this impressive, *perfect* creature didn't know how I felt about him, but on the other, I knew exactly why he didn't.

"Babygirl." I placed my palm on the shield, wishing he would lower it so I could touch him. "I..."

I...

Why can't I say it?

I saw his face fall as I failed to complete the sentence—failed to express just how deeply I cared for him—and my borrowed heart shattered along with his.

"Goodnight, Ziggy," Micah whispered, back to his impassive mask. "See you tomorrow."

Even though I knew this conversation was over for tonight, I stood in the gangway for a long time after the door closed, mentally replaying everything—the words said and unsaid.

I really fucked this up.

It was only after I returned to the cockpit that I realized the implications of Micah locking Pedro in the bedroom with him.

He was using his shields to protect *both* of them.

From me.

I was *pissed* at Ziggy Andromeda.

For real this time.

The betrayal I'd felt when he left me behind on Marox paled in comparison to the pure *fury* coursing through my veins.

I knew a lot of what I was projecting was my own family baggage getting stirred up again, but it wasn't unfounded. Ziggy *knew*. He knew how I'd been treated by my parents—like I was expendable—and, until now, he had always done his best to make sure I felt *worthy*.

Was it all just an act?

Despite how dismissed they were in the past, my powers *were* useful, and now, I couldn't help but wonder if that was one of the main reasons he'd kept me around for so long.

Don't spiral, Micah.

What Would Space Daddy Do?

Focus on the mission.

While the thought of never seeing Pedro again made me want to cry, I knew the safest place for the Trol would be among their own kind—away from anyone who only wanted to *use* them for what they could provide.

"You and I are more alike than I realized, huh?" I chuckled humorlessly, wishing the translator device allowed me to better communicate with my furbaby.

Pedro chittered in a way that made it seem like they understood before cuddling closer in the sleeping pod.

The sleeping pod I banished Ziggy from last night...

As extra as I was, I never thought I'd be one of *those* queens who kicked their partner out of the house and threw their clothes on the lawn. Even though I *had* kind of locked Ziggy out, I'd still spent the night cuddled up with his gray sweatpants instead of tossing them on the gangway.

I'm so fucking weak for this emotionally constipated alien.

I'd lowered the shields surrounding the bedroom at some point, mostly because it took a lot of energy to maintain, but also just in case Ziggy felt inspired to show up with a midnight grovel-slash-official marriage proposal.

That didn't happen, and I woke up this morning choosing to be big mad about it instead of acknowledging *I'd* been the one to tell that dumbass consent king I needed space.

Whatever.

I'm still pissed.

It wasn't only that he'd overreacted with Leeloo—effectively shutting down my space wizard lessons—but because I was starting to suspect my man was hiding more from me than just his desire to get mpregged.

I don't want to think about what it may be...

My negative thoughts were cut short when Ziggy's phone buzzed on the nightstand—right where he'd left it the entire time we were on Ekistron. I didn't make a habit of snooping, and he rarely used his phone to communicate with anyone anyway, but my curiosity got the better of me.

I deserve a little treat.

What I found were a series of texts from Gabe, all from the past 48 hours, all consisting of ridiculous cat memes and videos.

Okay, but this is adorable.

I knew the psychic supe sent cat content to Balty whenever he felt his older brother's anxiety spike, but I'd always assumed this had something to do with their unique brotherly connection.

Wait a minute...

Grabbing *my* phone, I tapped Gabe's name in my favorite contacts, smiling wide when he picked up on the first ring.

"Hey, cutie," he purred into the line, making my toes curl. "What's up?"

"Hi," I replied before clearing my throat. "Weird question, but... Were you keeping tabs on us the past few days?"

"Yeah," he murmured apologetically. "I'm sorry, dude. I just... I got worried after our family video call and just wanted to make sure you guys weren't in danger."

"You know I don't mind," I huffed before smirking. "How much did you see of our sex toy training session?"

Gabe groaned and laughed self-deprecatingly. "I only hung around for a min' before I peaced out but, dang... You're into some freaky shit huh?"

Pot calling the kettle black.

"Whatever, perv," I cackled, knowing he would never judge my three-pronged tentacle creation. Then, I sobered. "I'm actually calling because I saw the texts you sent Ziggy..."

Gabe sighed. "Yeah, I usually don't get much of a read on him because, you know, he's locked down tighter than Fort Knox... But whatever he's going through made him drop his defenses and... Is he *okay*, Micah?"

I swallowed thickly. "I-I don't know. He told me he's going through some stuff right now but isn't really elaborating on what's bothering him."

Even though I have my suspicions.

I should've known something was wrong with the way Ziggy reacted after entering Pedro's body—especially since it was rare to see my bad bitch mercenary flustered about *anything*. But then the space dads called with intel on Pedro, and the mission kicked into high gear from there.

If only I'd checked in more...

Ziggy *should* have been more open and honest with me, but I knew better than most that trauma could make even the simplest conversation seem impossible. While I preferred not to force my squirrely Stellarian out of his comfort zone until he was ready, this was clearly a situation where Dr. Micah needed to step in.

As soon as I feel like talking to him again.

"Do you want me to..." Gabe interrupted my chaotic thoughts, bringing me back to the conversation at hand.

"Yes!" I blurted out, more than happy to put my personal psychic to work for the greater good. "I mean, if you don't mind..."

Gabe was silent for a good 30 seconds before he sighed again. "He's still got his thoughts secured but, sheesh, his anxiety is through the goddamn roof. Are you..." He cleared his throat. "Are you *safe* with him, Micah?"

"Of course I am," I snapped, harsher than I intended. "Ziggy would never hurt me."

Pedro, on the other hand...

My Earthside bestie chuckled. "Hey, no judgment. Lord knows Theo tried to kill me a couple times before we became official, and he and Dre like to threaten each other as foreplay on the regular. It's all good."

No judgment, but... what?

I decided not to touch any of *that* hot mess in favor of keeping us on track. "Please don't worry about us. Even with all the anxiety he's burying beneath the surface, Ziggy's still taking good care of me... in his overly protective, emotionally stunted, lizard-brained way."

Gabe laughed. "Yeah, that tracks—not just with Stellarians, but supes in general. For real, dude, you're carrying the team here with your emotional IQ." When I huffed, his voice dropped a few octaves. "That's good to hear, though. Someone as sweet as you deserves to be treated sweet."

Omg, staaahp.

"Such a flirt," I teased, feeling one thousand percent better than before I'd called him.

Some may not understand our polycule situation—*hell, we were still figuring it out ourselves*—but it worked for *us,* and that was all that mattered.

Plus, I no longer want to murder Zig.

Win-win!

A knock on the door had me sitting up so fast, Pedro rolled off my chest with an indignant squawk. "Gotta go," I murmured as Gabe answered with his goodbyes. "Space adventure awaits."

Along with a good grovel, I hope.

"Micah?" Ziggy called out, earning a few points for not just barging or star hopping in. "We will be arriving on Lacertus in an hour or so, and I would like to... discuss the plan... *with* you."

That poor idiot is trying his best.

I still fully intended to make him talk, but I also knew Ziggy well enough to understand the reason he hadn't said anything up until now was because he'd still been working through his issues.

Time's up, Space Daddy.

Because partners work through things together.

First, I checked on Pedro's shields then set aside the breakfast tray that had magically appeared outside my Fortress of Solitude this morning. Then, I steeled my spine and walked to the door before sliding it open.

Ziggy was still wearing the same clothes from yesterday and looked noticeably exhausted for someone who didn't need much sleep. I forcibly tamped down the urge to comfort him —to *fix* things for everyone else—and simply stood there, waiting to hear what he had to say.

"I'm so sorry, Micah," he began, which was a good start. "For how I behaved on Ekistron—for ruining your training. I need to think things through before reacting, even when I feel you might be in danger... because I *know* you can handle yourself."

As the most impressive creature in all the galaxies, sure.

When I gestured for him to keep going, he continued. "I was being truthful when I told you I didn't feel like myself lately, but I should have explained why."

His gaze drifted over my shoulder to where Pedro was squeaking up a storm while running back-and-forth on the bed—unable to reach their favorite space dad because of the shields I'd sneakily activated around the sleeping pod before opening the door.

Because my trust has been broken.

In the interest of moving things along, I filled in the blanks for him. "It's because of Pedro, isn't it? Specifically the karnilian inside them..."

Ziggy winced, and my gut twisted at the realization my worst fears had come true.

Has he actually considered claiming the gemstone for himself?

"The stone has been calling to me ever since I encountered it inside him." His voice had a raw, wavering quality I'd never heard before. "Your shields help by blocking it, but the idea of anything happening to the Trol feels like I've turned my tendrils on myself. We *need* to return Pedro to their planet before... before I..."

Ohhh...

Oh, you ridiculously stacked, grab-bag of tasty idiot.

I knew exactly what was going on here, even if Ziggy was too emotionally stunted to see it for himself. My man was already deep in his—extremely satisfactory—grovel, however, and I didn't want to overwhelm him with the truth of what he was feeling.

Baby steps for the space dad.

It wasn't his fault he couldn't separate actual protective instincts from witchy, gemstone-induced possessiveness. If anyone was to blame, it was probably Theo, but it hurt my heart to know my true love had been dealing with such overwhelming feelings alone for so long.

"I've got you, Zig," I whispered, pulling him close for a Salah Squeezer hug. "We're going to figure this out together, and I do mean *together.* No more secrets, okay?"

Commander Babygirl is serious.

He collapsed all those hot muscles into my arms with a relieved shudder. "Anything you say, sunshine. Just... Please, let me in..."

For a moment, I was confused about what he was talking about, since I'd already opened the bedroom door. Then I remembered I'd *also* formed a mini-shield around the piece of his core lodged inside me, using a similar method to when I protected my thoughts from meddling psychics like Uulvin.

Or Dre.

"I'm sorry too, Zig," I replied, giving him another squeeze. "I shouldn't have accused you of trying to stunt my powers, since you've always been my biggest supporter. Ya boy's just a little nervous about how I'm going to dissolve the shields around Uuktar—especially once we have a bunch of over-grown lizards breathing down our necks."

For now, I released the shields still separating us, and Ziggy groaned, deeply inhaling my scent before taking a step back, smiling like he had a secret.

A good one this time.

"That was going to be my olive branch..." he murmured. "Offering to show you which skin suit I'd be wearing once we landed."

Once again, my interest is piqued.

"Lead the way, Space Daddy," I replied, waving my hand Leeloo-style and releasing a squealing Pedro from the sleeping pod shield, knowing the Trol was safe with *both* of us. "It's bad bitch mercenary time."

Micah was oddly unconcerned about me having access to Pedro again, especially after what I'd finally confessed, but I still insisted the Trol be left with the nanny bot while we went to the skinsuit closet.

Since I don't want to frighten them with my next vessel...

There was a time I'd worried about *Micah* being scared of me —of my true form in particular—but my mate had continuously demonstrated how much he accepted me, *desired* me, no matter which form I was in.

As adventurous as my Earthling was, he did have a few hard limits, which we luckily seemed to agree on. Spider-like Arachs were out of the question, as was any species that practiced ovipositing, and neither of us wanted me to inhabit a *Lacertus.*

For slightly different reasons.

Even if I had possessed a *Lacertus* skinsuit, it wouldn't have made sense to wear it for this stop on our mission—not with

Micah accompanying me. The "overgrown lizards" did not keep pets, and while their planet was *also* a popular outpost and refueling station along the Intergalactic Highway, they didn't make a habit of mingling with other species aside from business dealings.

Leaving Micah on the ship wasn't an option, not only because *he* would be dismantling the shields imprisoning Uuktar— despite inexplicably believing he *couldn't*—but because I knew how hurt he'd be if I left him behind again.

And I'm trying to do better.

Even if it kills me.

Despite my best efforts, my protective instincts were going haywire at the thought of my mate being surrounded by my kind's greatest enemy. I'd spent half the night flipping through my skinsuits, partly to distract myself from our separation but mostly to find a solution that would ensure his safety.

I think we have a winner.

"Keep in mind, I cannot expand this skinsuit to full size until we leave the ship..." I preemptively explained. "However, it belongs to a species the *Lacertus* consider allies, so there shouldn't be an issue with one appearing on their planet."

"The suspense is killing me, Zig!" Micah whined, flapping his hands impatiently as I pressed a panel to open one of the climate-controlled drawers built into the wall. "Show me, show me, show me!"

So fucking adorable.

I removed a suitcase-sized block of what appeared to be metal from the drawer, chuckling at his obvious confusion. "Now, I don't want you to get too excited, but this particular species is going to remind you of more Hollywood aliens."

If I couldn't already feel his eagerness through our bond, the sheer size of Micah's eyes would have given him away. I feared he might pass out completely when I unleashed a few tendrils to enter the skinsuit—just enough to unfold it into a kneeling version of its final form.

"IS THAT A GODDAMN TRANSFORMER?!" my mate shouted loud enough to echo off the walls. "Oh. My. *Gawd,* Zig. Are you for real, right now? Wait. Is it a mech suit too? Is this a Transformer-mech suit *hybrid*? I am legit losing my shit right now, ahhh!"

His description was fairly accurate, since the vessel resembled a cross between his beloved, heavily-armored *Transformers* and the sleek, futuristic mech suits favored by Earthling science fiction.

Either way, his joy was infectious, and I couldn't help the grin that stretched across my face. "Yes, the *Opertum* are fascinating. Despite the inanimate appearance, what you see here is actually the *organic* exoskeleton that melds with the species' non-corporeal core."

Micah hummed thoughtfully as he circled the towering skinsuit. "A non-corporeal core surrounded by living tissue, huh? That sounds familiar..."

Ugh.

I begrudgingly considered Leeloo's revelations about a

common ancestor, if only to humor my scientifically-minded stellar collision.

"I suppose they could be seen as similar to a Stellarian, or an Eki," I mused. *"Opertum,* however, consist of two separate but interconnected organisms—an outer shell and inner core— operating as one being through a synchronized mental connection."

"I'm sorry, what?" Micah choked out before craning his neck, trying to peer into the hollowed chest cavity faintly visible beneath the rigid metallic structure. "How would a Stellarian even take control of a species like this?"

I grimaced, oddly embarrassed to admit my failure, though I knew my mate wouldn't see it that way. Micah viewed every setback as an opportunity for improvement, and, in this case, *he* was quite possibly the missing piece to the solution.

He's always been my missing piece.

"It wasn't until I'd taken over completely that I realized this vessel requires *two* organisms with a shared consciousness to fully operate." I watched as understanding dawned on his perfect face before I dared to ask, "Do you... want to give it a try?"

Do you trust me?

Micah observed me for a long moment, his expression giving nothing away. "Will this require more of you inside me?"

I dropped my gaze, suddenly realizing how ridiculous it was for me to ask him for this—especially after how I'd been behaving recently.

Maybe someday....

"Fuck, yes," he whispered, and when my gaze snapped to his, I saw the same familiar mix of excitement and desire he brought to *all* our skinsuit encounters. "I've been dreaming about you stuffing more of your star stuff inside me since we took down Astrum Force."

My brow furrowed. "You... have?"

As much as I'd enjoyed that experience on a primal level, it had been a means to a bloody end. The fact it resulted in a piece of me remaining *permanently* inside him had been a bonus, but I'd never expected Micah to ask for more.

I should know better than to underestimate this Earthling.

"Of course, I have," he replied, smiling softly. "My true purpose in life is the same as yours—for us to be as closely connected as two incredibly impressive creatures in any galaxy can be."

Huffing, I quickly glanced away, hoping to hide the visual evidence of my emotions while also knowing there was no way to disguise the pure happiness radiating through our bond.

I love him.

This simple yet enormous revelation hit me with the force of a star exploding, but, luckily, Micah had already refocused on the skinsuit and the task ahead.

"Okay, let's do this." He cracked his neck before shifting from one foot to the other, like a boxer readying for a fight. "How do I get inside?"

I discreetly wiped my eyes and chuckled. "Let me discard my current skinsuit, and then I'll star hop us—" My words choked off as I felt the piece of me inside him forcefully *jump.*

Then Micah disappeared.

Where...

Before I could panic, his joyful voice called out from the chest cavity of the *Opertum.*

"Fuck. YAS! Did you see that? I star hopped, Zig! I mean, *we* star hopped—same diff..."

By Stellaria...

Needing to be with him, I shed my Earthling skin and joined Micah inside the vessel. Blanketing him in countless tendrils, I finally confessed everything I'd wanted to tell this perfect creature for so long, content in knowing he could understand every word.

He's the only one who's ever understood me.

"My mate." I cooed in Stellarian. *"My perfect mate. The only one for me in all the galaxies. I knew from the moment I saw you that you were mine. My sunshine, my stellar collision... Mine until I return to the stars."*

"Jesus, Zig..." Micah sniffled, removing his glasses so he could wipe his eyes with the sleeve of his sweatshirt. "Anything else you wanna say? I don't think you've emotionally wrecked me enough..."

Yes.

I took a deep breath. *"I love you."*

He dropped his arm to gape up at me, gaze darting around the pulsing mass of my starry core, as if unsure where to look.

Anywhere.

You've always seen all of me.

"Say it again," he whispered desperately. "I-I wasn't ready. Please, say it again."

I laughed, wondering why I ever thought this would be difficult. *"I love you."*

Micah nodded slowly, his eyes shining, locked on me as he magic-ed his harp out of thin air and mimicked my notes.

"I love you," he replied in Stellarian—the sweetest notes I'd ever heard in all my three hundred years.

The sound of my resonance was filling the *Opertum's* vessel, with Micah answering in kind, and despite my willingness to be vulnerable with my mate, I was thankful to *not* be inhabiting a skinsuit with tear ducts.

I do have a reputation to uphold.

"Zig..." Micah rasped, dissolving the harp and awkwardly pulling his sweatshirt over his head in the small space. "I need you inside me, stat."

I laughed again. *"Inside you how?"*

My stellar collision shot me a disbelieving look. "In *every* way. Get those tendrils all up in my guts, fill me with stars, connect our consciousness... Light me the *fuck* up, Space Daddy."

Such a perfect mate.

Such a perfect slut.

I backed off only long enough to help him out of the rest of his clothes, purring contentedly once he was gloriously naked and shivering with anticipation.

All mine.

Lifting him by the thighs, I spread him wide, securing his wrists overhead. He whined as I stretched him with more tendrils than usual, so I caressed his face and sent soothing energy through our bond.

"Open for me, my love," I cooed, gently prying open his mouth.

The last time I'd entered his body, I struck fast, before *either* of us could change our mind. This time, I slid in slowly, gliding down his throat and entering his bloodstream before branching off in every direction—attaching myself to any piece of him I hadn't already claimed.

Give me all of you.

Let me give you all of me.

He groaned as I backed off again, watching him closely for any sign his body was rejecting this larger piece of my core, even though I knew it wouldn't.

Because we're meant to be one.

"Zig... I can *feel* you. I can feel you everywhere. Holy shit. I'm so full. I... oh, *fuuuuck...*"

I mentally smirked as I breached his ass with another thick

tendril, pumping in and out at an agonizingly slow pace while he whimpered and writhed in my hold.

"More…" he croaked, barely coherent as I began to attach myself to the neurons of his brain. "F-fuck me… from the… i-inside."

What babygirl wants, babygirl gets.

I wasn't exactly sure how to grant his wish, because it wasn't something I'd ever done before. Then again, I'd never given pleasure to anyone in my true form before him—hadn't realized I was capable of *anything* good.

Not until he made me want to do better.

"Tell me how you knew I was yours."

Micah's voice *in my head* confirmed we'd successfully melded consciousness, and my core pulsed as the *Opertum* we were inhabiting powered to life.

All mine.

I wrapped another tendril around his leaking cock—twisting hard, just how he liked it—before answering him through our new connection.

"I knew before I consciously knew… From the first day we met. I remember feeling an unfamiliar pull in my chest, and, a moment later, you appeared to introduce yourself. When you shook my hand, when we touched, electricity shot through me and buzzed in my system for hours. After that, I couldn't take my eyes off you."

"Because I was fine as fuck, don't lie."

"That too. I assumed the interest would pass—or that we'd fuck and get it over with—but then I wanted you near me all the time, wanted to know everything about you... to make you mine."

"I was always yours."

Always.

Determined to satisfy Micah's latest fantasy, I resonated again, this time from where I was lodged inside him, letting him *feel* exactly how deeply my love for him ran.

Beyond the stars.

Knowing he was close, I increased my pace, massaging his p-spot with my tendril until he was sobbing, shuddering, spilling—until I felt his pleasure like it was my own, until I no longer knew where he ended and I began.

Now, we are perfect.

I waited until he'd come down from his orgasm to detach myself from the *Opertum,* gather his clothes, and star hop my mate to the sleeping pod.

Our nest.

"Don't go..." he mumbled sleepily, grabbing a tendril before I could hop back to the closet for my Earthling form. "Let me just... pretend I'm a True Stellarian like you for a little while longer..."

I didn't want to ruin the moment by asking what he meant. Instead, I allowed him to pull my true form close, marveling over how he never saw me as a monster—how he'd always accepted every part of me.

Inside and out.

Until we return to the stars.

"Are you ready, babygirl?"

"Is that a rhetorical question, Space Daddy?" I smirked up at the Stellarian-powered Transformer towering over me. "Since you could technically check for yourself now."

I hope he didn't. The truth was, I *didn't* feel ready to dismantle shields I hadn't created. Both Leeloo and Ziggy seemed to think I could do anything an Eki could, however, so I was willing to at least give it a try.

Do or do not...

Opertum Ziggy chuckled with a sound like a rumbling motor-cycle engine. "Just because I *can* read your thoughts when-ever I want doesn't mean I'll do so without your permission."

We stan a consent king.

I appreciated that and planned to give him the same respect, but I couldn't resist a little tease. "Oh? So you *won't* be snooping for clues during those times when you forget how to human?"

Ziggy cocked his enormous metal head and gazed down at me. "There may be times I need to check in without asking, but I will do my best to save that for emergencies only."

What my man considered an emergency was up for debate, judging by how he'd gone scorched earth on Ekistron when he couldn't find me for two whole minutes, but I usually liked how protective he was.

I *really* liked having more of him inside me. It was comforting, like a sentient security blanket, an ever-present reminder my stellar collision was a permanent part of me now and always would be.

Glancing at the Lodger, I nervously chewed my bottom lip. "Do you really think it's a good idea to leave Pedro on the ship? I mean, I know SWOL-E is in there with them, but what if—"

"Pedro will be fine, sunshine," Ziggy replied far too quickly.

I narrowed my eyes. "Are you saying that because you're worried about a *Lacertus* getting their claws on them... or is it about something else?"

Unfortunately, the giant robot alien I was attempting to stare down from far below had an even better poker face than Ziggy in Earthling form.

"Pedro will be safest on the ship," my man sneakily skirted the question. "Now, why don't you get inside me?"

Sir!

I dropped my head back with a groan, channeling all my incredibly impressive powers into *not* getting a boner. "You really don't play fair, Zig, but you're probably right..." I turned my back on the ship before refocusing on my newest party trick.

Star hopping, motherfuckers!

It had never occurred to me to try and manipulate my personal piece of Ziggy to enhance my powers—not until Leeloo suggested it in the most witchy space wizard way possible.

"You already have everything you need inside you."

Kind of on the nose, but whatever.

They also implied the secret sauce was *me* needing to trust myself—to trust what I was "made of."

Super slut alien DNA.

All jokes aside, self-confidence in my abilities was something I'd struggled with for almost my entire life. To add to the emotional soup, now I was linked with a Stellarian who had his own self-worth challenges—who didn't even trust himself to be around our temporarily adopted baby.

Why can't you see what I see, Zig?

I stared up at the *Opertum* for a beat longer, trying to gauge whether he was eavesdropping on my thoughts. When he simply gestured at his chest cavity again, I realized this was a conversation we would need to continue at another time.

With a quick scan of our surroundings to check there were no overgrown lizards to witness my Stellarian skills, I star hopped inside my man.

I'm a space wizard, y'all!

It was still wild to get dragged through the ether by someone else, but it was way cooler to be the one manipulating time and space, to hop there yourself.

As soon as I was settled in my cozy cockpit, Transformer Ziggy started plodding along, his giant robot feet rattling the wooden planks of the wharf we'd parked the Lodger on.

Lacertus was an aquatic planet—which tracked, since I'd grown up with Zion's "deathpond" beneath the house. With it being a convenient stop on the Intergalactic Highway, multiple rows of piers had been built for the visiting species who couldn't breathe underwater.

While Zig's current skinsuit was the opposite of inconspicuous, most of our fellow travelers didn't seem at all surprised or concerned by the sight of him.

The giant lizards lurking beneath the waves probably help with the shock value.

Zig had told me the *Lacertus* were a fairly antisocial species, but I still expected to run across at least one. Instead, I was getting strong Stellaria vibes from the melting pot of diverse aliens making pitstops for supplies and business opportunities.

Or... psychic readings?

Uulvin had given us the exact coordinates for their missing sibling, and the location was oddly accessible. Instead of being deep inside an underwater fortress, the shielded cell was apparently just off a bustling market square. This made me wonder if Uuktar was less a high-value prisoner and more of an indentured seer.

My Spidey sense was tingling the closer we got, and even though my partner and I had discussed this mission at length, I couldn't help "voicing" one of my concerns.

Through our new, witchy bitch bond of course.

"Are you sure this isn't a trap, Zig?"

"I'm not sure, and if it is a trap, it's hard to say who set it."

WHAT?!

"Well, why the hell are we walking straight into what could potentially be a trap?!"

He released another rumbling sound.

"Because sometimes, there's no better way to determine who your enemy is than to allow them to believe they've won."

Okay, fair.

I knew Ziggy pivoted—had witnessed him change his strategy mid-showdown before—so I knew I could count on him to keep a cool head no matter what happened.

As long as I'm not directly threatened.

Worst case scenario, we could always star hop back to the ship for a quick getaway.

Assuming we don't get trapped by a shield...

I didn't like how we'd left things with Leeloo, but I also didn't believe they, or their fellow Eki, meant us any harm. While many aliens were only looking out for themselves, we'd also met those who were welcoming to different species and more than willing to help.

The same could be said of Earthlings, I suppose.

> *"Are you open to the possibility that Leeloo was telling the truth?"*

This was a topic I'd attempted to discuss before we landed, but Ziggy had managed to avoid engaging.

Shocking, I know.

Unfortunately for him, there was no hiding from a session with Dr. Micah—not when you were sharing the same skin-suit—and I needed to be absolutely sure where my stellar collision stood before we confronted Uuktar.

"About what exactly?"

> *"About some species not being what they seem..."*

He was silent for so long, I wondered if we'd lost our mental connection—or if he'd tapped in to my thoughts to catch my subtext. But then, he rallied.

"It would be hypocritical of me to not be open to the idea. Stellarian history turned out to be more complex than what I was raised to believe so, of course, I am open to considering the same for other species."

I gasped, loud enough for him to hear me over the bustle of the bazaar—perhaps from outer space.

"Does this mean my superior Stellarian is acknowledging his imperial blind spots?"

He sighed in my head, equally loud.

"Let's just see what intel we can extract from Uuktar."

"Roger that, partner!"

Nothing better than interrogation time with my Space Daddy.

Soon enough, we'd reached the last pier in the row, closed in by shields and containing nothing but a small wooden hut and a meditation cushion with a snake-headed alien serenely perched on top.

"Ah, there are our rescuers," they hissed in unison from all six heads. "We have been expecting you."

Something was buzzing in my intuition, whispering for me to pay attention, but we'd agreed that Ziggy would do the talking to start.

"Let me guess," my man boomed in a truly terrifying voice, "your renowned psychic abilities foretold our arrival?"

The Hydrassian snickered. "Psychic abilities were to thank, yes. Now what can we humbly offer you in exchange for our freedom?"

"We seek a planet that has mysteriously disappeared," Ziggy continued, all business as usual. "The place where we can acquire a gemstone said to guarantee victory in battle for its owner."

Zig showing such single-minded interest in the karnilian would have freaked me out a day ago, but this angle was part of our agreed upon strategy.

And I trust my stellar collision.

Even if he doesn't trust himself...

Uuktar's set of smiles faltered as they rose from the cushion and moved closer. "What do you mean, *acquire?* I was told you already had the Trol in your possession..."

Told?!

The water beneath the pier began to churn and bubble, causing nearby aliens to run for dry land. Alarm bells were going off in my head, but I desperately needed to know how to get Pedro home.

I could *feel* Zig preparing to star hop us to the Lodger—to cut the action short once again—so I went off script.

Just like a True Stellarian.

Before he could catch on to my plan, I star hopped myself out of the skinsuit, landing directly in front of Uuktar with only the Eki-made shields between us.

Ziggy shouted as the mech froze in place, but we didn't have time to waste—not with how the entire pier violently swayed from the force of the waves.

"Who told you we were coming?" I demanded, quickly activating an extra filter on my glasses to block any hypnotism attempts, but the Hydrassian ignored my question.

They leaped forward and frantically pounded their clawed fists on the transparent walls of their enclosure. "I will tell

SPACE DADDY'S GUIDE TO THE GALAXY

you how to reach the planet of Karn, but you must let me out before they surface. *Please hurry!*"

Fuck.

Unlike the natural affinity I felt toward Leeloo, I did not trust *this* witchy bitch one bit, especially as we still didn't know *why* they'd been imprisoned here.

So, I switched gears once again.

"Do you trust me, Zig?"

"Of course I do, but we need to go. Now!"

The uncharacteristic *panic* I was feeling from my Stellarian almost made me abandon my plan, but I was determined to follow my intuition.

Here we go.

Three enormous *Lacertus* broke the surface of the water the same instant I conjured myself a Jedi robe of glittering, lava-infused space sorcery.

May the witchy bitch Force be with me.

36
ZIGGY

Without Micah physically in the *Opertum* with me, I was no longer able to move to defend my mate—at least, not without exposing my true form.

It was tempting to do just that, but the last thing I wanted was to be a lone Stellarian facing off against three *Lacertus*. This wasn't because I was *scared,* but because the sight of me would most likely ruin whatever plan Micah's beautiful brain had come up with.

And I need to show him respect by letting him lead.

My stellar collision disguising himself as an Eki lessened my anxiety for his safety, but only slightly—especially as our opponents finally appeared. It was difficult to explain exactly how large an adult *Lacertus* was, but the newer Earthling Godzilla movies came fairly close.

Just add horns and wings...

And intelligence, as loathe as I am to admit it.

I could feel my mate's instinctive terror at the sight of the beasts, but luckily, the hood of his robes hid his reaction.

"Holy shit, Zig... You weren't kidding when you said Zion is a miniature version of these lizards."

Of course, I wasn't kidding!

"What do we have here? An Eki?" a deep green *Lacertus* boomed in the trade language. "And what brings you to our planet today with your... Well, we have not seen one of these in many moons. An *Opertum!*"

They lowered their massive head to sniff at my skinsuit while I made myself as undetectable as possible. One of the Stellarians' greatest defenses against *Lacertus* had always been our ability to stay several evolutionary steps ahead, so I assumed —hoped—this species hadn't suddenly developed the ability to *smell* my kind.

That would be inconvenient.

"Yes!" Micah shouted, drawing the curious lizard's attention back to him. "The *Opertum* is simply a... creation of mine. But, to answer your question, I am here to check on the barrier containing this Hydrassian—to ensure everything is secure."

All three *Lacertus* stared at my mate with so much predatory intensity, it was all I could do to not star hop him all the way back to Earth.

I hope you know what you're doing, Micah.

The largest of the pack, a gigantic purple beast with coloring like Micah's eldest brother in his true form, shifted their attention to the Hydrassian in question.

"You told us your visitors would be a Stellarian and an... Earth-ling, whatever *that* is. You also insisted they would have a Trol with them. Do you *dare* lie to us again, Uuktar?"

Again?

I wanted to take advantage of the distraction to discuss this eerily specific intel with my partner, but Micah jumped on the chance to discredit the seer before I could check in.

"Can a Stellarian do this?" he huffed, expertly crafting a *katana* out of thin air to demonstrate his Eki-like matter manipulation powers. "Last I heard, *Trols* went extinct."

"Good riddance," the third, umber-colored *Lacertus* muttered under its breath, and the other two nodded in agreement.

What in Stellaria's name...

I could sense Micah's surprise at this statement as well, but I didn't have the chance to ponder its meaning before Uuktar joined the conversation.

"They are the ones who are lying!" they shrieked. "Check their ship for the Trol."

Micah scoffed. "Why would I require an entire ship when I can star hop to my destination? Not to mention, all I needed to bring with me for this maintenance visit was my powers and the shell of an *Opertum*—for protection purposes."

My mate was clearly making up his story as he went along while also being extremely careful in his responses. He wasn't quite lying, but he also wasn't completely telling the truth.

Dr. Micah would call it redirection.

The purple *Lacertus* cocked its head, observing my mate shrewdly. "I do not recall any mention of ongoing maintenance being required. In fact, the alarm system the original creator installed supposedly ensured *no one* would be getting close to our prisoner without our knowledge—not even a fellow Eki."

Fuck.

This did not look good, but I forced myself to defer to Micah's ability to handle it. As I'd hoped, Commander Babygirl had the situation under control.

"Our shields have improved over time," he elaborated. "So the focus of this visit is more of an upgrade."

Does he intend to fortify the shields?

Or just fool the Lacertus into thinking that's why we're here?

My mate had been undecided on what to do with Uuktar as we left the Lodger, although he'd also mentioned he didn't fully believe the Hydrassians' story, which was surprising coming from my normally trusting mate.

Either way, we *both* wanted to return Pedro to their home planet—for slightly different reasons—so we'd decided to assess the situation as it evolved.

Han Solo-style.

At the moment, we seemed to be at a standstill, as the *Lacertus* were still squinting suspiciously at my mate.

Micah sighed heavily. "If you prefer, I can leave the shields in their current state... That is, If you're unconcerned how your prisoner is somehow gathering intel..."

The Hydrassian froze as all three enormous reptiles swung their heads to peer into their transparent cage.

"Now that you mention it..." the head *Lacertus* snarled. "You never did name your source, Uuktar."

Perhaps I was being generous, calling these creatures intelligent.

The seer sniffed haughtily, even as they shifted on their feet. "Why would we share such information with those who've unjustly kept us prisoner?"

"Unjustly!" Micah scoffed, as if either of us knew the reason for the Hydrassian's imprisonment in the first place.

Sly smiles stretched across Uuktar's many reptilian faces. "However, we'll give you a hint. Our source is someone capable of *not* setting off the Eki's alarm, and who else would be able to accomplish that, aside from an Eki or a Stellarian... since both species are able to star hop?"

Micah laughed incredulously. "Before the *Lacertus* arrived, you implied you were receiving information through *psychic* means, and neither—"

"Oh, wait..." the Hydrassian interrupted as their smirks grew. "Star hopping is what the *Stellarians* call it. The Eki refer to it as 'particle leaping.' Odd that someone who claims *not* to be a Stellarian would use their term for the ability..."

"Is that true, Zig?"

"I... have no idea."

Cold dread skittered up my nonexistent spine as the *Lacertus* turned their unwavering focus back to my mate.

This is all my fault.

If I had simply allowed Micah to finish his training with Leeloo, he would have been better prepared for this confrontation. Instead, I allowed my false sense of superiority to put the man I loved more than anything at a severe disadvantage.

A disadvantage that could get him killed.

Despite the fear and anxiety swirling in our bond, Micah stood his ground. "Are you implying I am a rare hybrid of some kind—an Eki overtaken by a Stellarian who is still able to utilize my powers? Everyone knows Stellarians take complete control of their vessels, leaving nothing but an empty shell for them to inhabit, like a single-minded parasite."

Uuktar didn't reply, but what shocked me the most was the *Lacertus* not immediately agreeing with Micah's outdated assessment of my kind.

Interesting...

The seer made a disgruntled noise before their multiple gazes grew distant. "It will be simple enough for us to learn more about what you are..."

For a moment, I feared they were reading my stellar collision's thoughts, but Micah looked unconcerned. This led to me recalling how he'd formed shields around his own mind to block psychic infiltration on *Dionaea*—causing Uulvin to comment on how my mate's shields were "more advanced" than the ones surrounding their cave.

The ones created by the Eki...

That lying set of snakes!

Suddenly, I understood exactly where Uuktar had been getting their intel from, and I desperately hoped my mate hadn't already activated his mental shields so I could warn him.

"Micah! Uuktar's communicating with—"

"I know, Space Daddy. I've got this."

Of course, my incredibly impressive mate was already ten steps ahead of everyone else. Then, he turned his back on the *Lacertus* to face his opponent, because *my* greatest enemies were not his.

The Hydrassian was.

Both of them.

"So, you've been psychically communicating with Uulvin all this time, hmm, Uuktar?" Micah tauntingly ran his fingers over the surface of the shielded prison, causing the air to ripple between them. "Scheming to send us here to do their dirty work for them."

Do their dirty work for them...

"You were sent here by Uulvin?!" the head *Lacertus* growled, baring its fangs and causing my protective instincts to spike.

"Yes," Micah calmly replied, and my proverbial blood ran cold. "They sent us here to free their sibling."

Nonononono...

While I agreed the Hydrassians were the true enemy here, Micah wasn't completely understanding how volatile the situation still was. As "intelligent" as the *Lacertus* were as a species—still far less than Stellarians—if they sensed a threat, no amount of logic would get through to them.

"PUT UP YOUR GODDAMN SHIELDS!!!"

Luckily, I *felt* Micah instinctively obey despite his confusion, but my relief was short-lived. With a roar, the purple *Lacertus* grabbed my mate, bellowing with rage when they failed to crush him in their powerful grip.

"ZIG!!!"

Micah's cry of terror wasn't for himself. The claws of another *Lacertus* closed around the vessel I inhabited, but before I could escape, a violent jolt of electricity shot through me, whiting out my vision and rendering my powers useless.

Oh, fuuu...

Besides star hopping making us difficult to catch, Stellarians had long ago developed a resistance to the *Lacertus'* ability to drain another's powers on contact. Unfortunately, it appeared the *Opertum's* metallic skinsuit was enough of a conduit to make that resistance useless as well.

...uuuuuuck.

"So you *were* lying about the Trol."

I groggily regained consciousness, only to find Uuktar glaring at me from behind the safety of their shielded prison.

Why couldn't they have gotten trampled during the idiot lizard rampage?

The next thing I registered was the sound of claws scraping against metal, along with a familiar *pspsps*.

Peering out from what was left of my skinsuit, I discovered *Pedro* scratching at the vessel in a desperate attempt to reach me.

This does not bode well for the nanny bot.

Or my ship...

By some miracle, my powers had recovered, so I star hopped out of the mangled *Opertum* and scooped Pedro into my tendrils. In sharp contrast to the first time the little creature had encountered me in my true form, they chittered happily and snuggled as close to my core as possible.

Ugh.

Cute.

I could still *feel* Micah—*alive, thank fuck*—because of our stellar collision bond, but I couldn't check in with him otherwise.

He must still have his shields engaged.

All his shields...

This meant our mental connection was also disconnected, probably left over from Micah shielding his mind from Uuktar. While I understood the precaution, the current lack of communication was alarming, and with no clear sign of my mate in the surrounding wreckage, my gaze warily drifted to the deep, uninviting waters sloshing against the pier.

Looks like it's time for a different skinsuit...

I'd only just begun mentally flipping through my options, determining which aquatic species would be best for the battle ahead, when the Hydrassian spoke again.

"They did not take him underwater. At least, not here..."

I spun on the seer, ready to interrogate them until they cried for mercy only to remember they most likely wouldn't understand my native language anyway.

Sigh.

Apparently, Uuktar was feeling generous, as they pointed toward a far-off cave on the far end of a seemingly endless strip of sandy beach.

It's time for another skinsuit either way.

"Be sure to come back and rescue us!" the Hydrassian called out in a sugary sweet tone that grated on my nerves. "After you have rescued the... whatever they are."

My mate, you mean?

Seeing no need to acknowledge their ridiculous request, I star hopped Pedro and I back to my ship. Our first stop was the skinsuit closet, then the arsenal of weapons still scattered around the Lodger's kitchen, where I chose only the best artillery for confronting Micah's kidnappers.

It's time to reclaim what's mine.

So... deathponds are apparently a universal Lacertus thing.

When all hell broke loose at the pier, I'd worried I was about to be dragged underwater, never to be heard from again. My shields probably would've kept me from drowning, but now I realized I needed to conjure myself a scuba-style breathing apparatus, stat.

For future alien freak-outs.

Luckily, I hadn't met a watery grave at the hands—claws—of giant lizards. The worst that had happened was being carried off like that damsel in *King Kong* before ending up in this waterfront cave.

Zion would be way into this.

The space we were in was *massive*—close in scale to Nuclei City—and while the set up in here was way more primitive than what the Eki had going on, it had a deluxe grotto feel that was homey. Some of the inhabitants lounged on rocks near the mouth of the cave, soaking up the sun, while others milled about, socializing and performing other oddly domestic duties with water at their doorstep.

Extremely deep water.

I'd already turned down several offers to take a dip—not because I had any issue with swimming, but because it didn't seem like the smartest move to enter a bottomless deathpond with a bunch of unfamiliar, giant reptiles.

I do have some sense of self-preservation.

Although Ziggy would probably disagree...

The only reason I wasn't freaking out about my Stellarian's wellbeing was that I could sense he was okay. *Physically* okay, I should specify, because his *emotions* were borderline psychotic.

So... the usual, just enhanced for the current shitshow.

I'd momentarily panicked when the one *Lacertus* crushed his *Opertum* skinsuit, but then I recalled Zig mentioning Stellarians could quickly exit a compromised vessel—like a fighter pilot ejecting from their aircraft.

It was safe to assume he'd already returned to the Lodger to grab no less than 3000 weapons and come save me, but I was hoping to handle this situation before he tracked me down and showed up.

Hence why my shields are still firmly in place.

On the one hand, the idea of my man busting in with guns blazing—literally—made me *swoon,* but I also knew there was a long history between these two species. I honestly didn't know what would happen if a Stellarian showed up at the grotto, and the last thing I wanted was for my pseudo-kidnapping to start a war.

But if anything happens to Zig, I will go full Stellarian on these lizards.

Even though I knew my stellar collision was freaking out, I'd done my best to pump 'sign of life' vibes through our bond, determined to stand on business on my own.

Commander Babygirl has the situation under control.

I hope...

Yes, I could have star hopped—*particle leaped, whatever*—out of here if I'd wanted to, but my 'captors' and I had already resolved our differences. With the immediate danger segment out of the way, I could now focus on gathering useful intel for our mission.

Hopefully, before all hell breaks loose all over again.

"You should have better explained what you meant by Uulvin sending you here, little Eki," my big, purple kidnapper—Krunk, apparently—called out from where they bobbed in the nearby pool. "But you must understand why we cannot risk freeing the Hydrassian in our custody."

The issue was, I didn't fully understand *why* Uuktar ended up here in the first place, even if I had already figured out the Hydrassians were bad news. The larger issue was that I still needed those planetary coordinates to get Pedro home—to Karn—which meant I had to show my hand at least a little bit.

Maybe an intel trade would do the trick?

"I have no intention of freeing Uuktar," I reassured my scaly host. "Unfortunately, the seer has information I need. Information about the *Trols* they mentioned…"

So much for self-preservation.

That caught Krunk's attention. "What do the Eki want with Trols?" they growled.

Weirdly, I didn't feel threatened by their tone, probably because Zion threatened me with a similar tone on a regular basis.

Middle child problems.

I sighed, knowing Ziggy would *never* be so honest—especially not with a species *he* considered an enemy—but we'd already established Space Daddy and I did things differently.

"We have recently encountered multiple Hydrassians searching for both Trols and karnilian as mercenaries for other species." I blew out a slow breath. "Possibly including yours."

It was an assumption, and a potentially rude one at that, but I needed to see how Krunk would react to it.

To my relief, the giant lizard seemed more vaguely offended than anything. "You should know the *Lacertus* would *never* work with the Hydrassians, especially not to track down the cursed stone that has brought my kind nothing but despair."

Okay, now we're getting somewhere.

"I must admit," I slowly began, really playing up my hesitancy for maximum effect. "I don't personally know all the details about *Lacertus* history—with Trols or karnilian. If you would feel comfortable explaining it to me, I would appreciate it."

Krunk's expression softened—as much as it could, considering they naturally looked like they wanted to chomp on me.

"Of course, little Eki. Although, *I* must admit, I cannot recall a time when another species has ever asked for our side of the story."

I wish Zig was here to hear this...

"WHERE IS HE?!!!"

As if on cue.

With a tidal wave-level splash, Krunk spun in the water to face the intruder—*Ziggy, obviously*—but his big ass lizard head was blocking the action. Scrambling off my rocky perch, I raced along the deathpond's edge to get a better view.

And to put myself *in view.*

"WHERE IS MY... *WIFE?!"*

Wife?!

I assumed Ziggy was so upset, he was struggling to find the correct words in the trade language, but I'd be damned if I wasn't swooning like a motherfucker.

All my romance novel dreams have come true!

I almost swooned again when I caught sight of him. Not only was my man in full Space Daddy armor, but he was *flying,* with tendrils unleashed, an enormous gun in each hand, and a fanged, tentacled, battle-mode Trol perched on his shoulder.

Look at him, being a bad bitch space dad.

"Zig—I'm here! I'm okay!" I shouted, pulling off my hood

and waving my arms overhead. "It was all a big misunderstanding with the *Lacertus,* but we're cool now."

He landed beside me before loudly stating in his usual stubborn AF way, "I believe you are being held here against your will."

Sigh.

I couldn't help noticing every *Lacertus* in the vicinity had backed away from my lone Stellarian and his hissing sidekick, despite the size difference and how vastly outnumbered he was.

It's all that big dick energy.

As clan leader, only Krunk remained close, although they eyed my rescue committee warily. "So you *do* have a Trol in your possession? And this... *Stellarian* is your companion?" Their horrified gaze drifted to me. "A-are *you* also a Stellarian like Uuktar claimed, My-kuh?"

"Yes," Ziggy snapped the same instant I replied, "No!"

Siiiigh.

"I am an *Earthling* with Eki powers," I quickly clarified. "Ziggy here is my stellar collision—my fated mate. So, yes, there *is* a piece of him inside me, but I still have complete control, I swear!"

Most of the time...

But we're gonna leave the kinky shit out of this.

My confession spilled out in a rush. "Pedro... the Trol came into our possession by accident. The Stellarians were hired by a mysterious client to rescue an *egg* from the Maroxians, and the egg hatched en route, but when we brought the creature back to Stellaria, the Irathians attacked out of nowhere. There was also a rogue Hydrassian on the planet, claiming they could 'hear the call' of the karnilian, which we didn't realize was inside the Trol at the time. We still suspected Pedro was who everyone was after, so we decided to keep moving until we figured things out."

Krunk looked a little dazed by the infodump, and rightfully so.

It's kind of a hot mess.

"Listen..." I took a hesitant step toward the *Lacertus,* which caused Ziggy to growl low in warning. "The misinformation between your species runs deep, and it goes both ways." I pointedly looked at each of them in turn. "But I really hope we can *talk* to each other and set the record straight."

Please.

An insistent *knock* on my mental walls had me lowering my inner shields to let my stellar collision back in. I sent him an apologetic grimace, instantly realizing me shutting him out had probably made things worse, despite my good intentions.

"Are you sure you're okay, sunshine? I was so worried..."

"I am, and I'm sorry, Zig. I just wanted to discuss a few things with the Lacertus before I left... and before you showed up like... Well, like this."

Like always.

Ziggy removed his helmet, exhaling slowly and facing Krunk before speaking in the trade language again. "Very well. I am willing to listen." He shot *me* an apologetic look. *"Truly* listen this time."

Thank you.

A moment of awkward silence passed before I took charge again. "So, Krunk here was about to explain why the *Lacertus* actually have *no* interest in Trols or karnilian... which will hopefully explain why Uuktar is imprisoned here."

There's no point in hiding my cluelessness now.

Krunk chuckled. "Lucky for you, little Earthling, it is all related."

I laughed. "Yeah, I figured as much."

The *Lacertus* sighed, as if what they were about to share pained them. "Long ago, we were a warring species, single-mindedly focused on conquering other planets. I believe it was in response to our destructive actions that your recently fallen Astrum Force first came to power." They nodded at Ziggy before continuing. "It quickly became clear that Stellarians were one of the only species who could challenge us, which meant we needed to find a way to turn the tide in our favor."

"And that's where the karnilian came in, hmm?" Ziggy scoffed, crossing his arms as a deceptively cuddly Pedro draped themselves over his shoulders like a furry danger scarf.

Krunk growled, although I got the sense it wasn't aimed at anyone present. "My kind still curse the day karnilian was suggested to us by a pair of Hydrassian seers—powerful siblings who claimed the stone 'showed' them *proof* of victory in a great battle against our greatest enemies."

My heart sank at the clever deception. "Uuktar and Uulvin didn't specify *who* would be victorious, did they?"

"No," the *Lacertus* huffed. "And we were too blinded by our own sense of superiority to consider we might lose."

"Well, that sounds familiar doesn't it, Zig?"

My stellar collision didn't outwardly react, but I could *feel* his signature loving exasperation wrap around me, like a warm, starry embrace.

Like Tendril Huggy Time.

I nodded and Krunk continued. "While I *do* believe Hydrassians are gifted with The Sight, they realized long ago that coin was more plentiful when the fates of entire planets were on the line."

A chilling thought occurred to me. "Does karnilian even do what they claim it does?"

The *Lacertus'* gaze drifted to the purring Trol. "It is difficult to say, but with how skillfully they have twisted the truth about other matters, it would not surprise me to learn they fabricated the story about this supposedly powerful stone to line their own purses."

Creating supply and demand...

Ziggy piped in, much to my surprise. "I believe it was after that great battle when karnilian was outlawed in many galaxies." He cocked his head. "But not this one. Why is that?"

Krunk displayed a toothy grin. "Because we decided to lay a trap for those who had deceived us. We knew the Eki had the ability to create impenetrable shields, so we offered to pay them to construct a set of prisons—one here and one on *Dionaea.*"

"I knew it!" Ziggy hissed, getting Pedro all worked up again. "I knew Leeloo was lying when they said the Eki's shields weren't for sale."

"They are not," Krunk interrupted. "Once we explained the situation, the Eki offered to help us free of charge—to put a stop to the lies enabling highly destructive interplanetary wars."

Well, now I know where my insatiable need to fix everyone else's problems comes from...

Ziggy squinted at the enormous lizard. "Why is Uulvin's prison unfinished? They seem free to come and go from *Dionaea* as they please—free to welcome clients more than happy to pay for their false prophecies."

The *Lacertus* looked sheepish. "It was to give Uulvin a false sense of security. We had hoped that by allowing the Hydrassians to move freely, they would not only attempt to liberate Uuktar—giving us reason to retaliate—but reveal themselves as the manipulative masterminds they are..."

"They did..." Ziggy muttered, almost to himself. "Unfortunately, they sent *us* to do their dirty work for them—not just to free Uuktar here on Lacertus, but to Marox to retrieve the Trol egg in the first place."

38
ZIGGY

Now that I'd put the pieces together, it was painfully obvious who the "masterminds" were behind this entire situation. It was also slightly embarrassing, considering Stellarians had been outsmarted by a bunch of snakes.

Nearly outsmarted.

Micah gestured for me to elaborate, and I nodded. "Word must have traveled that a Trol egg had somehow ended up on Marox. With how valuable karnilian was to their *business model*—how they themselves had most likely driven Trols to near extinction—the Hydrassians would have been willing to do anything to claim that egg for themselves." I chuckled humorlessly. "Well... *almost* anything."

It didn't take long for my incredibly impressive mate to catch on to my train of thought. "They knew the Stellarians would be one of the only species that could go against the Maroxians..."

"Besides the *Lacertus*," I added begrudgingly, with a nod at the one before us. "But it sounds as if that wouldn't have been an option."

Krunk scoffed. "Absolutely not. When we captured Uuktar, the first thing they attempted to bribe us with were the coordinates for Karn."

Micah straightened to attention "Did they give you the coordinates?"

The *Lacertus* observed him silently for a moment before huffing. "No. Because we had no intention of ever tempting fate in that way again."

WHAT?!

This went against everything I thought I knew about our greatest enemies. They had a seer at their disposal—one who could lead them to the origin of untold power—yet they had apparently refused the opportunity. They had refused to take advantage of coveted intel that could have finally brought them victory over my kind.

> *"Not everything is as it seems when it comes to certain species."*

Honnor's words blended with Leeloo's in my memory, reminding me so much of my personal history was based on propaganda created by those who did not care what others lost because *they* had everything to gain.

And it sounds as if I'm not the only one.

I looked at the *Lacertus* in front of us—really *looked* at them. Not their outward appearance, but at how their history and beliefs were so similar to, so intertwined with, my own.

"Enjoy facing your greatest enemy, Zig-ee."

Leeloo hadn't mentioned the *Lacertus* when they said this, because that wasn't who they were talking about. They meant my own assumptions, the demons I hadn't yet exorcised.

They were talking about *me*.

"I... may have been wrong about the Lacertus, sunshine."

"It's okay, Zig. Once you know better, you can do better."

I cleared my throat, rallying to not only be vulnerable with my mate, but in front of a species who no self-respecting Stellarian would ever show weakness to.

Because they would never show us weakness either.

"I'm not entirely convinced *any* gemstone is needed for the Hydrassians' rituals," I carefully said. "But I understand better than most that the *pull* from karnilian is very real. When I was attempting to figure out what our... what this Trol was," I reached up to absently run a gloved hand through Pedro's fur, "I opened some sort of channel between us. The stone is all I can think about when Micah lowers their shields —like a maddening drumbeat. Therefore, I understand how some might stop at nothing to claim it for themselves, no matter how rare it is. No matter how one must *kill* a Trol in order to..."

My words lodged in my throat like the stone in question, but my stellar collision stepped in to support me.

As always.

"Can I please have Pedro, Zig?" he gently asked, and I gladly obeyed, snatching the squawking creature from my shoulder and handing them off to my partner.

I'd assumed Micah was simply giving me breathing room from my shame, but then he held the Trol aloft, so Pedro's owlish yellow eyes could meet mine.

Then, he lowered their shields.

I gasped, leaping backward as a wave of uncontrollable desperation washed over me, luring me toward my prize, promising me everything...

> *"MICAH! You need to shield them... No, shield ME! Trap my tendrils inside me, please..."*

"No."

> *"PEDRO IS IN DANGER—"*

"No, they're not," Micah brusquely made our conversation public, shoving the creature closer to me despite the obvious risk. "What are you feeling right now, Zig?"

Feeling?!

"What?" I snapped, my frantic gaze darting to our audience. "I... I do not believe *now* is the time for a session with Dr. Micah..."

Because that is a level of vulnerability I refuse to display in front of my enemy.

Former enemy...

Unfortunately, Dr. Micah's methods were unforgiving. "Is the first thing that comes to mind how you want to *cut* Pedro open and violently *tear* the karnilian from their chest with your tendrils?"

BY STELLARIA!!!

It absolutely was *not* what came to mind. In fact, the thought of harming one hair on Pedro's tiny body had my tendrils retracting so far inside my Earthling form, they practically disappeared into my core.

"No," I choked out, my body shaking with the effort needed not to snatch the creature away from someone willing to even suggest it. "I could never—"

"Because what you're experiencing isn't the blinding need to covet the stone for yourself," Micah calmly cut in. "It's called a protective instinct—specifically, a *parental* protective instinct."

WHAT?!

"B-but, Pedro is not my... our..." I sputtered, backing away.

"No, Pedro is *not* biologically yours." Micah smiled. "Or ours."

Ours...

"Buuuut..." my relentless mate continued. "I actually think by coming in contact with the stone, you activated a kind of reverso imprint on Pedro—making your true form believe they're actually your offspring."

Excuse me?

"Fascinating..." Krunk murmured, seemingly captivated by the free show they were receiving. "Do you believe that is the original purpose of the stone being embedded in this species, My-kuh?"

My scientifically-minded mate eagerly nodded his head. "I do! I'm also protective of the Trol, and they're obviously comfortable with me, but the bond between Ziggy and Pedro has been super strong since day one—"

"I disagree," I attempted to argue, but Micah was uninterested in granting me mercy.

"Almost since day one, whatever." He grinned, rolling his eyes good-naturedly before sobering. "Unfortunately, I don't think you've been the only one to mistake this pull, Zig, and the Hydrassians capitalized on that biological response for financial gain."

Sighing, I dejectedly stared at the squirming creature, unable to ignore how I found the odd ratio of their enormous eyeballs and furry face to be *slightly* adorable.

"What's the matter? Do you want upsies with your space daddy?" Micah cooed in the ridiculous, sing-song voice I'd often witnessed him use back on Earth with the babies in his family.

Which is slightly adorable as well.

Pedro responded with a squeal and a scrabbling of their claws until I retrieved the creature from Micah's arms, placing them back on my shoulders with a sigh.

Fine.

It's practice.

To my increased annoyance, the *Lacertus* chuckled. "Why are you seeking to return this Trol to Karn? Clearly, they have found loving caregivers in both of you."

Micah smiled softly. "Well, I don't know if life aboard the Lodger is the right kind of set up for a baby, no matter how much I want to..." He cleared his throat, blushing deliciously. "And we should at least try to reunite them with their own kind, right?"

The *Lacertus* stared at my stellar collision thoughtfully. "I have often wondered whether all the species in the galaxies should be as segregated as we are... While you both look similar at the moment, you are not the same."

You'd be surprised.

"Yeah, about that..." Micah rubbed the back of his neck. "Have you really not heard of Earth, Krunk? Or the *Lacertus'* history with Earthlings like me?"

The lizard cocked their head, visibly intrigued. "What are the coordinates for Earth?"

Even with this new ground between our species, I wasn't eager to give these lizards a map to my mate's home planet.

"It's difficult to chart to outsiders, since the locals call their galaxy 'Milky Way,'" I deflected. "But it's a fertile, blue planet with a single moon, about three or four galaxies past Taius."

"Gaia!" the umber-colored *Lacertus* from earlier called out, hesitantly lumbering closer. *"03-Via Lactea."*

Recognition lit up the purple *Lacertus'* reptilian eyes. "Ah, yes... I remember now. That was a colonizing mission that failed when the Stellarians appeared to claim supremacy once again."

Should I correct them?

I don't think I will.

Unfortunately, Micah did not share my deeply ingrained need to dominate when it came to the *Lacertus*.

"Actually." He raised a finger. *"Lacertus* DNA is still alive and kicking on my home planet. I can even show you proof!"

Here we go.

Micah dematerialized his Eki robe before wrestling his phone out of his pocket and swiping through his photos until he found one of him and Zion in full supe form.

"This is my eldest brother." He turned the device to show Krunk. "He has a deathpond too."

The *Lacertus* peered at the phone screen. *"Eldest* brother, you say? They are so small... like a baby."

Oh, I will *be sharing this assessment with Zion.*

Micah snorted. "I'm sure Ziggy can't *wait* to tell him you said that."

He knows me so well.

What followed was my mate convincing Krunk and several other *Lacertus* to pose for selfies so he could "show the haters back home how the big dogs hang."

Whatever that means.

After an hour of this, Pedro showed signs of fatigue, and that was as good an excuse as any to take our leave—although, where we would go from here was a mystery.

"Oh, Stellarian!" Krunk called to us as we prepared to depart the cave. "If you know how we might schedule an audience with the *new* Astrum Force Command, we would be grateful. The *Lacertus* wish to form an alliance between our planets and settle our differences once and for all."

I froze as the enormity of that request sunk into my borrowed bones. "Yes... I believe I could help facilitate a meeting with the new Head Commander."

Micah scoffed. "Of course, Honnor would be willing to meet, Zig! This is exactly the type of outreach they've been pushing for. Plus, you're their offspring. Plus, *you* were originally supposed to be Head Commander."

So ridiculous.

Krunk cocked their head again. "Is that so? I did not realize I was in the presence of such a prestigious Star Unit warrior! It is no wonder you were prepared to take on an entire clan of *Lacertus* by yourself."

I yanked my helmet on as my cheeks heated. "You kidnapped my mate," I grumbled as Micah snickered.

The *Lacertus* sighed. "We may have overreacted at the pier. My kind is known for our short tempers, unfortunately. The tiniest offense or threat could result in a rampage of epic proportions."

"Well, that sounds familiar—"

"Behave, sunshine."

"I would like to bestow a parting gift." Krunk gestured toward the scene of the crime. "Take Uuktar with you—to guide you to Karn."

Micah blinked. "Wha... you're *giving* us your prisoner? What about revenge on the Hydrassians?"

Krunk shrugged. "You have the power to remove the shields imprisoning them, so go ahead. It will help you get your Trol home." His mouth spread in a fearsome grin. "What you decide to do with the seer—with *all* of them—after that is entirely up to you."

39

MICAH

I usually preferred honesty and clear communication, but I also saw no problem in letting Uuktar believe we'd slaughtered a bunch of *Lacertus* so we could all track down a planet full of innocent Trols.

Snitches will get their stitches.

Dissolving the Eki-made prison surrounding the seer was way easier than I'd thought it would be. First, I got out of my head about it—that was key—then I focused on reverse-engineering my own creations.

Instead of gathering the particles on hand and either pushing or pulling them into a solid shape, I made contact with the existing barrier and then abruptly blasted it back into the millions of particles from whence it came.

Simple.

Besides feeling like a bad bitch, the exercise showed me exactly how *my* shields were "more advanced" than the Eki's.

And I will just tuck that intel in my pocket for later.

As soon as we were back on the Lodger, I repaired first the ship then SWOL-E—*again*—before putting Pedro in their questionable care, far away from our temporary guest. I also made sure the anti-hypnotism feature was still activated in my glasses, just in case the Hydrassian thought they were gonna pull a fast one on me.

I wouldn't put anything past this fool.

Ziggy had already told me Stellarians were immune to such tricks, so I wasn't worried about him. If anyone should have been concerned for their safety, it was Uuktar, but they were acting as self-righteous as ever.

"We assume there will be a great feast in our honor once we're safely returned to Dionaea..." the seer's voices filled the cockpit with a pompous chorus as Ziggy piloted the ship. "But to show our gratitude, we would like to offer you an in-depth reading from Ulvin and us, free of charge!"

"How generous," Ziggy murmured dryly, and it was all I could do to keep my laughter contained.

Ain't nobody judgier than my man.

"So why doesn't Uulvin also know the coordinates for Karn?" I casually asked. "You know, since you're siblings and all."

Since you can communicate telepathically with each other— even through an Eki's shield.

The Hydrassian rolled their eyes. Meaning, they rolled all twelve of them so I wouldn't miss how unintelligent they thought I was.

"For security purposes, obviously," they huffed. "We are incredibly valuable assets, as evidenced by our unjust abduction, so proprietary intel is divided equally between us."

I glanced down at my phone, positioned where Uuktar couldn't see the screen, to assess the validity of that statement.

EARTH ANGEL

They're telling the truth, at least about their sibling not knowing the coordinates.

EARTH ANGEL

Once you're back on the giant Venus flytrap planet, I can dip into the other one's mind to see what they know.

I smiled and shook my head, wishing it wouldn't distract the psychic supervillain for me to send him all my unfiltered thoughts of shock and awe—because what Gabe and his twin could do was amazing.

Even if they need a conduit like me standing in front of their mark at this range.

Uuktar grunted in annoyance, unaware someone light years away was rifling through their thoughts. "What are you looking at over there, Earthling? We are your honored guest and deserve your full attention. Must we remind you that you would not be able to find this planet if it weren't for—"

"And we are *incredibly* thankful for your sacrifice," Ziggy interrupted, without taking his eyes off the endless stars ahead of us. "However, you must be tired after your ordeal. Shall I return you to your room? Or perhaps I could star hop you to Dionaea—reunite you with your loved ones before *we* continue on to Karn with the coordinates you've already provided..."

Tricky Space Daddy.

I could understand why Uuktar wouldn't take Zig up on the offer to head to bed, since it was in the same prison cell we'd kept the original Hydrassian, but for someone who'd been so "unjustly" imprisoned for so long, they didn't seem in a rush to get home.

All signs point to bullshit.

"It's quite alright, Stellarian." They sniffed haughtily, settling further into the captain's chair I'd offered them. "We would rather guide you all the way to your destination—to ensure everything goes to plan."

"Do they honestly believe we are this unintelligent?"

Again, I had to swallow my reaction to Ziggy's words, especially as they were in my head.

No point alerting the seer on board to the psychic warfare already underway.

Zig and I had figured out that if I kept my general shields activated but *not* the one sealing off my mind, he was still able to telepathically communicate with me. I'd then asked Gabe to test if *he* could get into my mind while my main shields were up, just to be sure my thoughts were safe. While the supe could still use my proximity as a jumping off point for accessing Uuktar's thoughts, he wasn't able to read mine.

So Operation Oh You Thought is well underway.

I knew my Space Daddy's question was rhetorical, but I replied anyway.

> *"I honestly think Hydrassians believe everyone is less intelligent than them. I also think this inflated sense of superiority is shared by many species out here..."*

Cough, cough.

"Well, in the Stellarians case, it's a fact. Although, I have met a certain Earthling whose intelligence puts the rest of us to shame."

My gaze drifted to the certificate Zig had commissioned from the Kaalas, already getting ideas of my own for how I could return the favor.

I just love seeing him blush beneath those murder freckles.

"That's odd..." Ziggy abruptly muttered out loud, glancing at his dashboard and back to the Intergalactic Highway head. "The radar should at least be picking up on the planet, even if I don't have a visual yet."

"It's there."

I couldn't say *how* I knew, but I did. Despite the wide swath of stars outside the window appearing unbroken, I could sense *something* was directly ahead of us. Something big.

Like a whole ass planet.

"Can you see it, Earthling?" Uuktar whispered, and I didn't need to look at the seer to get a visual of their frothing eagerness. "Can you identify where Karn is hiding?"

Hiding...

"Can you?" I shot back, tearing my gaze from the window to arch a brow at their dumbassery. "Or is that where *your* powers end?"

The Hydrassian huffed, although they couldn't argue with facts. "Of course, we cannot! It wasn't *our* kind who created the shield—it was *yours*."

And that's why Uulvin sent us.

While most of this puzzle had been falling into place, I'd been stuck on wondering why the Hydrassians on Dionaea hadn't just stolen Pedro from us and used the creature to trade for Uuktar's freedom. It wasn't just because they already knew the *Lacertus* weren't interested in the coordinates for Karn, but because none of them could remove the planet's shields.

And the Hydrassians are who the Trols are hiding from.

"Stop here, Zig," I softly commanded, getting my usual kinky thrill when he obeyed. "It's going to take me a while to dismantle the shields, and since all my concentration will be needed..." I turned to Uuktar. "I will need you to wait in your room—"

"NO!" the seer hissed, rising to stand before creepily focusing all six heads in my direction. "You *will* reveal Karn to us. You *will* extract more Trols for our breeding program. And you *will* continue to provide this service for our kind in the future. You work for the Hydrassians now."

This fool.

I stared blankly at them for a full thirty seconds, letting them *think* they had me hypnotized. Then, I laughed. "Nope. Not happening. But it sounds like someone needs a nap."

Uuktar opened their mouths to argue, but they'd been too preoccupied with their own imperial blind spots to sense they'd already been defeated. Recognizing his cue, Gabe used the mental access he already had to send the alien into a deep sleep before Ziggy whisked them away to their new "unjust" prison aboard the Lodger 79.

Girl, bye.

Once Zig reappeared, he swept me into his arms to pepper me with adorably schmoopy little kisses. "You know I *love* it when Commander Babygirl comes out to play, don't you?"

"I do!" I laughed, cupping his handsome face in my hands so I could land some kisses of my own. "Buuuuut... I'm having a hard time remembering... What *else* do you love?"

Say it again.

He rolled his pretty blue eyes before clearing them to show me his true form beneath. "You. I love *you*, Micah Salah."

Never stop.

"I love you too, Ziggy Andromeda," I replied with one last kiss —for now. "Even if it's *my* very impressive powers that can sense there's a planet out there at all."

We both turned to gaze out the window as a heavy silence fell over the cockpit.

"What do you want to do, sunshine?" he finally asked, and I shattered.

"I-I don't know!" I wailed as the tears threatened to fall *yet again.* "It's not that I don't *want* to give up Pedro, even though that's part of it, but the Trols are hiding for a *reason,* right? And even if I *can* dismantle the massive shields somehow camouflaging an entire planet long enough to get them home, what if... what if I can't put the shields back in place?"

My bad bitchery only goes so far.

Despite what the certificate says.

Before Ziggy could reply, scratching at the cockpit door caught our attention, followed by a familiar *pspsps.*

RIP SWOL-E.

With an exasperated sigh that was one thousand percent for show, Ziggy opened the door so Pedro could gallop in with an excited squeak. Of course, the little Trol immediately climbed his number one space dad like a tree so he could take his usual perch on Zig's shoulder.

Okay, I need to take another photo...

After I took about 300 photos, I blew out a slow breath. "I wish we could ask Pedro—"

"*KRAWWWK?!*" the Trol released an ear-splitting squawk, cocking its furry little head and blinking owlishly, as if replying to something only they could hear.

Is that...

BABY'S FIRST WORD!

I desperately fiddled with my translator device, hoping it could now interpret what the creature was saying. "That's it,

Pedro," I urged. "Say it again—"

"Krawk?" they repeated, and my heart simultaneously warmed and broke to hear the translation in my ear.

Father.

"They're calling out for their father, Zig," I croaked, swallowing thickly. "I-I think they can still hear their fellow Trols, even through the shield…"

Ziggy's Earthling face remained as impassive as always, but I could *feel* his emotions, whether he liked it or not.

Pride. Resignation. Sadness.

I see you, Space Daddy.

"Do you want to go home, Pedro?" he murmured, gently removing the creature from his shoulder and holding them at arm's length, facing the window. "Is that what you want, little star?"

MY HEART!

The waterworks were *definitely* imminent, but I didn't want to upset Pedro—or sway their loyalties—by revealing how upset I was.

This has to be their decision.

Pedro dangled from Ziggy's hands for another minute, head still cocked as they listened to *whatever* frequency they were picking up on. Then, they twisted in his hold and scampered up his arm, but instead of returning to their usual perch, Pedro slung both pangolin claws around his space dad's neck and stared him down from two inches away.

"Krawk," they squeaked, and I officially lost my shit.

"Ohmyfuckinggawwwwd, Zig!" I wailed, drawing in huge, sobbing breaths as Niagara Falls poured out of my eyeballs. "Pedro knows *you're* their daddy. I can't. I cannot HANDLE THE CUTENESS! Hold up... I need to document this moment..."

After I was done taking 300 more photos and blowing my nose at least as many times, I triumphantly smiled at *my* Space Daddy, knowing exactly what I wanted to do.

What needs to be done.

"I think we need to leave the Trols alone," I decisively stated. "At least until we *know* it's safe for them to come out of hiding."

Ziggy was still staring into Pedro's big, yellow eyes, trying to act cool even as he pumped our bond full of happy feels. "If that's what you think is best, Micah."

I SEE YOU.

"I do," I replied before smirking. "Besides, with Pedro imprinting on you the way they have, it would make the handoff difficult."

My man sent me a sidelong look of such loving exasperation, I almost swooned. "Yes, well, it appears I've imprinted on them as well."

Okay, SWOON!

"Well, then it's settled." I clapped my hands together, excited for the vengeance ahead. "Next stop: *Dionaea.*"

"Then Stellaria," Ziggy added, turning his attention back to *his* baby.

Our baby.

"Home," I stated.

"Yes," he murmured, the tiniest smile twitching his lips. "Home."

A smile that could've spanned all three of Stellaria's moons stretched across my face as we watched Ziggy tear around the dune racing track on the vehicle *I* had built for him.

With my very impressive powers, of course.

I'd started with a classic tube-frame dune buggy design, then added a sheet metal body to mimic my man's armor—more for the aesthetics than him actually needing any protection. A pair of modded Torrid Blasters served as the dual exhaust-style propulsion system, with a bucket full of loose Iota Bombs placed on the roof, specifically to distract the competition.

Hey, we play to win around here!

Pedro squealed in excitement when their favorite space dad took the turn closest to us, spraying cinnamon-colored dirt into the air before rocketing away.

"Sorry I'm late!" Honnor abruptly materialized next to Bron.

"Krunk wanted to discuss our talking points again before tomorrow's press conference."

"I'm still amazed these prideful lizards are willing to admit they were wrong on the intergalactic newsfeed..." Bron mused with clear amusement in their disembodied voice.

I couldn't help rolling my eyes as I handed a squirming Trol off to their favorite space grandpa. "Aren't the Stellarians owning up to their past mistakes too? Isn't the entire point of this broadcast to show two former enemies admitting they were wrong about *each other?"*

Bron snickered, although their starry gaze was on Honnor tossing a joyful Pedro into the air. "Of course. But we True Stellarians already knew Astrum Force's narrative was deceptive, so it was less of a shock to our systems."

Fair.

The piece of starry core lodged inside me pulsed encouragingly as Ziggy sent comfort while aggressively leaving his fellow racers in the dust. My man knew not being a 'real' Stellarian was a sore subject, so he liked to remind me how connected we were—how, despite our biological differences, I was still his fated mate-slash-one true love.

He even uses his words sometimes!

I knew my genetic makeup was a silly thing to be upset about. It was luck of the draw—no different than being born either a supe or a normie back on Earth, or which superpowers you manifested.

Versus which ones you acquire from your mate.

Unlike with the Earthside *inventus* bond between supes, Ziggy couldn't wield my powers as if they were his own. The only reason I was able to mimic his powers, like star hopping, was because of *him* existing inside me.

Being stellar collisions was still a fun connection to experiment with. We'd recently discovered I could produce tendrils —*real* tendrils, as opposed to my mechanical ones—but, again, it was actually Ziggy doing the heavy lifting.

Even if I'm the one behind the wheel.

There was another Stellarian trick I'd been practicing on the sly, but I was waiting until we handed off Pedro for their sleepover at Honnor and Bron's tonight to try it out with Ziggy.

Breathe, Micah...

I was so nervous about my date night plan, I refocused on the conversation just to distract myself.

"So..." I awkwardly cleared my throat. "What talking points did you decide on for the Big Karnilian Debunking Campaign?"

Honnor chuckled before covering Pedro's ears, just like I'd taught them. "That we unanimously agree the Hydrassians are full of shit."

Amen to that!

We knew it would be a hard sell to convince countless planets this trusted source had been playing them all along, but we were confident it would resonate.

For lack of a better word.

The Stellarian-*Lacertus* rivalry being so well known added an almost indisputable weight to the announcement, because no one would expect these notorious hotheads to agree on *anything.*

It's a new era for both planets.

As promised, Ziggy had helped facilitate truce talks between Honnor and Krunk soon after we returned to Stellaria, and it was during this initial meeting that the two leaders decided to publicly throw the Hydrassians under the bus.

It's the least they deserve.

Ruining the seers' reputations would be the icing on the karma cake. Ziggy and I had already made a quick stop on *Dionaea* on our way home to enact some sweet revenge of our own.

More psychic warfare.

The last Uulvin had heard, we'd freed Uuktar, thanks to their sob story of "unjust persecution." With us presumably falling under their sibling's hypnotism trap, *of course* we would then do their bidding, removing the shield protecting Karn so these snakes could have an unlimited supply of innocent Trols at their disposal.

Sike!

Gabe kept Uuktar knocked out for the entire journey back to *Dionaea* so they couldn't warn their psychic sibling before we arrived. By the time we appeared outside the Hydrassians' half-shielded cave complex—with an unconscious seer in tow—it was too late for them to protect themselves.

All it took was for me to set eyes on Uulvin before Gabriel Suarez got to work. As soon as he was done extracting every shred of useful intel from their brain, I created shields around both Uulvin and Uktar's minds, barring them from not only telepathically communicating with each other, but accessing their psychic powers at all.

Because we want them to remember how it felt.

Needless to say, these personal prisons did not go over well with the elders, but Ziggy coolly stepped in to remind everyone the Eki could return at any moment to finish the shields, trapping them inside their caves permanently.

With a dozen hungry *Dionaea muscipula* to munch on 'em a little.

He is so effortlessly sexy and threatening, I cannot.

Uulvin had made one last ditch effort to plead their case, dramatically wailing that losing one's powers was a fate worse than death. This was a little hypocritical, considering they'd done exactly that to Ziggy the last time we were here, but I focused on pointing out that *they* were the ones who had defied destiny itself.

Zero sympathy for fools in the Find Out stage of Fucking Around.

Thanks to Gabe's espionage, we learned the sneaky snakes *were* the ones who'd anonymously tipped off the Stellarians to rescue the egg from the Maroxians. They also encouraged the Irathians to attack Stellaria—promising victory, of course— but that was done as a cover, to distract from the Hydrassian mercenary simultaneously harassing gem vendors in the bazaars.

To no one's surprise, denying their mercenary side hustle turned out to be just another lie on the pile. Just as Ziggy had deduced, the Hydrassians fabricated an entire mythology around Trols and karnilian for the sole purpose of lining their own pockets, and they were more than happy to sell their services to others to fund their lucrative scheme.

Not only did they hire themselves out as gemstone bloodhounds, haunting busy Muonovas, but they offered vague promises of victory during psychic readings to encourage the hunt. With how single-mindedly focused on intergalactic supremacy certain species were, it was unsurprisingly simple to trick them into believing the hype.

This cycle of deception and destruction would have continued indefinitely were it not for the Hydrassians finally ending up on the wrong side of fate.

What the seers hadn't counted on was their *own* imperial blind spot, in the form of a seasoned mercenary by the name of Ziggy Andromeda. While his deeply ingrained distrust was something Dr. Micah was privately working on, Zig's suspicious nature made him an excellent bloodhound as well.

My man has a PhD in sniffing out bullshit.

Uulvin *had* gotten one thing right about Ziggy: He *was* honorable, and despite the pain of dismantling his own systemic biases, he continuously chose uncomfortable truth over supposed supremacy. He bravely, if not begrudgingly, embraced his destiny as a *hero* to his own kind—a destiny that, ironically, had once been predicted by the Hydrassians to his former Astrum Force commanders.

If that's not poetic—petty—justice, I don't know what is.

What nobody predicted, including Ziggy, was that he would form a bond with the Trol at the center of it all. Even with him initially trying to claim the karnilian was to blame for awakening his previously nonexistent parental instincts, I knew there was more to it than that.

While my childhood was far from perfect, I'd grown up in relative comfort, and my older siblings had taken care of me. Both Zig and Pedro were orphans dismissed by their own kind, solo travelers adrift among the stars with no family to call their own.

Until they found each other.

Despite his generational trauma, Ziggy's ice-cold exterior had started to crack, just enough to allow a certain ferocious furbaby into his heart.

And this is why an official "Best Space Dad in All the Galaxies" certificate now hangs in the Lodger cockpit.

We were still unsure *where* Pedro's egg had originally come from. The Eki's shield stopped anyone from entering or *leaving* Karn, so the little Trol being blasted into space like Kal-El in their Kryptonian Rocket was out of the question. A more likely scenario was Pedro's birthing parent being held in captivity somewhere with the egg either lost or stolen from there.

It was a moot point anyway. Pedro had found their family, and the general plan was to leave Karn alone until long after our Hydrassian smear campaign went live. Only when it was deemed safe for Trols to be seen in public again would the Eki even *consider* removing the shields keeping the planet undetectable and safe.

We knew this because we'd also made a stop on Ekistron on our journey home—mostly so Ziggy could swallow his pride and *apologize* to Leeloo, but also so I could beg the Jedi Master to let me train with them again.

I wanna be a space wizard, goddamnit!

True to form, that shit-stirring Eki let me *sweat* for a good sixty seconds before they replied. Right as I was about to go lie down on the Intergalactic Highway, Leeloo cackled from deep within their sparkly robes and cheerfully agreed to teach me the ways of the matter manipulator Force.

To start, I got a quick lesson in detaching myself from my creations, which conserved my energy while ensuring my shields stayed intact, even when I wasn't around.

Aside from the Hydrassians and their mind-shields, SWOL-E was the first lucky recipient of this new trick. In the interest of giving adoptive parents and grandparents across the universe a break, I upgraded the alarm system and created miniature, and *hopefully* indestructible, shields around the long-suffering nanny bot's wiring.

My money's still on Pedro's two rows of fangs, unfortunately...

As we said our goodbyes, Zig politely asked Leeloo to tell him more about their common ancestor, but the Eki simply pointed to the endless stars beyond Nuclei City's open hatch.

Much to learn, we still have.

That mission would have to wait. Honnor had insisted we hurry back, specifically so they could promote Ziggy to an official Astrum Force position.

Interstellar Ambassador.

He hates it, of course.

"How are you settling in at your new lodging?" Honnor breezily asked as he fed Pedro a strip of raw meat.

Despite being allergic to any mention of his hero status, Zig and I agreed the fancy new high-rise housing that came with the gig was worth the hit to his bad bitch reputation.

There's even a roof deck!

"We love it," I truthfully replied. "And I appreciate Ziggy getting the recognition he deserves."

My man deserves all the kudos.

"Well, now that the Stellarian-Lacertus Peace Accord has been finalized, that humble mercenary will get another chance to earn his keep," Bron joked as the merc in question appeared, proudly waving the bag of CSI remains he'd just won.

Looks like we'll be dining on corpus spongiosum tonight!

"You have a new mission for me?" Ziggy asked, and I couldn't help rolling my eyes at the blatant eagerness in his tone.

Bron chuckled, but Honnor replied in a somber tone. *"Indeed. It appears Karn is not the only planet disappearing off the map. The difference is that the others all sent out distinct distress signals beforehand."*

Yikes.

Ziggy hummed distractedly, attention already on his Celestial Cube, no doubt cataloging which weapons would be joining us for the job. "When do we begin?"

His creator huffed. *"Tomorrow. I believe your stellar collision specifically asked for a date night tonight..."*

"Oh, yes," Ziggy murmured, tearing his gaze away from his cube to fix his attention on me. "What did you have in mind, Micah?"

Eek!

The full weight of three Stellarian stares almost had me star hopping back to our new apartment alone, but then I was saved by a signal from a galaxy far, far away.

"Hold that thought!" I squeaked, fumbling my buzzing phone out of my pocket, smiling when I saw who the text was from.

KING OF THE MONSTERS

> You know, Meeks... if I were a lesser man, I might get offended at the message you sent with that photo.

I snickered. The photo Zion was referring to was me posing with Krunk and a few other *Lacertus,* which I'd sent with the caption, "If you can't run with the big dogs, you'd better stay on the porch."

Even though I knew I was playing with fire, I couldn't help replying with some sass.

> Were any lies detected, big bro?

KING OF THE MONSTERS

> Absolutely none. I'm glad you're enjoying yourself out there, even though I miss having my favorite little bro around...

He probably says that to all our brothers.

Three dots appeared and disappeared a few times, which was strange behavior from the self-confident supe, but I patiently waited him out.

It's better than answering Ziggy's question.

> KING OF THE MONSTERS
>
> On that note, the family's about to get a little bigger.

"WHAT?!" I shouted, even though he couldn't hear me.

Unable to resist the tea, Ziggy peered at my phone screen over my shoulder.

> Are you and Balty adopting? What does Daisy think? When is this happening? When can we meet the baby?!!!

My man sighed heavily, but I couldn't help noticing he remained invested in the conversation.

I see you, Space Daddy.

> KING OF THE MONSTERS
>
> It's a biological kid. Your Space Husband gave us some mpreg pointers.

Ohhh?

Ziggy tensed beside me as I turned, horror movie slow, before lecherously assessing my man from top to bottom.

Especially his bottom.

"You wanna know what I had in mind for tonight, Zig?" I smirked before grabbing his arm and holding on tight. "Let Commander Babygirl debrief you."

And then I star hopped my stellar collision straight into bed.

Rude of me to leave you hanging like that, hmm? You can get your claws on **Commander Babygirl Reporting for Booty** *by subscribing to my newsletter* **HERE.**

If you want more space sloot schmoop and spice, head to my Patreon! *I recently shared the (mostly SFW) bonus special -* **The Most Impressive Meet-Cute in All the Galaxies** *(Micah & Ziggy's ACTUAL meet-cute!) for all paid tiers, and the second installment of NSFW alien polycule filth -* **All I Want Before I Die** *- for MVPs of DP and above (and here's a quick link for part 1 -* **Horny F*cking Glo Worms***).*

Yes, we will have ONE MORE **Villains in Space** *mission in this trilogy, called* **Interstellar Love Song,** *before we head elsewhere in this universe (subscribe* **HERE** *for preorder and release alerts).*

If you felt you missed important information (despite my best efforts), orbit back to the main **Villainous Things** *series, starting with* **Not All Himbos Wear Capes** *to catch up on the backstory (and to meet Zig all over again).*

And be sure to share your love (through reviews and word of mouth) for **Space Daddy's Guide to the Galaxy***—thank you for reading!*

AUTHOR'S NOTE & ACKNOWLEDGMENTS

I'm not crying, you're crying...

I actually don't know *why* I'm surprised by the amount of schmoop that made its way into this book (since I am the schmoop_simp), but here we are, and I only have myself to blame.

That and an emotionally constipated alien.

Because *Ziggy* is the one getting me all up in my feels—especially with just how far he's grown as a character... *especially* with how he's now let not just Micah into his borrowed heart, but an entire family as well!

A common "complaint" I heard about **Earth Boys Are Easy** was that there wasn't enough Rabble Chat (or general meddling from the main **Villainous Things** characters). It was an easy enough fix for our resident "space wizard,"Micah to fix the WI-FI situation (more on *his* personal growth in a minute), and while I still kept the focus of this tale on Ziggy and Micah's relationship, it felt... *symbolic* to allow their ridiculous families in.

You see, the Earth Boys storyline was insular and cut off from the world—much like Ziggy and his emotions—but **Space Daddy's Guide to the Galaxy** was purposefully expanded to allow these connections (or reconnections) in, to make our sad boi Stellarian's world that much brighter.

There are a loud few who love to hate on our precious alien polycule (and polycules in general), but this supposedly out of character situation was actually an essential part of Ziggy's character growth.

He didn't "do a 180" (as one tone-deaf hater boldly and incorrectly commented on an Instagram post of mine), didn't magically turn into someone he's not just to add more spice. This is Ziggy becoming who he was meant to be, surrounded by the extended family he always deserved, especially after being emotionally closed off for so long.

With Micah's unconditional love and support (and SO much consent & communication) Ziggy has been willing to lean into this unconventional situation and re/connect with his true family. Anyone who *actually* understands my characters will be able to comprehend the incredible amount of bravery and vulnerability this required from our proud Stellarian.

If you're here, I'm going to assume you *get it* (unless you're purely hate-reading, in which case, yikes!), and you support these characters growing and changing in ways that benefit them in the end (even if it's a little uncomfortable along the way as they figure things out... *just like in real life!).*

Despite Micah being the one "carrying the team" when it comes to the emotional IQ, he had his *own* battles with self-worth to fight (thanks to his terrible parents), and I *loved* being able to offer our favorite space slot the opportunity to level up his powers—to become the "most impressive creature in all the galaxies" that Ziggy has always known him to be.

And, of course, they did it together, because writing these two "green flag men" has been a balm on my soul during these turbulent, frightening times, and I hope they have brought you the same level of comfort.

As of press time, Villains in Space has *not* seen the same success as Villainous Things, but I remind myself that VT didn't *really* take off until book 2 (Gentlemen Prefer Villains), so maybe (hopefully!) I'll see the same success with Space Daddy.

Either way, I fully intend on diving directly into writing book 3 of this space adventure trilogy, because it's important to me to give these two idiots-in-love the *true* happily ever after they deserve.

Micah getting space married to his space husband, of course! (Aaaand... maybe a lil mpreg to rival his big bro's...)

There will be a perilous plot, as I do, and spice. So. Much. Spice. Ziggy's skinsuit closet continues to provide us with all the fancy accessories our slooty hearts desire.

Excuse us, C? You can't just mention book three of **Villains in Space** and not drop the title!

Why, it's **Interstellar Love Song** (because the schmoop must go on!), and as always, you should subscribe **HERE** for preorder and release alerts. And if you were one of the strategic ones who preordered a "deluxe" ebook **direct from me**, you should plan on doing that again (for spicy art and extra goodies, not to mention an earlier release!).

As always, I will continue dropping spicy (and/or schmoopy) bonus specials on Patreon (like the alien poly-cule encounters: **Horny F*cking Glo Worms** and **All I Want Before I Die**) or the *real* meet-cute of Micah & Ziggy: **The Most Impressive Meet-Cute in All the Galaxies.**

There will also be a verrrry special special edition (or three) for Villains in Space being announced in the coming months, so be sure to **lovingly stalk me everywhere**.

What's next for this universe? How does dark academia sound (at least, *my* spin on it)? Or more contemporary tales from the "normies" stuck dealing with these superpowered idiots on Earth? Or superhero hockey? (Jk...)

Wherever we go, I know you ride-or-die Weird-Ho's will be with me, because YOU believe in love is love in ALL forms (and no matter how many individuals are involved)!

HOW ABOUT SOME SCHMOOPY ACKNOWLEDGMENTS?

Despite ongoing subpar service provider experiences (for real, what rock are these dusty grifters crawling out from under?), I have been #blessed by adding two new rockstars to my team: My PA, Krys, and my Patreon/Store Manager, Shawna. These lovelies have taken *such* a load off my back and I am forever thankful for them.

Vikki from Literati Media continues to pound the pavement to find me foreign rights and translations deals and I'm still optimistic that *this* year is when it will happen! My alpha readers returned with much hype, and I added some new blood to the mix: Adrienne, Amanda, Billie, Kris, Season & Sophie. And an extra acknowledgment to Bermi for patiently answering random pronoun questions and Dee for swooping in with the sensitivity read!

Of course, my stellar collision, Lem (aka @lemonade_doodles) gets extra sloppy smooches—not just as my Villainous Illustrator but as my creative partner (in crime) and bestie for life.

I'm forever thankful for my author friends and the various group (or one-on-one!) chats we inhabit. Writing can be such a solitary adventure, it's comforting to know I have others at my back who get it, and who are more than willing to offer support and advice when needed.

These acknowledgments wouldn't be complete without mentioning my ARC and Street Team lovelies (some of whom have been here since book 1—Shadows Spark). It's because of YOU loud, proud Weird-Ho's that others have taken the chance on my dirty little books! Thank you.

And last but certainly not least, my superfans on Patreon—those willing (and able!) to support me in this way. I won't sour this section with too much doom and gloom, but with times being so turbulent right now—especially for us indie authors writing LGBTQIA+ stories—my Patreon (and direct sales store) have become not just my safety net but my safe space.

Speaking of Patreon... all my Va Ju-Ju Queens and above get their NAMES listed here *(with the list growing longer every time!)*: Adrienne, Alaina, Ali, Amanda H., Amanda Q., Amber, Amy, Ashe L., Ashe B., Beth, Bree, Brooks, C8, Carlee, Charlotte B., Charlotte M., Chelsi, Christina, Ciara, CJ, Claudine, Crystal, Danielle C., Danielle D., Danielle W., Dedicatedzombie, Elizabeth, Elle, Emily, Erica S., Erica C., Erica T., Erika, Erin, Fawn, Gigi, Haley, Heidi, Hillary, Hope, Jamie A., Jamie V., Jessica, Jessyca, Jo, Kai, Kaitlin, Kala, Karen, Kat, KayBee, Kayla, Kaylah, Kellpool, Kelly, Kelsey H., Kelsey M., Kelsi, Kit, Krista, Kristina P., Kristina S., Laura B., Laura T., Laura W., Lee, Leigh, lsmain, Mandy, Melissa H., Melissa L., Melissa T., Mercedes, Natalie, Nereyda, Nita, Paige, Paula, Rannveig, Rebecca A., Rebecca H., Roxanna,

Samantha, Sarah B., Sarah K, Season, Selena, Shawn, Shawna M., Sophia, Sophie, Steph D., Steph P., Stephanie, Syn, Tamara, Taylor, Vickie, Victoria, Wraithy & Yi.

And just a reminder that—for my own mental health— I've started putting up preorders only about a month before release. It's a bit nerve-racking for me to not see those preorders building over time, but I have to trust that you lovelies will still want to read my unhinged fuckery on shorter notice.

Be sure to *(politely) stalk me everywhere* and *subscribe to my newsletter for pre-oder alerts* to stay *in-the-know on Micah & Ziggy's next book, more in the Villainous universe, and anything else I dream up for you!*

Keep your fangs sharp!

XXX
-C

(Pedro Pspspscal by Lemonade Doodles, ofc)

REVIEWS

If you have enjoyed **Space Daddy's Guide to the Galaxy**, be sure to show your love for our Space Daddy and his babygirl, through word of mouth and reviews! It helps other readers find my work, which helps me as an indie author. *Thank you!*

Amazon
Goodreads
Bookbub

But don't stop there: Tag me in your reviews, stories, edits, videos, and fan art on social. I love to share these posts with my followers!

VILLAINS IN SPACE PLAYLIST

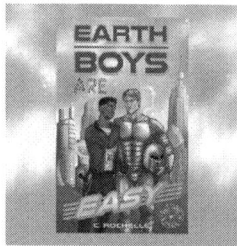

Please enjoy the Spotify playlist that inspired the Villainous Things series *(and let me know if you have a song to add to the retro space vibes!).*

SPACE DADDY PRINTS
AVAILABLE
BY LEMONADE DOODLES

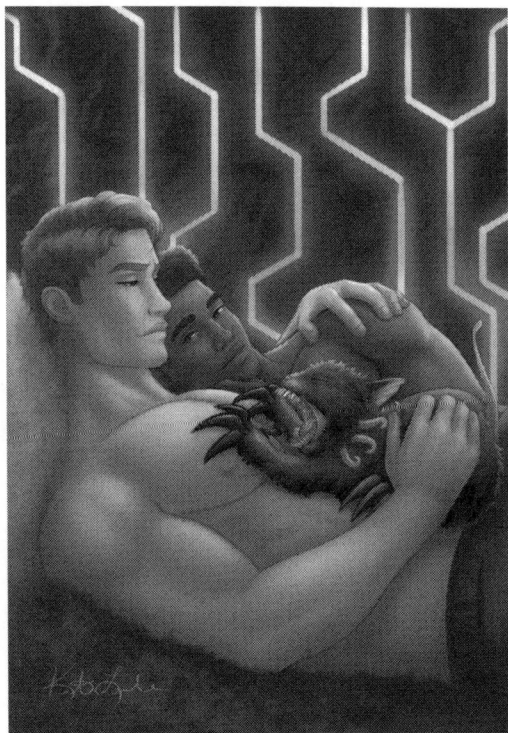

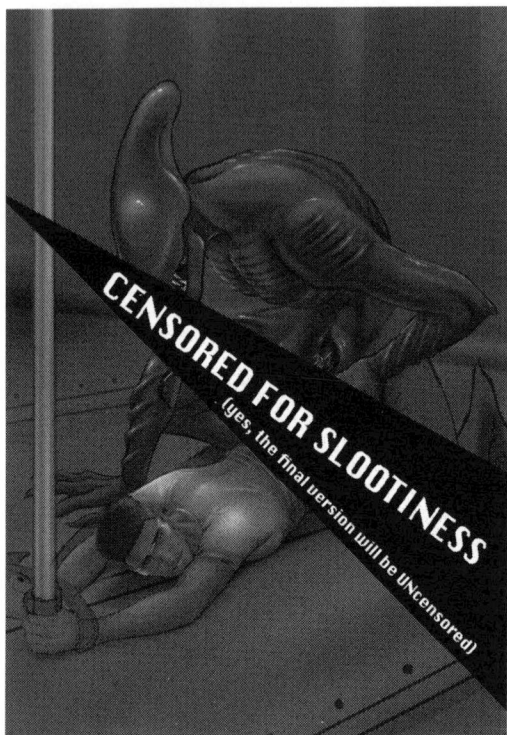

And more!

Order full-color 5x7" art prints at **C-Rochelle.com/shop** (and **join Patreon** at MVPs of DP+ to see UNcensored art)

Looking for signed paperbacks, N/SFW art prints, bookplates & other goodies? My store can be found at **C-Rochelle.com/shop** (and **Patreon** members get discounts on art prints and signed books with extra swag, plus exclusive special editions!)

Be sure to *(politely) stalk me everywhere and **subscribe to my newsletter for pre-oder alerts** to stay in-the-know on what's next!*

VILLAINS IN SPACE TRILOGY - SUPERHERO/ALIEN MM ROMANCE (ALSO ON AUDIBLE):

- **Earth Boys Are Easy** *(sign up for the newsletter to get the Meet-Cute at the Muonova bonus epilogue)*
- **Space Daddy's Guide to the Galaxy** *(sign up for the newsletter to get the Commander Babygirl Reporting for Booty bonus epilogue)*
- **Interstellar Love Song** *(subscribe to the newsletter for preorder and release alerts)*

Want the series that started it all?

(While you wait for more Villainous spin-offs—like Supe Academy—to come?)

VILLAINOUS THINGS - SUPERHERO/VILLAIN MM+ (& FF) ROMANCE (ALSO ON AUDIBLE):

- **Not All Himbos Wear Capes** *(sign up for the newsletter to get the Only Good Boys Get to Top Their Xaddys bonus epilogue)*
- **Gentlemen Prefer Villains** *(sign up for the newsletter to get the Yes Sir, Sorry Sir bonus epilogue)*

- **Putting Out for a Hero** *(sign up for the newsletter to get the Idiots in Love bonus epilogue)*
- **Enter the Multi-Vers** *(sign up for the newsletter to get the Among the Stars bonus epilogue)*
- *If you're reading chronologically, Earth Boys Are Easy goes here!*
- **Rabble: End Game** *(subscribe to the newsletter to get the Husbands, Assemble bonus epilogue)*
- **BONUS! Villainous All the Way: A Sweet n Spicy Celebrations Collection** - *order it direct from me (with extra goodies) or from **Amazon**.*

MONSTROUSLY MYTHIC SERIES - POLYAM WHY CHOOSE (ALSO ON AUDIBLE):

- **The 12 Hunks of Herculeia** (Herculeia Duet, Book 1)
- **Herculeia the Hero** (Herculeia Duet, Book 2) *(sign up for the newsletter for the bonus epilogue: Three Heads Are Better Than One)*
- **Herculeia: Complete Duet + Bonus Content** *(includes Calm Down Monster-Fucker, Three Heads Are Better Than One, & the Thanksgiving Special: Get Stuffed, plus UNcensored art)*

More Monstrously Mythic Tales:

- **Valhalla is Full of Hunks** (Iola's standalone, Norse Mythology Why Choose) *(sign up for the newsletter for the bonus tale: The Yule Log in Jör's Lederhosen)*

STRANGE VACATIONLAND MONSTERVERSE (MMF, MF, MMF):

The previously published anthology tales **Be Not Afraid, You Can't Get There from Here**, and **Vampires Totally Suck** are now available to be purchased directly from the author's website in a

Tales from Strange Vacationland ebook collection. *Stay tuned for more in the future.*

The Yaga's Riders Trilogy - Polyam Why Choose (Also on Audible):

- **Rise of the Witch**
- **A Witch Out of Time**
- **Call of the Ride**
- **The Yaga's Riders: Complete Trilogy + Bonus Content** *(The Asa Baby Christmas Special & the Too Peopley Valentine's Day Special)*

More Yaga's Riders Tales:

- **A Song of Saints and Swans** *(Anthia spin-off novella, which includes From the Depths & the Halloween Special: It's Just a Bunch of Va Ju-Ju Voodoo)*

Wings of Darkness + Light Trilogy - Polyam Why Choose:

- **Shadows Spark**
- **Shadows Smolder**
- **Shadows Scorch**
- **Wings of Darkness + Light: The Complete Trilogy + Bonus Content** *(Oversized Cupids V-Day Special, The Second Coming Easter Special, & the Sexy Little Devil Halloween Specials Pt. 1 & Pt. 2)*

More from the Wings Universe:

- **Death by Vanilla** (Gage origin story novella)

ABOUT THE AUTHOR

C. Rochelle here! I'm a naughty but sweet, introverted, Aquarius weirdo who believes a sharp sense of humor is the sexiest trait, loves shaking my booty to Prince, and have never met a cheese I didn't like. Oh, and I write extra spicy paranormal, monster & sci-fi love-is-love romance with epic plots and dark, unhinged humor.

Want More?

- **Join my Clubhouse of Smut on Patreon**
- **Subscribe to the Weird-H0 Bi-Weekly**
- **Find all my books at C-Rochelle.com**
- **Join my Little Sinners Facebook group**
- **Stalk me in all the places on Linktree**

GLOSSARY & REFERENCES

I created the companion glossary below, to hopefully enhance your (unhinged) reading experience of Space Daddy's Guide to the Galaxy.

FIRST, A NOTE ON ALIEN LANGUAGES/SPECIES: Unlike with Earth Boys Are Easy, I chose to show all conversations in alien languages being translated into American English (thanks to Micah's handy translator device!), with Stellarian being italicized (see **Formatting Notes**), but we do still have occasional "sci-fi" words thrown in to keep things interesting.

- **Andromeda** *(Greek):* A spiral galaxy (also called Messier 31 or M31) and our closest major galaxy neighbor at 2.5 million light years away from Earth. It is also a northern constellation directly south of Cassiopeia between Pegasus and Perseus, as—in mythology—Andromeda was an Ethiopian princess of great beauty who was rescued from a sea monster by her future husband, Perseus. *This is also what*

Ziggy chose as his last name on Earth, since Stardust was already taken.

- **Apotelesma** *(Latin):* The effect of the stars on human destiny. ***Stellaria's** largest moon.*
- **Arach** *(Latin):* Spider-like alien species that I *refuse* to describe in detail because I am deathly afraid of spiders.
- **Astrum Force Command:** The fictional military dictatorship of **Stellaria** and Ziggy's former/current employer as a mercenary. The old (evil) Astrum Force was dismantled at the end of Earth Boys and recently relaunched as the benevolent (but still violent, when needed) fighting force of **Stellaria**, with Honnor as the new Head Commander.
- **Black-bagged** *(Slang):* This is used in reference to covert operations obtaining information for human intelligence, including (but not limited to) kidnapping someone to make them disappear (as opposed to ransom). It's like that scene in *V for Vendetta* when Evey Hammond is captured outside Deitrich's house for questioning.
- **Borque:** A fictional alien species that is tall and lean, with a glossy, chestnut brown pelt and vampire-length canines (despite being vegetarian). Think a cross between a Wookie and a Sasquatch, but sexier. They also possess two dicks, complete with knots, although DP is highly discouraged due to the girth *(cue sad Micah face).*
- **Celestial Cube:** A fictional device that resembles an all-white Rubik's cube, where the various squares are tapped in just the right order to activate different functions and engage weapons.

- **Corpus Spongiosum** *(Latin):* A column of spongy tissue that runs through the shaft (body) and glans (head) of the penis, and surrounds the urethra. It contains blood vessels that fill with blood to help make an erection and keep the urethra open during the erection. Since you're in this deep, you may as well Google it. *Also: Micah's favorite Stellarian street food.*
- **Deathball:** A fictional supe sport that's a cross between American football, rugby, and MMA (mixed martial arts). Ziggy was playing it as part of his cover on Earth (to keep a close watch on Zion Salah, who also played), but he also enjoyed the violent (although not violent enough) outlet it provided.
- **Deathpond:** Those who've read the main Villainous Things series will recognize this slang reference to the aquatic pool located beneath the Salah mansion, built for Zion's needs as a super who turns into a *Lacertus.*
- **Dionaea muscipula** *(Latin):* Aka, Venus Flytrap, a carnivorous plant native to the temperate and subtropical wetlands of North Carolina and South Carolina, on the East Coast of the United States *(or... the planet of **Dionaea**, depending on who you ask).*
- **Eki:** A fictional alien species whose appearance is undocumented, thanks to their identity-shielding, glittery space wizard robes (which may or may not have been loosely based on the Dinks from *Spaceballs).* The Eki have "matter manipulation" powers suspiciously close to Micah's (the ability to create anything from inorganic matter), and our boys discover some shocking truths while visiting their planet *(which will be explored more in book 3!).* The

planet they inhabit is **Ekistron,** which suffered an ice age at some point in history, forcing the Eki underground, to their lava-fueled **Nuclei City.**

- **Felis catus** *(Latin):* A house cat—a small domesticated carnivorous mammal (and *not* what Pedro is, despite Ziggy's disgruntled comments).
- **Gaia** *(Greek):* In Greek mythology, the personification of Earth—the ancestral mother of all life. *Also what many alien species refer to Earth as.*
- **Genero** *(Latin):* Creation. *One of **Stellaria's** three moons.*
- **Genus** *(Latin):* A taxonomic rank above species and below family as used in the biological classification of living and fossil organisms as well as viruses.
- **Hatini:** A fictional alien meal first encountered in Earth Boys on Kaalanesea—an "unexciting grain dessert puréed with spices and topped with local fruits," according to Ziggy. *Micah enjoyed it and it's the perfect thing to feed a newborn Trol!*
- **Homogenous:** The same or having a similar kind or nature. In biology, possessing the same genetic structure.
- **Hydrassian:** A fictional alien species with a scaled, humanoid body (with lizard hands, feet, and claws) and six Hydra-style snake-heads. They possess psychic and prophetic powers and are sought out by other species for their predictions (especially for the outcomes of battles). They live on the planet of **Dionaea**, and were first spotted in the "safest bazaar" in Earth Boys, as a sneaky reference to **my Herculeia duet**.
- **Igneous** *(Latin):* Rock solidified from lava or magma.

- **Intergalactic Highway:** Exactly what it sounds like. The ambiguous thoroughfare used by space travelers to traverse the galaxies.
- **Interitus** *(Latin):* Destruction. *One of **Stellaria's** three moons.*
- **Invenio-Astralis** *(Latin):* Genius related to the stars. *In this universe, it's directional coordinates to the galaxy containing **Stellaria** and its three moons.*
- **Inventus** *(Latin):* Find/discover. Perfect passive participle of invenio and the word used to describe supe soulmates.
- **Iota Bombs:** Fictional, acorn-sized explosives that are more of a distraction than anything. The flashes of light they give off are enough to temporarily blind someone, whether hot-bod **Xenomorphs** in pursuit of their prey or dune racing competition.
- **Irathians:** A fictional, flesh-eating species of alien who Stellarians don't consider a threat in the least.
- **Iridium** *(Latin):* Considered one of the rarest metals on Earth and, presumably, on other planets, since we see it here in a form of currency (coins) used for paying the **Hydrassians** *(and possibly "printed on demand" by a certain matter manipulating supe).*
- **Kaala:** A fictional alien species, always born as twins who remain together for life. Micah (me) eloquently describes Kaalas as having alien emoji faces 👽 with silver skin covered with a thin layer of velvet, like a young buck's growing antlers. And while their bodies are fairly humanoid, their hands consist of only three fingers and their feet have no toes at all. *Kaalanesea is their home planet while **Kaalanesean** is their "tinkling chimes" language.*

- **Karn:** The fictional planet where **Trols** originate from *(interesting that it's named after the stone inside them, hmm?),* but not much more is known, since the **Eki** hid it behind a cloaking shield to protect the Trols from extinction.

- **Karnilian:** A fictional stone found inside **Trols,** characterized by its glowing red color and almost maddening "pull" to those who encounter it. This stone is highly coveted as the **Hydrassians** can supposedly use it in their rituals to predict (or, determine...) the outcome of battles.

- **Katana** *(Japanese):* A sword characterized by a curved, single-edged blade with a circular or squared guard and long grip to accommodate two hands. Katanas were used by **Samurai** in Feudal Japan.

- **Lacertus** *(Latin):* In this case, it's derived from *lacerta* ("lizard") and is a lizard-like species that originally landed on Earth during the Stone Age. In the Villainous Things series (*Gentlemen Prefer Villains,* specifically), we see cave drawings of them, with wings and claws and faces that look like the Incan god Supay. Micah's eldest brother Zion looks like a (smaller) version of *Lacertus* when he's in his supe form. In this book we also get to visit the aquatic planet of **Lacertus,** a convenient stop on the Intergalactic Highway, multiple rows of piers had been built for the visiting species who couldn't breathe underwater. The differentiation between the two is that the species is *italicized* and the planet name is not.

- **Maroxian:** A fictional alien species described as vaguely humanoid, only because they are bipedal. They are as close to a xenomorph as ~~copyright allows~~

possible, with an inky-black exoskeleton, sleek aerodynamic head, disconcerting lack of eyes and an extremely impressive tongue (Micah approves—when it's Ziggy). They also have sharp fangs and claws, a tail, and a cock-cage like structure surrounding other appendages (MICAH DEFINITELY APPROVES!). They live on the planet **Marox** and *eat* most every other species, which is why Stellarians are needed to go up against them (and why Ziggy insisted on Micah staying with the ship).

- **Metamorphic** *(Greek):* Rocks that have undergone changes due to heat and pressure.
- **Mica** *(Latin):* A group of crystalized silicate minerals with the notable physical characteristic of individual crystals being easily split into fragile elastic plates. The word is derived from the Latin *mīca,* meaning "crumb," and probably influenced by *micare*—"to glitter."
- **Muonova:** A chain of fictional, city-sized, floating rest-stops along the **Intergalactic Highway**, which include bars, by-the-hour hotel rooms, red-light districts, sprawling markets, and more...
- **Neluth:** A fictional alien species with flippered hands known for their luminescent skin and extra-long appendages—like Micah's favorite tentacle dick delicacy—and the ability to camouflage themselves as a defense mechanism.
- **Nova** *(Latin):* New. What Stellarians call their young. Also an astronomic term given to bright stars that appear suddenly in the sky and release powerful energy.

- **Nuclei** *(Latin)* **City:** A fictional lava-fueled, alien city located beneath the snowy surface of **Ekistron.** While it probably started with existing caverns and lava tubes, the **Eki** used their matter manipulation powers to create not only the structures but everything they needed to be a self-sufficient society.
- **Ogorn's milk:** A fictional alien beverage that I never fully explain (but I feel like we can all agree on what this might be, hmm?).
- **Opertum** *(Latin):* A fictional alien species that's "a cross between [Micah's] beloved, heavily-armored *Transformers* and the sleek, futuristic mech suits favored by Earthling science fiction" (according to Ziggy). I called them this based on the Latin word for "covered," and included them to try and quiet the Transformers-style plot bunny that's been running around inside my head since before the Villainous series was first published. It only helped a little...
- **Ovipositing:** The act of using a tube-like organ to lay eggs inside your mate. (Micah's swiping left on any skinsuits with this feature...)
- **Padawan** *(Star Wars):* An apprentice Jedi (aka, a space wizard).
- **Pangolin** *(Malay):* The only mammals covered in scales, a unique adaptation that serves as armor and allows them to curl into a ball for protection. They are also one of my illustrator, Lem's, favorite animals. Just Google them and enjoy the cuteness overload.
- **Parasitic symbiosis** *(Greek root):* A symbiotic relationship in which a **symbiote** lives all or part of its life in or on a living host, usually benefiting while harming the host in some way.

- **Pumice:** A low-density, volcanic glass full of porous cavities that has long been used as an abrasive in cleaning, polishing, and scouring compounds. You probably have a pumice stone hanging in your shower.
- **Raspun:** A fictional, domesticated alien species that I imagine look like Highland cattle—just woolier and scarier.
- **Samurai** *(Japanese):* A member of a powerful military caste in feudal Japan.
- **Sedimentary:** Rock that has formed from sediment deposited by water or air.
- **Sensei** *(East Asian):* Teacher.
- **Star Hopping:** The universal term for how Stellarians teleport by following unique vibrations along the path to his destination. ***Star Hopper*** *was also the name Ziggy went by on Earth while moonlighting as a Deathball-playing superhero.*
- **Stellar collision:** What Stellarians call their fated mate bond. Also, the coming together of two stars caused by the dynamics within a star cluster, or by the orbital decay of a binary star due to stellar mass loss or gravitational radiation, or by other mechanisms not yet well understood.
- **Stellarian/Stellaria:** A fictional alien species (Ziggy's species!) that resembles a spiral galaxy—with starry tendrils that fade from gold to mauves, deep purples, teals and more as they spiral inward to a central core. They are incorporeal symbiotes, who are drawn toward other species to inhabit their bodies as vessels. ***Stellarian*** *is also their language and* ***Stellaria*** *is their home planet, located in the* ***Invenio-Astralis*** *galaxy.* **P.S.** In my many rabbit

holes of research, I discovered that Stellarians exist, as a non-binary gender from the *galactian alignment system* (a system created for non-binary people to describe their gender without having to use binary terms), specifically someone who is abinary/unaligned, or neutral-aligned. I hope anyone on *this* planet who identifies as such knows I borrowed the term with the upmost love.

- **Symbiote/Symbiotic** *(Greek root):* An organism living in symbiosis with another.
- **Taius:** Random galaxy mentioned for directional purposes to **Via Lactea** & **Gaia** (Earth).
- **The Knowledge:** The legendary Kaalanesean library first visited in Earth Boys Are Easy, housing archives in both bound and digital format, and collected from across the galaxies. Ziggy describes it as having "walls of alternating concave and convex glass panels allowed sunlight to filter in while creating a soft, rippling effect to disguise the sharp angles required for book storage." Very aesthetically pleasing (if not life-changing in the secrets revealed within).
- **Torrid Blaster:** A fictional weapon similar to a rocket launcher. Very effective in turning Maroxians into green goo (and for serving as the dual exhaust-style propulsion system in a modded dune racer).
- **Trol:** A fictional alien species from the planet **Karn** and containing the coveted **karnilian** stone, deep within their chest cavity. Trols are characterized by a thick coat of shaggy, chestnut-colored fur, pointed ears, large yellow eyes, a thin, hairless tail, pangolin claws on their front and hind feet, and a suspicious resemblance to a **Felis catus.** When threatened, they first attempt to curl themselves into a ball or scare

away their attacker with an ear-splitting yowl. As a last resort, the fur hanging from their face parts to reveal thick tentacles while the end of their tail balloons, creating a ring of spikes, like a medieval morning star. Their jaw can also hinge wide, like a snake swallowing its prey whole, while tiny fangs extend to enormous canines nestled in two rows of equally deadly teeth. They're really just a baby.

- **Via Lactea** *(Latin):* Known as the Milky Way Galaxy, containing Earth, our sun and moon, at least 100-300 billion planets and at least that number of stars. Just a stop on the **Intergalactic Highway**.
- **Yaaritzi:** A fictional galaxy mentioned only briefly by Ziggy for having metalworkers capable of creating grates strong enough to stop Pedro from infiltrating the air ducts again.
- **Zeanidion:** A fictional alien species that looks like a cross between a gargoyle and a Minotaur. The texture of its skin seems almost stone-like, and its craggy face is bovine than anything, with its massive size making it look like one of Notre Dame's gargoyles come to life. *(**Zeanides** is what they call their home planet, located in the **Crux-Aldebaran** galaxy, and the language is **Zeanidese**.)*

Random references:

- Again, I'm fairly certain Dr. Suess is universal, but if you were confused by my mention of **Who Hash** and **Roast Beast,** those are in reference to *How the Grinch Stole Christmas.*
- Perhaps less universal were my Candyland (boardgames) references: **Candyland Court** and

    Gumdrop Pass are stops in the game. Micah uses these to describe Stellaria because it's similarly (and deceptively) pastel.

- Not-Hoth and the "slutty books about strapping blue aliens fucking Earthlings" Theo teases Gabe about is, of course, **Ice Planet Barbarians by Ruby Dixon.**

- A **Nelson hold** is a grappling hold executed by one person to immobilize their opponent from behind. There are a few different versions of this, so if you're interested in learning more, go forth to the internet!

- Once again, we get to see Micah's ***Trumpet of the Swan*** harp in action, which is called that in reference to the children's novel by E. B. White published in 1970, where a swan is born without vocal cords (or something equally traumatizing) and gets himself a trumpet so he can call to his mate.

- **Carl Jung** (the Swiss psychiatrist, psychotherapist, and psychologist who founded the school of analytical psychology) comes up during Chapter 31, while Ziggy is musing about his existence. The "collective unconscious" & "synchronicity" (both Jung concepts) are mentioned, but I suggest falling into your own internet rabbit hole on this fascinating Earthling.

- **Kal-El** is Superman's birth name and the **Kryptonian Rocket** is the vessel he arrived on Earth in as a baby (along with the goodest boy, Krypto the Superdog, of course). The **Fortress of Solitude** is Superman's remote (usually arctic) top-secret sanctuary.

- ***MTV Cribs*** was a documentary show that originated on MTV and featured tours of the private homes of celebrities. It originally aired from 2000 to 2010, so yeah, I'm old.

- Even older is the **ACME Corporation** reference, which is from Looney Tunes. It's a running gag that the company produces a wide range of outlandish products, and a giant neon ray gun felt like it would fit.

- Miscellaneous sci-fi entertainment references include *The Fly* (starring Jeff Goldblum), *Little Shop of Horrors* (starring a Venus flytrap looking, "mean green mother from outer space" named Twoey), *WALL-E* (in the form of SWOL-E), *Lily & Stitch, The 5th Element* ("multipage!"), and another childhood favorite of mine—**Transformers**—starring robot aliens who turned into Earthling cars.

- We also get Ziggy's nickname of "Alien Rambo," which originated with Micah's brother-in-law, Baltasar Suarez and of course, references the cinematic masterpiece, *Rambo: First Blood* (which was really just called *First Blood...* it's complicated).

- A reminder that Ziggy's spaceship—**Lodger 79**—was named after the 1979 David Bowie album, *Lodger.* Speaking of Bowie, *Ziggy Stardust and the Spiders from Mars* (album) and *The Man Who Fell to Earth* (movie) are also mentioned in this book.

- The **Xenomorph** in this book is only loosely inspired by the *Alien* franchise (and more in reference to the Greek definition for xenomorph), and not meant to encroach on any copyrights by H.R. Giger or Carlo Rambaldi.

- On that note, I shall mention again that **this book is a *PARODY,*** so any references to the media mentioned above or Star Wars—including Jedis,

Wookie's, Anakin/Luke Skywalker, Obi-Wan Kenobi, Yoda, Grogu, or the author's Space Daddy babygirl Mandalorian/Din Djarin/Pedro Pascal—are also **protected under the First Amendment** and and not to be confused with licensed use of material owned by Lucasfilm/Walt Disney Company, etc.

Made in the USA
Columbia, SC
28 April 2025

57271098R00263